OHIO'S HISTORIC HAUNTS

· JAMES A. WILLIS ·

OHIO'S HISTORIC HAUNTS

Investigating the Paranormal in the Buckeye State

Black Squirrel Books™ 🐿™

Kent, Ohio

© 2015 by The Kent State University Press, Kent, Ohio 44242
All rights reserved
Library of Congress Catalog Card Number 2014049487
ISBN 978-1-60635-260-1
Manufactured in the United States of America

BLACK SQUIRREL BOOKS™ 🐿™

Frisky, industrious black squirrels are a familiar sight on the Kent State University
campus and the inspiration for Black Squirrel Books™, a trade imprint of
The Kent State University Press.
www.KentStateUniversityPress.com

This book is intended as entertainment and as a historical record of ghost stories, legends, and folklore from Ohio. Many of these stories cannot be independently confirmed or corroborated, and the author and publisher make no representation as to their factual accuracy. Readers should be advised that some of the sites described in this book are located on private property and should not be visited without the permission of the owners, or visitors may face prosecution for trespassing. Sites open to the general public should be visited only during normal hours of operation or with special permission from the owners.

Library of Congress Cataloging-in-Publication Data
Willis, James A.
  Ohio's historic haunts : investigating the paranormal in the buckeye state /
James A. Willis.
     pages cm
  Includes bibliographical references.
  ISBN 978-1-60635-260-1 (pbk. : alk. paper) ∞
1. Haunted places—Ohio. I. Title.
  BF1472.U6W55545 2015
  133.109771—dc23

                              2014049487

         19 18 17 16 15   5 4 3 2 1

For Steph—Thank you for your unconditional love, your unending support, and for never letting me give up, no matter how many times I tried to.

I still have no idea what I did to deserve you, but I'm glad I did it.

CONTENTS

INTRODUCTION

Ghosts exist.

There, I said it.

I'm guessing that since you're flipping through a book about ghosts and ghost hunting, you're probably not too surprised by that statement. So I'll do you one better: not only do ghosts exist, but I know what their purpose is.

Ghosts exist to help us keep history alive.

OK, so now that I've probably got more than a few of you scratching your heads (or shaking them in disgust), allow me to demonstrate with an example.

Let's just say that there is a famous plantation in Ohio, the Willis Plantation. According to legend, the Willis Plantation is supposed to be haunted by Harry Willis, who built the plantation in 1904. During construction, Harry Willis lost his left hand in a bizarre gardening accident and had it replaced with a hook. He died on March 25, and ever since then, people visiting the Willis Plantation on the anniversary of his death are chased off the property by Harry Willis's ghost, who has a hook for an arm.

OK, so now let's look at that little ghost story. In fact, let's take the ghost out of the story. What are we left with? Historical facts. Anyone hearing that ghost story for the first time walks away from it knowing the name of the building, who built it, that he lost his hand, and when he died. You could probably make a pretty good case that the ghost is the least important aspect of the above-mentioned story. But that would be shortchanging the ghost, especially since it's been my experience that it's the ghost that lures people in.

Think about it: interest in ghosts and ghost hunting is at an all-time high right now. Back in the 1980s when I started ghost hunting, it would be years before I ran into someone who also shared my obsession with the paranormal. Now they are everywhere. These days, it seems like everyone loves a good ghost story. But here's the kicker: most people think they're just reading. What they fail to realize is that they're getting a history lesson disguised as a ghost story: history wrapped in a funeral shroud, if you will.

Once I had that unique premise for my book, I made the decision that, as a whole, I wanted this work to be different from any other ghost-hunting book I'd read over the years. I didn't want this to be merely a collection of rumors and secondhand stories. I decided I wanted to focus on a set number of historical locations in Ohio that were reportedly haunted and then immerse myself in each location, soaking up the actual history as well as the firsthand stories from employees and owners who genuinely believed that they had encountered something unexplainable. And then I wanted to spend the night inside each location to see what, if anything, would happen.

So while each chapter will focus exclusively on a specific historical location in Ohio, I divided each chapter into three sections. It's my desire that you read all three of these sections together as opposed to only one or two of them as I believe you need all three to get the full picture of each location:

The History

Far too often, people get caught up in the ghost stories associated with a location without looking into the history. To me, that's getting only half the story. Often if you know the history of a location, what might seem like random ghost activity suddenly makes sense. For example, a rocking chair that rocks on its own at night might be interesting, but if you have historical documentation that states the woman who once owned the chair liked to rock herself to sleep in it every night, well, that might not prove that ghosts exist, but it certainly helps build the case that they might!

The Experiences

More often than not, books on ghost lore will fall into the trap of simply retelling the same stories that have been handed down from generation to generation. I've been guilty of doing that my-self. There's nothing wrong with it when you are merely trying to chronicle or document the stories associated with a specific location. But for this book, I wanted to go beyond that. For that reason, I made the decision that when it came to collecting the ghost stories, I wanted to interview each and every person and hear his or her stories firsthand. And I didn't want people who had been in the building for only an hour or so (or not at all). I wanted the people who owned the building or who worked there—the ones who knew the building inside and out. The ones who knew the normal noises the building made . . . and what wasn't normal.

The other reason I wanted to interview everyone was so that I could look them all in the eye while they were telling their stories to see if they were being honest with me. Did these people really see a ghost? I'll leave that up to you to decide. What I can tell you is that, without a doubt, each and every person who told me about the ex-periences was convinced that he or she had an encounter with the unexplained. They might not have all said the word "ghost," but they all said they had no explanation for what they experienced.

The Vigil

This is where I feel my book is breaking new ground. I'm not just going to tell you stories about these locations, I'm going to spend the night inside each and every one of them. I chose to call it a "vigil" because, despite what certain ghost reality shows will tell you, a proper ghost investigation takes longer than a few hours. Often it takes multiple visits and weeks and weeks of research.

Also, the purpose of the vigil is not to determine whether or not any of these locations are haunted. Again, that would take multiple visits and research. Rather, I simply wanted you to get an idea of the sights and sounds of all of these locations. Oh yeah, and I dragged a whole mess of equipment in there with me, too, just in case I got lucky and there were some ghosts hanging around the night I was there.

So are you ready to join me on the ghostly adventure of a lifetime? Great! Then let's grab some equipment and get going!

EQUIPMENT USED

Since so much has been made about "ghost-hunting equipment" and its importance in an investigation, I thought it would be helpful to explain the different types of equipment I took with me on my overnight vigils. More importantly, I will explain why I chose to use this equipment.

First, it is my opinion, regardless of what others will try to tell me, that there is no such thing as a device that can detect ghosts. Sure, on the Internet you can find all sorts of equipment that will claim to detect ghosts and even allow them to speak directly to you. But here's the thing: we don't know what ghosts are (or, to be honest, if they even really exist in any sort of tangible form). So how can someone claim to have a device that can detect something we don't even know exists?

For that reason, the vast majority of equipment that I use is designed to detect atmospheric/environmental changes that are caused by energy. I base this on the idea that we are all forms of energy. Since you can't destroy energy (only change its form), where does our energy go when we die? It's my personal belief that it's the energy people are seeing/feeling/sensing and calling a "ghost."

HAND-HELD DEVICES

Infrared (IR) Thermometer

These are handy because you can just point them at the area you want to get a temperature reading from, pull the trigger, see where the laser beam hits, then read the back of the thermometer to determine the temperature reading of that area. You can also hold down the trigger, which will allow you to take constant readings from entire areas as you scan the beam across them.

The downside to this device is that it needs a solid object to bounce off of in order to give a reading. So if you point it across a room and the beam hits the far wall, the device's signal will bounce off the wall, giving the temperature reading of the wall. And since it needs to read off a solid object, you're getting a specific temperature from a specific location, so you won't be able to pick up things like breezes. Still, I like to use the IR thermometer if I'm working a case where people have reported objects moving of their own accord. As far as I'm concerned, if something has enough mass to move an object, then it should also alter the surface temperature of any object it's trying to move.

Ambient Temperature Devices (Weather Stations)

Unlike the IR thermometer, which needs a solid surface to produce a reading, ambient temperature devices take readings from a general area in space. I like to put several of these sensors along a hallway or some other location where people have reported unexplained cold breezes. Lining up the ambient temperature sensors allows me not only to detect any temperature changes, but also find out where that change originated and, more importantly, where it went.

EMF Meters

EMF stands for electromagnetic field, a real field of energy that is essentially made up of anything that has an electric and/or a magnetic charge. EMF meters measure the strength of the field in milligauss.

I use EMF meters because it's my belief that what we call a ghost is nothing more than a form of energy, and as such, we should be able to measure that energy. In terms of the reading, I don't care how high or low it is—there's no number that means "ghost." Rather, I'm just looking for a strange spike or drop that I can't account for. Most locations will be loaded with things that will give off EMF (pretty much every electronic device in your house), so most of the time, I end up getting high readings that are nothing more than a bad air-conditioning unit or poorly wired outlet. But hey, it's all part of the job.

I usually bring a wide variety of EMF meters into the field with me— some with lights, some with digital printouts—since some will end up being better suited for the job at hand (the ones with lights, known as ELFs [electromagnetic low frequency], are especially handy when you're in the middle of a dark basement, for example).

Natural Tri-Field Meter

This functions like an EMF meter, with the added bonus of being able to detect changes in the levels of "natural" DC fields. Again, I'm not looking for a specific reading of number, just a weird variance. The cool part about the tri-field meter is that it is incredibly sensitive and has a squelch knob so you can adjust the threshold when an audible sound occurs. In other words, you can put this device on top of a solid object and leave it there. If, at any point during the evening, the energy levels happen to go up, the device will sound the alarm, so to speak.

K-II Meter

Basically, K-II meters are just EMF meters with lots of pretty lights on them. Somewhere along the line, it was decided that ghosts could communicate through the K-II and would make the lights flash in response to questions. Incredibly, ghosts will flash the lights in the exact same pattern as the K-II makes when you first turn it on, which you can do by simply exerting the tiniest bit of force on a pressure plate. In other words, if someone is holding a K-II meter and it's flashing like crazy, make sure the person isn't turning it on and off inadvertently. Even the newer versions with on/off switches flash their lights like crazy whenever they get too close to someone's cell phone or if someone is using a walkie-talkie.

Still, the K-II is a handy way to detect sudden EMF changes when you turn it on and leave it sitting on a table.

MEL Meter

Touted as the only professional measurement tool designed exclusively for paranormal research, the MEL meter is basically a two-in-one device: an EMF meter and an ambient temperature device. The MEL meter has quickly become one of my go-to devices simply because it means I no longer have to keep juggling between using my temperature gauge and my EMF meter.

"Ghost Meter" (Cell Sensor)

Most of the world knew these devices as cell sensors until someone realized they could sell them for a lot more if they stuck a "ghost meter" sticker on them. As I mentioned earlier, there is no device that can detect ghosts. What this device does detect is EMF, although it really likes cell phones and cell towers (hence the "cell sensor" name). I treat these just as I would any other EMF meter, but as it's called a ghost meter, I thought I should give it its own section just so I could clarify it.

Laser Grids

These are a trip to use on investigations, even if they don't end up helping you find a ghost. Essentially, these are laser pointers with a type of prism at the end of them, which creates a kaleidoscope-type effect— dozens upon dozens of tiny red (or green) beams of light. We project this grid across a room onto a solid object like a wall. If something— hopefully, a ghost—walks in front of the grid, it will break the beams, allowing us to see it. Trippy, huh?

Dowsing Rods

These are nothing more than a pair of L-shaped pieces of metal that you hold out in front of you in order to find something. They've supposedly been used in the past to find everything from underground water supplies and hidden land mines to ghosts. People who use dowsing rods to find ghosts will often hold the rods straight out in front of them and then ask the ghosts to move the rods to reply to "yes" or "no" questions. Every time I try to use them, I can never go more than ten seconds without the rods swinging wildly about. Simply put, they are too easy to manipulate simply by twitching your fingers, even accidentally.

Pendulums

Pendulums function in much the same way as dowsing rods do, except rather than a bent piece of metal, you hold a piece of string at the end of which is attached a crystal, rock, or other heavy (and sometimes pointy) object. You just let the crystal dangle in midair and the ghost will manipulate it in response to your questions. Again, I don't put much stock in this, but I keep it around because I'm always willing to try anything.

AUDIO

Digital Voice Recorders

Digital voice recorders are all the rage when it comes to capturing electronic voice phenomena (EVP). They are based on the idea that ghosts can somehow imprint their voices onto the recording and you will hear them during playback, not "live" when you're recording. But how is something like that possible? Back in the day, people believed ghosts could manipulate the electromagnetic field—a field made up of anything with either an electric or a magnetic charge—and that since old-fashioned cassette decks often incorporated magnetic tape heads or magnetic tapes, ghosts could manipulate them. It's a stretch, I know, but it sort of makes sense in a weird kind of way, except digital recorders don't have tape or tape heads, so how do the voices get there? No idea. My only reason for rambling on and on about all this is to say that I haven't found one particular digital voice recorder that is especially good or bad for ghost hunting. Rather, I've found that the cheaper the device, the more ghost voices you're going to get, as the devices tend to garble or misinterpret what they're recording, so I prefer to use rather expensive stereo digital voice recorders.

Something else I should touch upon is the notion that most people, including those on ghost reality shows, choose to walk around with these devices, pointing them into every nook and cranny while they're walking through a haunted location. The result is that they pick up everything from wind resistance to their own footsteps, all of which could be mistaken as voices or sounds from the Other Side. For that reason, when I'm using a digital voice recorder in an investigation, I try to put it in one central location and leave it there.

Superlux CM-H8C Condenser Microphones

I'm constantly trying to reduce the amount of noise and feedback I get from various digital voice recorders. The Superlux microphones help me do just that. Designed for the recording studio, these microphones deliver excellent quality audio. I use microphone cables with these, as opposed to going wireless, to further cut down on any potential interference. Finally, I also mount every microphone on its own stand, complete with a shock mount, which cuts down on vibrations from people walking around it, etc.

Korg D888 Studio Mixer

All studio microphones used on the vigil are hardwired into a studio mixer, a Korg D888. It can handle up to eight microphones at once, each with its own channel. We can listen to all eight channels live at once or isolate what a specific microphone is picking up. Everything is burned onto the mixer's internal hard drive from which we can extract sounds, uncompressed, to be further analyzed.

Frank's Box

Of all the devices being used in ghost research today, none is more con-troversial than the Frank's Box. Also referred to as a Shack Hack or an instrumental transcommunication (ITC) device, the Frank's Box, which is essentially a small AM/FM radio, is said to be designed to allow ghosts to communicate with you. How they are able to do that is open to debate— a lot of debate. Fans of the Frank's Box will tell you that the ghosts are able to somehow use the white noise/static and convert it to words and phrases that you can hear in real time by simply turning the device on and listening for the words between all the noise. Skeptics, including myself, counter by saying the Frank's Box is nothing more than a radio that has had its auto-tune function disabled, causing the device to continually scan across all the radio frequencies. Because of that, the "ghost voices" you're hearing are nothing more than snippets of conversation from local DJs that the radio manages to pick up as it's whizzing around the dial.

Even after all that, I still keep a Frank's Box in my equipment bag, just in case.

VIDEO

Lorex Multi-Channel Digital Video Recorder with Infrared Cameras

Think closed-circuit security system and you'll get the idea here. I use infrared night-vision cameras, all of which I hardwire into the monitor/ DVR to cut down on any possible interference. Each is also equipped with a microphone, so I can record both audio and video. I can use up to eight cameras at once, but each time you add a camera, you lose some resolution, so I tend not to use more than four cameras at a time if possible.

The hard drive on the DVR holds up to fifteen hundred hours of video, which I can also download for further review analysis.

Sony Infrared Night-Vision Cameras with IR Extenders

All of these cameras are mounted on tripods to reduce any bounce and vibration. It also reduces the amount of videos taken by wildly swinging cameras featuring out-of-focus ghosts to a minimum.

Unless forced to, I prefer to record using external DVD burners, if for no other reason than it helps cut down on the internal noises that are sometimes picked up when you're recording internally.

Digital Still Cameras

Over the years, I have shot everything from 35 mm film to Polaroids, all with limited success. So I tend to use digital cameras now, if for no other reason than I shoot a lot of photos while on a ghost hunt—an average of 250 photos a night. At the end of the night, I can delete all the ones that didn't turn out right without having to worry about old-school things like film processing (I feel old just saying that).

While I've found that digital cameras are really good at picking up dust orbs, flash reflections, and a whole array of non-ghostly debris often referred to as ghosts, I've yet to find any type of camera that is the best for getting prize shots of ghosts.

Vernier LabPro

This is really the crown jewel of all the pieces of equipment I use on investigations. Essentially the Vernier LabPro is a data-logging system that allows for multiple remote sensors to be plugged into it. These sensors are capable of recording two readings per second, essentially allowing me to record in real time. By connecting the data logger to a laptop, I can also monitor the readings in chart form, again in real time.

The sensors are interchangeable, so I can use whichever ones the investigation calls for. For example, if someone is experiencing cold breezes on a staircase, I can use multiple ambient-temperature sensors/probes and run them up the entire staircase, which will allow me to detect and record not only any temperature changes as they happen, but also the direction in which the temperature changes are moving.

NORTHWEST

OHIO

THE HAUNTED HYDRO

Fact: Every October, the building located at 1333 Tiffin Street in Fremont becomes infested with not only ghosts, but ghouls, monsters, and every imaginable creature of the night. It's been that way for over a quarter of a century. That's because since 1989, Bob "Crazy Bob" Turner has been operating his massively popular spook house, the Haunted Hydro, on this site. The Haunted Hydro has grown every year since its inception, with thrills and chills spilling out of the building itself and out into the neighboring property. It's not uncommon to hear screams from terrified patrons echoing through the cold night air even before the Hydro is in sight.

Of course, there are those who say that after the final guest has left for the evening and the last bit of grease paint has been wiped from the actors' faces, that's when the real show begins. For that is when the real ghosts of the Haunted Hydro get up and walk around.

THE HISTORY

You wouldn't know it by looking at it today, but the land the Haunted Hydro sits on had much humbler and quieter beginnings. Due to its close proximity to the Sandusky River, the area was popular with the Wyandot Indians, who would often hunt, fish, and even set up camp along the water's edge. After the Indians were forcibly relocated from the area, the land stood vacant for some time before being purchased by a farmer, who was also drawn to it because of its close proximity to the river.

The property's location would also gain the attention of local officials in the early 1900s. They discussed the idea of building a hydroelectric

The original hydroelectric power plant, still visible on the grounds of the Haunted Hydro.

power plant to harness the power of the Sandusky River to produce electricity to power Fremont and the neighboring towns. In 1909, plans were drawn up and reviewed. The property where the Haunted Hydro currently stands was purchased after taking into consideration the size of the property required and how close the power plant would need to be to the Sandusky River in order to feed the water in and out of the building. The following year, in 1910, construction on the building, officially named the Hydro Electric Power Plant, began. In 1911, the gates to the plant cranked open and water from the Sandusky River rushed in. Once the water was inside the building, turbines spun, generators whirred, and Fremont, Ohio, lit up.

Shortly after the power plant opened, the decision was made to dam up a portion of the Sandusky River to ensure there would be enough water to continually feed the plant. The Ballville Dam, named after the next town over from Fremont, was constructed in 1912 out of concrete and featured an earthen embankment. All seemed to go according to plan, yet less than a year later, all hell would break loose in Fremont.

March 1913 had been unusually wet and warm in Ohio. In Fremont, the ground was already waterlogged, to the point where it would squish whenever people walked on it. As a steady rain continued to fall across the area, often for days on end, area streams and even the Sandusky River swelled to levels much higher than usual. As March wore on, the sun decided to make a rare appearance. But on the morning of Easter Sunday, March 23, the skies over Fremont once again grew dark. A short time later, a light rain began to fall. And fall. Before long, a hard, steady rain was beating down on the ground. Over the course of the next forty-eight hours, the rain continued without end.

On the morning of March 25, the rain was still falling and nearby streams had already overflowed their banks and started spreading across fields. The Sandusky River had swollen to great heights, its mighty waters crashing against the banks, removing huge boulders and uprooting trees as it went. Initially, people had gone out to the Ballville Dam to stare at the fierce water rushing past. But by noon on March 25, people saw that there were nearly five feet of water spilling over the top of the dam. Many began to seek higher ground, fearing the dam would not be able to continue holding back so much water. They were right. As those standing alongside the dam looked on in horror, the Sandusky River started washing away large earthen sections of the dam. Within minutes and with a mighty rumble, a large hole appeared and water began rushing through. The Fremont Flood had begun.

Once free of the dam, the swollen waters of the Sandusky headed straight for the power plant, slamming into it with a force so mighty that the plant's giant gates, which were designed to keep out the water, were ripped from the building. Likewise, the tubes that fed the water into the plant were pulled loose and washed away. Large portions of the building itself were also destroyed, crumbling under the massive strength of the rushing water.

By late afternoon on March 25, the entire town of Fremont was in deep trouble. The Sandusky was now flowing freely through the streets of downtown, sweeping away anything in its path, including entire houses. Fremont mayor C. Stausmyer issued a statement, officially appealing for aid. Almost immediately, citizens from neighboring towns and cities such as Port Clinton and Toledo responded and sent boats and personnel to help. A special train bearing relief personnel and supplies was even dispatched from Sandusky.

It would be another two days before the rain finally stopped falling on March 27. It was estimated that during those five days, over seven inches of rain fell in Fremont. Before the flood waters began to recede on March 28, the river gauge in the Sandusky River showed that the water had risen to 21.5 feet, almost seven feet higher than it had ever been. Reports throughout Fremont put the water level even higher.

When all was said and done, the Fremont Flood was the worst flood in Ohio history. Statewide, the flood had been responsible for millions of dollars' worth of damage and the loss of over 460 lives. In Fremont, over 550 homes were flooded, with fifty of them completely destroyed. There were also three confirmed deaths. One estimate listed the total damage done to property, including the Ballville Dam and the power plant, at well over $1 million.

As soon as the water was cleared out of the power plant, the decision was made to rebuild it. Once reopened, it served as the main source of Fremont's electrical supply until 1925, when more modern methods became the primary means of supplying Fremont with electricity. The plant enjoyed a resurgence and hummed back to life during World War II, when it was needed to help supply extra electricity during wartime. It remained in operation until approximately 1954, when the generators were removed from the building, making the plant inoperable. For the next few decades, it functioned as a warehouse and storage facility with some of the property containing a clubhouse for the neighboring golf course. Then, in the late 1980s, Crazy Bob Turner, who had the even crazier idea of turning the building into a haunted house attraction, purchased the plant and the property. And the place has been filled with ghosts ever since.

Or maybe the ghosts were already there. Truth be told, stories of the power plant being haunted date back long before it became the Haunted Hydro. In fact, some stories claim the ghosts are those of the displaced Wyandot Indians who roamed the area many years ago. According to tales told locally, when the sewer line was being dug for the building, an Indian burial mound was disturbed, resulting in the entire property being cursed. Still others will tell you that the farmer who once owned the property died an unnatural death in his home and that his spirit still lingers inside the Hydro. And then there's the tale of the worker who was helping repair the flood-damaged power plant when he slipped off the outside wall, falling to his death on the rocks below.

THE EXPERIENCES

Of course, like most ghost stories, there are no records that verify any of the deaths alleged to have happened on the Hydro property or that confirm there's a curse on the area. But if you want to separate fact from fiction and truth from rumor at the Haunted Hydro, the man you need is Jeff Joerg. A teacher and a certified golf-club builder, Jeff was working in the golf clubhouse when Bob Turner first bought the power plant. According to Jeff, since he had a lot of tools at his disposal in the clubhouse, Bob and the Hydro staff would often stop in to borrow some of them while they were doing repairs. That's what started Jeff's involvement with the Hydro, and he's been there ever since.

As soon as you bring up the topic of ghosts, Jeff is quick to point out that even though he's spent years inside the Hydro, even spending hours on end sitting in the dark supervising a "ghost hunt," he's never seen anything.

"I'm one of these people who's never met a ghost," Jeff told me, although he was quick to add, "Ask me if I've ever seen anything that would cause me to step back and think for a second, my answer to you is 'yes.'"

When asked to elaborate, Jeff explained that he thinks there possibly could be something to the legend of the curse, at least in theory. According to Jeff, a worker operating a backhoe did indeed uncover human remains when digging for the new sewer system. "They unearthed a whole lot of stuff," Jeff told me. "And they must have disturbed something because from that point on, believe it or not, there were a lot of things that happened." When I asked him to explain what sort of things happened, Jeff pointed to people suddenly becoming ill for no apparent reason and even the Sandusky River rising and flooding the golf course. Jeff said that in the 1990s, when Bob Turner found out that graves had been disturbed, he called in a Wyandot shaman who re-blessed the land. As soon as the shaman left, "all the strange things around here stopped," Jeff said. Or, that is, the strange things associated with a potential curse stopped. The ghost stories, however, were just getting started.

One of the oldest ghost stories associated with the Hydro is that of a little girl seen roaming the building, often after it has been closed. But that's not to say that she doesn't make herself known to guests. Workers are often stunned when people exiting the Haunted Hydro remark at how scary the "little girl" was, even though the Hydro does not employ children.

"I do know that people who work here have reported, at least a dozen times, the ghost of a little girl walking around in here," Jeff said. He continued that most times, they describe her as a girl about ten or eleven years old wearing a dress, although the dress appears to be "a costume," which may account for why some witnesses believe she is an actor working at the Hydro. Oddly enough, the patrons' descriptions never go further than that, although Jeff remembers one patron saying the dress was white.

One employee who got a closer look at the ghostly girl is Tony Johnson. An actor, builder, and licensed fire performer with well over a decade of experience at the Hydro, Tony is quite familiar with the building, so he's comfortable moving throughout its maze-like corridors, even in the dark. Yet one evening, several years ago, Tony was walking through the building when he said "I just got this eerie feeling I was being watched." Looking back over his shoulder, Tony was shocked to see a young girl standing right behind him. "She was just on the other side of the hallway," Tony said. "I felt she was looking right at me."

Before he had time to react, the girl disappeared. "She was gone so fast, I couldn't even see what she was wearing," Tony said. "Couldn't even tell hair color. It was almost like it was in black and white." Tony was so shaken by the encounter that he spent the rest of the night avoiding that part of the hallway altogether.

So who is this ghost girl? And what is her connection to the Hydro? According to local legend, she was the daughter of the farmer who originally owned the property, but nothing has been uncovered yet to verify that. One darker legend says that the girl was living on the streets of Fremont at the time of the flood and that she was swept away by the Sandusky River, taking her name with her. The result is that she haunts the property lest people forget her entirely. It's a sad and creepy story to be sure, but again, there is no historical evidence to support it. The truth is, no one really knows who this girl is, and perhaps we never will.

Yet even though we don't know her name, one thing is for certain: the ghost girl was responsible for bringing the Haunted Hydro to the attention of local ghost hunters. According to Jim Bevens, the ghost girl was the one ghost hunters first came looking for. With well over fifteen years of service at the Hydro under his belt, Jim said he hadn't heard any stories about the building being haunted prior to his working there. "I don't know how the stories of the little girl got started," Jim said, "but one day, they told me a paranormal group was coming in here. And when they got here, they wanted to know about the little girl ghost."

It seems as though once the ghost groups started showing up, their attention began to shift away from the ghost girl and over to more "traditional" haunted locations within the Hydro. Specifically, an old hearse used as a prop during Halloween season and stored inside the building when not in use. Jim said that ghost hunters would put "their meters" on top of and even inside the hearse and "get all sorts of readings," although they never told Jim what the readings were or what they meant.

Another prop the ghost hunters fixated on was Ralph, an old skeleton resting inside a small wooden coffin. In this case, I could see why they would want to take a closer look at Ralph. You see, unlike most of the props inside the Haunted Hydro, Ralph is real. Or at least he was real at one time. According to Bob Turner, who acquired Ralph, the skeleton dates back to the late 1800s or early 1900s and was used as part of the secret rituals carried out by the fraternal organization, the Independent Order of Oddfellows. The casket Ralph calls home at the Hydro is original, too, and was also allegedly an integral part of the Oddfellows' rituals.

Jeff Jeorg was present the night a group of ghost hunters decided to place one of their meters on the Plexiglas lid of Ralph's coffin. Jeff never heard the results, but he says that "supposedly, they got all sorts of stuff."

In speaking with Jeff about the skeleton and why people think it might be causing paranormal activity, he brings up an interesting point that also raises more than a few ghostly questions. According to Jeff, there is some speculation that Ralph might not be all he appears to be. Jeff claims that a woman from the Forensics Department in Toledo came down to view the skeleton and believes the remains belong to a young female. So Ralph might actually be a she. Of course, there is no way to prove this conclusively without removing the skeleton from the coffin and taking it away for more tests, so for now, Ralph is still a guy. But Jeff brings up an interesting theory: If the skeleton really does belong to that of a young girl, could this be the little girl who's said to be haunting the Hydro?

In 2009, it would appear that someone or something new started hanging around the Haunted Hydro. That was the year the decision was made to open up the old hydro plant's basement. While most employees found the basement to be a rather dull place (despite the fact that someone had carved "Water Level 1913" into one of the beams near the ceiling and it was still clearly visible), there were others who sensed that something foreboding was lurking down there, and that by opening up the basement, they had essentially let it out.

To date, no one has ever seen anything in the basement. Rather, they feel it. Extreme temperature fluctuations are common here and were present from the day they opened it. According to Jim Bevens, when the trap door to the basement was opened for the first time, "it was like walking into a sauna," which was perplexing not only given the time of year, but also because the basement is below ground. So they left the door open overnight and when they got back the next day, things had cooled down. For a while. But from time to time, from no apparent cause, the temperature would ratchet up almost immediately, often while people were working down there. Other times, the temperature would suddenly drop, once again without any known reason. As with most of the ghostly activity said to take place at the Haunted Hydro, no one is quite sure why this happens or who is responsible.

That's not to say that all of the ghosts here are unknown. Spend enough time with the people of the Hydro and one name keeps popping up: Artie.*

In life, Artie was a gifted Hollywood special-effects makeup wizard who, upon retiring from the business, made his way back to Ohio. He fell in love with the Haunted Hydro and came to work there, quickly becoming a beloved fixture about the place. Artie also developed a reputation as a bit of a prankster, but one with a heart. Artie would remain an employee of the Haunted Hydro until his death and is still greatly missed by the people I interviewed, even though Artie had been gone several years by that time.

Jim Bevens really put things in perspective when he mentioned "it definitely changed the year we opened after Artie wasn't here. It felt different. There was something missing—it was Artie." Of course, immediately

*I have used a pseudonym out of respect for the individual.

after making that statement, Jim smiled and said, "I have my suspicions that he's still hanging around here, though."

Indeed, while Jeff Jeorg has never seen Artie since his passing, he has spoken with several Hydro employees who have gotten up close and personal with Artie's ghost without ever realizing it. "It's usually the new employees," Jeff told me. "They'll come up to you and say 'Who's the guy with the funny-looking glasses? He just came by and smiled at me.' It was Artie. And then we have to tell them he's no longer with us."

LaRue Van Fleet is another Hydro performer who had a close connection to Artie while he was alive. So close, in fact, that he was set to marry LaRue and her husband, but Artie passed away before he could perform the ceremony. Still LaRue believes Artie comes back to the Hydro from time to time and lets his presence be known in typical Artie fashion. For example, LaRue and some other employees had been giving fire performances for several years in the Hydro courtyard when, in 2010, they received their licenses and were permitted to take their show inside. They set up a stage in one of the end turbo cells, which shared a common wall with the rest of the Hydro. The cell itself was fully enclosed with a simple archway through which to enter. Almost all of the fire shows would go off without a hitch, but every once in a while, something weird would happen.

"Something would mess with our fires," LaRue explained. "We'd be out there and all of a sudden, our torches would start acting funny. They'd be perfectly fine, and then they'd just start going crazy on us. Or they would just go out."

The fire's odd behavior puzzled the actors. This was in an enclosed space where no wind could get at the flames. Plus, the flames had never acted like that before, not even when they were out in the open-air courtyard. On top of all that, on certain nights, their metal staffs would start humming and rattling. LaRue and her fellow performers were at a loss as to what was causing it until they took a few photos of the flames and saw a familiar face smiling down at them: it was Artie.

"That's the kind of guy Artie was," Jim Bevens added. "It was in his nature to mess with people and then come in later and say 'Got you, didn't I?'"

Needless to say, Jim is pretty convinced that Artie is hanging around and messing with him, even if he has yet to see him face to face. Take, for example, the wooden door near the back of the Hydro that leads to the makeup area where Artie used to work (and where a small memorial to him still remains). Jim said that door will close on its own all the time, especially when he's alone in the building. He's convinced it's Artie's ghost messing with him. "Whenever that door closes, I'm like 'Come on, Artie, knock it off.'" Jim was quick to mention that while there had been ghostly activity reported prior to Artie's passing, that particular door never closed on its own until after Artie's death.

Artie also apparently likes to mess with Jim by moving things around the building when no one is watching. He also enjoys rattling the shutters and making somewhat random banging noises, as if to startle someone. Jeff Jeorg admitted to being in the building late one night with a group of ghost hunters and hearing odd banging noises. He's not ready to say it was Artie's ghost, though. "I thought that people could be throwing things at the building, trying to scare us."

Yet another member of the Hydro family who's not ready to pin the ghostly activity on Artie is Janet Gnepper. "I know a lot of people think that he haunts these walls. But I've known Artie personally and don't think it's him," Janet remarked.

Janet has been at the Hydro since 2001. During that time, she has had more than her fair share of strange activity, most of it centered around the common wall that runs between the turbo cells and the rest of the building. Usually Janet can pass through that area and feel absolutely nothing. Yet every once in a while, when she's walking in that area, especially on the outside of the wall in the turbo cells, Janet gets a really weird feeling: "I get goose pimples. It's not like anything's really touching me, but it's sort of like a gentle sweep across my face."

Janet has had this experience numerous times over the years. The odd thing, though, is that while the occurrences don't seem to be tied to any particular time of the day, there is one thing that's consistent: Janet doesn't feel anything unless she's in makeup. If she passes through the area dressed in street clothes, she feels nothing. "One time," Janet recalled, "we did a live news report at 7:00 in the morning and I wandered back there in full clown makeup and I felt it. So it doesn't matter what time, just that if I'm in makeup. That's when I feel it the most." Stranger still, Janet claims that sometimes the weird feeling is accompanied by the sound of a grown man giggling, "like an older man giggling at you when you do something wrong." The giggling, she told me, does not sound like Artie.

But the real reason Janet is convinced that she's not feeling the ghost of Artie is a simple one: "I would feel that stuff on the back wall while he was still alive." In fact, Janet mentioned that while Artie was alive, he also felt something in that same hallway. According to Janet, Artie "would always lean up against that wall and say 'Don't you feel the energy it in? Can't you feel the energy?'"

At the end of the interviews, I was left with so many questions: Is Artie haunting the Hydro? Who is the ghostly girl people keep seeing? One thing was for certain, though. Whoever or whatever might be lurking inside the Haunted Hydro, there was no doubt I would be in for a truly memorable evening.

THE VIGIL

To say that I was looking forward to the unique opportunity to spend the night inside a "haunted" haunted attraction would be an understatement. Not even the odd, yet somewhat stereotypical, cold Ohio temperatures that accompanied my arrival on that April afternoon could calm my excitement.

Strangely enough, while the day I arrived for the vigil was bright and sunny, a steady rain had fallen over the course of the previous few days. As a result, I was barely out of my car when I heard the Sandusky River as it rumbled past the Haunted Hydro. Walking over to the embankment, I stood there transfixed for a moment. I could almost close my eyes and imagine what it must have felt like standing here days before the Great Flood of 1913.

Returning to the car, I met up with Samantha "Sam" Nicholson and Ted Seman, two members from my group, The Ghosts of Ohio, who would be accompanying me on this vigil. From there, we headed toward the back door of the Haunted Hydro, where we were met by Hydro owner Bob Turner. Unlike his Crazy Bob alter ego, I found Bob to be warm, soft-spoken, and very passionate, both about the Haunted Hydro as well as the history surrounding it. Bob then handed us off to Jim Bevens, who would be our host and guide for the evening.

In order to determine where we should set up our equipment, Jim gave us the grand tour of the building, pointing out any areas where he thought we might have the best chance of experiencing something paranormal. That was the first time Sam, Ted, and I realized that running video and audio cables through all the twists and turns of a haunted attraction would be a logistical nightmare. On top of that, even though it was off-season for the Hydro, some of the animatronics and bloody props were still hanging inside the building, which I was sure would scare the heck out of me around 2:00 A.M. when I'd forgotten they were there. (Hours later, I'd prove myself right when I rounded a corner too quickly and walked head-first into some sort of skeletal clown thing. The results, which were captured on video, weren't pretty.)

At one point during the tour, we had just come out of the basement and were discussing where we could set up our video cameras when Jim and I both heard a very strange noise, so strange that it caused me to stop in mid-sentence to ask if anyone else heard it. To me, it sounded like someone was moving around in the other room, even though we were alone in the building. Jim said he had heard it, too, but had no idea what it was. "But those are the kinds of sounds you hear in here all the time," he said.

Based on the information we'd gathered from the interviews, our setup for the evening included:

Main Hallway
· two DVR night-vision cameras, one facing in each direction
· two Superlux condenser microphones, one at each end of the hallway

Rear Hallway
· two DVR night-vision cameras, one facing in each direction
· two Superlux condenser microphones, one at each end of the hallway
· Vernier LabPro sensors, including two ambient temperature devices, one electromagnetic sensor, and one static charge sensor running across the hallway toward the basement door

Shared Wall Between Hydro and Turbines
· one infrared video camera at the near end of the wall, facing the studio microphone
· one studio microphone at the far end of the wall, facing the video camera

Basement
· one infrared video camera at the bottom of the stairs, facing the rear wall
· one studio microphone against the rear wall, facing the stairs

Ralph's Coffin
- · digital voice recorder on top of the coffin
- · tri-field meter on top of the coffin

Once everything was set up and ready to go, Jim wished us luck and locked us in the building. It was time to get started!

For the first session, Ted decided to stay inside while Sam and I elected to walk the cemetery and the turbo cells, including where the fire performers' stage was set up. I took with me a set of hand-held devices, including an EMF, an ELF, a non-contact thermometer, digital camera, and digital voice recorder.

The first stop for Sam and me was the fire performers' stage. Standing atop that stage inside the cell, I immediately had a newfound appreciation for these performers. The area was cold, dark, and somewhat cramped. Certainly not the place I'd feel comfortable having open flame shot at me. But then again, they're the professionals, not me.

Either way, I had no weird feelings that we weren't alone or that something was going to jump out at me. While sitting quietly on the stage and looking up toward the open sky, it finally made sense what LaRue Van Fleet was trying to impress upon me: the way this part of the building was designed, it would be nearly impossible for any wind to get in here. In fact, I was almost completely surrounded by walls, all of which were several stories tall. Regardless, I held my hand in the air and even dangled the cord from my digital camera to see if I could detect even the slightest breeze. I couldn't.

Next, we tried an EVP session. We called out for Artie to come and join Sam and me. I asked the little girl what her name was. I even spent a good ten minutes telling any ghosts who happened to be listening a little bit about myself and the book I was writing, further explaining that they were welcome to come forward and be interviewed so they could be included in a chapter. During the entire time, the EMF remained flat and there were no temperature changes detected. Realizing there was nothing going on in this area, Sam and I decided to move on.

Upon leaving the stage area, Sam and I continued down the outside of the building, stopping at each cell to ask questions, take readings, and snap photographs.

By the time we entered the third cell, I had already taken twenty-one pictures, all normal-looking with nary a ghost in them. The first two

I snapped in the third cell were normal, too. But the third one I took revealed an odd white misty shape in the bottom right corner of the photo. Realizing I might have just captured something weird (but also aware that it was just one picture), I called Sam over and we launched into an impromptu set of pseudo-experiments to see if we could recreate the misty shape in the photo. We first looked to see if the image could have been caused by my flash bouncing off something that was on the section of wall visible in the photo. Finding nothing there, we then tried to see if Sam and/or I could have caused the image with our breath, which is most often the culprit with these types of misty photos. Over the years, I've learned to hold my breath before I take any photo, but still, I wanted to be sure breath wasn't involved. So I took a series of pictures, one right after the other, during which I did something different to see if I could recreate the mist. Here's what I took pictures of:

- Sam and I exhaling at the same time behind the camera
- Sam standing in front of me, but off camera, and breathing directly toward the camera
- Me exhaling heavily from behind the camera
- Me breathing normally behind the camera, but exhaling over the top of the camera
- Me holding my breath with the flash turned off
- Me holding my breath, but waving my free arm around as I took the picture
- Sam and I both breathing normally with me behind the camera and Sam in front of the camera

While some of the above-mentioned pictures did result in white shapes and forms, none of them bore the same characteristics or density/thickness that appeared in the original photograph. They weren't even close. So for now, the photo remains unexplained.

Leaving the cells altogether, Sam and I made our way out to the cemetery. There had not been any reports of ghosts in this area, but since I'm of the mind-set that ghosts go into hiding whenever I'm around, I decided to see if I could find some out in the cemetery.

I wandered around the stones, pausing to take photographs along the way. When we reached the far end, Sam and I decided to split up, with Sam returning back through the cemetery and me sitting down in the corner and conducting an EVP session.

Unexplained mist captured near the turbo cells. Despite all attempts, I was unable to recreate this "mist."

As I sat there in the darkness, I asked for any spirits that were present to make themselves known to me. I told them that I was here only to document the history of the building and, as such, wanted to tell their stories since they were part of that history. I asked for names, ages, if they were married, how many of them were here—anything I could think of, all the while staring down at the EMF and ELF in front of me. I even asked for them to come stand in front of me so I could at least take their picture, telling them to say "cheese" and counting "one, two, three" before I took the photo. Nothing out of the ordinary appeared in the photos, and days later when I reviewed the audio, the only voice on the recording was mine.

Heading back inside, we reset the Vernier LabPro (after checking to see that there had been no odd variances), swapped out the DVDs, and made sure the DVR was still running. Then we decided to split up again. This time, Sam and I would stay inside while Ted investigated the graveyard alone.

Once Ted had left, Sam said she wanted to spend some time over in the garage area where Artie's makeup area had been. So while she headed in that direction, I decided to go to the opposite end of the building and see if I could make contact with the ghost girl. I started by walking up and down the hallway where Tony had his encounter. I even went so far as to walk halfway down the hall, stop, and then look over my shoulder. When that didn't work, I sat down in the middle of the hallway and asked if the girl would come and talk to me. Then I just sat quietly in the darkness, listening. The whole time, none of my hand-held devices picked up even the slightest variance.

At that point, I decided to move again. Working my way along the other wall, I had just made my way to the farthest point of the building and was turning to head toward the basement when I heard an extremely loud bang followed by what sounded like metal bouncing on the floor. It was so loud that at first I thought Sam or Ted had knocked over an entire display.

I immediately called out, "What was that?" to which I heard Sam respond "I'm not sure, but it sounded like it came from in here with me." Hearing that, I immediately wound my way through the maze over to the makeup area where Sam was. As I was making my way over, I noticed a metal angle iron lying in the middle of the hallway. I left it there, but it seemed odd and out of place, and I remembered thinking that I hadn't seen it there before.

When I got to the makeup area and asked Sam what happened, she said she'd been standing over along the wall and was attempting to talk to Artie's ghost—saying aloud how people had told her what a good makeup artist he was. It was then that she heard the bang, but she couldn't tell exactly where it came from. As Sam walked over to show me where she had been standing, it suddenly dawned on her that at the moment we heard the noise, she had been standing right next to Artie's old makeup station.

Standing in the makeup area, we reviewed the audio on our handhelds to see what they recorded. On our recorders, we clearly heard a very loud bang, as if something slammed against wood, followed by what sounded like metal bouncing on concrete. Hearing that, I immediately thought of the angle iron I had seen earlier in the hallway. I went back and retrieved it and we dropped it on the concrete floor to see if it sounded like the noise on the recorder. It did. From what we could gather, what we heard sounded like something had hit the wall, causing the angle iron to fall off the wall and drop to the floor. But as to how all that happened, we didn't have a clue, although when Jim returned at the end of the night to let us out, he had an interesting theory. The wall where we thought the sound had originated from divided the makeup area from the rest of the building. According to Jim, Artie would sometimes bang on that wall when the Hydro was in operation, just to give the guests an extra scare.

Upon deciding that we wouldn't be able to learn anything else about the cause of the bang, Ted, Sam, and I decided we would stick together the rest of the evening. I'll admit that based on how the night had started off, I was convinced things were going to continue to get more and more intense. But it was not to be. In fact, after the bang, absolutely nothing happened, even though we spent time trying to coax the ghosts out, both from inside and outside the building. We even made our way out to the old hearse that was parked in the maze and spent some time sitting inside it. I even spent time alone in the basement, talking to no one in particular, asking them to adjust the temperature for me. Again, nothing.

After the vigil, we reviewed all the materials we'd collected to see if we had captured anything paranormal. I initially had high hopes for the recorder we had set up on top of Ralph's coffin, but Ralph must not have been in the talking mood that night. As for the Vernier Lab-Pro sensors that were running in the basement, the only variances they detected during the night were when we were down there. Other than that, the temperature and electromagnetic levels remained fairly constant throughout the night.

None of the video cameras stationed throughout the building picked up anything abnormal. Interestingly enough, while they all picked up the sound of the mysterious bang, nothing can be seen moving on any of the cameras, leaving the source of the sound a mystery.

When it came to the studio microphones, they too managed to pick up the banging sound, but that was it. None of them picked up any other noise that might have provided clues as to the origin of the sound. However, one recorder that night did manage to pick up something odd. At one point, Sam's recorder recorded the discussion that she and I had about where the sound came from. Right after Sam makes the statement that "Whatever it was, it sounded like it came from over there," a very loud, very breathy voice seems to say "yeah."

FINAL THOUGHTS

Looking back on the Haunted Hydro, I think that going into it, I was fairly convinced I would come face to face with Artie's ghost. Granted, given my past history of ghosts avoiding me like the plague, I should have known better. But I guess I just felt that since Artie so loved the Hydro and I was coming in to bring the Hydro's history alive, Artie would accept me and he'd appear before me, asking me to help keep his memory alive, too. But then I remembered something that Jim had mentioned to me about how Bob Turner throws an annual banquet for Hydro employees. And every year at that banquet, they always have a special tribute to Artie. "It's just something we do," Jim told me.

It was then I realized that Artie didn't need my help to keep his memory alive. His Hydro family has already taken steps to ensure Artie will never be forgotten.

The Haunted Hydro
1333 Tiffin Street
Fremont, Ohio 43420
www.hauntedhydro.com

SULLIVAN-JOHNSON MUSEUM

There are different theories as to why ghosts choose to haunt where they do. According to one theory, ghosts will return to haunt places they knew and loved while they were alive, like the old family homestead, for example. Still another theory is that ghosts will hang around their prized possessions, just to make sure they're being looked after and taken care of. Well, in the case of the Sullivan-Johnson Museum, you can test out two theories at once. That's because the Sullivan-Johnson Museum is a former private residence that has been turned into a county museum, filled with historical treasures. Knowing that, is it any wonder that some believe there's a ghost or two hanging out there?

THE HISTORY

The building known today as the Sullivan-Johnson Museum was built in 1896 as a private residence for Daniel W. Sullivan (1847–1906) and his wife, Louella Mohr Sullivan (1857–1947). Daniel was a saddler by trade and, judging by the looks of the house he had built, he was quite successful. Of course, the fact that his wife "came from money" didn't hurt, either, especially since rumor has it that Louella brought quite the dowry with her to the marriage.

When Daniel and Louella moved into their new home, they brought with them their sixteen-year-old daughter, Edna. She would live in the house several years before she married Dr. Burke L. Johnson. Eventually, Edna and Dr. Johnson would move into and take over ownership of the Sullivan house, thereby unofficially changing its name to the Sullivan-Johnson House.

The former Sullivan-Johnson home, today one of Hardin County's historical museums.

The good doctor and Edna had two children: a son, Daniel, and a daughter, Mary Lou. Mary Lou would marry briefly, then return to the Sullivan-Johnson House after her divorce, where she remained until her death in 1977. She would be the last family member to live in the house.

Upon her passing, the house was deeded, per Mary Lou's request, to Hardin Memorial Hospital. After a period of time, the hospital gave it to Hardin County, which made the decision to lease it to the local Historical Society so they could operate it as a museum—the Hardin County Museum.

Today, nearly every room of the Sullivan-Johnson Museum is filled with artifacts and other items of historical significance to Hardin County. While some exhibits change throughout the year, such as the Local Business Room, others, like the Indian Relic Room and the recreated parlor, remain unchanged. As does the Military Room, which proudly displays medals belonging to Jacob Parrott, who was given the nation's first Medal of Honor (Army) for his participation as one of Andrews Raiders during the Civil War.

Andrews Raid refers to a brazen hijacking of a locomotive, the General, in Marietta, Georgia, on April 12, 1862, by Union sympathizer James J. Andrews and his band of "raiders," of which Parrott was one. The plan was to take the General north toward Chattanooga, Tennessee, stopping to destroy the tracks behind them, thereby cutting off the Confederates' supply chain between Atlanta and Chattanooga. While the initial hijacking was successful, Parrott and others were eventually captured. Parrott received constant beatings in an attempt to get him to give up information, but through it all, Parrott remained silent.

After the war, Parrott returned to Kenton, where he lived until his death in December 1908. He is buried in Grove Cemetery in Kenton.

But if there is one thing that drives most of the traffic to the museum, it is the amazing Kenton toy collection. In the late 1800s, the Kenton Company was producing cast-iron locks when they made the decision to start selling a few cast-iron toys. When they noticed the toys were outselling the locks, they decided to produce cast-iron toys almost exclusively. By 1910 or so, they were the largest producer of cast-iron toys in the world. Today, the toys are some of the most collectible and sought-after by toy collectors, especially the Gene Autry line of guns.

THE EXPERIENCES

With all of the historical pieces on display throughout the Sullivan-Johnson Museum, one might assume that the ghosts said to haunt here showed up when a haunted item was donated to the museum. But that's not the case. In fact, the ghosts here all date back to a time when the building was still a private residence. The problem is trying to determine how many ghosts are actually here and who they are.

The first known mention in print of a ghost at the Sullivan-Johnson House came in 2003 with Chris Woodyard's *Haunted Ohio V*. The book describes an incident where a group of schoolchildren walked into the sitting area and saw a woman matching the description of the woman "for whom the house was built." As the children watched, the woman simply disappeared.

With no other description given, people just began assuming the ghost was Louella Johnson, the woman who, along with her husband, built the house. "Louella is the ghost that is seen in the house," said museum director Linda Iams. "Not by me personally. I have never seen her, and I have been here over a decade." In fact, other than a former maintenance man, who told Linda he once saw Louella's ghost standing at the top of the main staircase, no one has ever reported seeing any ghost inside the Sullivan-Johnson Museum.

That's not to say there isn't something ghostly going on here. Linda herself has encountered several strange things that left her scratching her head. On more than one occasion, Linda has heard people walking back and forth upstairs on the second floor, usually when she's down on the first floor. Every time she goes up to look, there's no one there. Other times, she will hear what sounds like the back door open and close, like someone has come in. "Only I know that door hasn't opened since it's hooked up to the security system and it beeps whenever you open it," she said.

Stranger still, Linda has heard voices in the house when she's there all alone. And they're talking to each other as well, as if engaging in a conversation. She has no idea what they are talking about, though. "I've tried," Linda said, "but you can't ever make out what they're saying."

And then there are the smells that seem to disappear as quickly as they appear. Linda has encountered two specific smells within the walls of the Sullivan-Johnson Museum, both of which appear to be centered in the same areas. "Sometimes," Linda began, "on the second floor, you will get a whiff of perfume. Just a passing whiff. And if you stop and think, 'Oh, what was that smell?' You can't smell it again."

Linda has also smelled tobacco smoke in the area between what would have been the kitchen and the dining room—never anywhere else in the house, just in that specific area, and only first thing in the morning, just as Linda is opening up for the day. It's as if she's interrupting some specter having his or her first smoke of the day, although Linda's quick to point out that she doesn't smell cigarette smoke. "It's like from a pipe or a cigar," she mentioned.

Over the years, whoever is haunting the Sullivan-Johnson Museum has made it a point to let museum employees know that he or she likes for things to remain calm and peaceful inside the house. The ghost does not take kindly to arguing of any kind. Case in point: the Historical Society has their board meetings in the museum library. Linda says that if any arguing takes place during the meeting, for the next few days, doors in the museum will slam closed of their own accord. "They don't like arguing in the house," Linda said.

The ghosts also aren't opposed to doing a little remodeling or letting people know exactly where they think a museum piece belongs. The museum's Collections Committee meets in the museum on Wednesdays. One Wednesday morning, the group arrived as usual and headed up the main staircase to have their meeting. All of a sudden, Linda said she heard one of the committee members yell down to her, "Is there a reason why the settee is across the doorway?" Linda went upstairs and found that a wooden settee had been moved from its usual spot near the top of the stairs to across one of the doorways, barring entry to the room. "It moves on its own," Linda remarked. "And it does it periodically."

A few years ago, Linda decided she would try to get to the bottom of who was haunting the house. She began by digging a little deeper into the house's history and even speaking with former employees. First there was Charles, a former museum curator who lived in the Sullivan-Johnson House until the late 1990s, when he moved to Maine. Linda said that a few years ago, Charles was back in the area and had stopped in for a visit. As they were chatting, the subject of ghosts came up and Charles mentioned that on several occasions he heard a strange "whoosh" noise on the main staircase, starting at the bottom and going toward the top, as if someone were rushing up the stairs. "And I hear that, too," Linda told me. "I'll just be sitting down here, and I'll hear this 'whoosh' going up the stairs." Ever the skeptic, Linda tried to find a rational explanation for it, but came up empty. "I tried to see if the noise is in time with the air conditioning, but it's not."

Linda also recalls another former curator who, upon hearing what she took to be ghosts roaming around inside the house at night, decided it was time to move out. "She was the curator, so she used to live here. But she finally moved out because she got so scared in the middle of the night that she hit the panic button. She kept hearing what she thought was someone moving around on the first floor." After a thorough search, the building was found to be secure with no one else inside.

Linda also began researching who the ghost could be, including the possibility that it was another former lady of the house: Mary Lou

Johnson. It seemed to make sense. After all, Mary Lou was not only the last member of the Sullivan-Johnson family to live in the house, but she also reportedly died there.

During her research, Linda unearthed an interesting tale regarding the local library and a painting of Mary Lou. Linda said, "Over at the library, they had a picture of Mary Lou hanging there, and one time, they decided to put up a new picture. They came in the next day, and the new picture was on the floor, so they put it back up. Came back in the next day, and it was down on the floor again."

Apparently, the library staff got to thinking and decided that maybe Mary Lou's ghost was trying to tell them something. Namely, that she didn't want a new picture put up. "So they put the old one of Mary Lou back up," Linda said, "and it's been there ever since."

Of course, not everyone who has spent time inside the museum has had a ghostly encounter. Mike Elwood, who has volunteered at the museum since around 2007, has spent the night inside the building with numerous ghost groups and tours and has yet to experience anything. "I've been up here with all these ghost groups and nothing has ever happened to me," Mike sighed.

Bottom line is that no one's really sure who the ghost is. Or if it even exists at all. Linda's fairly convinced there's a ghost here, though. "I know it's an old house. But there are things that happen here that you just can't explain," she stated matter-of-factly.

THE VIGIL

When I first arrived at the Sullivan-Johnson Museum on the night of the vigil, I admit that it was initially hard for me to stay focused on the task at hand. The museum is filled with such amazing pieces, all centered around Hardin County history. Everywhere I turned, there was something new and intriguing to see and read more about.

For the vigil, I was joined by three members of The Ghosts of Ohio: Kathy Boiarski and Adam and Sheri Harrington, the first husband-wife duo The Ghosts of Ohio has ever had. While getting the grand tour from Mike Elwood, we ran into a bit of a problem. Since the ghosts said to haunt the building seemed to be tied to a period in time when it was a house, not a museum, we were looking to set our equipment up in specific areas such as bedrooms. However, everywhere we looked, we just saw a museum and displays. In short, while the physical features of the rooms were still mostly intact, it was hard to determine what the purpose of each room was "back in the day." That's when Mike suggested consulting with Charlene Hilty, a local woman who also volunteered at the museum. Mike said that Charlene had spent a lot of time inside the house when it was still a private residence, so perhaps she could help us identify what each room was originally. I thought it was a great idea, so as Mike went off to phone Charlene, Kathy, Adam, Sheri, and I began unloading the equipment.

Charlene arrived at the museum a short time later and was more than happy to give us her version of the tour. Just as Mike had predicted, Charlene knew what each room originally was. She also managed to add another name to the list of potential haunters: Lucia.*

According to Charlene, Lucia was a family friend who, as Edna Johnson grew older, would come up to the Sullivan-Johnson House and help Mary Lou care for her. She would even handle all the cooking since, as Charlene tells it, "Mary Lou couldn't even cook a can of corn." When Edna passed away in 1960, Mary Lou was left all alone in the big house and she wanted company . . . and something to eat. Charlene remembers: "After Edna Johnson died, Lucia would come up here, cook, and then go back home. And eventually, Mary Lou just told her to move in."

Charlene and her husband, Kenny, who was also the local pharmacist, became close friends with Mary Lou and Lucia. The foursome would often go out together for dinner or spend long nights inside the Sullivan-Johnson House, playing cards. Interestingly enough, Charlene doesn't ever remember Mary Lou or Lucia talking about seeing ghosts in the house but said that Lucia would sometimes say the house was haunted. "She was a cusser and she would say, 'That 'gd' house is haunted.' She never said why she thought that. Just that the place creaked."

The four remained close friends until Mary Lou passed away. Sadly, barely a month after Mary Lou passed, Lucia also died. Unfortunately, it was Charlene who discovered the body. Charlene's son had just gotten a new puppy and he brought it over to the Sullivan-Johnson House to show Lucia. When he got there, all the lights were on, but Lucia was nowhere

*This is a pseudonym.

to be found. When he returned and told his mother, Charlene went out
to the house. Finding the back door unlocked, she climbed the back stairs
up to where Lucia's bedroom was. That's where she found Lucia, lying
motionless on the bed. "She'd had a massive stroke," Charlene told us.
"But really, I think she was just heartbroken over Mary Lou. They were
pals. They went everywhere together."

At the completion of Charlene's tour, based on the information she
provided us, as well as the list of potential "hot spots" in the building,
here's where we set up the equipment:

Main Hallway, Second Floor
   · two DVR night-vision cameras in the main hallway, one at each end
   · one DVR night-vision camera, pointed directly at the settee
   · one DVR night-vision camera in the doorway of Mary Lou's room,
     pointing into the room
   · two Superlux condenser microphones in the main hallway, one at
     each end
   · Vernier LabPro sensors, including two ambient temperature de-
     vices, one electromagnetic sensor, and one static charge sensor, run-
     ning from the settee all the way down the hallway
Sitting Room, Second Floor
   · one infrared video camera in the sitting room, pointing into Mary
     Lou's room
   · one Superlux condenser microphone pointing into Mary Lou's room
Parlor, First Floor
   · one infrared video camera at the back of the parlor, facing the door-
     way
Rear Staircase
   · one Superlux condenser microphone at the bottom of the back
     staircase, pointing up the stairs
Former Dining Room/Kitchen
   · one Superlux condenser microphone in the area between the old
     dining room and kitchen

As the vigil was about to officially start, an interesting thought popped
into my head. Knowing that Charlene had a personal connection to two
women who had passed on in the house, I asked if she would be inter-

ested in taking part in the vigil. She eagerly accepted, although she sheep-
ishly said, "But I don't know what to do."

I made the decision that I would take Charlene up to the second floor
and the two of us would sit on the couch in the sitting room that looked
into what had been Mary Lou's bedroom. Sheri and Kathy would go
up to the attic while Adam would don the headphones and watch and
listen from the first floor.

Once the lights were out and Charlene and I were sitting comfort-
ably next to each other on the couch, she looked at me and awkwardly
asked, "What do we do now?" I took out a digital voice recorder, set it
on the table in front of us (with it facing toward the bedroom), and as I
turned it on, I explained that some people believe that if you ask ghosts
questions, they can respond, and their voices will somehow show up on
the recording, even though they won't be heard in real time.

"What do I say?" she asked me. I told her, "Just talk as if you're having a conversation with an old friend. That's what I normally do." Charlene nodded and then sat back quietly. After a minute or two, she began
to speak. "Mary Lou, are you there?" she began. There was no way I
could have been prepared for what Charlene said next.

Charlene began to pour her heart out to her old friend, Mary Lou.
She spoke of the fun nights she and her husband had while playing cards
in the old house with Mary Lou and Lucia. She mentioned how she had
enjoyed Mary Lou's friendship over the years and even went so far as to
admit snatching up Mary Lou's souvenir pen from Hawaii after Mary
Lou had passed on. "When you went to Hawaii," Charlene said into the
darkness, "you said you were going to bring me something back. But you
didn't. So after you'd gone, I took that pen. I hope you're not mad at me.
It's a nice pen, and I still use it. And I think of you whenever I do."

At this point, I felt my lips begin to quiver and noticed that my hands
were visibly shaking. Then the tears started flowing. But this had nothing to do with any paranormal activity. Rather, I was overcome with
emotion while listening to an intimate conversation of a woman trying
to reconnect with a dear friend. I felt as though I were eavesdropping. It
was at this point that Charlene dropped a bombshell.

"Mary Lou, you remember my husband, Kenny? Well, he's gone now.
It's just me now," she said. "I'm all alone, Mary Lou. And I just want to
make sure you're all right."

At that point, I lost it. I remember thinking I needed to get up, excuse myself, and pull myself together. But I was afraid to open my mouth in case I broke down. But I had to get up. I had to get out of that room.

I had managed to put the clipboard I was holding down on the table in front of me and was just about to stand up when the most amazing thing happened: something started walking around in Mary Lou's old bedroom.

When I heard the first "footstep," I immediately thought it was just the house settling. But then came the second step. And then another. And another. Slow, deliberate steps that not only caused the floor to creak, but also seemed to be coming closer.

"Are you hearing that?" I asked Charlene. It was the first time since she had begun having her conversation with Mary Lou that I was actually able to turn and face her. I was hoping the darkness would conceal my tear-stained eyes. As soon as I saw the wide-eyed look in her eyes, I realized Charlene didn't have to give me an answer; she heard the noises. But she answered anyway: "I am. It's in that room. Someone's in that room."

Instantly, the tears dried up and I snapped back into investigator mode. I reached into my pocket for a flashlight, never taking my eyes away from the open archway that divided Mary Lou's bedroom from where Charlene and I were now sitting. As I did, there were four more footsteps, each one sounding closer than the one before. The last step sounded like it was on the thin piece of flooring directly under the archway. Then all was quiet.

"Someone's standing in the doorway," Charlene whispered to me. I turned my flashlight on and directed the beam toward the archway. There was no one there. Shining the light around the other room, I could see it was empty. When I called down to Adam, he confirmed two things for me: he had heard the noises through the headphones (meaning the studio microphones had picked them up) and Charlene and I were the only two people on that entire floor.

"Mary Lou, are you here?" Charlene asked. There was no response. No more footsteps. For the next twenty minutes, Charlene continued to try and talk to Mary Lou (and I was able to keep myself together this time), but we heard nothing else. While she was talking, I positioned myself in the old bedroom and placed an EMF, an ELF, and a K-II meter along the floor, including around the archway between the rooms. The readings never fluctuated. Whatever had caused those footsteps had moved on. Later, when we reviewed the audio and video we took during this part of the vigil, other than the footsteps picked up by multiple audio and video devices, we did not "capture" anything else. Video recorded in those rooms did not show anything out of the ordinary, even when the footsteps occurred.

As exciting as the footsteps incident was, Charlene told us that she had to go. At this point, Kathy, Adam, Sheri, and I decided our best bet would be to spread out across the building to see if we could hear those footsteps again. So as the night wore on, each of us spent time either alone or with a partner on each level of the house.

Toward the end of the night, Adam and I were up in the attic area on the third floor and Kathy was alone in the front part of the second floor, near Mary Lou's bedroom. Sheri was down at the monitors, watching and listening.

Adam and I had been walking around in the attic for approximately ten minutes when we both heard what sounded like footsteps below us. It sounded like someone was walking around on the first floor, near the back steps. We both stopped, and I remember thinking that either Kathy or Sheri was coming up to ask us something. As Adam and I stood there waiting, we heard two more footsteps, followed by Sheri radioing up to us from the first floor, telling us to stop walking around.

As I started to radio back to tell her we weren't moving, the footsteps started up again. This time it was three distinct steps on the back staircase, so heavy that you could hear the wood creak and strain underneath the weight. The footsteps were so loud that Sheri was obviously convinced Adam and I were causing them. That is, until Kathy let her know that from her vantage point, it sounded like the footsteps were on the first floor, toward the back staircase.

Just like earlier in the evening, the footsteps suddenly stopped. Standing motionless for several minutes at a time tends to make me quite restless, so I eventually called for a break and we all headed back to the front room on the first floor. We had a brief conversation as to where we all felt the footsteps were coming from, and the general consensus was that they were centered around the back staircase, somewhere between the first and second floor. Interestingly enough, Charlene had told us that the back staircase was the one Mary Lou and Lucia used most often as they liked to park at the back of the house. What's more, Lucia's bedroom, where she was found deceased, was the first bedroom at the top of the stairs.

Stranger still, when we went back and reviewed the audio from that part of the vigil, we found something odd on the recording made by the microphone that was positioned near the back staircase. Approximately five minutes before the footsteps are heard, there is a loud feedback-type buzzing noise that lasts for roughly three to four seconds. My initial thought was that the microphone and/or cable had gone bad or they were no longer grounded. Neither turned out to be true. I also checked the sound mixer itself, and it was fine. Even the dedicated surge protector that we use for the mixer on investigation checked out.

Perplexed, I sent the audio clip with the buzzing on it for analysis. I made no reference to "ghosts" and simply wanted to know what caused it. The official results I got back were that based on the sound heard, as well as its cadence, it "appeared to be an electrical disruption caused by the microphone picking up the output from an electrical device that came too close to the microphone as it passed through the area."

Sounds good, but there was only one problem: no electrical device "passed through the area" near the microphone. All of our microphones are mounted directly onto mic stands that even have shock mounts attached to them. Once we have a microphone in place for a vigil, it stays there the entire night. Video taken that night at the moment the buzzing sound is heard shows nothing out of the ordinary anywhere near that microphone or even moving, for that matter. And the sound was picked up only by that microphone, not the external microphone that's part of the video camera.

The case could be made that there's something wrong with the microphone or one of its components. But that night, we recorded for over six hours with that microphone and that noise was heard only once. We've also continued to use that same microphone on investigations, as well as the same cables and mixer. We've yet to hear that noise again.

There was one last bit of weirdness that we discovered while reviewing the materials from the vigil. Or perhaps I should say from the day of the vigil, since this happened even before the rest of my team had shown up.

I was sitting out on the front porch of the Sullivan-Johnson Museum, talking to Linda Iams about her personal experiences in the house. At one point, Linda was discussing how none of the activity in the house is particularly frightening and in fact she has almost made a game of it, talking aloud to the ghosts and even thanking them for making her laugh at their ghostly antics. On my recorder, immediately after Linda says "and I've gotten to the point where I'll just say, 'Thank you, Mary Lou, I really needed my laugh for today,'" there is a loud, drawn-out whistling sound, quite loud and clearly in close proximity to the recorder, which was sitting on a ledge directly between Linda and me. No source for the whistling sound has been found yet.

FINAL THOUGHTS

As I mentioned earlier, the purpose of this book is not to declare any of these locations as "haunted" or "not haunted." To be honest, there's no way anyone can do that after just one night inside a place. Still, the evening I spent has left a permanent mark on me. The emotions I felt that night have made me rethink how I conduct my paranormal research, so much so that I feel it's my duty to share my thoughts with all of you.

Today, most ghost reality shows and books will tell you that to get results while on a hunt, you need to be aggressive. Confront the ghost, yell at it, and taunt it. Get right up in its ghostly face and challenge it to a fight if you have to, the idea being that you need to get a rise out of the ghost in order to get it to perform.

If my night at the Sullivan-Johnson Museum taught me anything, it's that one need not engage in all that browbeating to get a ghost to react. Maybe all it takes is loved ones telling ghosts how much they meant to them and that they're not forgotten.

Sullivan-Johnson Museum
223 North Main Street
Kenton, Ohio 43326
www.hardinmuseums.org

MERRY-GO-ROUND MUSEUM

I'll let you in on a little secret: I've always had this weird love-hate relationship with old merry-go-rounds. The craftsmanship that goes into making them, as well as the beautiful colors and even the music bring back memories of childhood. And yet, some of those carved horses are pretty creepy-looking. Don't even get me started on the non-horse creatures you see on some of the carousels, too. Seriously, who thought kids would enjoy riding on a hippo or an ostrich? OK, I admit it: I have issues.

Still, even I couldn't walk into the Merry-Go-Round Museum in Sandusky and not be swept away by the nostalgia. Ornate carved animals, some dating back hundreds of years, all lined up for inspection. Horses being carved and painted right before your eyes. And oh yes, the massive 1939 Allan Herschell carousel front and center in the middle of the building, just waiting for you to hop aboard and take a spin. It's an adventure few can resist, even if you are a ghost.

THE HISTORY

Most people who stand in front of the Merry-Go-Round Museum and admire the building's curved portico just naturally assume that it was built specifically to house a carousel. It wasn't. In truth, the massive neoclassical-style building was built in 1927 to serve as Sandusky's Post Office. Well, at least that was the main function of the building. It also served as a business center from which merchants could both receive and ship goods. U.S. Customs also had an office here, as did the Federal Bureau of Investigation and even armed forces recruiting. But while all the other businesses continually moved in and out, the one thing that remained

Entrance to the Merry-Go-Round Museum. Some of the neoclassical elements incorporated into the building when it was first erected as a post office are still visible today.

constant was the Post Office—that is, until 1987, when they relocated and closed the building. It would sit vacant for the next three years until a makeshift celebration brought the painted ponies to Jackson Street.

In September 1988, the United States Postal Service announced that they would release four special-issue stamps, each featuring a famous carousel animal. One of the four was the Daniel Muller–carved King (or "lead") Armored Horse, which at the time was on the Kiddieland carousel at Cedar Point in Sandusky, Ohio.

When the decision was made to have the October 1 First Day Issue Ceremony at Cedar Point in Sandusky, area residents got together to see how they could make the ceremony even more special. They decided that they would create a special display, highlighting the Cedar Point carousel, as well as some of the more valuable and historic carousel horses and animals. But where to put the display? Well, what better place to celebrate the release of new stamps than a Post Office? And wouldn't you know it, Sandusky just happened to have a giant old Post Office that nobody was using!

The group responsible for pulling the display together (and for pulling the strings to get permission to use the vacant Post Office) said that they originally thought maybe a hundred people or so would show up for the event. In truth, several thousand came by. Based on those numbers and the sheer looks of delight the visitors had on their faces, the group decided the carousel display needed a more permanent home. Not quite two years later, on July 14, 1990, the old Sandusky Post Office was no more as the doors to the Merry-Go-Round Museum swung open for the first time.

For the rest of 1990, the museum began acquiring various carousel-related memorabilia and artifacts. In 1991, they purchased the frame-

Two of the museum's carousel animals pose in front of a replica of the stamp that renewed interest in carousels and would eventually lead to the creation of the Merry-Go-Round Museum.

work of a 1939 Allan Herschell carousel and installed it in the middle of the museum. All of the original horses were missing from the carousel, so in addition to restoring the framework, scenery panels, and even the main platform, the museum set about trying to hunt down the original horses. Over the years, some were found and returned to their rightful place on the carousel. But joining them were various other horses and creatures that, while not original to the carousel, are from the same time period or in the same style. Today, the carousel is fully operational and visitors to the museum are able to have a ride.

THE EXPERIENCES

While the carousel is situated on the main floor, most of the ghost activity seems to be on the floors above and below. On the top floor, which houses mainly offices and a large painting room, the activity seems to emanate from one room in particular, although the ghost here has been known to roam the building sometimes. The room in question is at the far end of the hallway and is currently used as the archives. It is said that back when the building was still functioning as a Post Office, a janitor died of a heart attack in this room. What's worse, he is said to have died during the night and his body was not found until the following morning.

There are no records to support the man's passing inside the building, so if he did indeed die there, his name is currently lost to the ages. Perhaps that's why his ghost is apparently still making his appointed rounds. There have been sightings of an older man walking around the museum, often accompanied by the sound of jingling keys. Sometimes, though, only the keys are heard and nothing is seen.

One man who might have caught a glimpse of the old janitor's ghost was Dave, the former custodian of the Merry-Go-Round Museum. Kate Adam, the museum's artist in residence who has worked at the museum for well over fifteen years, remembers the time the two of them were chatting and Dave mentioned that he thought he saw a ghost in the museum.

"Dave used to have a desk down in the basement, in the back," Kate told me. "One day, he was sitting down there and he said he saw an elderly man standing in the doorway down there, near the stairs."

Thinking one of the museum's visitors had gotten lost, Dave stood up and asked if the man needed any help. In response, the man simply backed out of the doorway and appeared to go into the room to the left. "So Dave kind of chases after the guy, you know, to usher him back upstairs," Kate explained. "Only when Dave got to that room, there was nobody there and no way for the old guy to have gotten past Dave."

Museum curator Kurri Lewis is quick to tell you that next to nothing about this janitor figure is known. That said, if the janitor enjoyed a good cigar while he was alive, Kurri just might have busted him on one of his ghostly smoke breaks.

Kurri was working in his office one day when a woman who was working in the upstairs paint shop came in and said, "Come here, I want you to smell something." Intrigued, Kurri followed her back to the paint shop and stood in the middle of the room with her. "She asked me, 'Do you smell cigar smoke?' And you know, I did! You know how cigar smoke has a distinct smell? Well, it smelled exactly like that."

Not wanting to automatically jump to conclusions that this was para-

The 1939 Allan Herschell carousel on display inside the museum. Visitors to the museum are given the unique opportunity to ride the carousel as part of their paid admission.

normal activity, Kurri began looking around the room, checking pipes, and just generally trying to uncover the source of the smell. He never found one. "And then," Kurri added, "maybe five or ten minutes later, the smell was gone." When I asked him to describe the smell to me, he replied very matter-of-factly, "It was like someone was there in the room, smoking a cigar."

Cigar smoking aside, far and away the most impressive act of ghostly strength ever reported at the Merry-Go-Round Museum and attributed to the deceased janitor involves brooms. Ten of them, to be exact.

"We used to keep two brooms upstairs," Kurri explained, "and both of them disappeared. It got to the point where I could never find a broom anywhere in the building." One day, Kurri was working in his office when an employee came in and said, "Are you trying to give us a hint or something?" Perplexed, Kurri asked, "About what?"

"All the brooms you put down in our room," the woman said. "There's like ten of them in there." Sure enough, when Kurri made his way down to the painting room on the second floor, there were ten of the missing brooms, all neatly stacked in the corner. To this day, no one knows how they got there . . . or where they were before they appeared in the painting room.

Another area of the museum that seems particularly active is the basement. Home to offices, painting and carving areas, and general storage, there is one area that, in recent years, has been home to several bizarre events. The area in question is the section of hallway to your left as you descend the stairs. Down that hallway and to the right is a small pass-through room that has also seen a lot of activity.

Inside this room is a set of security lights that seem to have a mind of their own. They are motion-sensitive and will go on when no one is in the area . . . at least not anyone who can be seen with the naked eye, that is. Kate Adam got so annoyed with the lights that she thought she'd try an experiment just to make sure a critter hadn't gotten into the building and was setting it off. Since it was the holiday season, Kate went and found a round plastic Christmas tree ornament and rolled it across the floor. The security lights never came on. But a storage door in the corner suddenly opened on its own.

Kate figured that since the door led to an old shaft that runs up the side of the museum, perhaps a draft was blowing it open. She couldn't feel any breeze, though. Still, she decided to wedge the door closed. Didn't help. Every so often, she'd come into the room and find the door wide open, with the piece of wood she used as a doorstop lying on the floor.

Kate told me that she felt like something was messing with her by playing tricks with the door. Perhaps this is why employees have reported hearing the sounds of what appears to be a child in this room, giggling.

But if you want a chance to see a ghost down in the basement, your best bet appears to be to hang around the main staircase.

Kate Adam was working down in her basement office one Friday afternoon. Around 5 P.M., she decided to call it a day and made her way to the main staircase. But no sooner had she reached the landing when she heard what she described as "a scream from a little girl" coming from the far end of the basement.

Stunned, Kate froze on the stairs. She thought for a second and then started to tell herself that maybe it was just someone outside, playing around. But then came a second scream and at that point, Kate said she could tell it was coming from the hallway. By the time the third scream came, as Kate puts it, "I was done. I was up the stairs and out."

Before leaving, though, she took a look around the outside of the building just to see if anyone was messing with her. There was no one in sight. "That was probably the most dramatic thing that's ever happened to me here," she said.

Another time, Kate was coming down those same stairs and saw something standing to her left, near the entrance to the pass-through room. "Just as I got to the basement, I see something out of the corner of my eye, just standing there," she began. "I couldn't tell you what it was, but it was white. And as soon as I saw it, it went real fast down the hallway and disappeared. I didn't even have enough time to be able to tell you it was a solid form or anything."

Another time, Kurri Lewis's wife had a similar experience in almost the exact same spot. "She said it was about knee-high and as soon as she saw it, it took off down the hallway. And it kind of like evaporated as soon as it took off," Kurri explained. "She couldn't really see what it was except that it was white."

Of course, the main attraction at this museum is the carousel. So it should come as no surprise that even the ghosts appear to want to ride it.

One Tuesday after Labor Day, Kate went in to the museum to catch up on some work, even though the building was closed. She was painting one of the horses over in the carver's station on the main floor, near the carousel. Kate had propped the horse up so that she could paint the underside of it. Still, at one point, Kate had to climb under the horse in order to see what she was painting.

As she was working, she heard the telltale sounds of someone climbing onto the carousel. Peeking up, half-expecting to see a fellow employee standing there, Kate was shocked to find the carousel empty. And yet, the noises continued. "I can hear the sounds of someone walking on the carousel platform," Kate remembered. "It sounded like someone walking from the left side of the carousel to the right. I could follow the noise with my eyes, but there's nothing there. And there's no movement."

Why would a ghost be climbing up onto the carousel? Well, it could be the janitor, making sure everything is working fine. Or perhaps it's the ghost of a former patron, wanting just one more ride. Or maybe, as some people suggest, the ghost has simply dropped by for a look at the famous Muller Military Horse.

Created around 1917 by famed carver Daniel C. Muller, this horse is truly a sight to behold. Designed to look like a military steed, the horse comes adorned with swords and guns—not the type of things you'd traditionally expect to see on a carousel horse. Oh yeah, and according to legend, it also comes complete with its very own ghost.

Like all good ghost stories, the one attached to the Muller Military Horse has mutated over the years. But in the original version, upon seeing the horse for the first time, a woman (in some versions, it's Muller's wife) immediately fell in love with it. So much so that she would stop at nothing to ride it . . . and to keep others from riding it, too. Apparently, even after the woman died, her fascination with the horse continued from beyond the grave, as did her possessive nature. It is said that back when the horse was still installed on the carousel, people would report seeing a ghostly woman sitting or standing alongside it. Sometimes, late at night, the carousel would start up on its own. Oh yeah, and don't even think about trying to take a picture of this horse. The ghost will have none of that, and all attempts to photograph it will leave the photographer with nothing but blurry or dark pictures.

THE VIGIL

I was first introduced to the Merry-Go-Round Museum back in 2001, when I stopped in while hunting down the truth behind the Muller Military Horse. Several years later, I was honored that The Ghosts of Ohio was asked to be one of the first paranormal groups to investigate the museum. During that investigation, nothing much happened, although we did manage to capture what sounds like a woman's voice on one of our video cameras (more on that later). So I was anxious for a return visit to see if we could capture that woman's voice again, especially since none of the ghost stories associated with the building mentions a woman.

A few weeks before the vigil was to take place, I got a call from Kurri Lewis that immediately sent me packing up my trusty 1997 Honda Accord, Ol' Blue, and heading north toward Sandusky: the Muller Military Horse was going to be on display in the museum.

Before we go any further, I should probably give you the skinny on this infamous "haunted horse." First off, the whole "can't take a picture of it" rumor is pretty easy to dismiss. Over the years, I've taken literally dozens of pictures of the horse and only one or two came out blurry. But that was due to user error as opposed to anything paranormal, although I'd love to be able to blame my poor photography skills on a ghost!

Anyway, I'm pretty much convinced that the reason people started saying you couldn't take a picture of the Military Horse was because it was hard as heck to find the real one!

You see, the original Muller Military Horse was, for many years, happily going round and round on the Frontiertown Carousel at Cedar Point in Sandusky, Ohio. That carousel would eventually be sold to Dorney Park, and the whole thing was shipped off to Pennsylvania. Well, everything except for the Military Horse, which was put into storage at Cedar Point. To further confuse things, a fiberglass replica was created and put on display at the Merry-Go-Round Museum. Eventually, the original horse was taken out of storage and put on display in the Frontiertown Museum.

I mention all this so you can see why I was so excited that the original horse was going to be at the museum. I am a firm believer that if a ghost is supposed to be capable of interacting with physical objects (in this

Daniel Muller's infamous "haunted" Military Horse, on display at the Merry-Go-Round Museum.

case, climbing up onto a carousel horse or making the entire carousel move), it needs to have energy in order to do that. Further, you should be able to measure that energy whether it is in the form of electromagnetic energy or even heat. So this was the chance to measure the Military Horse to see if there might be something attached to it.

When I got to the museum, I put every type of hand-held device I could think of around the horse: two EMFs, two ELFs, one tri-field, and two ambient temperature devices. I also used the data logger from the Vernier LabPro and put some EMF and temperature sensors around the horse. I wanted to surround the horse with remote sensors and probes, but I had to keep reminding myself that this was a piece of history—a museum-quality piece of history, for that matter.

While I was letting the meters do their thing, I talked to Kurri to see if there had been any increase in the ghost activity since the Military Horse had come for a visit. "Not really," he said. He mentioned that almost all the recent activity was down in the basement, in and around that pass-through room. I found that interesting, since the first time we had been out to the museum, the only thing we captured—the woman's voice—was from near the carver's station on the main floor. That led Kurri and me to talk about what had changed at the museum since we did our last investigation. And that's when Kurri told me something rather intriguing. It seems that after our first investigation, pieces of a children's carousel that were being stored in the carver's station had been moved. Get this: they were moved downstairs and were currently being stored in that pass-through room! Needless to say, I made a mental note to take a closer look at that children's carousel when I returned for the vigil.

Gathering up all the hand-helds, I was a little disappointed to find that there had been no unexplained changes. In short, the data seemed to suggest that there was nothing out of the ordinary around the horse. But perhaps since the horse had been at the museum for only a few days when I got there, the ghosts were just making a conscious effort to be fashionably late.

For the vigil itself, I was joined by The Ghosts of Ohio team members Wendy Cywinski, Samantha Nicholson, and Ted Seman. Based on the interviews, as well as our previous visit, this was the setup we decided on:

Carousel
 · two DVR night-vision cameras on opposite ends of the main floor, each facing the carousel
 · one Superlux condenser microphone in front of the carver's station, facing the carousel
 · Vernier LabPro sensors, including two ambient temperature devices, one electromagnetic sensor, and one static charge sensor, running across the carousel
Main Staircase
 · one DVR night-vision camera on the main floor, pointing up the main staircase

- one DVR night-vision camera on the main floor, pointing down the main staircase

Archives Room (Second Floor)
- one infrared video camera in the archives room, pointing toward the door

Hallway (Second Floor)
- one infrared video camera in the second floor hallway, pointing toward the archives room
- one Superlux condenser microphone in the second floor hallway, pointing toward the archives room

Painting Room (Second Floor)
- one Superlux condenser microphone in the back of the painting room, pointing toward the door on the second floor

Basement
- one infrared video camera in the basement hallway, pointing toward the pass-through room
- one infrared video camera inside the pass-through room, pointing across the children's carousel toward the closet door that opens on its own
- one Superlux condenser microphone in one corner of the basement, facing out into the basement

If that looks like a lot of equipment, it is. And if there's one thing I wanted to find more than a ghost at the Merry-Go-Round Museum, it was an elevator. One was not to be had, though, so Sam, Wendy, Ted, and I had to lug a lot of equipment cases up and down the stairs. But when all was said and done, we all broke off and got down to trying to make contact with the Other Side.

I started off in the archives room. One of the things I like to do whenever I'm looking for ghosts is to sit quietly and get a feel for the location. I did this for about fifteen minutes and then started trying to contact the janitor. Sounds simple, right? Just turn on the recorder and go to work. It's not that easy, though, even when you've been doing it for so long that you finally get over the fact that you're essentially sitting in a dark room, talking out loud to yourself.

In this case, I didn't have a name or even validation that the ghost in this room was indeed a janitor. So not wanting to insult the ghost, I decided to begin by introducing myself and explaining that I was writing a book about historic buildings and interviewing people associated with the building. And then I said something strange: "May I interview you, sir? Can I ask you a few questions?" Thus began my first attempt to officially interview a ghost.

Looking back, I don't know why I hadn't hit on this approach before. I merely pretended that the ghost was sitting there in front of me—just your average, ordinary interview. Suddenly, the questions just came pouring out: What is your full name? How old are you? How long have you been here? Do you have any hobbies? The questions just rolled off the tongue. Before I knew it, I had been conducting an EVP session for a full thirty minutes straight. Unfortunately, it didn't appear as though the ghost was in a talking mood as no unexplained voices or noises showed up on the audio.

Throughout the night, Sam, Wendy, Ted, and I took turns crisscrossing the museum, spending time in each part of the building, both alone and in pairs. We stared at the monitors and waved our hand-helds around. We even had Kurri fire up the carousel at one point to see if that would wake any ghosts up. It didn't. Nine hours after we arrived, we packed up our equipment and headed home. A thorough review of all the audio, video, and photographs taken during the course of the evening revealed nothing out of the ordinary.

FINAL THOUGHTS

The popular theory is that there are two main types of ghosts: intelligent and residual. The intelligents are the ones who tend to like hanging around people and places they loved when they were alive. Residuals, on the other hand, are nothing more than a form of energy that got left behind (like "residue"). Residuals tend to be in locations where sudden, violent deaths occur or, at the complete opposite end of the spectrum, in places where there's a lot of energy in the air. Looking at the Merry-Go-Round Museum through that lens, there's no reason why the building shouldn't be haunted, whether by intelligent or residual ghosts.

I say that because there is just so much history in this museum. But what sets the Merry-Go-Round Museum apart is the vast majority of its holdings are such that multiple ghosts might be interested in attaching themselves to them. For example, take any one of the carousel horses. There are multiple ghosts that could possibly attach themselves to it: the carver who considered it his best work, the child who loved riding on it, even the janitor who helped keep it clean and running smoothly.

And as far as there being energy in the air, well, one need only open the front door to the museum. You'll feel that energy long before you've even got your ticket in your hands. But don't take my word for it. Take a trip out to the Merry-Go-Round Museum and climb aboard the carousel yourself. And as you're wildly spinning round and the music is coursing its way through your body, don't forget to take a quick look around. You just might be surprised at who's sitting there beside you.

Merry-Go-Round Museum
22301 Jackson Street
Sandusky, Ohio 44870
www.merrygoroundmuseum.org

NORTHWEST OHIO LITERACY COUNCIL

Here's a weird thought for you to ponder: Ever wonder what your house thinks about you? You know, like if it likes the color you've chosen for the master bedroom or if it's annoyed that you still haven't bothered to fix the leaky faucet in the upstairs bathroom? Even if you haven't, you've undoubtedly walked into a house or building and immediately picked up on the vibe of the place. It will feel warm and cozy or sad and depressed or somewhere in between.

Some people have told me that when I feel those vibes, it's not coming from the house. It's actually the energy from the ghosts, reacting to the current state of affairs going on inside the house. If that's the case, and if ghosts really do exist, then they must be over the moon at the Northwest Ohio Literacy Council. That's because not only has a once-decaying house been brought back to its former glory, but it's also now used to give area adults the chance to better themselves.

THE HISTORY

The building that would become the Northwest Ohio Literacy Council was the original brainchild and home of Clair and Lulu Tolan. Clair Tolan was the son of D. H. Tolan, founder and operator of the newspaper, the *Delphos Herald*. As his father grew older, Clair stepped in and took over the newspaper, becoming a successful businessman in his own right.

At the dawn of the twentieth century, Clair and his wife, Lulu, moved to Lima, Ohio, and in 1903 began building their dream house on West Spring Street. The stunning home was completed the following year. And

Once a private residence, the building at 563 W. Spring Street in Lima is now home to the Northwest Ohio Literacy Council.

while Clair was still reaping the rewards of his newspaper, which he had renamed the *Delphos Daily Herald,* he was looking for something a little closer to home to keep himself busy. With that in mind, Clair decided to get involved with the banking industry, taking a job as the head teller at the Lima Trust Company.

With all their successes, the Tolans quickly became known as movers and shakers in Lima. The fact that they loved entertaining meant that their West Spring Street house was almost always filled with family, friends, and laughter.

Around 1910, Clair extended his little empire even more with the formation of the Delphos Printing and Publishing Company. He and Lulu also began looking at acquiring commercial property in downtown Lima and would eventually become owners of what became known as the Tolan Block of buildings near Spring and Main streets in downtown Lima.

Clair passed away inside his family home on August 13, 1932. Lulu continued to live in the house until her death in 1954 at the age of ninety. After her death, the house remained vacant for several years until it was purchased by Kenneth Chapman in 1956. Chapman lived in the upstairs portion of the house while he operated his Kirby Sweeper business out of the ground floor, complete with a small showroom. Chapman stayed in the house until 1958, when he sold it to accountant Fred John. At that point, the house ceased being a private residence and functioned solely as a business office when Fred and Doty Accountants began operating out of the building. The accounting firm was in operation for several decades, until approximately 2005, when the firm ceased operations. At that point, the building was boarded up and abandoned.

The house remained abandoned for over three years until it was purchased by the Northwest Ohio Literacy Council, an organization dedicated to teaching adults to read. That summer, Literacy Council executive director Ken Blanchard and a group of trustees from nearby Lima Correctional Institute dug in and started repairing the building—everything from burst pipes to wallpaper and painting. Amazingly, most of the original woodwork was left intact, although it was buried under years of paint and drywall. During this renovation/restoration, it was discovered that the brown plastic wall covering going up the main staircase was actually incredibly rare pressed Spanish leather.

Some of the beautiful pressed Spanish leather that adorns the walls along the main staircase.

In the summer of 2011, the West Central Ohio Adult Basic and Literacy Education/General Educational Development (ABLE/GED) Program moved their administrative offices into the building. With this collaboration, the building has become the perfect setting for teaching adults.

THE EXPERIENCES

Prior to the Literacy Council taking over the building in 2008, there were no reports of it being haunted—at least none known to the general public. Ken Blanchard remembers talking to family members of people who worked in the building when it was an accounting firm: "They just talked about playing in the house when they were younger, running around and having fun because the house was so big." There was no mention of ghosts or anything out of the ordinary. So the paranormal was the last thing on Ken's mind when he was in the building. He has never had any strange experiences at the house either, even though he has been in the building at all hours of the night. "I can't say I believe or I don't believe. But as far as this house is concerned, I've never noticed anything weird."

Like Ken, Laura Ball was unaware of any ghosts in the building prior to 2011, when she moved her office in. Of course, it didn't take long for her to hear her first ghost story. "I guess it was maybe a week or ten days after we moved in. I was talking to a woman who used to work in the building. And she told me, 'There's some bizarre things that go on in that house.' I'm a skeptic, so I was like, 'Um, OK,' and she just dropped it."

Not long after, Laura would have her first experience that made her just a wee bit less skeptical. She was working in one of the upstairs offices with several other employees when they all began to feel hot, even though the air conditioning was running. Looking up at the ceiling, Laura could see daylight coming through the air vent. "So I asked our IT person, Steve,* if he would go up into the attic and take a look," Laura said.

When Steve climbed up to the attic, he was met by a puzzling sight: the flexible tubing had been removed from the vent and was now lying to the left of the vent itself. Stranger still, the O-ring clasp used to clamp the tubing onto the vent had been removed and was now sitting on top of the insulation on the right side of the vent. Close inspection of the O-ring found that its screw was loose—as if someone had unscrewed it in order to remove it from the tubing. Finding it odd, but not necessarily paranormal, Steve put the O-ring back onto the tubing and screwed it back down onto the air vent.

About a week later, it happened again. "Steve said it wasn't like the O-ring just came off. The parts were all over," said Laura. "So I was like, 'OK, something here doesn't want us to have air conditioning.'" Later that day, Laura remembered something strange that had happened to Steve when he first started working in the building. "I was giving him the big tour," Laura began, "and when we got to the attic, he opened up the door and went, 'Whoa!' When I asked what was wrong,

*This is a pseudonym.

he said, 'Something doesn't want me to go up there.' He didn't say what it was, just that it was something."

Intrigued, Laura asked Steve about the incident and if he had felt the same thing when he went up to the attic to fix the tubing. "He said that he didn't feel anything up in the attic except for that one time. But that one time, he said he had a feeling that there was definitely a presence that did not want him up in the attic."

"Steve's also told me that he's seen shadows moving around at the end of the hallway near the attic door," Laura mentioned. "One time, he said he saw a shadow down at the end of the hall near the plants in front of the window." Another time, Steve said he saw a shadow that moved down the hallway and appeared to make the houseplants at the end of the hall move and shake. Intrigued, Steve went down the hallway to get a closer look. "He told me that as he went down the hallway, it got really cold all of a sudden," Laura recalled.

Like Laura and Ken, Janette Ford knew nothing of ghosts in the building when she first came to work here. That didn't stop her from having her own experiences, beginning with the attic door.

"Nobody will have gone up into the attic and yet, one day, you'll come in and the door is wide open," said Janette. "At first, I would think, 'OK, maybe someone did go up there,' and I would just close it. But then it would pop open again." Even though this happened numerous times, Janette was still unwilling to believe there was a ghost in the house. That is, until it began speaking to her.

"I was working in my office one Friday afternoon and all of a sudden, there's a man's voice coming through my computer speaker. Just the left speaker," Janette recalls. She couldn't make out what the man was saying, though, and after only one sentence, the voice fell silent. At least for a while.

It would return, though. The odd thing was that neither the computer nor the speakers needed to be on in order for the voice to come through. "But it was always the same voice," Janette said. "It sounded like the same man, talking in a low, raspy voice." On one occasion, Janette wasn't even in the office and her computer and speakers were completely turned off when another employee who had been working in Janette's office came in and told Laura she had just heard something.

"She told me she heard a man's voice coming through Janette's computer speakers," said Laura. This time, the voice could be understood. "She told me the voice said, 'Come upstairs and meet me,' Laura recalled. "It really freaked her out because upstairs from the office is the attic."

Over the course of the next few months, both Janette and Laura would hear a man's voice coming through Janette's left computer speaker. "The only explanation we could think of," Laura surmised, "was that we were picking up a truck driver on his CB or workers on their radios." Seemed like a plausible theory except according to Janette and Laura, the voice never said anything that could be taken as workers talking or someone on a CB.

"He never says anything like 'What's the address?'" Janette confirmed. "Just things about 'going upstairs.'"

Just across the hallway from Janette's office are Ken and Laura's offices and the landing for the main staircase. It was here where, it would appear, the ghost of the house decided to turn another skeptic into a believer.

The woman, who shall remain nameless, had come up to the second floor and was standing between the offices, talking to Laura and Janette. "I was standing in the doorway to my office," Laura began. "Janette was out in the hallway, standing right next to the woman. The three of us were just talking about nothing in particular when she [the woman] brought up the idea of ghosts."

"She was kind of being flippant about the whole thing," Janette added. "She was saying things like, 'How are the ghosts coming?' and 'Anything spooky happen yet?'" All of a sudden, as if in response to the woman's questions, the door to Ken's office, which had been standing almost completely open, slammed shut. There was no one inside the office, either.

"It was violent," Laura stated. "It slammed so hard that we all jumped. It literally blew the woman's hair back." Apparently, that was all the proof the woman needed because after standing there silently for a moment, she simply told Laura and Janette "I gotta go" and left. She hasn't been back up to the second floor since.

If there is indeed a ghost hanging around the house, it also apparently likes to mess with clocks, especially if that clock's hanging in Laura's office.

"It was right after we moved in and were refurnishing all the rooms," said Laura. "One of the things I ordered was a clock for my office—

your typical, standard, battery-operated wall clock. And I hung it in my office. It was great for about one or two weeks."

But then the clock started acting weird. One morning, Laura came into the office to find that the clock had stopped at 11:11:11. Even the second hand wasn't moving. Thinking the battery had died, Laura replaced it with a new one and reset the time.

"Next day, I come in, and it's stopped at 11:11:11 again," Laura recalls. "She called me into her office and showed me the clock," Janette chimed in. "It was weird. I have the identical clock and mine was fine."

Laura once again replaced the battery. The following day, the clock was still running. But over the next few days, it would randomly stop at 11:11:11, 3:11:11, and 9:11:11. "At that point, I was thinking the clock was defective and there was something wrong with the hands," Laura told me. "So I called up Tony, the guy who brought the clock in, and said, 'I've got a defective clock.'"

The next day, Tony showed up at the house with a new clock. After hanging it up, he took a look at the "defective" clock, and everything seemed to be in working order. "So he grabbed the old batteries I had thrown away out of the garbage and put them back in the clock. And the clock worked fine. But he took it back to his store with him," Laura said.

When Tony got back to his store, he hung up the clock and waited for it to stop running. It never did.

On the main staircase, there is a landing between the flights of stairs. Feeling the need to fill some empty space on a shelf on the landing, Ken Blanchard brought in some tabletop electric chimes from home. "They came from my mom," Ken told me. "There's no significance to them, and my mom's still alive. I just put them there to fill some space."

"There's a little fan on the base and when you turn it on, the chimes ring," Ken explained. "But I don't even think they are plugged in. Nobody uses them. They are kind of annoying."

While none of the employees seems to like the chimes, something in the house apparently does.

"One time," Laura began, "our IT guy, Steve, was just starting to go down the stairs and all of a sudden, the chimes just start going off. We all just froze because we'd never heard them go off before. But this time, they were just swinging wildly around. That went on for almost fifteen seconds."

The electric wind chimes, located on the landing between the first and second floors of the Literacy Council. These wind chimes are said to ring on their own.

Janette added, "It was weird. You can slam doors or even blow on those chimes and they won't move. But they were really moving that time and there wasn't anyone even close to them."

A final story Janette shared with me, reluctantly at first, was about the time she thought a ghost locked her in the upstairs bathroom.

"The upstairs bathroom has a skeleton key," Janette remembered. "You just go in and turn the key and you can lock the bathroom door. So I went in one time and turned the key and it turned easily and locked." But when she went to leave the bathroom, Janette suddenly found that, try as she might, the key wouldn't turn. "At first, I was thinking, 'It's just an old lock and an old key.' But I was trying for like five minutes and it wouldn't budge."

Panic started to set in when Janette suddenly realized she was essentially locked in the bathroom. "Then, all of a sudden, I turned the key and it turned easily and I got out." Relieved (no pun intended), Janette decided to just chalk it up to old mechanics in an old house. However, the next few times Janette used the bathroom, she had no problems locking or unlocking the bathroom. For a while. "Every once in a while," Janette explained, "I would still get locked in. It's gotten to the point where I just don't lock the door anymore."

THE VIGIL

For this vigil, Ghosts of Ohio team members Sean Seckman and Amy Kaltenbach were with me. I was also joined by Aubree Kaye and Cara Stombaugh from Downtown Lima, Inc., a local organization that promotes a positive image of the city. I had met them both several years ago when I participated in the October Lima Lantern Tours. Even though, for the purpose of this book, I wanted to focus mainly on my personal experiences on these vigils, I thought it would be interesting to get the viewpoints of some non-ghost hunters.

The Northwest Ohio Literacy Council building falls into a category that I like to call "Haunted by Unknown," in that no one seems to know who might be haunting the building or why. The building does not have any sort of dark history, and there are no recorded deaths happening within its walls. In fact, based on the interviews, one would be led to believe that the haunting started only in recent times.

When conducting investigations in these types of locations, I determine where I would place the equipment based solely on where people have reported possible paranormal activity. So based on the interviews that I had conducted, the equipment setup for the house ended up looking like this:

Ground Floor
- one DVR night-vision camera, pointing up the staircase and focused on the wind chimes
- one Superlux condenser microphone in front of the main staircase, facing upwards toward the wind chimes

Main Staircase
- one DVR night-vision camera on the second floor landing, pointing down the staircase and focused on the wind chimes

Second Floor Hallway
- one DVR night-vision camera, pointing toward Ken and Laura's office doors

- one infrared video camera, pointing down the hall toward the plants at the back window
- one infrared video camera, pointing toward the bathroom door
- one Superlux condenser microphone in front of Ken's office, pointing down the hall
- Vernier LabPro temperature, EMF, and static charge sensors running up and down the second floor hallway

Janette's Office

- one DVR night-vision camera, pointing through the doorway of Janette's office and focused on the speakers

Attic

- one Superlux condenser microphone in the center of the attic

In addition to all this equipment, I decided to set up a Frank's Box in Janette's office on her desk near the computer speakers that the man's voice came through. I wasn't going to use the Frank's Box the way ghost hunters intended it to be used, though, partly because I don't think they really allow ghosts to speak through it (I'm 99 percent sure that what people think are ghosts are nothing more than fragments of speech from DJs that the radio picks up as it rapidly scans through the stations), but also because I had a better idea.

To be honest, I thought that the voice Janette heard was from the CB radio of one of the many trucks that pass by the house on a fairly regular basis. So I figured that if the CB signal was strong enough to interfere with the computer speakers, maybe if I tuned the Frank's Box to nothing but static and left it there, I might hear some CB chatter bleed through. Hey, it was just a thought! So basically, that's what I did. I put the Frank's Box in Janette's office, tuned it way down the dial until there was nothing but constant static, and left it on.

For the first part of the vigil, I asked Amy to play the role of Janette and sit alone in Janette's office to see if anything would talk to her through the computer speaker. I would stay downstairs, eavesdropping through the headphones plugged into the mixer. Cara and Aubree would stay with me while Sean positioned himself near the back of the house. After listening to Amy try to talk over the constant static of the Frank's Box for a good forty-five minutes, I called everyone back downstairs to regroup.

For the next session, I went upstairs with Sean and we each spent time alone in the offices. Eventually, we both ended up in Janette's office. With the Frank's Box still hissing away, I sat at Janette's desk while Sean positioned himself against the windows, about six feet away from me. It was then that I decided to try and do an EVP session.

I began by introducing myself and Sean and explaining why we were there. Then I started asking questions. After approximately twelve minutes, I asked, "Are you the man who speaks through the computer speaker? Are you the voice?" No sooner had those words left my lips when something truly bizarre happened: the static from Frank's Box shut off. No, it didn't just drop in volume—it turned off. There was nothing but dead silence.

Allow me to explain. The static volume didn't go down, as if another station was coming through or "stepping on" the station we had it tuned to. Usually when that happens, while the static level goes down, it's because you hear the other station coming in louder. We didn't hear that. There was no other station. Rather, it sounded like someone had walked up to the Frank's Box and either turned it off or else turned the volume all the way down. So it wasn't like we were still hearing static. We weren't hearing anything at all. But after a few seconds, the static would pop back in again, as if someone had turned the device back on.

Since this incident, The Ghosts of Ohio has conducted numerous experiments to see if there is any way Sean or I could have been inadvertently blocking the static signal. We found that while we could sometimes cause the level of static noise to go up or down by moving or repositioning ourselves while in very close proximity to the Frank's Box, the best we could do was to lower the static. We could never get it to turn off completely. What's more, we could do it only by standing right over the top of the Frank's Box. Reviewing the video from that night, as well as the audio from the studio microphone, while Sean and I do shift our weight from time to time, we do not appear to have been close enough to impact the static. Plus, whenever the static disappeared, neither Sean nor I was moving at all.

But back to the vigil.

Seven seconds after the static stopped, it came back on, just as loud as before. Over the course of the next thirty-four minutes, Sean and I continued to ask questions. Most of the time, the static remained constant.

But every once in a while, seemingly in response to "yes" or "no" questions, the static would suddenly stop. The following is taken from the transcripts from that vigil, noting the questions where the static seemed to respond:

12:28 (Jim): Are you the gentleman who is talking through the speakers? (static stops for twelve seconds, then returns)

14:38 (Jim): Do you like the woman who works in this office? (static stops for seven seconds, then returns)

15:14 (Jim): Is she your favorite one in the office? (static stops for sixteen seconds, then returns)

18:00 (Jim): Are you still here? (static stops for fourteen seconds, then returns)

18:17 (Jim): Sean says that's a "yes." Is that a "yes"? (static stops for five seconds, then returns)

25:48 (Jim): Are you still there? (static flutters for four seconds, then returns)

25:55 (Jim): Was that a "yes"? (static stops for three seconds, then returns)

33:29: End of session

In addition to the seven questions above, as well as the original "Are you the voice?" question, there were twenty-eight other questions asked during this part of the vigil. The static level did not fluctuate at all when any of those twenty-eight questions were asked.

Looking over the questions we asked that the static seemed to respond to, one could say that something was responding to those questions with a "yes" answer. One could also say that we're reading too much into it and it was all just a coincidence. What I can tell you is that during the entire vigil, the above-noted instances were the only times the static fluctuated at all. The rest of the evening, the static remained constant. We've used the same Frank's Box on subsequent investigations to attempt to get the same result. To date, we've been unsuccessful.

After the vigil, while we were reviewing all the materials we recorded during the course of the night, we discovered two pieces of intriguing data. To begin with, at approximately 10:24 P.M., while everyone in the building was downstairs on the main floor, the video camera on the second floor—the one positioned in front of Ken's office and pointing down the hallway, past the attic door—recorded what sounds like heavy boot steps walking toward the camera. There are five distinct steps, each one louder than the next. After the fifth step, they simply stop. This was also recorded by the studio microphone that was positioned in roughly the same location as the video camera (the microphone stand was immediately to the left of the video camera tripod).

It is interesting to note that while the video camera picked up the noises, there was no one visible in the hallway at the time. In fact, the time stamps on the other video cameras (as well as the audio from the studio microphones from the same time) show that everyone was on the first floor and we were all accounted for. Stranger still, although the noise sounds like boots walking on a wood floor, the second floor hallway is carpeted.

Finally, while Sean and I were up in Janette's office, listening to the Frank's Box, something odd was happening in the hallway just outside the office door. Specifically, one of the ambient temperature probes from the Vernier LabPro, the one in the second floor hallway (and the one closest to Janette's office) registered an eight-degree temperature drop over the course of four minutes: from 74 degrees to 66 degrees. While that might not sound all that significant, it represents one of the biggest drops The Ghosts of Ohio organization has ever encountered during an investigation. All the other remote sensors in the hallway, including the ambient temperature device at the opposite end of the hallway, remained fairly constant, meaning that the temperature drop was confined to that specific area of the hallway.

FINAL THOUGHTS

When I was a child, my mother used to tell people, "My son doesn't read books. He devours them." Truth be told, my love affair with books began at the age of six, when I was reading at a fifth-grade level, and most of what I was reading had to do with ghosts and the paranormal. It was as if by reading about them, I might be able to feed my bizarre desire to find answers to all that is unexplained. So it seemed like it was destiny to eventually find myself looking for ghosts in a building whose main purpose is to help adults learn how to read.

Perhaps it was that very desire that drew the ghosts in to play with the Frank's Box that night, if that's indeed what happened. Maybe they looked upon me as something of a kindred spirit (no pun intended) who, like so many others, comes to the Literacy Council building with a thirst for knowledge and a desire to learn. Maybe they were trying to help me fulfill that desire.

Along those lines, I remember a conversation I had with Ken Blanchard in the kitchen of the Literacy Council building. He confessed to me that he wasn't sure how he felt about the building becoming known as a haunted house. "But," he said, "if it helps get the word out about what we're doing here and how we're trying to help people, then I'm all for it."

And that's when it hit me: for years, I have been telling people that ghosts and ghost stories are an important part of our culture because they help keep actual history alive. At the Literacy Council, the ghosts are doing that and so much more. Here, the ghosts are indirectly working to try and help raise awareness about adult illiteracy and what can be done to put an end to it.

Northwest Ohio Literacy Council
563 W. Spring Street
Lima, Ohio 45801
www.limaliteracy.net

OLIVER HOUSE

If you're ever in the Toledo area and can't decide what you're in the mood to eat, head over to Oliver House on Broadway Street. Inside the giant brick building are several eateries, each offering its own unique brand of cuisine—everything from a casual sports bar and a brew pub featuring local beers to a five-star steakhouse and even a café and patisserie. It has been said that no matter what you're hungry for, you'll find it at Oliver House, even if your appetite originates from beyond the grave.

THE HISTORY

The Oliver House was the brainchild of Cincinnati entrepreneur William Oliver. During the War of 1812, Oliver was a serviceman stationed at Fort Meigs in northern Ohio. After the war ended, Oliver decided he wanted to purchase some land around Toledo for development. Returning to Cincinnati, Oliver gathered several backers and together they purchased some land, including that on which the Oliver House currently stands.

The first building they erected was a warehouse whose image is still visible today on the official seal of Toledo. But then some of his backers began to lose interest and, to be honest, so did Oliver. So for the next few years, nothing was done with the property. Then in 1835, the Ohio General Assembly designated Toledo the county seat of Lucas County. Looking at where his land was, Oliver was convinced that the state would soon be building the county courthouse right next door to his property. And since all those people would most certainly need a place to stay, Oliver decided to build a hotel on his property.

But this was to be no ordinary hotel. Oliver wanted to spare no expense and erect a marvelous hotel that would attract people from all over the state. To do this, Oliver hired the man many now consider the father of the modern hotel, architect Isaiah Rogers.

Construction began in 1853 and would continue almost nonstop for the next seven years. When completed, close to a million and a half bricks had been used to create a massive hotel complete with over one hundred guest rooms, each with its own fireplace. Oliver even created an omnibus system that could shuttle guests from the train station directly to the hotel.

The hotel welcomed its first guests in June 1859, and they all raved about its opulence. Local newspapers praised the hotel's amenities and drooled over the hotel restaurant's cuisine. But as the years went by, more and more of the hotel's neighbors began moving away and closer to downtown Toledo. The area where the hotel stood, commonly known as the Middle-grounds, began to become a destination for manufacturing plants. Slowly but surely, Oliver's hotel began to lose business and the rooms themselves

The exterior of the Oliver House as seen from Broadway Street.

started falling into disrepair. By the late 1800s, the once-opulent hotel was now known simply as a rooming house. Some even called it a flophouse.

With the outbreak of the Spanish-American War in 1898, the plethora of rooms made the hotel an ideal location for a makeshift infirmary. Although the war lasted only a few months, the building continued to help heal its veterans, many of whom had contracted yellow fever while fighting overseas. Soon, though, the hotel returned to its rooming-house status.

Around 1915, Edward Riddle, owner of the Riddle Gas Fixture Company, began to take an interest in the Oliver House. Having heard all the buzz about the crazy notion of electricity going into people's homes, Riddle was looking for a location to expand his business. Some time later, Riddle purchased the Oliver House and turned it into the headquarters for his new company, the Riddle Electric Company.

But in order to transform a hotel into a manufacturing facility, Riddle had to do some major renovations, or destruction, depending on how you look at it. Riddle gutted most of the building in order to install a foundry. During this time period, all of the hotel rooms were demolished.

Riddle would own the building until 1947, when he sold it to Toledo Wheel and Rim, a company that manufactured wheel axles. They would remain in the building for two decades until they sold it to Successful Sales, a local manufacturer of various novelty items. Successful Sales used the building primarily as a warehouse, although some of the building housed a showroom for their products.

Finally, in 1990, the building was purchased by Pat and Jim Appold, who made the decision to return the Oliver House to its former glory. They also wanted to transform the Oliver House into a social and entertainment center. And that's exactly what they did. Today, in addition to the famous Maumee Bay Brewing Company, hungry and thirsty patrons can stop by Oliver House and have their pick of wonderful places to enjoy, each offering its own unique culinary delights: Maumee Bay Brew Pub, Mutz Sports Bar, Petit Fours Patisserie, Rockwell's Steakhouse, Rockwell's Lounge, and The Café.

EXPERIENCES

One of the places in Oliver House where ghosts are said to congregate is an area that used to function as the lobby when the building was a hotel—an area now referred to as the Historic Lobby. Today, the space is used to hold meetings, banquets, and wedding receptions. As such, it's normally filled with large circular tables with formal white dining tablecloths on them.

"It just seems like the temperature is never right in that room. It's always cold in there," said Ariel Kynard, who has worked at many functions held in the Historic Lobby.

"Things tend to move around on their own in that room," added Dawn Cahill. "Especially the curtains and tablecloths." Dawn explains: "We used to have curtains that were in there and they would be hand-tied. When we would have programs, we would untie them so they could be down. Now, at the end of the evening, when we would be cleaning up, if you were to leave the room and forget to tie them back up, when we would come back for an inspection, they would be tied back up."

Dawn further explained that the first time she noticed the curtains had apparently tied themselves back up, she was initially willing to dismiss it as something one of her fellow employees did. That is, until she untied the curtains again, only to find them tied back up again when she turned around.

The tablecloths in the Historic Lobby sometimes seem to have a mind of their own. "You could just be in there working, or even standing at the top of the stairs, looking into the lobby, and the tablecloths would all be going up and down. It reminded me of the Parachute Game—up and down like that," Dawn told me. "Some of the staff would get freaked out because they would see the cloths, and they would say, 'But there's no one there,' and yet the cloth would just be like floating above the table. It was like if the spirits were trying to straighten the table-cloths out."

On either side of the Historic Lobby are staircases, one leading to the Oliver House offices and the other leading toward Rockwell's Steakhouse. Guests and employees have reported feeling as though someone is staring down at them from those staircases, even when there's no one there. On more than one occasion, shadowy figures have been seen at the top of the stairs leading to the offices, looking down into the Historic Lobby, as if just making sure the event is going off without a hitch.

There are also reports of a ghost child inhabiting Oliver House. Or perhaps it's ghost children. That's because some people report seeing a little boy; others, a little girl.

"What I saw, I took to be a little boy," said Ariel Kynard. "I was over in the server aisle [in the kitchen] when I saw it. It was like he just stuck his head in, looked around, then poked back out. I couldn't see a face or anything, but it looked like a little boy wearing something dark blue, like denim or overalls."

Dawn Cahill has seen a child's ghost in the same area as Ariel. Only Dawn sees a little girl. "Sometimes when I first see the ghost, I think it's just one of the girls that works here. But then I think, 'Why is she bent over like that, so low?' Then I realize she's not bent; it's a little girl. Then the girl kind of cackles at me and disappears. It's kind of creepy."

Oliver House owner Pat Appold adds an interesting side note to the ghost child story: "When we were renovating the fourth floor upstairs, we found an old crutch, a child's crutch. It's weird, but I don't know if there's any connection. People were seeing ghosts here before we found the crutch."

Ghostly children aren't the only paranormal activity supposedly taking place around the kitchen server aisle. There are reports of glasses, plates, and even silverware seemingly moving on their own. Servers often report having to plug appliances back in, only to return a few minutes later to find them unplugged again. Ariel Kynard even remembers a time when an entire tub of salad dressing appeared to have been thrown across the kitchen. "It was one of those big plastic containers and it just came flying off the shelf. It didn't slide off. It was like it was thrown. Dressing just went everywhere," she said.

And then there was the time where the kitchen door started misbehaving. One night in 2010, Ariel was in the server aisle with two other employees when the kitchen door just flew open. "That door's hard to open. Most times, I have to kick it to open it," Ariel said. "You can open it by pushing it, but it's hard. It was like someone shoved the door open, but there was nobody there."

One of the more unusual sightings, yet one that has been reported by numerous people, both employees and customers, is a ghostly woman. What makes this apparition so unusual is that she likes to hang out in the women's restroom.

Dawn Cahill is one employee who has encountered this ghost several times, always in the Rockwell's women's restroom. "The first couple of times something weird happened, I would just be using the restroom and I would hear knocking, like someone knocking on the door. Didn't really think anything about it at the time," she said.

"But one time," Dawn recalls, "I'm in the bathroom and I hear that knocking. But then I heard what sounded like the bathroom door unlatching. So I looked out and I see this woman. But I only see her from the shoulders up; the rest of her is a blur. She's a gorgeous gal—all done up makeup-wise, and she has beautiful blonde hair." The ghostly woman appeared to look in Dawn's direction and then simply vanished.

Dawn continued to see this woman several more times, always in the Rockwell's restroom. Each time Dawn saw her, the encounter always ended the same way: "She just sort of pokes her head in and pokes out," Dawn said. "She never speaks. Just looks at you and then just disappears."

Ariel Kynard is another employee who encountered this ghostly woman. It was an encounter that, even as I interviewed her well after the fact, still causes Ariel's voice to quiver when she retells the tale.

It was around midnight. Rockwell's was closed for the night, and Ariel had just finished her shift and was heading out to the parking lot with two coworkers. When she reached her car, Ariel couldn't find her car keys. Thinking she must have left them back in Rockwell's, she returned to the darkened restaurant. Finding her keys, Ariel decided to use the restroom before the long ride home. As she went into the women's restroom, Ariel had to turn the lights on since she was the only one in there. That would soon change.

"So I'm using the restroom and all of a sudden, it just started to feel weird in there," Ariel told me. "I kind of peek through the crack in the stall door and over near the lounge chair near the door, I see a shadow. It was like someone was moving around."

Ariel continued, "And then I saw what appeared to be a woman, sitting down in that chair. She didn't seem transparent, you know, like see through. It looked like a person, like a dark figure—a person. So I get up and I look through the crack some more and I can see her now, you know, like moving, and she's still sitting."

Knowing that she was the only one in the restroom, Ariel was soon overcome with fear, unable to move. "Finally, I get up the nerve to open the door to the stall. The woman just looked up at me and disappeared."

When I asked Ariel to describe what the woman looked like, she said, "Her hair was like a dirty blonde and it was down and in her face. I could see the bridge of her nose, but not her face. Her hands were very skinny."

It is not known who this woman is or why she chooses to haunt the bathroom. Some believe that she might be somehow connected to that specific chair that's located near the door. Dawn Cahill doesn't think that's the case, though. "Even before that chair was in the bathroom, people were seeing a ghost in there. But she was in the closet back then," she said.

Intrigued, I asked Dawn to expand on her "closet" comment. She told me that before the chair was added to the Rockwell's restroom, employees and patrons would claim to see the ghost of a woman in the restroom closet. "She would just be standing there," Dawn said.

"I've had customers tell me that the door to the closet opened while they were in there. They close it and it opens right back up again," Ariel added.

There is another ghost said to haunt the Oliver House: a spectral figure known simply as the Blue Man. Frank Chenetski III is a former employee who had two memorable encounters with this spirit.

"I started working here in 2002, so my first experience would have been at the end of 2002, early 2003," Frank began. "I used to be the valet here, so I would hang around out front, outside the bar, near the front entrance."

It was the end of the night, so after bringing in his "valet" sign, Frank rode the elevator upstairs to drop off the reservation book. After leaving the book in one of the upstairs offices, Frank took the elevator back down to the entrance lobby. As he exited the elevator and headed into the lobby, Frank said something in the corner of the lobby caught his eye. "I turned my head and there was a guy standing there. But I could see through him. Bluish kinda guy. And he didn't have any feet. It was weird because even though I could see through him, I could see a lot of detail. He looked like he was in his forties. He was dressed like a worker from like the 1920s, a worker with overalls on."

Obviously, such a sight would stop anyone dead in their tracks. That's exactly what happened to Frank. "I just stopped and stood there, staring at him. He's staring right back at me, too." Then, ever so slowly, Frank began moving toward the elevator. "I just kept backing up toward the elevator. I never took my eyes off of him and he didn't take his eyes off me. Finally, I got in the elevator and went upstairs."

Later that night, Frank made himself a promise: "I told myself, 'I'm not telling anyone about this.' I didn't want anybody thinking I was crazy." Frank told me that the morning after the encounter, he was able to brush it off, even though he still wasn't sure what he had seen. Two weeks later, almost to the day, Frank would get another chance to get a closer look.

Once again, it was the end of the night and Frank was coming down in the elevator after having dropped off the reservation book. "I get off the elevator, and there he is again," Frank remarked. "He's in the same spot, too, like he never moved. Gives me the goose bumps just thinking about it."

Just like last time, Frank started to back toward the elevator. Only this time, Frank had an idea. "I went back upstairs and grabbed a manager," Frank explained. "I said, 'You might think I'm crazy, but you have to come downstairs.' So we go back downstairs together: he's gone. There's no one there. And I've never seen him again."

I asked Frank why he thought the ghost would have appeared to him twice in the space of a few weeks and then never again. Frank had a theory about that. "I did something on each of those days that I had never done before," Frank began.

"Our wine cellar is right below the main entrance, in the sub-basement. And there's a little hole out there that goes down into the wine cellar. And every once in a while, we'd have our host stand out there, and so I would always have little things of garbage, and if I didn't want to throw it in the can I would just kind of push it down the hole. You know, little wads of paper or something."

Frank continued, "But those two times, I took a highlighter, a yellow highlighter, and dropped it down the hole. Both times. I don't know if that really had something to do with it, but I've never done it before or since. I've worked here for years and I've never had anything else ghost-related happen to me. I've always thought that since I have a deep respect for this building that it leaves me alone. Maybe it thought the highlighter thing was being disrespectful," he concluded.

About a year or two after his encounter, Frank would find out that he wasn't the only one to have seen the Blue Man. "After my ghost sighting, I sort of became the unofficial ghost historian for the Oliver House," Frank joked. "People would come up and tell me their stories.

One day, the bartender asked me to tell him about the Blue Man, so I told him. When I was done, he said, 'That sounds exactly like what that manager saw.'"

The bartender then proceeded to tell Frank that one night, one of the managers was carrying a tray into Rockwell's kitchen when she saw a man with a bluish tint to him, standing over near the mop sink. According to Frank, the bartender said the woman "threw down her tray, ran out of the kitchen, and left the building. She ended up quitting and never came back."

There is a popular legend making the rounds on the Internet that claims Oliver House was built on top of an Indian burial ground. What's more, the spirit of an Indian chief is angry over his final resting place being disturbed and is therefore haunting the building. To begin with, there has never been a single sighting of a Native American ghost inside Oliver House. So how did this story get started? Well, as is the case with all good legends, there's a tiny kernel of truth to it. Sort of.

As you leave the Maumee Bay parking lot and make your way down the concrete steps to the entrance, take a look in front of you. Over in the corner, sticking out above the concrete is part of an old tree stump. According to legend, there is a Native American Indian chief buried under that stump and he uses the stump as a conduit between the land of the living and the dead. Or so they say.

"It's not even confirmed that it's an Indian out there," Pat Appold said. "But what I do know, based on what the former owner told me, was that when they were excavating out front, near the Maumee Bay parking lot, they found bones." Pat was told that the bones were sent to the University of Toledo and confirmed as being human. "And because of that, they were able to go back and make an educated guess that it was an Indian. I don't believe they called it a 'chief,' though," Jim Appold added.

The former owner also told Pat that after the University of Toledo returned the bones, he reburied them in the same spot, right under the old tree stump. "I don't know if there was a tree there that they took out when they were excavating," Pat said. "But that stump's been there since we've owned the building."

Pat said that when she and Jim were preparing to do some renovations out front, she started to worry a bit. She still wasn't convinced there were bones buried out front, let alone those of an Indian. Still, she wanted to do the right thing, just to be on the safe side. "So I contacted a tribal association in Toledo, and they said they would come down and help appease the spirits with a sage and tobacco ceremony," Pat explained. The following Saturday morning, several elders from the tribal association arrived and together with Jim, Pat, and several Oliver House employees, they performed a special ceremony near the tree stump. "I told [the spirits] that we were sorry for disturbing them with the renovations, but that it would be better in the end." As far as anyone can tell, the ceremony worked as there were no reports of angry Indian chiefs inside Oliver House. But maybe that's because they were never there to begin with.

But perhaps the most enigmatic and widely known ghost at the Oliver House is the one referred to as The Captain. A quick online search will reveal dozens of references to a ghostly man dressed in a military uniform wandering the hallways of the Oliver House. Some will claim that this ghost is connected to the period when the building was used as an infirmary during the Spanish-American War. Others will tell you that the

The entrance near the Maumee Bay parking area. The object near the corner is an old tree stump said to mark the grave of a Native American Indian chief.

ghost is none other than Capt. William Oliver himself, despite the fact that William Oliver was a major.

Simply put, no one seems to know who this captain is or where he originated from. And with good reason. For you see, no one I interviewed, including owners Pat and Jim Appold, have ever seen such a ghost or even spoken with someone who claimed to have seen him. There is not a single, verifiable encounter with a ghost dressed in any sort of military uniform, captain or otherwise.

So how did such a story get started? Pat Appold believes it dates back to the early 1990s, when a woman who claimed to be able to see spirits was visiting the restaurant. On her way to the restroom, she reported feeling as if there were suddenly a man standing close to her, just over her right shoulder. As Pat recalls, the woman described the man, whom she could see only in her mind's eye, as a "middle-aged man, possibly in his sixties, who was wearing dark clothes and hat." The woman further said the man's appearance reminded her of a sea captain. Neither Pat nor anyone else was able to see this ghostly figure at the time.

Several years later, when Pat heard about Frank Chenetski III seeing the figure he referred to as the Blue Man, she wondered aloud if perhaps Frank had seen "that captain." And the moniker stuck.

Frank also agrees that this was where the idea of a captain haunting the Oliver House originated. He's also pretty convinced that whatever the psychic woman saw on her way to the restroom, it was not the Blue Man. "The guy I saw didn't look like a sea captain or like he was wearing a uniform. The guy I saw was dressed like a worker."

THE VIGIL

The odd activity at the Oliver House would present itself to me even before I began my vigil. Earlier that afternoon, I was conducting interviews up in the office area. I had been sitting in the same chair, back to the windows, facing the office door, for approximately thirty minutes when I began to interview Dawn Cahill. Fifteen minutes into the interview, I suddenly got a big whiff of what I could only describe as pipe smoke, specifically cherry pipe tobacco. And it was as if it were right in front of me. It was so strong that I stopped the interview and said, "I'm sorry, but do you smell a pipe?"

Dawn took a couple of sniffs of the air and said she couldn't smell anything. As she was talking, the smell seemed to move over to my left, still in front of me. I mentioned to Dawn that I could still smell it and for her to come over to my side of the table and see if she could smell it. Dawn got up, walked around the table, inhaled deeply and said "I can smell it now. It's like cherry pipe tobacco." Once she said that, the smell disappeared.

"I don't smell it anymore," I told Dawn. I got up and looked out the closed window, as my first thought had been that someone was smoking outside and somehow the smoke had drifted through the window. There was no one out there. Dawn must have guessed what I was doing because she said, "I didn't smell it behind you. It was right in front of you. But it's gone now," and returned to her seat on the other side of the table.

About twenty minutes later, Ariel Kynard joined the interview . . . and the pipe smell returned, again almost out of thin air. Once again, I stopped the interview and asked if anybody else could smell it. Both Ariel and Dawn said they could smell it, but it was only concentrated in a small area, about eighteen inches wide, right in front of me. Like before, the smell abruptly vanished. I was never able to determine a cause for the smell.

But things were to get even weirder during the interview. Several minutes later, Dawn, who believes she can see and sense spirits, told me that, unbeknownst to me, I had had some ghostly company. "I didn't want to say anything, but earlier, when you were talking, a black orb flew behind you. At first I thought it was a fly or something. But then it got bigger, and as it went toward that Buckeye bottle (which was on the shelf behind me), it disappeared. Unfortunately, I wasn't able to capture any of that on video." In all honesty, I didn't see or feel anything near me.

Toward the end of the interview, Dawn let me know that the ghosts of the Oliver House were apparently growing weary of my droning on and on about the paranormal. "Sorry to have to tell you this," Dawn interrupted me, "but someone out in the hallway just 'shhhhhed' you twice. I don't see anyone out there, but someone 'shhhhhed' you."

Ghosts or not, I took that as a not-so-subtle hint that I should end the interviews there.

Later that afternoon, I was getting a tour of the entire facility by Pat and Jim Appold. When we descended the steps from Rockwell's into the Historic Lobby, I instantly felt the temperature drop, to the point where it gave me a shiver. Having never been in the building before, I thought the room was normally that cold. But as Pat was telling me about the lobby, she suddenly stopped and said, "Why is it so cold in here?"

I told Pat I felt the cold, too, and suggested that it might just be the air conditioning. "No," she said, "the air conditioning doesn't feel like this. It's like there's a door open somewhere. It's like a draft."

Jim Appold pointed up to the vents and said, "It's not a ghost. It's the air conditioning." At which point, the lights in the room began to flicker, causing me to utter a very professional-sounding "What the— are you kidding me?"

Quickly realizing I was in danger of losing my ghost-hunting street cred, I immediately dropped my voice a few octaves and said, "Has this happened before? Do those lights normally flicker like that?" Pat responded, "Maybe during a storm, but not normally."

After a few seconds, the lights stopped flickering. The cold, however, still lingered in the room. But all at once, it appeared to move across the room and up the stairs leading to the offices. Climbing the stairs, Pat remarked, "It's still cold up here."

"There's vents up there, too," Jim remarked. Pat replied, "I know that, Jim, but it's never been this cold up here before." Realizing I might soon be finding myself in the middle of a believer versus skeptic battle, I started considering how long it would take me to get back to the car to retrieve an ambient temperature gauge in order to try and track the cold spots. But before I even had a chance to make a dash for the car, I heard Pat say, "It's gone." And it was. Yes, the room still felt cool, but the extreme cold spot I had felt earlier was no more. Before we left the Historic Lobby, I took one last look around at the air vents, making a mental note to come back later during the vigil and see if I could recreate that cold spot.

This vigil would be unique in that I was flying solo. So I was probably looking at about two hours of setup time before I could try to capture a ghost. Still, before I started to set things up, I wanted to see if I could uncover any information about the chair in the ladies' room that employees kept seeing the female ghost sitting in. I was trying to determine if there were a connection or a reason why the ghost was showing up sitting in that particular chair.

According to Dawn Cahill, the chair originally sat in the lobby, near the entrance to Rockwell's. It was moved to the ladies' room around

2005. She could not recall anyone reporting seeing a ghost sitting in the chair prior to it being moved to the ladies' room. She did say, though, that on occasion, a guest would sit in the chair when it was in the lobby and say things like "I can feel them [the ghosts]." But Dawn chalks that up to overactive imaginations. "For me," Dawn said, "it was like they had heard the stories about the place being haunted and were just making things up because they wanted to feel something."

With that out of the way, I took a look through my interview notes and decided that for me to have the best shot at capturing some evidence, here's where the equipment needed to go:

Historic Lobby
- two DVR night-vision cameras in the center of the Historic Lobby, pointing in opposite directions in order to cover the whole room
- one DVR night-vision camera, pointing up the staircase leading to the offices
- one DVR night-vision camera, pointing up the staircase leading to Rockwell's
- one infrared video camera, angled upwards toward the old safe/common wall shared with the women's restroom
- one Superlux condenser microphone in the corner of the Historic Lobby, pointing into the lobby
- one Superlux condenser microphone at the top of the stairs in the Historic Lobby, pointing down the hallway leading to the offices
- Vernier LabPro sensors, including two ambient temperature devices, one electromagnetic sensor, and one static charge sensor running across the old main lobby from one staircase to the other

Office Hallway
- one infrared video camera in the hallway outside the offices, pointing toward the back door
- one Superlux condenser microphone in the hallway outside the offices near the back door, pointing toward the lobby

Rockwell's Hallway
- one infrared video camera in the Rockwell's hallway, pointing toward the kitchen
- one Superlux condenser microphone in the Rockwell's hallway, pointing toward the kitchen

Now I know what you were thinking as you were looking over that list: Shouldn't he have put a video camera in the women's restroom? Yeah, right. I could just see myself trying to talk my way out of that one: "No, really, officer. I was just looking for ghosts. Yes, in the women's bathroom. Yes, I needed a camera that could see in total darkness." I could just about hear the "click" as the handcuffs were being slapped on me. Don't worry, I had plans for the women's room. I just needed to wait until the restaurant was closed.

In all seriousness, I was planning on waiting until the end of the night before putting any audio or video in the bathroom, partly to avoid an embarrassing situation but also because, according to Ariel Kynard, the restaurant was closed and it was close to midnight when she had her encounter.

But I had a lot to accomplish before midnight. Working all alone, it took me a while to get everything set up. Once I did, I decided to just sit quietly in the center of the Historic Lobby and watch and listen. For the first hour or so, everything was quiet. But then I caught something out of the corner of my eye. Turning, I noticed that the bottom of one of the tablecloths on a table near me was starting to flutter. It almost looked as though there was someone or something under the table.

One of the infrared DVR cameras was within reach, so I spun it around in its tripod and focused it on the tablecloth, which was still moving. After watching it for almost a minute with it showing no signs of slowing down, I began to notice a consistent pattern to the ripples in the tablecloth. I got up and walked toward the tablecloth and as I got closer, I immediately felt a slight breeze about waist-high. Turns out there was an air vent close to the table that was causing the tablecloth to flutter.

Having solved that little mystery, I began to walk around the room to see if I could determine where the other vents were blowing. The motion that I witnessed was no way near the violent "flapping" employees had reported the tablecloths doing in this room, but it was a start. I also thought that if there were enough vents blowing at once, it might explain the icy cold temperatures Jim, Pat, and I had experienced earlier in the day. I did manage to find a few more vents, but while they were all blowing cold air, none of them, save the one that I found first, was causing any of the tablecloths to sway, let alone flap. The room also never got as cold as it had been earlier.

Around 11:30 P.M., with Rockwell's closed for the evening, I decided it was time to investigate the women's restroom.

I think this is probably a good place to state that while I have been involved with organized ghost research since 1985 and have in my personal library thirty-nine books (yes, I counted them) that discuss how to conduct a ghost hunt, I have yet to come across any type of standardized procedures and protocols concerning how a middle-aged man should investigate a women's restroom. Alone. With video and audio equipment.

That said, I figured it would be best if I kept the restroom door slightly ajar. Once inside, I took baseline reading of the chair with my EMF and non-contact thermometer. The chair's temperature matched that of the rest of the restroom, and the EMF wasn't picking up anything at all. Next, I put a tri-field meter on the seat of the chair and turned the squelch up to the point that if the meter detected any changes in the electromagnetic field, the tri-field would emit an audible alarm. Next, I made sure the closet door was firmly closed. Finally, I went inside the stalls, closed the doors, and tried to see in which one I could peek through the crack in the door and still see the chair. Once I found one, I first turned on my digital voice recorder, then my IR video camera. Pointing the camera through the crack in the door and focusing on the chair, I began what was, hands down, the most bizarre and uncomfortable EVP session I have ever conducted. Thirty minutes later, not having heard or seen anything strange, I opened the stall door to find the closet door still closed. Somewhat relieved and yet disappointed, I returned to the Historic Lobby to finish the vigil.

Days later, I finished reviewing all the materials I had collected during my vigil at the Oliver House. There was nothing out of the ordinary.

FINAL THOUGHTS

Even though I walked away from the Oliver House having had several strange things happen in my presence, none of it was captured on video or in any other form that could be presented as evidence. As such, they amount to nothing more than personal experiences.

It doesn't matter if you're in the mood for a cup of coffee or a pint of local brew, a salad or a steak. It's all waiting for you at the Oliver House, all just a few steps from each other. It's the kind of place where you could enjoy breakfast, lunch, dinner, and an after-dinner nightcap without ever having to leave the building. It's a foodie's paradise and a place that keeps people coming back time and time again. It's a place so popular, you could say some people don't even let a little thing like their death get in the way of them coming back to hang out at the Oliver House.

Oliver House
27 Broadway Street
Toledo, Ohio 43604
www.theoliverhousetoledo.com

McKINNIS-LITZENBERG HOUSE

There is an interesting phenomenon in paranormal research that I can best describe as ghostly role playing. Basically, researchers will dress up in costumes from the same time period as the ghosts are believed to be from and see if they can get the spirits to react. It's something that's practiced quite a bit, especially at Civil War sites. Personally, I've never been one to engage in this practice, mostly because I think it's almost like you're playing a dirty trick on the ghost by pretending to be something you're not. Of course, there's always the notion that if ghosts have the intellect and ability to see you, then wouldn't they be able to tell you were just dressing up in a costume?

There is, however, a historical location in Ohio where it would seem that the ghosts do respond to people in period costumes. That place is the McKinnis-Litzenberg House.

THE HISTORY

In 1821, Robert McKinnis wanted relocate his wife, Betsy, and his family from Chillicothe, Ohio. With his grown son, Charles, Robert set out across northern Ohio, seeking out a large tract of land for himself and his ever-growing family. The two men finally settled on a gorgeous piece of property in Hancock County, nestled alongside the Blanchard River. While its exact location has been lost to the ages, it is believed that Robert McKinnis built a cabin for his family on the south side of the Blanchard. Charles, as the only one of Robert's children who was fully grown at the time, chose to build his own cabin, erecting it on the north side of the river, near where the current home now sits.

The beautifully restored McKinnis-Litzenberg House, the result of many years of hard work by the Hancock Park District and volunteers.

The following year, the whole McKinnis clan moved out to their new homes and became well-respected members of the new community. Robert would be elected justice of the peace and, in 1928, associate judge.

Charles McKinnis was also very busy from the moment he arrived in town. In 1824, he married Mary Vail, and she came to live in the cabin Charles had built. Charles, like his father, took an interest in becoming an elected official, and in 1828, he succeeded in being elected county commissioner. He did such a fine job that he was reelected two years later.

Over the years, as Charles's achievements continued to stack up, so did the number of children living in his cabin. In all, Charles and Mary would have six children. So it came as no surprise in 1847 when Charles announced that he was going to have a larger house built on the property to accommodate his entire family.

Built in the Vernacular Greek Revival style, the home mirrored the look of many rural farmhouses of that period. It might not have been the most elegant, but Charles and his family loved the home, so much so that it would remain in their family for over eighty years.

In the 1920s, the house and surrounding property were purchased by a local probate judge, Theodore Bayless, who was also the owner of Riverside Flower and Garden. Records show that for the most part, Bayless used the house as a rental property.

In 1953, the entire property, including the house, was sold to Otta and Ruby Litzenberg. Even though it had been a private residence for nearly a century, records show that the Litzenbergs used the home solely for storage and that they lived somewhere else.

In 1985, Otta Litzenberg passed away (his wife, Ruby, having passed years before). In his will, Litzenberg bequeathed the house and property to the Hancock Park District with the stipulation that it be sustained as a forest preserve. Beginning in 1989, the Hancock Park District started work on the property, creating paths, installing public restrooms, and even rebuilding a barn. The house itself was another story. In order for it to be restored, practically the entire structure had to be gutted. It was a long, slow, and painful process. But thanks to the hard work and dedication of the Hancock Park District and countless volunteers, the Litzenberg Memorial Woods opened to the public in 1995, with the McKinnis-Litzenberg House out front and center.

THE EXPERIENCES

Casey Lauger started volunteering at the McKinnis-Litzenberg House in 2005 before getting a part-time job there as an assistant to the living history coordinator. While Casey admits she has always had an interest in ghosts "and that sort of thing," prior to 2005 she hadn't heard any stories about the McKinnis-Litzenberg House being haunted. But she said it wasn't long before she began to wonder if there was something paranormal going on in the house. And for her, it all started with the house's security system.

"The first time anything happened to me in the house was when I was there alone and I had set just the perimeter on the alarm [meaning only the doors and windows were armed] so I could keep working inside. So I was in there working, and all of a sudden it was like the door jiggled or something and the alarm started going off. It really scared me because I thought someone was trying to get in the house," Casey continued. "But there was no one there, so I sort of convinced myself that it was just a false alarm."

Casey would find it harder to keep telling herself that it was a false alarm since the system started to take on a mind of its own, going off at all hours of the day and night and even flashing out alerts that people were moving inside, even when the house was empty. There were so many incidents that the Park District investigated to verify that the system was running properly. It was.

"Then one night I was out at the house cleaning. When I finished, I was getting ready to lock up and went into the kitchen to set the alarm," Casey told me. "I went to turn the alarm on and as I did, for whatever reason, I said something like, 'Well, I hope you like your house, it's nice and clean now.' All of a sudden, the alarm, which had been counting down, started flashing 'BAD—BASEMENT,' meaning it had detected movement in the basement. As I'm sitting there watching the keypad, it starts flashing 'BAD—BED CHAMBER,' and then it goes 'BAD—HALLWAY,' 'BAD—PARLOR.' So it was like something was moving through the house toward me. Then it said 'BAD—KITCHEN,' which was where I was. That was it! I just hit 'bypass,' and the alarm started counting down again, so I just ran out and slammed the door behind me," she concluded.

Chris Allen has been volunteering at the McKinnis-Litzenberg House since 2001. She remembers hearing the forest rangers who patrolled the property telling stories about seeing shadowy figures moving around inside the house late at night. "But I'd never heard anything from people inside the house," Chris admits. That would soon change.

Several years ago, Chris was upstairs with another volunteer, discussing the best way to store the materials they had been using for a recent sugar maple collection demonstration, when all of a sudden, they heard something hit the floor right behind them. They looked, and lying on the floor was the spindle from the spinning wheel that was on the other side of the room.

"That's not something that can come out on its own," Chris confided. "It literally has to be pulled out because it has a shaft on it—it has to be pulled up and pulled out. So it was like something pulled it up and out and threw it at us. It literally flew several feet across the room at us."

"I didn't know what to do, so I just picked it up, put it back in the spinning wheel and said, 'Please don't ever throw that at me again.' And it never happened again," Chris concluded.

Well, at least not to Chris. Casey confirmed that other volunteers have reported having the spindle thrown at them. "It's weird because the spinning wheel is a reproduction, so I don't know why they would pick that as the thing to mess with. But it keeps happening. And it's being thrown far. After the last time, I actually went upstairs and told the ghosts, 'This has got to stop because if it breaks, I don't know where to go to get it fixed.' But that didn't help. They still throw it," Casey said, shaking her head.

Robert Sims has been a ranger for the Park District since 2007, although he's been inside the McKinnis-Litzenberg House since the late 1980s. He doesn't recall having any ghostly encounters in the house back then but is quick to point out that "that was before we fixed the house up. Back then, the house was absolutely dilapidated. So if anything weird had happened to me in the house back then, I would have attributed it immediately to a falling-down house."

Once the house was restored, Robert began to experience things that, while he's not prepared to call them ghostly, he would certainly classify as odd. "The first time I experienced something I'd call 'odd' in the house was several months after I started working for the park service. Part of the service ranger thing is we go out and check the buildings, usually on nights and weekends," Robert explained.

"So one time, it was probably evening, I go out to the house, go inside, and shut off the alarm. And then I hear what sounds like someone walking around in the next room. So I go 'Hello?' and of course, I don't hear anybody. So I walk in there—nothing. Next room over, I hear it again. So now I'm thinking we have mice or something."

Mice or not, Robert began to engage in a weird game of cat-and-mouse, chasing the sound of footsteps from room to room. No matter what room he thought the sounds were emanating from, as soon as Robert got there, the footsteps would stop, only to continue again in another room.

"Finally, I walk into the storage room upstairs and then I hear the footsteps back downstairs. They're pretty loud, too," Robert continued. At that point, I said, 'I'm not playing this game,' and I walked out."

It would not be the last time Robert would hear the footsteps. In fact, he would hear them as he was getting ready to meet me for the interview for this book.

"Just this morning," Robert explained, "I was out there and some people wanted to see the barn. So I showed them and then went to check on the McKinnis house. I walk in there, and sure enough, I hear footsteps in the other room. The footsteps move from room to room, but they always sound the same to me. You'll hear the floorboards creaking. It's not like the wind blowing or anything. It sounds like actual footsteps. And they are never in the same room with you."

Casey knows those footsteps all too well. "It's like they're messing with you," she told me. "You'll be in the parlor and you'll hear it in the bedchamber. So you go in the bedchamber and then it's upstairs. Then it's in the kitchen." Casey also vividly remembers an occurrence in 2009 that, while I didn't know it at the time, I played a major role in.

In October 2009, Casey had invited me to speak at the barn at Litzenberg Memorial Woods about my book, *Weird Ohio*. After the presentation Casey asked if I wanted a quick tour of the McKinnis-Litzenberg House. Two members of The Ghosts of Ohio, Darrin Boop and Steph Willis, went to the house with Casey, Chris Allen, and me. "We had a lot of cleaning up to do, so we just sort of let you guys in the house and then let you go wherever you wanted."

Returning to the house a short time later, Casey said she and Chris thought we had left already. "We were downstairs and I remember telling Chris, 'I don't know where James is.' But then we heard walking around upstairs and we were like, 'OK, he's upstairs.'" Not wanting to disturb me, Casey and Chris left the house and went to finish packing up the barn. When they got there, they found Darrin, Steph, and me waiting for them. We'd been there for about fifteen minutes. "I don't know who we heard walking upstairs," Casey said, "but it couldn't have been you guys. Turns out, there wasn't anyone upstairs."

"All my pictures from that night turned out bad," Chris chimed in. "None of them were good. They're all fuzzy or blurry. Some even look like they have other images on top of them. That's never happened before," she added.

Over the years, Casey has also encountered something else in the house that sends her from room to room, searching: disembodied voices. "I've heard voices in the house, probably four or five times. It's always two men talking. The first couple of times I heard them, I freaked out. I told my dad, and he said, 'Are you sure it's just not someone standing outside the house, talking?'"

Casey told me that even though she thought it would be highly unlikely that someone would just walk up to the McKinnis-Litzenberg House since it stands alone, she took some comfort in her dad's words. "I figured that if I ever heard the voices again, I could go look out the back window because you can see the parking lot from there. If there were cars there, that would tell me I was hearing people, not ghosts."

So the next time Casey was alone in the house and heard the men talking, she immediately went to the back window. There were no cars in the parking lot. Undaunted, Casey tried to make contact. "I said, 'Hello?' and then the voices just stopped. It was like they suddenly knew I was there or something. It got real quiet," she said.

Since that incident, Casey told me that every time she heard the voices, she would call out to them: "I'll say things like 'I know you're there' or something like that and then just go back to whatever I was doing. And the voices will just stop—it will get really quiet. But then, and here's the weird thing, sometimes they'll just start talking again!"

When I asked Casey to describe the voices, she said, "They're not loud. You can't ever make out what they're saying. But it's always two men talking. It's not gruff or mean, it's just a normal conversation. It's the strangest thing, and it's like they know you're there, but they don't care."

Not being able to determine what the men were talking about led Casey to do a bit of research, as well as figuring out where the voices were coming from. "A couple of times, the voices move from room to room. But most of the time, I only hear it coming from the downstairs bedroom, which we believe used to be Mr. McKinnis's office, where he would have done most of his business. So maybe it's Mr. McKinnis, conducting business. I don't know," Casey concluded.

Casey also mentioned a recent event that still has her scratching her head. "It was this past November," she began. "I had gone out to the house to get an extension cord from the upstairs storage area, where we keep all the costumes. I go upstairs, and I happen to look down at the floor near one of the windows and there's a little wet footprint there! It looked just like a footprint from a small child! You could see toes and everything! But the rest of the floor was dry."

Casey continued, "I called to the girl who was with me to come look at it, but then I ran down to my car and grabbed my camera. By the time I got back, most of the toes were gone. But I got a picture of it. On closer inspection on the computer, it looks like it's two—like one was kind of dry and one was at the window."

After the footprint dried up and disappeared, Casey and the other girl looked around the room to see if they could determine how the footprint got there. "We have no idea," Casey admitted. "It wasn't near anything that was wet. The closest wet anything was downstairs in the bedchamber. We don't even have running water in the house."

"It was the weirdest thing," Casey said. "It looked as if a barefooted child stepped in something wet and then went over and stood in front of the window that looks out over the garden. We looked on the window for fingerprints or something, but there was nothing."

Just as the interviews were coming to an end, Casey said she wanted to tell me one last story, something that happened to her and her then-boyfriend, Jim, one September evening. Before telling me her story, Casey told me it was "the weirdest night of my life. I don't think whatever was in the house was purposely trying to scare me, but it really freaked me out," Casey admitted.

"So we go in the house, and we each have a lantern—we have plugs in the house, but it's usually just easier to use candles and lanterns. As soon as we go in, there was just a creepy feeling to the house. I can't explain it. We go upstairs and there's still this creepy feeling. I remember getting nervous and not even wanting to leave the room because I just had a bad feeling. But anyway, we leave the storage room and we start walking down the stairs."

Casey paused, took a deep breath, and then continued: "I went down the stairs first, and Jim was behind me. I was about halfway down the stairs. I didn't know it at the time, but Jim had stopped at the top of the stairs and was looking toward the middle window. He thought he saw a head—a little head—pop out of one of the door frames—like a child's shadow head or something. And he was squinting to see what it was.

"At the same time, I had stopped halfway down the stairs because I swear it was like someone was just standing there. The light from my lantern was reflecting back at me except for on these three windows at the bottom. And I just stopped and thought, 'That's not right.' As I did that, it was like whatever it was stepped out of the way and into the parlor."

Casey paused here, so I asked her to further describe what she saw to me. "It looked like a man, but not with a hat on. It looked like a bald head. But he was clearly inside the house. And he stepped back, like he stepped back into the parlor. Like, if it was an actual person—if you were standing there and saw us coming down the stairs and you knew I was going to go into the parlor, you'd step out of my way. That's what it did—it stepped out of the way and into the parlor.

"That really freaked me out because I knew to get out of the house, I had to go through the parlor," Casey continued. "So I just ran. I ran down the stairs and just left Jim there. I didn't even look up as I ran through the parlor. I just kept my head down and ran."

Her harrowing encounter wasn't over yet, though. "So I get to the keypad in the kitchen and I start to punch in the code to set the security system. Jim comes up behind me, but then I felt like someone else came up behind me and was standing right there, looking over my shoulder and almost breathing down my neck. And it wasn't Jim.

"I get the alarm set, and I run out the door. But as I turn around, I see Jim struggling to shut the front door. It's like something is on the other side of the door, inside the house, holding the door open. Finally, he jerks the door and it's almost like he fell backwards, but he gets it shut. So I run up and put the key in and lock it. Then, as we're walking away, we both hear a noise. We look back, and I'm not kidding you, the doorknob had started shaking back and forth. We're not even near it. It was like something was on the other side, moving the handle. It was like the creepiest thing that ever happened to me in my entire life."

THE VIGIL

The McKinnis-Litzenberg House was not as large as some of the other buildings I've had the pleasure of being inside of, so rather than jam every single room with equipment, I decided to go more bare bones and simply focus on the specific areas where activity had been reported.

For this vigil, Amy Kaltenbach from The Ghosts of Ohio was with me. We decided to put the command center—the place where we keep the DVR monitors, sound mixer, and laptop screen for viewing the Vernier LabPro sensors—in the kitchen area at the back of the house. This would not only allow us to monitor things while not being in the way: sitting in the kitchen also gave us a clear view of both the security system keypad and the door that featured so prominently in Casey's creepy encounter.

The setup for the McKinnis-Litzenberg House went something like this:

Parlor
- one DVR night-vision camera, pointing across the parlor toward the front of the house
- laser grid in corner of parlor, pointing across the room toward the front of the house

Downstairs Bedroom
- one Superlux condenser microphone in the corner of the downstairs bedroom, pointing out into the room

Main Staircase
- one DVR night-vision camera at the bottom of the main staircase, pointing up the stairs
- one Superlux condenser microphone at the bottom of the staircase, pointing toward the second floor
- one Superlux condenser microphone at the top of the staircase, pointing toward the first floor
- Vernier LabPro temperature, EMF, and static electricity sensors running up the main staircase

Second Floor
- one DVR night-vision camera in the storage/dressing room, pointing toward the back window where the wet footprint had appeared
- one DVR night-vision camera focused on the spinning wheel
- one infrared video camera on the second floor landing, pointing down the stairs toward the front door

Setup was going smoothly, and we were just about to kill all the lights and get started, when all of a sudden, the laser grid started pulsating. It was almost strobe-like. It was the first time I had ever seen it do something like that. (For a description of how laser grids work, see the chapter "Equipment Used.")

The laser grid I was using for this particular vigil was fairly new, although I had used it before on several private investigations with The Ghosts of Ohio. It was during those investigations that we learned something interesting about the laser grid: it burns through batteries fast. With only two AA batteries to run it, having the laser grid constantly on meant the batteries would die in just a few hours, hardly the length of time we needed the grid to be on during an all-night investigation.

For that reason, I had Ghosts of Ohio team member Mark DeLong modify the laser grid so that we could run it off good, old-fashioned electricity from the wall. I only mention this because, even though we had tested the laser grid twice since Mark modified it, this was the first time we had used it in the field. So even though setting it up is fairly straightforward, when I saw it flashing, my initial thought was "user error."

So I texted Mark and told him what was going on. He texted back with all sorts of questions like "Is it connected to a surge protector?" and "Are the cables connected?" The answer was always "yes," leaving Mark to reply, "That's odd," which it was. But not as odd as when it suddenly stopped flashing and began working normally again. And certainly not as odd as what it was about to do next.

About thirty minutes later, Amy and I were sitting in the kitchen, staring at the monitors, which were showing nothing out of the ordinary. I had just looked down to start logging in the probe readings from the Vernier LabPro when I heard Amy say, "Look at the laser grid." I looked up and into the parlor, where the grid was projecting onto the wall. At first, it looked the same as it had been: a whole bunch of green dots, illuminating, from left to right, a portion of the back wall of the parlor, part of the entryway in front of the main staircase, and the front wall of the house. But something didn't look right. That's because a portion of the grid was now missing. Put another way, it appeared as though roughly twenty laser points were being blocked, except there was nothing blocking that portion of the laser.

In previous tests, whenever we aimed the laser grid at the wall and then moved an object between the laser and the wall, while the object created a black shape on the wall, you could also see the laser points of the grid on the object. In other words, the laser points were not being absorbed, just blocked. Try this little experiment on your own: take a laser pointer and point it at the wall. Then move your hand in front of it. The laser point will disappear from the wall, but you will then see the laser point on your hand. Well, that night in the McKinnis-Litzenberg House, something appeared to have absorbed a portion of the grid.

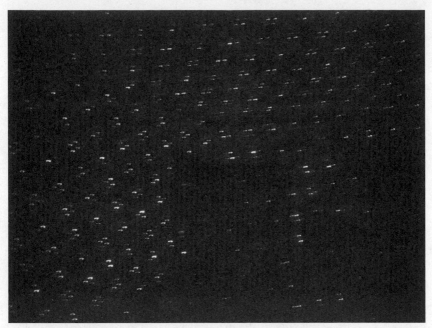

A laser grid anomaly, photographed near the main staircase where Casey Lauger had her encounter. Note the dark areas of the grid, where it appears something is literally blocking out the laser beams even though there was nothing between the beams and the wall where the grid was pointing.

I was standing there in the kitchen, looking at the grid itself as well as its image on the DVR monitors and couldn't make sense of it. You could actually see the laser originating from the device and shining brightly across the room. Yet, somewhere along the way, something that was not visible to my eyes or to an infrared camera was blocking part of the light.

Not knowing what to do next, I figured I should document this as best as I could. Knowing that we've had investigations where we've seen things on the monitors that do not show up later when we review the footage, I decided not to assume that what I was seeing on the monitor would be recorded. So I took a picture of the DVR screen. Next, I walked to the edge of the kitchen, leaned into the parlor, being careful not to get too close to the laser grid, and took three pictures in quick succession of the area where the laser was being blocked out. As I was about to take the third picture, I noticed that the grid was once again complete; whatever had been blocking or absorbing it was now gone.

In reviewing the photo I took of the monitor, you can clearly see that part of the grid is missing. Since we were using four cameras, though, the screen is in "quad mode," meaning the screen is divided into four, so the image in question is rather small.

However, in two of the digital photos I took of the grid, you can clearly see that part of the grid is missing; it's all black. The rest of the grid is bright and strong. Some people who have seen the photograph say that the dark section looks like the outline of a person, peeking around the corner. Some even point out what looks like the outline of a second person. I'm not sure I'm ready to go that far yet. But I can tell you I have no explanation for what caused a portion of the grid to appear blacked out. All the manufacturer could tell me was that it did not appear to have been "caused by a malfunction." Since this vigil, I have used the laser grid in fifteen other investigations, including at some of the other locations featured in this book. It has yet to perform the way it did that night at the McKinnis-Litzenberg House, including the strange strobe-like flashing. In fact, I haven't had a single problem with the laser grid since.

FINAL THOUGHTS

I still have no explanation for the laser grid "malfunction." When I showed the photo to Casey, she didn't say it looked like what she saw on the stairs that night with Jim. But she did say the picture gave her chills.

Still, it was the only thing out of the ordinary that happened that night. There were no jiggling door handles, no ghostly footsteps, no disembodied voices. We didn't even have anything chucked at us. I didn't really have an explanation as to why none of that happened while I was there either. But then I looked back at my notes and recordings I took while conducting a group interview with Chris, Casey, and Robert, and the answer became clear.

"It's almost as if—if the ghosts don't know you, they don't do anything or respond to you," Chris had told me.

So maybe that had something to do with it; the ghosts are responding to people they know. But there had to be more. I mean, I make it a point at the start of each vigil to introduce myself to any spirits that might be hanging around. So it's not like I was a total stranger to the ghosts. Why do the spirits continually interact with Chris, Casey, and Robert?

At one point during the interviews, Casey pulled out a photo of what the McKinnis-Litzenberg House had looked like when the Park District first took it over. It was a mess and looked like the whole thing might collapse in a strong wind. I asked the group what motivated them to help preserve a building such as this. "It's the importance of keeping things alive," Robert said without hesitation. "This was just a farmhouse. It was nothing like a presidential memorial or anything, but it has history. It's a neat piece of history, and it's a small slice of what people were like 160 to 170 years ago, and that's worth keeping."

Chris echoed that sentiment: "I think it's very important to keep the family memory alive. You know, who lived there and what they did for the community. I think that's very important. They were one of the backbone families of Hancock County, so I think it's very important to keep that history alive."

And there was my answer.

"I think I've got it figured out," I told them. "I think maybe they appear to you because of all the hard work you've done in this house. You have a special place in their ghostly hearts."

Casey, Chris, and Bob all looked at me and smiled. Then Casey whispered softly, "I hope so."

McKinnis-Litzenberg House
6100 U.S. Route 224
McComb, Ohio
www.hancockparks.com/YourParks/LitzenbergMemorialWoods.aspx

NORTHEAST

OHIO

PUBLIC LIBRARY
OF STEUBENVILLE AND JEFFERSON COUNTY

There are some who believe that ghosts are nothing more than leftover energy that has somehow managed to leave an imprint on a location. Often referred to as "residual energy," this type of haunting is said to sometimes be caused by the act of repetition—people doing the same action over and over again, leaving behind trace amounts of energy that manifest long after that person is gone. This type of ghost is most often reported in high-traffic areas or in areas where there are normally high levels of excitement or energy, like battlefields, for example.

Keeping that notion in mind, wouldn't it stand to reason that public libraries would have a couple of residual spirits hanging around? I mean, think of it: the excitement of a new book, the happiness over being able to rent movies for free. Most of all, the sheer number of people who pass through the front door on a daily basis. Add the fact that the Public Library of Steubenville and Jefferson County has been in operation for well over a hundred years, and you'd have to admit there's no reason why the building shouldn't be haunted!

THE HISTORY

Even though he would eventually be known as one of the richest, most successful businessmen of his time, no one could say that Andrew Carnegie was born with a silver spoon in his mouth. Born to dirt-poor parents on November 25, 1835, in Dunfermline, Scotland, Carnegie immigrated with his family to the United States in 1848. With no means to support themselves, all members of the Carnegie family, including thirteen-year-old Andrew, immediately started looking for work.

After several attempts to get and hold a job, in 1850, Carnegie found employment as a telegraph messenger boy for the Ohio Telegraph Company. The following year, 1851, Carnegie traveled to Steubenville to help after a flood downed the telegraph lines between Steubenville and Wheeling, West Virginia. Carnegie remained in Steubenville for nearly two weeks before returning home.

Fast-forward to the late nineteenth century: Andrew Carnegie is now a successful businessman, having made a fortune in the iron and steel business. Rich and powerful as he was, Carnegie never forgot his modest beginnings and remained a very humble man. He also believed that it was the responsibility of all people of wealth to help those less fortunate. One of the ways Carnegie liked giving back to the community was to fund the building of local libraries. Eventually, he would help fund the construction of well over 2,500 libraries throughout the world. Initially, Carnegie chose the cities and towns that would receive funds based on ones he was familiar with. So in June 1899, when Steubenville resident Dr. A. M. Reid wrote, asking for funds to build a library, Carnegie remembered the time he had spent in Steubenville after the flood many years ago and sent a check for $50,000 to construct a library.

Contrary to what some have claimed, Carnegie didn't design the Steubenville Library (or any other library, for that matter) himself. Rather, the money was to be used for the construction of the building itself. The Steubenville Library was designed by the Pittsburgh architectural firm of Alden & Harlow, who chose to incorporate the Richardsonian Romanesque style into the building.

As the building was nearing completion, Steubenville officials noticed that the city's coffers were looking a little empty and the library had yet to be completed, so they wrote to Carnegie, asking for additional funds. He responded with a second check, this one in the amount of $12,000, making Steubenville one of the few libraries to receive a second check.

The original plans for the building called for a four-faced clock to be installed near the top of the tower in the front of the building. According to legend, the last thing that needed to be installed for the building was the four-faced clock. Low on funds once more, the story goes that Steubenville again wrote to Carnegie, asking for money for the clock. While this is not documented, it is said that instead of sending a check, Carnegie simply wrote that instead of purchasing four clock faces, Steubenville should just "buy a watch."

Today, the Public Library of Steubenville and Jefferson County looks much the same as it did when it was first erected in 1902, save for the top of the tower.

True story or not, the tower would eventually be completed with glass windows in place of clocks. Today, nothing remains of that portion of the tower. Roughly thirty-five feet of the tower, including the glass windows, were removed over fifty years ago.

When all was said and done, the library building was completed in early 1902. It officially began admitting patrons on March 12, 1902. It has remained in constant operation ever since. And while, in addition to the removal of the top of the tower, other renovations have taken place in the library over the years—most notably office spaces and a garage for the bookmobile—the original structure has remained remarkably intact. Some would say that one of the biggest changes, however, was to the library's name. Originally known as the Carnegie Library of Steubenville, the name would eventually be changed to the Public Library of Steubenville and Jefferson County.

THE EXPERIENCES

Alan Hall has been at the library since 1983 and is the current director of the Public Library of Steubenville and Jefferson County. He told me that when he first arrived, he had no idea that there might be a ghost or two lurking among the shelves. He said that he'd been at the library for only about a month before someone made a comment to him about "the ghost in the attic." "I think the people who first told me about the ghosts were members of the staff," he said.

Intrigued by the thought of a ghost in the attic, Alan climbed up the spiral staircase that led to the attic. That was the first time he saw the sign on the attic door: "Home of the Attic Ghost." "I opened the door and went into the attic and went, 'Wow, OK. If I were a ghost, this looks like where I would live.' I didn't see or feel anything. It just looked like the kind of spooky attic where a ghost would like to live."

Alan decided to ask around about the sign and if there really was supposed to be a ghost in the attic. "When I first started working here, there were a lot of employees who were older and had been here a long time," Alan said. "They told me that while the sign had been replaced over the years, the original one had been put there in the 1950s. But when I asked if anyone had ever seen the ghost, no one had. They would just tell me about the strange noises they would hear coming from the attic."

At that point, Alan said he was about ready to, as they say, give up the ghost. "This is an old building and it makes a lot of racket, partly because it has big steel I-beams and it has brick and mortar. And up in the attic, the trusses are wood, but there's steel and concrete, and it probably all rubs against itself." Besides, Alan thought, the stories about the ghost seemed to be something only the employees themselves were talking about.

All that would change in 1997.

"I guess the first time that the story about the library possibly being haunted made it into print was *Haunted Ohio IV*." Alan said that when Chris Woodyard's book *Haunted Ohio IV,* which included the story about the library, was first released in 1997, it was initially business as usual at the Public Library of Steubenville and Jefferson County. But then people started stopping by, wanting to see the ghost that they had read about. Alan said he didn't like disappointing them, but had to be honest and tell them there's usually not much to see, ghost-wise, at the library. "I didn't have much to tell them," Alan admitted. "There wasn't much in the way of a blood-and-guts kind of story. Just some noises and an old sign on the attic door."

Then two locals came in who claimed they could get to the bottom of things.

"I guess it was around 2000," Alan stated. "A local pair came in on a Saturday night and set up some sort of equipment. I don't know what it was, but you could hear them bumping around upstairs. So I finally went up and said, 'How's it going?' and one guy was as white as a sheet and he said, 'The energy levels!'"

Thinking the pair had actually captured something, Alan asked the man for more information. "He didn't tell me anything else, and they left soon after. They promised me a full report, but I never heard another thing from them, so I have no idea what they found, if anything."

Alan is quick to point out to me that since he has been at the Public Library of Steubenville and Jefferson County, he hasn't seen a single ghost. That doesn't mean that he doesn't think there's one here, though. "From time to time, I will feel like a presence here. It's hard to explain, but just sometimes, I feel like I'm not alone here," Alan told me.

One memorable instance when Alan thought he might have been aided by a ghostly presence was the time he was confronted by a very irate library patron.

"A couple of years ago," Alan began, "a woman came into the library, wanting to return some materials that were two or three years overdue. In cases where they are that overdue, we sometimes turn them over to a collections agency. Turns out she had tried to buy a washer and dryer and her credit was rejected, so this woman was not happy. She came in the library and demanded to speak to the director of the library. She wasn't going to mess around with any staff member at this point."

Alan said that when he came upstairs to talk to the woman, he had no trouble identifying which one she was: "She was the one who looked like she was ready to explode."

"I tried doing the customer service thing," Alan continued, "but she was really angry. I almost thought she was going to take a swing at me."

But then something strange happened. "All of a sudden," Alan explained, "it was like I sensed a presence behind her. And then her whole attitude just changed and she calmed down. She even smiled at me and said, 'Well, you know, I shouldn't be so nasty about it. It was my own fault.' Her whole demeanor just suddenly changed after I felt that presence. I never saw anything behind her. I just felt it. I couldn't help thinking, 'Did a former librarian just come up to you and put her hand on your shoulder to calm you down?'

"That's the sort of things that I feel here," Alan explained. "I just sometimes sense that there's someone else here with me. I don't really know who it is or even if I'm feeling something that's really here. But whatever it is, it's never a bad feeling. It doesn't scare me, even being in the building alone. It's a good feeling."

When I asked Alan if there was anywhere in particular that he feels something, he thought for a moment and then said, "When I feel it, it's almost always in the spiral staircase," referring to the old staircase that leads to the library's upper storage areas and attic. "But then again, I think just climbing those stairs would make you feel weird."

Christy Williams is the daughter of the library's treasurer, who also started working here in 1983, a mere two weeks after Alan Hall did. As such, Christy told me she feels like she sort of grew up at the library. "I would come here after school and hang out. Sometimes I would run around and go places I wasn't really supposed to go." On several occasions, Christy said, she would pick up on what she called "energy" in the building: "It always felt like female energy, though. But sometimes, it felt younger—like five or six years old—and sometimes it felt older."

Christy says that when it comes to the younger energy, if she tries hard enough, she can see what she describes as "almost angelic-like. She had very long blonde hair and an older-looking dress. Almost like a little Amish girl," Christy said. While she has felt and seen this ghostly girl in different places in the library, most of the encounters happen in the Children's Room.

When the library first opened in 1902, the area now known as the Children's Room was actually an auditorium, complete with a stage. In 1925, the children's area was relocated here from its original location on the main floor. "When I see the girl in here," Christy told me while standing in the middle of the Children's Room, "she's usually over in one of the corners."

Another area where Christy sometimes senses the girl ghost is around the staircase that runs along the outside of the building, just outside the Children's Room. "This staircase is part of the original building," Alan told me, "so maybe it was used as an entrance to the auditorium."

As for the older energy, Christy says she feels it most often around a certain room up in the tower.

"We call it the Tower Room," Alan said. "We use it for storage now, but back then, it was the librarian's office. It's a hard room to get to— you have to go up that spiral staircase. Even in 1902, it was difficult to get to the room. Even the librarian didn't like climbing all those steps. We used to try to hold board meetings up there, but eventually it reverted back to storage," Alan said.

"That's the room where I feel her energy the most: the Tower Room," Christy says of the older energy. "Sometimes, I will see her up there, just standing there. She's an older woman, wearing a long dress that sort of flares out and then layers of sweaters on top. I never see her face for some reason.

"I don't know who this woman is," Christy said, "but I somehow get the impression that she is somehow associated with the library."

So who is haunting the Steubenville Main Library? Good question.

Regarding the little girl, if she is indeed haunting the library, it is unclear who she is or why she's hanging around the building. "I do know I've checked the history and as far as I can tell, there's no records of a little girl dying here," Alan said.

"I don't get the feeling the little girl died here," Christy chimes in. "I think she just feels comfortable here."

As for the older female ghost, Alan also admits that when it comes to the older female ghost, while he can name two possible "suspects," no one knows who the ghost is either.

The first name ever attached to the ghostly woman of the library was Ellen Summers Wilson. "I guess I am partly responsible for that," Alan admits.

Alan told me that while Chris Woodyard was writing *Haunted Ohio IV*, she called and asked him who he thought the ghost was. "I kept saying, 'I don't know,' but at the very end of the conversation, I evidently said, 'Maybe it's Ellen Summers Wilson.' I was doing a lot of research on

The library tower minus the top floor that had originally been designed to house a four-faced clock.

Ms. Wilson at the time and to me, she just seemed like the logical person to be the ghost."

Ellen Summers Wilson was the first head librarian of the Steubenville Library. She had previously worked at several other Carnegie libraries, but the Steubenville Library was the first one she was in charge of. Tragically, Wilson's time at the library was cut short when she passed away suddenly in November 1904. "I guess I just thought, boy, if there's an essence that should still be around, that would be it. So maybe she's still here, watching over things," Alan said. "Plus, her office would have been in the Tower Room, where people report feeling weird."

Another woman whom Alan feels might fit the ghostly bill is a former librarian named Eleanor.* Interestingly enough, Eleanor actually worked at the library during Ellen Summers Wilson's short tenure here. "Eleanor worked here from 1902 until around 1936, and she appar-

Eleanor's last name is withheld for privacy.

ently loved this place," Alan told me. "The board minutes even have a one-year gap because she got too ill to work, but she wouldn't quit."

Alan continued, "I believe Eleanor passed away around 1940. But even after all that time, as soon as I started working here, people would tell me stories about Eleanor and how she loved the library. She was supposed to have had a very rough exterior, but deep down inside, she was very gentle and nice.

"I can remember a patron—he must have been in his eighties at the time—telling me about the time when, as a child, he dropped his library book in a mud puddle, ruining it. He said that Eleanor really let him have it," Alan explained, "but in the end, she whispered to him softly, 'Don't worry about it. It's OK.'

"So maybe she's still here, just watching over the library," Alan told me. "Again, I have no proof that it's her. But she does sort of fit the bill."

THE VIGIL

The vigil was conducted by me and Ghosts of Ohio member Sean Seckman. With most of the ghost activity reported in areas that could be reached only via a small spiral staircase, Sean and I had a dilemma: how to get all of our bulky equipment cases up there. We came up with a unique solution: tie a rope around them and pull them up through the center of the staircase.

It was rough going for a while, but when all was said and done, we had everything set up and ready to go:

Children's Room
- · two infrared DVR night-vision cameras in the Children's Room, pointing in opposite directions in order to film the entire room
- · one infrared video camera outside the Children's Room, pointing toward the external staircase
- · one Superlux condenser microphone in the corner of the Children's Room

Tower Room
- · one DVR night-vision camera on the landing in front of the Tower Room, pointing down the spiral staircase
- · one DVR night-vision camera on the landing in front of the Tower Room, pointing up toward the attic door

- one infrared video camera in the corner of the Tower Room, pointing across the entire room
- one Superlux condenser microphone on the landing in front of the
Tower Room, facing the attic door

Spiral Staircase

- Vernier LabPro sensors, including two ambient temperature devices, one electromagnetic sensor, and one static charge sensor, running up the spiral staircase

Attic

- two infrared video cameras in the attic, pointing in opposite directions in order to film the entire attic
- one Superlux condenser microphone in the center of the attic

One of the more intriguing things that we encountered right off the bat
was the legendary attic door sign in the shape of a ghost with the name
"Herbie" written up the side of it. To the ghost's left is a thought bubble

*Meet Herbie, the un-
official library ghost.
The sign hangs on the
door to the library's
attic, located off the
top of the tower.*

with the words "I'm the library ghost—do not disturb" written inside of it. The sign looked rather old, but Alan didn't think it was the same one that he saw back in 1983. Christy agreed that it wasn't the original sign. Neither one of them recognized the handwriting on the sign. Personally, I was intrigued with the notion that the ghost's name was Herbie, while the only ghosts that had been reported at the library were all females.

Later on in the vigil, while in the Children's Room, both Sean and I heard what I described as "circus music." It seemed like something you would hear at a circus, like a combination of a brass band and a calliope. I heard it first along the left wall of the Children's Room. I was walking alone along the shelves, maybe ten feet from the wall, when I heard it. When I got closer to the wall, the music became louder. Even though the music sounded old-fashioned, my immediate thought was that it was coming from a car outside the library.

I called Sean over and he heard it, too. It was weird because not only did the music seem to be dated, but there had also never been any reports of ghostly music coming from anywhere in the library. True, Christy Williams had reporting sensing things in the Children's Room, but she never mentioned music. The external stairs outside the Children's Room were on the complete opposite side of the room, too.

With the music still playing, Sean and I decided to utilize those external stairs to go outside and see if we could determine the source of the sounds. We climbed to the top of those stairs and walked around outside a bit, but didn't hear anything. Going back inside, we could still hear the music, coming from the same area along the far wall. Our hand-helds didn't register any anomalies. After a few more minutes, the music faded away. The only explanation we could come up with was that it was just caused by the heating system, blowing air through old pipes and tubes. It is interesting to note, however, that while we remained in the building several more hours, we never heard the music again. Nothing was picked up by the studio microphone or DVR camera positioned in the room, either—not even the original music Sean and I both heard.

While in the Children's Room, I tried to get the ghost girl to come and play with me. If you watch any of these ghost reality shows, you'll notice that they sometimes employ "trigger objects," objects that they hope will be familiar and/or intriguing to the ghost, thus triggering a response—specifically, that the ghost will interact with the object, causing it to appear to move on its own.

With that in mind, I thought it would be interesting that since there was supposed to be a ghost of a little girl in the Children's Room, I might be able to find out why she hung out here. Perhaps she liked reading books. Or maybe she liked the fact that the room was also filled with various toys and games.

I started by talking to the little girl, explaining who I was and that I had a little girl of my own whom I liked to read to. I asked the ghost if I could read to her and that if she wanted to hear a specific story, could she move that book or else make some sort of noise to guide me to that book? I tried that for about fifteen minutes with no results.

After that, I said, "OK, if you don't have a favorite, I'll just read you some of my favorites. Why don't you come and sit with me?" With that, I grabbed a couple of books off the shelf, sat on the floor, and even attempted to sit cross-legged. I then began to read aloud, pointing to the illustrations that accompanied the storyline as I went. I read four books in total. After each one, I said, "Thank you for listening to my story. Can I take your picture to show everyone what a good listener you were?" I then pointed my digital camera at the area of carpet in front of me and took a picture. When reviewed, none of the pictures showed any anomalies.

Finally, I moved on to the games and toys. I spread them out on the floor and asked the ghost girl to come play with me. For each game I played, I would "lose" something (the last puzzle piece, one of the dolls, a toy car, etc.) and then ask the ghost girl if she knew where it was. And if she did, could she show me where it was or bring it to me? I had also put an EMF and an ELF in front of me to monitor things. By the end of the night, nothing had moved, not even the readings on the EMF and ELF.

With the vigil rapidly coming to an end, and when Sean and I realized that we needed to drag all that equipment down from the Tower Room, we decided to call it a night. Days later, upon reviewing all the audio and video from the vigil, there was only one thing that seemed a bit odd. During our initial tour of the building, Christy Williams and Alan Hall were showing Sean and me the outside steps that run from the Children's Room to the ground level. When Alan remarks, "These would have been part of the original building," something that sounds like a voice saying "Yeah" can be heard. The "voice" is very loud and appears to be rather close to the microphone. However, this was, admittedly, recorded on a digital voice recorder that was in my hand and we were walking at the time. So without a stationary recorder, the possibility that the "voice" was actually caused by one of us moving or inadvertently rustling is something that cannot be dismissed. Other than that, the library was very quiet that night, as all good libraries should be.

FINAL THOUGHTS

You know, if I were to ever come back as a ghost, I don't think I'd mind haunting a library. In fact, I think it would be a pretty sweet gig. After all, I'd have an unending supply of books, either to read or to use for symmetrical book stacking, just like the Philadelphia Mass Turbulence of 1947—you didn't really think you'd get through an entire book by me without a single *Ghostbusters* reference, did you?

All joking aside, it's endearing that what drove some people to the library was the fact that they read about it first in a book, *Haunted Ohio IV*. So this could be one of the first times that history was kept alive by a book about ghosts instead of simply a ghost.

Put another way, I've never understood why libraries aren't always standing room only. There are books, movies, computer games, all for free. Free! For whatever reason, libraries seem to remain one of Ohio's best-kept secrets. But it's a secret that the ghosts of the Public Library of Steubenville and Jefferson County are trying to let people in on. They're trying to lure people in with ghostly tales and then keep them coming back for more when they realize all the cool stuff waiting for them inside.

Perhaps Alan Hall said it best when he told me, "I'm hoping when people come for the ghosts, they stay for the books."

Public Library of Steubenville and Jefferson County
407 S. 4th Street
Steubenville, Ohio 43952
www.steubenville.lib.oh.us

FAIRPORT HARBOR MARINE MUSEUM

I've always found lighthouses a little spooky. I'm sure part of it is due to my never having fully recovered from sneaking downstairs as an impressionable child and watching John Carpenter's *The Fog* during an HBO Free Weekend. But there's also something sad and forlorn about lighthouses. I guess it's the whole notion of a solitary lighthouse keeper, cold and lonely, climbing the lighthouse stairs during a terrible storm, trying desperately to keep the light lit to prevent a ship from crashing into the rocks and sending sailors to a watery grave.

The lighthouses that dot the landscape around Lake Erie are no different. I've visited several, and they all just feel weird to me. It's like they're all haunted simply because they look and feel like they should be haunted. That said, one lighthouse in particular stands out among all the others on Lake Erie: the one at Fairport Harbor. What makes it so unique is that the ghost said to haunt here prefers to walk around on four legs as opposed to two.

THE HISTORY

There are actually two lighthouses in Fairport Harbor. The first one, the Grand River Lighthouse—known today as the Fairport Harbor Lighthouse—was designed by architect Jonathan Goldsmith and erected in 1825 at a cost of $5,000. When it was completed, the lighthouse sat over one hundred feet above lake level and could be seen for almost eighteen statute miles. To reach the top of the lighthouse, keepers needed to climb sixty-nine steps. A small, two-story building was also constructed next to the lighthouse to serve as a home for the lighthouse keeper and his family.

The first lighthouse keeper assigned to Fairport Harbor was Samuel Butler. Butler would become a firm supporter of the abolitionist movement and actively help slaves escape north via the Underground Railroad. It is said that Butler often resorted to transporting slaves himself across Lake Erie to Canada.

In all, fourteen lighthouse keepers would keep the light lit for one hundred years. The last keeper was Daniel Babcock, who served until 1925. That year, the Fairport Harbor West Breakwater Light was erected, making the Fairport Harbor Lighthouse obsolete. Soon after the new light was lit, the Fairport Harbor Lighthouse was officially decommissioned.

Once it was abandoned, plans were underway to have both the lighthouse and the keeper's house demolished. Several Fairport Harbor residents wouldn't stand for that, though, and petitioned to have the structures protected. In June 1925, the U.S. government decreed that it would allow the structures to remain standing "for the time being."

Twenty years later, while the lighthouse and keeper's home were still abandoned, they had finally found their savior. In 1945, the Fairport Harbor Historical Society was officially formed, and it had a primary goal in mind: preserve the lighthouse.

That they did, even going so far as to move historical artifacts into the lighthouse keeper's former home and turning it into the Fairport Harbor Marine Museum, which is open to the public. The lighthouse is also open to the public and available for tours.

THE EXPERIENCES

The ghost stories associated with the Fairport Harbor Lighthouse are a wonderful example of how, with time, history and folklore can become intertwined. All the ghost stories center on an actual historical figure: lighthouse keeper Joseph C. Babcock, a man with the distinction of having held the position of lighthouse keeper at Fairport Harbor twice.

Babcock first held the position from April 1871 until March 1881, when he stepped down and took the position of assistant lighthouse keeper so that he could move his family out of the lighthouse and into a more traditional home in Fairport Harbor. Babcock would move his family back to the lighthouse in 1900, when he accepted the position of lighthouse keeper once again.

The Fairport Harbor Marine Museum, comprises the lighthouse keeper's house (left) *and the lighthouse* (right). *(Courtesy Fairport Harbor Lighthouse and Marine Museum)*

According to legend, Babcock's wife, Mary, was a cat lover and kept several as pets. So when Mary fell ill and became bedridden, Babcock presented his wife with several new cats to keep her company in bed.

Fairport Harbor Historical Society historian John Ollila told me that while they have established that Babcock's wife was indeed bedridden for a time, it's unclear what she suffered from. "All of the documents we have say Mrs. Babcock was bedridden. They don't say why she was, but then again, back then, if you were sick with anything, they said you were bedridden."

Former Fairport Harbor Historical Society president Valerie Laczko adds: "There is no documentation that Mrs. Babcock was terminally ill or completely bedridden. She was bedridden, though. It could have just been a bad cold or something. But maybe she really was sick and they just didn't mention it. All we really know was at some point, Mrs. Babcock spent some time in bed."

Either way, the museum does have several pictures that show Mr. and Mrs. Babcock posing outside the lighthouse with several cats visible in the background. There's even a photograph in the museum's holdings that show two cats that belonged to Mary Babcock.

According to the legend, Mary soon picked out one as her favorite: a plump gray cat. The cat apparently took a liking to Mary as well as it rarely left her side, which is why both Babcock and his wife thought it strange when one day, the gray cat simply disappeared and could not be found.

Fast-forward now to the late 1980s. The lighthouse has long been decommissioned, but still remains a popular destination as it has become part of the Fairport Harbor Marine Museum. The majority of the museum's historical pieces are displayed on the first floor of the old lighthouse keeper's home with the second floor used for storage and, from time to time, housing for the museum's curator.

The curator living in the building at the time was Pamela Brent. As the story goes, she was in the upstairs kitchen when she saw something "small and dark" dart by. Going to investigate, Brent saw nothing there. Brushing it off, Brent returned to the kitchen and went about her business. But this would not be the end of it. Over time, Brent would continue to see this small shape dashing about the second floor. What's more, with each encounter, more and more of the shape became visible: that of a small cat—a cat with gray fur, gold eyes, and no feet!

Brent even reportedly played with it one night, throwing her balled-up sock down the small hallway, and the cat scampered after it. Brent would continue to see the ghost cat for the next few years until she moved out of the museum. With that, the reports of the ghost cat ceased.

As to why the sightings suddenly stopped, Valerie Laczko wonders if it was because after Brent left, the second floor was used for storage and meetings. "Maybe we weren't seeing it because we weren't up there as much," Laczko speculated. "The areas where Pamela was seeing the ghost cat aren't open to the general public." The ghost cat was also apparently confined to the upstairs floor as it was never seen in the museum itself. "All of the sightings of the cat were upstairs. Never downstairs," Laczko stated.

Carol Bertone has been involved with the lighthouse since 1998, and she has yet to have an encounter with the ghost cat. "Personally, I've never seen anything. I'm certainly not afraid to come in here by myself.

The only person I know who's claimed to have seen anything in here—the ghost cat—is Pam."

In early 2001, work was underway to install air conditioning at the lighthouse keeper's former home. In order to do that, workers had to crawl through the basement and up under the floors in order to install the ductwork. One morning, a worker was lying on his back in the small crawl space under the floors when he started to feel as if he were being watched. Turning his head, he was horrified to find what appeared to be the remains of a mummified cat staring back at him.

John Ollila remembers the first time he laid eyes on the mummified cat: "I came in one morning and went down into the basement, where they were working. At the bottom of the steps, we had a model of a riverboat. Well, leaning on this boat was what looked like a pure white cat. It looked like someone had stretched white canvas over the frame of a cat. Not a hole in it. Just perfect and just as white as white could be," Ollila said.

Ollila continued: "I asked one of the workers, 'Where did this come from?' and he said, 'Under the floor. I almost had my head on it.'"

Examining the remains, it soon became apparent that the cat hadn't actually been mummified. It appeared as though it had just died in the crawl space and the conditions under the house were just right so the body dehydrated. As evidence, Ollila said that once the remains were brought up from the basement, it began to weather and deteriorate. "Once we got it upstairs, it started to turn gray and got holes in it," he said.

In an interesting move, the cat's remains were put on display inside the museum.

Historical Society member Carol Bertone has no doubt that the discovery of the "mummified" cat resurrected the ghost stories about the lighthouse. "When we found that mummified cat, all of a sudden there's a big legend around the whole thing. People started believing that maybe there was a connection between the mummy cat and the ghost cat."

In the early 2000s, the mummy cat was removed from the museum and put on display in the mayor of Fairport Harbor's office. When patrons who came to the museum specifically to see the cat were clearly disappointed, it was returned around 2008. Now safe and secure under its own glass display case, visitors from all around the world can come and gaze upon the museum's unofficial mascot, Sentinel the Mummified Cat.

During the interviews, I came across a lesser-known ghost story associated with the lighthouse. Once again this one centers on the family of Joseph C. Babcock. It's also one that is grounded in history.

During Joseph Babcock's tenure at the lighthouse, he and his wife Mary endured the painful loss of a child, Robbie Babcock, who passed away at the lighthouse. According to legend, he died inside the caretaker's house. Some say he's still there, too.

Carol Bertone has heard people who have claimed to have encountered the boy's ghost: "People have said that he's here—weird feelings, weird smells, that sort of thing. They say that's Robbie."

John Taipale, who has conducted extensive research on the Babcock family, confirms: "Robbie Babcock passed away here, we think from smallpox. I have talked to a lot of people who think he's still here."

John himself admitted to me that he has heard some strange things in the museum. "Sometimes I'll be here late at night, and I'll hear things that make me think that maybe there's something here," he explained. "Sometimes it will sound like someone walking. But it sounds more like it's in the walls. I think it's kind of neat."

But as for whether or not he believes there are ghosts in the museum, John remained uncommitted: "In a building like this, you hear all sorts

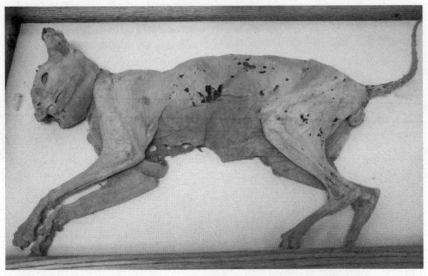

Sentinel, the mummified cat, said to be the cause of most of the hauntings allegedly taking place at the Marine Museum. (Courtesy Fairport Harbor Lighthouse and Marine Museum)

of creaky things, so it's fun. But if there are ghosts here, I don't think we have any that are bad."

One other thing that John points out: none of the ghost stories involve the lighthouse itself. "I never heard about anyone talk about a ghost in the lighthouse itself. It's always in the building," he said. Carol Bertone agrees. "I've never heard any ghost stories about the lighthouse being haunted. It's just the house," she confirmed.

Valerie Laczko is also on the fence when it comes to ghosts in the museum: "I will tell you that if you're here all alone, especially in the fall, and it's starting to get dark, it's a little spooky here. But the building is over a hundred years old, so it's going to make noises. But you know, we don't know the whole history of the building, so who knows who might be here?"

Through all of this, John Ollila remains skeptical: "I never heard of any stories about ghosts in this building prior to Pamela Brent. There may have been stories, but I never heard them. Even after I heard them, I'm still waiting to see something here," Ollila told me.

THE VIGIL

For the vigil, I was joined by Ghosts of Ohio members Wendy Cywinski and Samantha Nicholson. Two members of the Fairport Harbor Museum were also in attendance.

This vigil was interesting for several reasons. To begin with, while we were dealing with a two-story house with a basement, not to mention a giant lighthouse, other than vague references to hearing footsteps or creaks, all the activity was limited to the second floor of the house. So since there would be five people crammed into a rather small space, we had to choose our equipment and where to place it wisely to avoid potential contamination of any evidence.

The decision was made to put our command center in the far corner of the main room on the second floor. This would allow us to gather there and watch the monitors while being far enough from the Vernier LabPro remote sensors so they would not pick up our movements. It also provided us a clear view of the second floor landing and hallway, two areas where the ghost cat was said to roam.

This is where we ended up placing the equipment:

Kitchen Area (Second Floor)
- one infrared night-vision camera in the corner of the kitchen, facing the door
- one Superlux condenser microphone in the corner of the kitchen, facing the door

Office #1 (Second Floor)
- one infrared night-vision camera in the corner of the office, facing the door
- one Superlux condenser microphone in the corner of the office, facing the door

Office #2 (Second Floor)
- one infrared night-vision camera in the corner of the office, facing the door
- one Superlux condenser microphone in the corner of the office, facing the door

Second Floor Hallway
- one infrared night-vision camera in the second floor hallway
- one infrared video camera on the second floor landing, facing down the stairs
- Vernier LabPro temperature and EMF sensors running up and down the second floor hallway; static electricity sensor in the middle of the hallway

Sentinel's Display Case
- one tri-field meter on top of the display case
- one digital voice recorder on top of the display case

Another reason why this vigil was so interesting to me was because it was one of the first times I would be trying to track a non-human ghost. Several nights before the vigil, while I was sitting in my office thinking about what equipment to bring to the lighthouse, I was suddenly distracted by the sound of scampering feet behind me. Turning, I saw two of my normally lethargic cats, Ernie and Maddy, running amuck, playing with one of the foamy feathery cat toys that litter my house. And then it hit me: I needed to pack some cat toys for the lighthouse vigil!

Investigators will usually use trigger objects—items for a ghost to interact with—on investigations. But those are usually things human ghosts would want to interact with (dolls, books, balls, etc.). So I thought that if my cats like these toys, maybe a ghost cat would, too! I even decided to bring along some catnip since that tends to bring out the wildness in my narcoleptic cats. I was hoping it would do the same for the ghost cat, too.

I have to be honest: I was a little nervous breaking out the cat toys and catnip on the vigil, not because I didn't think it was a good idea. Rather, it was because there were representatives of the museum present. I was trying to present myself as a serious, professional researcher (not as easy as it sounds when you throw ghosts into the mix), and yet here I was sprinkling catnip onto a napkin, wadding up pieces of paper, and purring, "Here kitty, kitty, kitty" while lying on the floor. Oddly enough, the guys from the museum didn't even bat an eye.

Wendy and Sam got into it, too, especially Sam. She spent a good thirty minutes on all fours, batting the toys and wads of paper and encouraging the cat to come out and play. Wendy came up with a brilliant idea: to use our non-contact laser thermometers as cat toys to see if we could get the ghost cat to chase the beam. Sadly, the ghost cat didn't appear to be in a playful mood that night as nothing out of the ordinary happened.

When I wasn't rolling around on the floor, I took turns with the women roaming around the main floor of the museum. I spent time in each room, sitting on the floor and calling out for both the ghost cat as well as Robbie Babcock. When I got no response the first hour I was down there, I returned later in the evening and went from room to room, asking if there was anyone in the room with me and if they were attached to something in the room. I figured that with so many relics in the museum, perhaps the ghost here wasn't related to any of the lighthouse keepers and instead showed up when an item they loved was brought to the museum.

I sat there alone in the dark and asked whoever was in the room with me to give me a sign of their presence. I asked for them to knock on the wall or to simply make a sound so that I knew I wasn't alone . . . or crazy for sitting in a room, talking aloud to no one in particular. I even said that if they would just make a noise for me, I would leave them alone and stop asking silly questions. It didn't matter. I never got a response.

Toward the end of the vigil, I was sitting alone in the office that overlooks the lighthouse. To be honest, I was a little disappointed since I really thought the cat toys would get us a response. It was then that I heard a soft "meow" behind me. I had my back to the window, so I turned around and listened. I heard it again, just as soft. This time, I could definitely tell it was a cat and that it was coming from the lighthouse. Just as I was getting ready to punch myself in the head for not putting any equipment out in the lighthouse, I saw a dark shape dart away from the lighthouse and out toward the road. It was a cat—a very live, non-ghostly cat. At that point, I became convinced the lighthouse was just messing with me and perhaps it was time to call it a night.

At the end of the night, after everyone had left, I stayed behind to take some nighttime shots of the lighthouse exterior. It was after 2:00 A.M. and everything was still. There wasn't another living soul in sight. Trying to get just the right shot, I had my camera on a tripod and was on my knees in order to tilt the tripod up to just the right angle. After about five minutes in that position, I finally had the shot and stood up. That's when I felt something hairy rub against my leg.

Jumping up, I looked down and saw a chubby gray cat staring back at me. After checking to make sure I hadn't just soiled myself, I once again realized that this cat, like the one I had seen earlier in the evening, was alive and well. I looked down at the cat and laughed. It meowed back as if to say, "Gotcha, didn't I?"

The cat followed me to my car and watched as I packed the rest of the equipment. I even gave him a couple of the leftover cat treats to eat, telling him, "You earned it." As I started the car and got ready to leave, I watched my new friend trot slowly to the apartments across the street. I started to pull away, but then stopped to watch, just to make sure the cat didn't suddenly disappear into thin air. It didn't.

FINAL THOUGHTS

A review of the materials we collected during the lighthouse vigil revealed nothing out of the ordinary. I can't say I was surprised by that. Truth be told, since Pamela Brent's sightings, no one has seen the ghost cat in over twenty years.

Still, there's no denying that the story of the ghost cat, complete with a mummified cat, makes for one of the most unique ghost tales out there. What's more, the stories are all intertwined with the very real history of Fairport Harbor and its lighthouse. It stands as a perfect example of how ghost stories work to keep actual history alive, as echoed in the words of

John Taipale: "Because of the ghost story, we've looked a lot more into the Babcock family history."

Of course, there's no denying that a good ghost story is also good for business. But that doesn't mean it has distracted the Historical Society from its goal of educating people. As current Historical Society president Daniel Maxson put it, "Part of our mission as a historical society is to educate people. So if this ghost story turns out to be somewhat true, we'll all be educated."

Fairport Harbor Marine Museum
129 Second Street
Fairport Harbor, Ohio 44077
www.ncweb.com/org/fhlh/

ANNA DEAN FARM

If there was ever a place in Ohio where ghosts would have their work cut out for them trying to keep history alive, it would be Anna Dean Farm. I'm ashamed to say that prior to starting work on this book, I had never heard of Anna Dean Farm or the man responsible for its creation. But in yet another prime example of ghosts helping to keep history alive, I was drawn to the farm by the ghostly stories that had been passed down to me. To be honest, there wasn't much to the ghostly tales, but man, was there a lot of history, so much so that it could, and has, filled several books and still has only begun to scratch the surface.

THE HISTORY

I'd like to introduce you to the man with one of the coolest names in all of Ohio's history: Ohio Columbus Barber. Ohio, or O. C. as he was known, was born in 1841 in a small town that would eventually become part of Akron. O. C.'s father, George, made matches by hand, which he sold door to door. When O. C. reached his teenage years, his father's business had grown considerably, so O. C. went to work for the Barber Company. By 1880, the Barber Company had become the largest match manufacturer in Ohio and one of the biggest in the United States. The following year, it merged with several other companies to form the Diamond Match Company, making O. C. and his family very rich in the process.

By 1890, O. C.'s manufacturing facilities had all but outgrown Akron, so he started looking at neighboring areas where he could relocate. In 1891, O. C. purchased a large area of land from Norton Township and founded the town of Barberton, naming it after himself. He named the lake in the center of town Lake Anna, after his daughter.

Three years after founding Barberton, O. C. moved the Diamond Match Company's manufacturing facilities to town. A new facility in town meant new jobs and soon, people began relocating to Barberton in droves. The town literally seemed to spring up overnight, almost by magic, earning Barberton the nickname "The Magic City." O. C. found the relocation so successful that from that point on, every time he acquired or expanded a company, he would relocate it to Barberton.

Around 1905, Barber started to entertain thoughts of retiring. Of course, when you're as driven as he was, retirement means anything but relaxing and taking it easy. Sure, he did start to buy up land on the east side of town with the idea of building a new home there, but this was not to be what one would call a retirement home. Far from it. Rather, Barber wanted to use the land to test out a new idea he had: applying business practices to agriculture.

Most industrial farms at the time focused on only one crop. Barber had the idea that if he created a farm that provided a multitude of crops, they would be more profitable. Barber also disagreed with the current method of farming, which was to stay on one plot of land until you had exhausted the soil. He felt that if crops were rotated instead, the yield could be improved. When it came to livestock, Barber also had some ideas that were considered radical at the time, including raising cage-free, free-range chickens.

Altogether, Barber purchased over 3,500 acres, most of which would be dedicated to his farm. Forty acres, however, would be set aside for his private home. In March 1909, construction began on the Barber mansion. Over eighteen months later, in October 1910, the mansion was complete. It is said that Barber moved into his new home on Halloween.

At a cost of over $400,000, the mansion was a sight to behold: fifty-two rooms situated on four floors with well over fifty thousand square feet of living space. The mansion featured Italian marble, walnut and oak woodwork, gold leaf in the library and bathrooms, even an elevator with a glass roof. The following spring, Barber named the thirty-five acres surrounding his mansion Barber Park and had the entire area landscaped with flowers, bushes, and trees. *The New York Times* took one look at Barber mansion and declared it "the finest mansion between New York and Chicago."

When people think of the Anna Dean Farm, this building, the Piggery, is usually the first thing that springs to mind.

As for the farm itself, Barber spent $7 million on its construction. He named the farm Anna Dean Farm—"Anna" after his daughter and "Dean" after Anna's husband (and O. C.'s son-in-law), Dr. Arthur Dean Bevan. Over the years, Barber would erect thirty-five buildings on the property, all of which were designed in the French Renaissance Revival style of architecture. All these buildings featured terra-cotta tile roofs and were constructed using red bricks and white concrete blocks.

Anna Dean Farm was an immediate success. The farm's initial yield was such that it was able to provide fruits and vegetables to all the big hotels in Cleveland, Pittsburgh, and even Chicago. Barber even went so far as to erect greenhouses on the farm property so that he'd be able to provide fruits and vegetables off-season.

Sadly, O. C. Barber would not get to fully enjoy the success of Anna Dean Farm. In 1920, only ten years after opening the farm, Barber died. In his will, he had asked that the entire Anna Dean Farm be given to Case Western Reserve University to be used as an agricultural college. The problem was that prior to his death, Barber had neglected to get all his finances in order. As a result, most of the estate was tied up in the courts for years. Neither Barber's family nor the university was able to successfully operate the farm either. So little by little, buildings and property began to be sold off. By the time Barber's estate was finally settled in 1946, Anna Dean Farm was but a shell of its former self. It had not functioned as a farm for many years, and it never would again.

In 1974, the Barberton Historical Society began taking steps to try and save Anna Dean Farm's remaining buildings. Sadly, by then only eight of the original thirty-five French Renaissance Revival buildings were still standing. Even Barber's mansion was no more, having been demolished in 1965. Realizing that the best way to preserve a building is to buy it outright, the Historical Society starting holding fund-raisers to purchase the remaining buildings. Today, the Historical Society owns six of the remaining eight buildings and conducts two different types of tours of them, one historical and one based on the ghost stories and folklore.

THE EXPERIENCES

If there ever were two individuals who could tell me not only the straight history of the Anna Dean Farm, but the ghostly side as well, it would be Steve Kelleher and Jessica King. Steve was instrumental in the formation of the Barberton Historical Society back in 1974 and has been involved with the organization ever since. Jessica has been with the Barberton Historical Society since 1996. They both collaborated on the 2009 book, *Ghosts Along the Tuscarawas,* which features some of the ghost stories associated with Anna Dean Farm.

Steve is quick to point out that for the most part, even though he tries to dig into the history of the buildings, he has yet to find anything that might explain why there are ghosts present. "Honestly, we don't know why some of these buildings are haunted," he said. There is one exception, though: the Feed Barn. Steve and Jessica are pretty confident they know who haunts that particular building.

As recounted in *Ghosts Along the Tuscarawas,* the woman's name was Nellie Brown. She came to work as a cook at the Barber Hotel around 1915 and soon became known for her pastries. By all accounts, she was a friendly, kind person, making it all the more painful to hear about the taunting and teasing she was forced to endure from her coworkers. You see, Nellie was what was referred to at the time as a "hunchback dwarf," which made her, sadly, an easy target for heartless individuals. Barber himself was said to have been so appalled when he heard about the teasing that he chastised the entire staff, telling them all in no uncertain terms that the taunts must stop immediately.

And stop they did, at least for the next few years until Barber passed away in 1920. Shortly after, the hotel employees, perhaps bitter over the fact that the hotel would close and they would be out of work, began taking out their aggression and anger on Nellie Brown. The teasing quickly returned with a vengeance. The hotel would close down the following year, but Nellie remained in the area, unable to find work.

In 1925, Barber's family allowed all the former Anna Dean Farm employees back on the property for one last reunion. Nellie made the fateful decision to attend, too. She wasn't there long before she probably realized it was a mistake. Several years away had done nothing to curb the viciousness of some of the workers, and they began making mean and crude remarks about Nellie, both behind her back and to her face. Sadly, Nellie couldn't take anymore and she cracked.

Nellie left the reunion and returned home. Several nights later, she returned to the property, wearing a white dress. It is believed that Nellie first made her way down to the Barber Hotel. Unable to get inside the now-closed building, she tried entering several other buildings, which were all locked. Eventually, she found that the door to the Feed Barn was unlocked. Going inside, Nellie found a length of rope, which she took over to the nearby smokehouse. Tying one end of the rope to the roof beam of the smokehouse, Nellie next fashioned a noose out of the other end. Climbing up on a table and then tightening the noose around her neck, Nellie paused for a moment before stepping off the table and ending her life. Her body would not be found for several days.

Today, there are some who believe that since the smokehouse no longer exists, Nellie's ghost has chosen to take up residence inside the Feed Barn. "We think that maybe because none of the other buildings associated with her death are still around, Nellie's ghost came to the Feed Barn," Steve surmised.

Nellie's ghost or not, whatever is haunting the Feed Barn likes to snack on batteries—any size battery, even huge ones for tractors. "We can't keep our tractors in here," Steve told me. "We put a tractor in here and even if it has a new battery in it, you come back and they won't start. We need to jump-start them.

"One of the gentlemen in the Historical Society is a GM-certified mechanic—he can fix anything," Steve continued. "So we asked him to go down to the Feed Barn and see if he can figure out why the tractors won't start. He gets there around 3:15 in the afternoon, but he can't get any of them to turn over. So he works on them for a while, but he still can't figure it out, so he decides it's time for dinner. He looks at his watch; it still says 3:15. Whatever had drained the tractor batteries was also messing with his watch battery," Steve concluded.

Jessica King remembers a time when someone or something started messing with the batteries inside a visitor's digital camera. "He was down at the Feed Barn, taking pictures," she said, "and all of a sudden, I see him pulling the batteries out of his camera. He said, 'These are really hot.' They were so hot that when he put them on the windowsill, I thought they were going to burn it [the windowsill]."

"Also," Jessica adds, "I don't know if it's related to the batteries heating up or not, but one time in the Feed Barn, we got weird temperature readings. It was over in one specific corner, and the temperature went up like twenty degrees. It's weird because there's not electricity in the building."

When the spirit or spirits of the Feed Barn aren't fiddling about with batteries, they sometimes like to make an appearance in photographs. Steve showed me a series of pictures that he took of a car in the Feed Barn, mere seconds apart. In the first picture, there's nothing out of the ordinary. But in the second, there is a very pronounced white, misty substance. "It was only in that one picture," Steve said. "The mist looked like it was forming outside the car."

Another building on the former Anna Dean Farm property that is said to be haunted is the Colt Barn. Originally built in 1912 as a barn to house bulls, Barber eventually moved the bulls to another barn on the property and began housing horses here. Today, it is the only remaining barn from Anna Dean Farm that has its original interior still intact.

According to *Ghosts Along the Tuscarawas,* a fatal accident took place near the Colt Barn in 1911 that might have resulted in a haunting. Eighteen-year-old John Papasky was driving a team of horses that were pulling a heavy wagon up the street. As the wagon reached the spot where the Colt Barn would be erected the following year, a wild dog suddenly darted out into the road, spooking the horses. Papasky was thrown from the wagon and crushed under its wheels. He died on the spot. The team of horses came to a stop right in front of where the Colt Barn would be erected less than a year later. Some believe that upon seeing the new Colt Barn, Papasky's ghost quickly moved in and has been there ever since.

Steve showed me a photograph that might just prove that. It's a picture of the windows of the Colt Barn. In one of the top windows, there appears to be a human face—one with a very long nose. "Some people think this is John Papasky," Steve told me. "They said that he had an elongated nose."

Jessica related a tale to me about a group of ghost hunters who decided they would try to capture the Colt Barn ghost on video. The group set up a video camera on the roof of an old car and left, leaving the camera running.

When they returned to review the video, they found they had captured something strange. "It was like a white mist," Jessica told me. "It sort of forms, goes away, comes back, stays for about twenty seconds,

Anna Dean Farm's Colt Barn. Built in 1912, today it is said to be home to several spirits, including that of John Papasky, who died in an accident near where the barn now stands.

and then leaves." Unable to explain what they had recorded, but trying to find answers, the group decided to see if perhaps the mist was created by reflections from the headlights of cars driving past the barn. "We drove back and forth past the barn over and over again, but we couldn't recreate it or figure out what caused that mist," Jessica said.

Jessica also said that numerous people have seen a dark shape darting back and forth between the windows on the second floor. "They see it dart between the three front windows and the front wall. Now, we do have birds that get in the Colt Barn, but it doesn't look like birds. It's different. It's dark and it darts," she said.

The last Anna Dean Farm building that is believed to have a ghost or two inside is the Heating House. This building, which was erected in 1821, got its name from the simple fact that it used to supply heat to the farm. The original boiler is still inside the building. In addition, Barber also used a portion of the building as a boarding house.

Jessica told me that many times, people visiting the Heating House will hear what sounds like someone or something walking around downstairs. The funny thing is that people hear it only when they are upstairs. "You'll hearing walking around and what sounds like feet shuffling," Jessica said. "You'll hear it from upstairs, but when you come down to check, there's never anyone here."

Jessica remembers the time she was on a tour of the Heating House and something made contact with her, literally. "It was the first night-time tour that Steve [Kelleher] gave, and I came with my aunt," Jessica begins. "We were standing over near the stage, listening to Steve talk, when all of a sudden, I just started feeling sick. I remember thinking I needed to go outside because I thought I was going to throw up. Just as I was turning to leave, something poked me in the side. I looked around, but my aunt was nowhere near me. There wasn't anyone within arm's length of me. But something poked me in the side."

On another tour, a woman in the group managed to snap a picture of what looks like a person sitting over in a corner. "She was just taking pictures and in one of them, it looks like there is someone sitting off in a corner by themselves," Jessica told me. "I personally tried to recreate it, but I couldn't. Any way you look at it, it doesn't look like anything other than a real person sitting there. But there was no one there when she took the photo," Jessica attested.

"The strange thing about this building," Steve mentioned, "is that unlike the Colt Barn and the Feed Barn, there's no record of any tragedy here, so I don't know why there'd be ghosts in here."

THE VIGIL

The vigil at Anna Dean Farm was by far the most elaborate one I have ever taken part in. This is because the locations we intended to cover—the Colt Barn, the Feed Barn, and the Heating House—were nowhere near each other. In fact, the Colt Barn was almost a mile away from the other locations. Given that, for security reasons, we could be in only one building at a time, we needed to come up with a setup that would allow us to investigate multiple locations at once. We decided to set up equipment in the Feed Barn, lock it inside, then go and investigate the other buildings, so in essence we were creating a "rolling vigil."

Another challenge was limited access to electricity at most of the locations, meaning we would have to use battery power for most of the night. We'd also need to build breaks into the vigil so that we could return to the Feed Barn to make sure things were still running properly and that the batteries hadn't died. Although given the fact that some of the unexplained activity in the Feed Barn included batteries dying, perhaps if ours died, that in and of itself could be considered evidence!

Ghosts of Ohio members Wendy Cywinski and Samantha Nicholson joined me on this vigil. We started setting up the equipment in the Feed Barn first, which included the following:

- one infrared video camera (running on batteries) in the doorway, pointing into the room
- one infrared video camera (running on batteries) on the left side of the room, pointing toward the car stored inside
- two digital voice recorders (running on batteries), one on either side of the room
- Vernier LabPro temperature, EMF, and static electricity sensors (running on batteries) in the center of the room, radiating out across the main floor

Once we had all that set up, we locked it all inside and headed over to the Colt Barn. For the Colt Barn vigil, we decided that we could go "old school" and use mainly hand-held devices. But in addition, we quickly set up the four-camera DVR and also two studio microphones. Here's where we placed the equipment:

- one DVR night-vision camera on the main floor in the back corner, facing the front of the barn
- one DVR night-vision camera on the main floor in the center of the floor, facing the front of the barn
- one DVR night-vision camera on the second floor in the front corner, facing the back of the barn
- one DVR night-vision camera on the second floor in the back corner, facing the front of the barn
- one Superlux condenser microphone on the main floor in the back corner, facing the front of the barn
- one Superlux condenser microphone on the second floor in the center of the floor, facing the back of the barn

In addition, we set up our command center in a corner of the second floor, allowing us to monitor the cameras and microphones on both floors at the same time.

For the Colt Barn vigil, Wendy, Sam, and I took turns sitting on each floor, asking the ghosts to make themselves known to us. I even went down and implored whatever the mist that had been photographed previously on the first floor was to come and see me. I asked for permission to take its picture and even did the "OK, ready? One, two, three" before I took the pictures. It didn't help.

When I was up on the second floor, I sat in the middle of the room and placed several EMFs and ELFs in a circle around me, asking whatever might be in the room to come closer. The meters never budged.

Not getting any results at the Colt Barn, we decided to pack up things quickly and swing by the Feed Barn to check on things before heading over to the Heating House for the next part of the vigil. Finding everything running smoothly at the Feed Barn, we made our way to the Heating House.

Once there, we decided that in order to spend the most time possible focusing on the vigil itself, we weren't going to set up much equipment at the Heating House. In fact, here's all we went with:

· one infrared video camera (running on batteries) on the first floor, pointing toward the front door and windows

· one infrared video camera (running on batteries) on the second floor, pointing toward the stage where Jessica felt she was poked

· one digital voice recorder (running on batteries) on the first floor near the boiler

· one digital voice recorder (running on batteries) on the second floor near the area where people report hearing footsteps

For the Heating House portion of the vigil, Wendy, Sam, and I each armed ourselves with our own EMF, ELF, and voice recorders. I also took a non-contact thermometer with me. We took turns with two of us walking together while the third person went solo. For my solo part, I went back near the original boiler and into a room where people sometimes report feeling "weird." It was an odd room, but other than a creepy feeling (mostly because it was dark and smelled musty), I didn't have any experiences here—despite the fact that I sat there in total darkness and called out to someone, anyone, to come and talk with me.

After packing up the equipment from the Heating House, we went back to gather the equipment from the Feed Barn. For better or worse, I found that all the batteries in the equipment we left inside the Feed Barn were dead, including the twelve-hour batteries in the video cameras—and they'd been running for only approximately six hours. All the other equipment was running on standard AA, AAA, and/or nine-volt batteries. I'm not willing to claim that the battery drain was paranormal, but it does seem strange that all the batteries died, including the twelve-hour ones. I had personally checked all the batteries before the vigil, and they were either brand new or else fully charged.

FINAL THOUGHTS

After the vigil, we reviewed all the materials and did not find anything out of the ordinary. All in all, it was a very quiet night, albeit a rather hectic one.

It is interesting to note that of all the locations covered for this book, Anna Dean Farm was the first one at which I conducted a vigil. Since then, Anna Dean Farm has opened up the buildings to even more tours, including some ghost hunts, too. Based on the amount of buzz on the Internet, it would appear that people taking these ghost tours are not only walking away with their own personal encounters with ghosts, but the tours seem to be becoming quite popular, bringing more and more people to Anna Dean Farm to learn about O. C. Barber and his legacy. The farm ghosts are doing their job well.

Anna Dean Farm
P.O. Box 666
Barberton, Ohio 44203
www.annadeanfarm.com

FARNAM MANOR

Who doesn't love a good party? I'm not talking about a music-blaring, beer-guzzling type of party. More like the good food, good conversation, good friends type of party—the kind where you just sit around and enjoy each other's company, not ever really wanting the night to end.

Those are the type of gatherings that used to take place at Farnam Manor years ago. So when the current owners took over, they figured they'd carry on that tradition and started holding their own festive gatherings, which everyone seemed to enjoy. Even the ghosts of Farnam Manor.

THE HISTORY

John Farnam was born in Connecticut in 1761. A highly motivated young man, Farnam enlisted to fight against the British in 1777, when he was only sixteen years old. After the war, Farnam married Mary Everett and began a career as a successful businessman and landowner. In 1812, Farnam and his wife decided to purchase a large tract of land in the Western Reserve—over twelve hundred acres—and moved their family to the area known today as Richfield, Ohio.

When the Farnams arrived at their new home, they built a simple log cabin to live in. But before long, Farnam was building himself a little empire, complete with the area's first sawmill, just down the street from their house. By the 1830s, the Farnams' estate had grown to thousands of acres. In 1833, Everett Farnam, one of John and Mary's nine children, began building his dream home, a manor house, on the property. By early 1834, Everett's home, known as the homestead or the manor

Since its construction over 180 years ago, Farnam Manor remains a sight to behold for anyone driving along Brecksville Road in Richfield.

house, was completed. In May of that same year, John Everett died, willing Everett the entire Farnam estate.

Everett Farnam lived alone in his manor house until 1841, when he married eighteen-year-old Emily Oviatt, a woman more than half his age. Together, the couple raised five children, including a son who was born when Everett was sixty-three years old. Everett thoroughly enjoyed living in his manor house, referring to himself as the Squire or even the Lord of the Manor. Successful business ventures allowed Everett to purchase even more land for his manor, which he furnished with lush gardens and even a carriage house adjacent to the main house. In fact, the Farnam Manor property became so large that Everett had to build roads to accommodate all the people who wanted to come out and tour the grounds.

In 1858, tragedy struck Farnam Manor. Everett's six-year-old daughter, Emily, fell into a cistern on the property and drowned. She was buried in the Farnam family plot at the local cemetery nearby. Some say that Everett never recovered from the loss of his daughter, especially since he had been traveling abroad at the time of her death.

Everett Farnam died in 1884. His wife, Emily, followed him to the grave a short time later. Farnam Manor and the surrounding property was passed down to his family members and remained with the Farnams until the early twentieth century.

In 1910, the house was purchased by Ella J. Mayer. After living in the house for about a decade, Mayer decided she needed a change. In 1921, she began extensive remodeling of both the manor house and the adjacent carriage house, the most extensive addition being the enclosed porch, which ran across the entire front of the house. There are stories that Mayer was, in fact, a madam, and used the manor as a house of ill repute. This has never been proven, though, and many believe the house was nothing more than an exclusive club.

Over the next several decades, the manor house would pass through several different owners until August 1948, when it was sold, along with several acres surrounding it, to Theodore and Marie Kirk. While the Kirks were planning on living in the house, they also had unique plans for it. Shortly after moving in, renovations began and the house was transformed into a restaurant. Soon afterwards, the Kirks welcomed all their friends and neighbors to the grand opening of their new restaurant, the Danish Smorgasbord.

The restaurant was an immediate success and was a local hot spot for many years. When Theodore and Anna Marie retired, they continued to live in the house while their daughter and son-in-law ran the restaurant. The Danish Smorgasbord would close for good in 1972, at which point the house became a rental property. During this time, it began to fall into disrepair. In 1980, Bill Cummings leased the property and sank an estimated $50,000 into repairs. It didn't help, though, and as the 1980s were drawing to a close, it looked as though the manor house's days were numbered. But in 1989, it was purchased by Harry and Susan Zaruba, who wanted to turn Farnam Manor into a bed-and-breakfast and began the painstaking process of restoring the property to its former glory. It was hard going, and it would take almost four years until the Zarubas were able to renovate the house to the point where they could live in it.

Little by little, the renovations started to take a toll on the Zaruba family. By 2003, after spending a small fortune on renovations, the Zarubas decided they had had enough. They put Farnam Manor up for sale and moved out. Over the course of the next few years, the house sat abandoned. Eventually, it fell prey to the elements as well as to those who grew curious as to what lay inside the house with the giant stone lions out front. Before long, vandals started having their way with Farnam Manor.

In 2006, Tim and Kathy Magner were living across the street from Farnam Manor in a house on the property that once housed Farnam Gardens. Curious as to what was going on across the street, the couple went over to look at the old house and were shocked at what had become of the once-majestic home.

While they originally intended only to lease the house for a while in order to fix it up and save it from ruin, Tim and Kathy eventually decided to buy Farnam Manor outright, creating the Farnam Manor Museum in the process, celebrating the Farnam family and their wonderful house. The museum is open for tours year-round and can also be rented out for private events—ghosts thrown in at no extra charge.

THE EXPERIENCES

Teri Gorecki has been living in the area her entire life—over fifty years—and can remember coming to the Farnam house back when it was the Danish Smorgasbord. She also remembers the first time she heard there might be ghosts in the house.

"I guess the first time would have been around 1978," Teri began. "In high school, I was friends with a girl who lived in the Farnam house. Her bedroom was upstairs. One night, she said she got up and went to go use the bathroom and she saw a candle, and it was just floating down the hall. She swore to me up and down. And I just went, 'Oh yeah, right. Candle floating up and down the hallway.' But she grabbed me and said, 'No, really. I don't like living there.' They only lived in that house one year," Teri concluded.

Neither Tim nor Kathy Magner had heard anything about the house possibly being haunted when they bought it. In fact, ghosts were the furthest things from their minds. "We never even thought about spirits," Kathy admits. It didn't take long, though, for the ghosts to start making themselves known, even if Tim and Kathy weren't taking notice yet.

"When we first took over the house, we started taking pictures," Kathy told me. "You know, like taking 'before' pictures to show what it was like before we started fixing it up. In some of those pictures, we would get weird mists and things like that. Looking back, it seems like there was something here, even in the first pictures we took."

Kathy recalled that even though she and Tim didn't know any of the ghost lore associated with Farnam Manor, soon after purchasing the building, the locals were more than happy to fill them in. "People would just stop by and tell us ghost stories about the place," Kathy explained. "In the beginning, we just sort of laughed it off after they told us their stories. But the more you heard, you started to think maybe there really are ghosts here."

Kathy also remembers the first day she believes she had a personal encounter with a ghost. There was a closet at Farman Manor, located off the kitchen. It was full of stuff, so Kathy decided one day to clean it out. "This would have been back in 2006. I just started going through the closet when all of a sudden, I felt something touch my arm. I thought it was one of the kids trying to get my attention. I turned around and there was nobody there."

Kathy didn't really give the incident too much thought until a few weeks later, when she was talking to a woman who had worked at Farnam when it was still a restaurant. She told her, 'Whatever you do, don't go into the cooler. Don't go into the cooler.' Kathy continued: "I asked her why not, and she told me that she went in the cooler one day and saw the ghost of a man standing there. She said, 'I dropped everything, ran out, and I'd never go back in there again.'"

When Kathy asked the woman where the cooler was, Kathy learned something very intriguing. "Turns out that when it was a restaurant, there was a walk-in cooler where the closet I was cleaning out stands today. So maybe it was the man in the cooler who was touching my arm that day," Kathy surmised.

While there are several spirits said to roam Farnam Manor, none is more popular than the ghost of Emily Farnam, the six-year-old girl who drowned after falling into the cistern back in 1858. The cistern was eventually covered over and now lies beneath the wood flooring in Farnam Manor's kitchen area. Some say that did nothing to prevent Emily's ghost from coming out to play.

Emily's ghost has been seen all over Farnam Manor and even outside on occasion. She has been known to tug on people's clothes, move objects, and even giggle on occasion. In fact, the only thing that remains constant about Emily's ghost is what she's wearing. "Every single person that sees Emily describes her the same way: she's wearing a white dress with flowers on it," Kathy told me.

Emily's ghost does seem to spend a lot of time in the room that's been dubbed Emily's Room. Perhaps that's because she's attracted to all the toys in the room—toys that often get moved by unseen hands. In particular, there's a certain ball that seems to be Emily's favorite.

"That ball moves all around the house by itself," Tim Magner told me. "They say Emily likes to play with the ball in her room, but we've found it in all different rooms of the house. We never see it move. It just shows up."

Steve Jones, a ghost hunter who often volunteers at Farnam Manor, decided to try an experiment to see if the ball would move if it was in a room other than Emily's. He put the ball in the middle of the parlor floor and trained a video camera, one with a motion detector, on it. "I'd probably done that experiment a hundred times before and nothing happened," Steve began. "One night, I'm sitting there watching the ball and I get bored just watching it, so I go outside to have a smoke. I come back inside and the ball is gone."

There were other people in the house at the time, so Steve said his first thought was that someone came in and took the ball. One problem: the motion detector never went off. No one admitted to taking the ball either. So Steve went to the videotape and looked at what had been recorded. "The video didn't show the ball moving at all. It was there one second and the next, it's gone. I can't explain it," Steve admitted. He would eventually find the ball underneath one of the loveseats in the parlor. How it got there, though, remains a mystery.

Sometimes, Emily's ghost appears to want something new to play with. When that happens, other toys in Emily's Room will move on their own. One fall, Joe Dutt was working as a tour guide at Farnam Manor's fall lantern tours when someone or something appeared to be playing with the toy train in Emily's Room.

"I brought my first tour into Emily's Room and the train is on the floor, sort of facing the bathroom in like an arc shape," Joe began. "I get done with that tour group, send them all back downstairs, and then I go into the back bedroom to wait for my next group."

After waiting alone in the back bedroom, Joe's next group came up to meet him and he took them over to Emily's Room. "I'm the first one to walk into the room to walk into the room and right away, I see that the train has flipped and is now facing the front of the house in a com-

Emily's Room at Farnam Manor, the room where the ghost of six-year-old Emily Farnam apparently likes to play.

plete arc. All the tours were taking the same route that night, so nobody could have gotten up into that room," Joe admits.

That wasn't the end of it, though. The rest of the evening, every time Joe left Emily's Room, he'd come back to find that the train had moved again. "The train would be in an 'S' shape and then you'd come back in and the train would be in an arc. Leave and come back and it would be in a straight line. It wouldn't move while you were looking at it. But turn your back for a minute and it would move."

Laura Soucek was at Farnam Manor one August, helping out on a ghost hunt. Needing a break, she went outside for a breath of fresh air. "I was just sitting out near a tree in front of the house, playing on my phone," Laura told me. "Then I just happened to look up and I see a little girl in a white dress over near the steps. She was just sitting there. Then she looked directly at me, jumped up, and started skipping into the backyard. She kind of just faded away when she went into the grass."

Several years ago, the local historical society came across a faded white dress that had clearly belonged to a little girl at one time. The dress was adorned with little flowers, birds, and a small tag that bore the name Emily Farnam.

"My heart just sank when I saw the dress," Kathy told me, "because so many people have told me on different occasions, 'I saw the ghost of a little girl wearing a white dress with flowers on it.'"

"It's the same dress everyone describes," Tim chimed in. "The historical society still has it and they keep it in a glass case now."

Not all the ghosts of Farnam Manor come with as much history as Emily's ghost does. In fact, Emily is the only ghost who has a name attached to it. As for the rest, no one is really sure who they are. For example, climbing the back stairs off the kitchen will lead you to a small hallway. People standing in the bedroom immediately to the left of the top of the stairs have seen an extremely tall, human-like shadow in the hallway. Some estimate the height at seven or eight feet tall. Other than the height, there are no distinguishable features, although sometimes there are reports of the shadow's arms being outstretched.

That bedroom leads to another bedroom, often referred to as the Soldier's Room. It is said that the presence of a man dressed in a Civil War uniform is felt here. Psychics have stated that the man actually died in this room, on the floor in front of the fireplace. No documentation has been found yet to substantiate that, though.

There is also the ghost of a woman in a long white dress. Who she is or even what time period she is from remains a mystery. There are stories that say she is a member of the Farnam family, while still others say she is one of the many women said to have been employed by Ella Mayer back in the day. Truth is, though, next to nothing is known about this particular ghost. "But we see her here a lot," Tim Magner told me. "People usually see her upstairs, although I guess she likes to hang out on the porch sometimes. Someone told me they got a picture of her out there one time."

The spirits of Farnam Manor also don't appear to be confined to the house itself. For many years, even before Tim and Kathy bought the building, people from the area would talk about the ghosts. Deirdre Pasko has lived in the area her whole life and can remember as far back as the 1970s that people said there were ghosts in the woods around Farnam Manor. "I can remember my brother telling me that you could see ghosts of Indians in the woods, walking around at night," she said.

The idea of Native American spirits in the woods seems to stem from the fact that they had inhabited the area long before the Farnams. In fact, there are stories that, as a child, Everett Farnam befriended a local Indian

Farnam Manor's "signal trees," trees said to have been groomed by Native American Indians so that the trunks would point north and south.

boy, who taught him many of the methods of farming and planting trees. As an adult, Farnam would incorporate these methods on his property.

It is also said that there are Native American "signal trees," or trail markers throughout the Farnam property. Most notably, the twin pine tree near the front of the house, which is said to have been groomed and bound by the Native Americans in order to make the one trunk branch into two fully grown trunks that would point north and south. This truly unique tree is considered to have created a sort of portal or ghostly trail through which Native American spirits can come and go.

In the years since they have taken over Farnam Manor, both Kathy and Tim have witnessed numerous shadows, which they take to be those of Native Americans, moving through the woods around and behind the house. Tim said that one night, they built a campfire in the backyard. While they were sitting around, chatting and enjoying the warm glow of the fire, someone mentioned that they had brought along some traditional Native American music that they'd like to play, which they did.

No sooner had the music started when people started seeing movement among the trees. "There were all sorts of shadows out there, moving around," Tim explained. "It was like there were people walking around in the woods, but all we could see were their shadows. As soon as we stopped the music, the shadows disappeared."

Another area on the Farnam property where ghosts are said to dwell is the carriage house. No one is sure who the ghost is, but people have heard footsteps echoing through the building, and objects stored here have been known to move even though there's no one around them. The ghost also apparently likes to snack on batteries, especially ones inside digital cameras. Visitors often report their cameras acting strangely or having their brand-new batteries suddenly drain.

Steve Jones remembers one ghost tour during which one visitor still might have managed to get a picture of the carriage house ghost even though the cameras were acting up.

"Nobody's camera was working that night in the carriage house," Steve reported. "People were taking pictures and they would be completely white, completely black, or just so out of focus you couldn't tell what it was a picture of." One woman, however, managed to get a picture and showed it to Steve. He wasn't impressed . . . at first. "She showed me a picture of a woman sitting in one of the chairs and I told her, 'That's a nice picture of Kathy [Magner].' But it wasn't Kathy."

Taking a closer look at the picture, Steve noticed that the woman in the chair was older than Kathy. That's when Steve realized the woman in the photo wasn't anyone who was in the carriage house with him at the time. At least not anyone he could see. "I was there when she took the picture," Steve said, "and that chair was empty."

Kathy and Tim both told me that the longer they were inside Farnam Manor, the more they experienced things they couldn't explain. But they did seem to notice a pattern developing. Oddly enough, the activity seemed to happen when there was a lot going on in the house. When Tim or Kathy were just sitting quietly in the house, hardly anything happened. It was almost as if the ghosts wanted to be involved if there was something going on in Farnam Manor; otherwise they would just lie low.

Steve Jones believes that to be true, too. "You think when you go on a ghost hunt, you've got to sit there and be quiet. But I think I've actually seen more the more active you are in the house."

The fact that the ghosts of Farnam Manor appear to be more active when the living are also active has led Tim and Kathy to believe that the ghosts appreciate what is being done with the house. "It was abandoned for so long," Kathy explained, "that I think the ghosts are happy there are people here again. It's like they enjoy the company."

Tim and Kathy have taken things a step further by playing period music and inviting visitors to dress up in period clothing. The idea is that by filling the house with laughter and good cheer, the ghosts will want to join in the festivities. Tim and Kathy even keep a supply of old-style "fancy hats" at the manor for guests to wear, should they so choose. Sometimes those hats seem to take on a mind of their own.

"We had a group of people over and we were all carrying on, having a good time. And we all had our hats on," said Tim. "At one point, I looked over and saw there was this one black hat over in the corner of the dining room on the floor." "We didn't know how it got on the floor. It was just there all of a sudden," Kathy added.

Later in the evening, the entire group went upstairs for a tour. After spending several minutes in the bedrooms, the group came back downstairs. "That's when I saw that the black hat was now in the living room," Tim said. "At that point, I thought maybe somebody had kicked it or something, even though we were all upstairs. But then we all went into the other room and when we came back, it was on the other side of the room, on the floor in the middle of the doorway."

Tim said at that point, he decided that maybe it would be best if he just returned the hat to where he had seen it at the beginning of the night: on the couch. Leaving the hat there, Tim turned and went to rejoin the rest of the group, who were all back in the kitchen. As he walked through the rooms, something caught Tim's eye: the hat was back on the floor, in the middle of the doorway! "No idea how it got there or who put it there," Tim confessed.

THE VIGIL

Ghosts of Ohio members Mark DeLong, Samantha Nicholson, and Wendy Cywinski would join me for this vigil. As soon as we arrived at Farnam Manor, I knew we were going to be in for a very memorable evening, ghosts or no ghosts. We were greeted by Kathy Magner, who was in full

The current owners of Farnam Manor believe the ghosts enjoy parties and the company of others. For that reason, they keep a wide selection of "fancy hats" on-site for guests to wear to add to the celebratory atmosphere.

costume. Tim Magner was not, but he showed Mark, Sam, Wendy, and me where all the hats were should we wish to wear one to create a party atmosphere that might help bring the ghosts out. How could we resist? Of course, I had to wear the infamous black hat that Tim told me he had chased all around the manor that one night. But after Kathy told me that, in keeping with the party theme, she and Tim would be preparing a special dinner for us, I decided to leave the hat on the floor with a motion detector nearby to see if it would move while we were eating dinner.

We did most of our setup before dinner was ready. Based on the interviews I had conducted, this was where we decided to place the equipment for the vigil:

Downstairs Parlor
· one infrared video camera in the back of the parlor, facing the front of the room
· one Superlux condenser microphone in the center of the parlor

Back Bedroom (Second Floor)
- one DVR night-vision camera in the doorway, pointing into the hallway
- one DVR night-vision camera in the doorway between the back bedroom and the Soldier's Room, pointing into the back bedroom
- one Superlux condenser microphone in the doorway between the back bedroom and the Soldier's Room, pointing into the back bedroom

Soldier's Room (Second Floor)
- one DVR night-vision camera against the far wall, pointing across the room toward the back bedroom doorway (fireplace was in the frame, too)

Main Staircase
- one DVR night-vision camera on the second floor landing, pointing toward the staircase
- one Superlux condenser microphone on the second floor landing, pointing toward the staircase
- Vernier LabPro ambient temperature EMF and static charge sensors running up and down the staircase

Emily's Room (Second Floor)
- one infrared video camera, focused on the toys on the floor
- one Superlux condenser microphone in the corner of the room, facing Emily's bed
- one motion detector, focused on the toys on the floor
- laser grid focused on the toys on the floor and on Emily's bed

Kitchen
- one infrared video camera, pointing toward the remains of the cistern

We decided to place our command center in the kitchen area, off in the corner. As for the carriage house and the woods, we decided those areas would be covered by individuals with hand-helds.

After a spectacular dinner, I rolled myself away from the dining room table and headed into the other room to check on the status of the black hat. Since I hadn't heard the motion detector go off since I placed it there, I wasn't surprised to find that the hat hadn't moved. At that point, I decided that the easiest way to keep track of it during the night was to put it on my head. I figured that way if it ever were to move, I'd feel it.

And with that, we started the vigil.

I began by spending some time in the parlor. We had placed a ball on the floor and I asked Emily if she would be so kind as to move it for me. After staring at the ball for a good half hour without so much as a wobble, I began asking if perhaps there was another spirit in the room other than Emily. During the interviews, Kathy Magner had mentioned to me that a psychic told her other child spirits had taken up residence inside Farnam after initially being attracted here by Emily's ghost. So I thought maybe it wasn't another child spirit who was moving the ball. I wasn't able to figure out if that was true or not because this night, no one moved the ball.

Thinking Emily might be up in her room as opposed to in the parlor, I next spent some time in Emily's room. The problem with that is since we had the laser grid running in the room, the beams were spread out across the entire room, leaving only a small area where one could sit without breaking the beams. For a portly man such as myself, it was a little tough trying to fold myself up to fit in that area, but in the name of science, I did it!

Just as I did in the parlor, I began this session by asking Emily to come and play with me. I asked her if she could touch or push her favorite toy so that I could see it move. Nothing happened. After a while, I resigned myself to the fact that Emily wasn't in the room with me, and I started asking if there was perhaps another child with me instead. I asked the ghost his or her name and age. I conducted an interview with them. During the interview, I never heard a response live (nor did any of The Ghosts of Ohio members who were listening down at the command center). When we reviewed the audio and video afterwards, there was nothing out of the ordinary to be heard or seen.

When I made my way back down to the kitchen, I overheard Kathy Magner and Mark DeLong, who were sitting near the fireplace. Kathy was telling Mark how some people on the ghost tours had claimed they had gotten "responses" by using dowsing rods. Since I had my dowsing rods with me, I decided to give them a try. Mark had brought along his pendulum, so he said he would try that.

I should probably mention here that while I have two sets of dowsing rods, I personally don't put much stock in them. Dowsing rods have supposedly been used over the years to find everything from ghosts to underground water supplies and even landmines, but for me, it's way too easy for the person using them to influence what the rods are doing. I can't even hold them steady when I'm trying to keep them from moving! The slightest twitch or breeze and off they go. So I wasn't surprised at all that after a quick tour of Farnam Manor, I didn't feel like the dowsing rods had detected anything other than the fact that perhaps I had ingested far too much caffeine and my hands were jittery.

I was, however, surprised at what Mark told me when I returned to the kitchen. Mark said that he was using his pendulum (meaning he was basically holding one end of the string and letting the pendulum itself dangle freely from the other end) in front of the fireplace with Kathy Magner, and that all of sudden it felt like someone was pulling on the pendulum. Mark said that he and Kathy would ask questions and every once in a while "it felt like something was pulling on the pendulum."

What makes that interesting is that I've never experienced what felt like something "pulling" on a pendulum. They don't work like that. Since the pendulum is hanging freely at the end of a string, it usually swings, but it always moves from side to side, never up and down. When I asked him what it felt like, Mark equated it to holding a fishing pole and having a fish pulling on the line. Unfortunately, the answers Mark felt like he might be getting were too confusing for him to glean anything concise from them.

Leaving the kitchen area, I decided to go outside to see if I could contact some Native American ghosts. Before that, though, I did something special that I had promised my sister, donna, I would do. donna is a bit of a hippie who has always done things her own way (including legally changing her name to be spelled with a lowercase "d"). Ever since I was a child, I knew my sister was infatuated with the Native American culture, so much so that she would refuse to play cowboys and Indians with me until I acknowledged that, as she put it, "The cowboys were the bad guys because they stole all the Indians' land." So as soon as she found out I was going to search for Native American spirits, she made me promise to leave them an offering. When I asked donna what kind of offering, she suggested tobacco.

Not being a smoker, I wasn't sure what type of tobacco to offer, so I settled on American Spirit because there was an Indian on the front of the pack . . . and I thought the word "Spirit" seemed appropriate.

The night before the vigil, I cut open each cigarette and dumped the tobacco into a Ziploc bag. As the vigil began, with Tim and Kathy's permission, I sprinkled the tobacco around the Signal Tree, saying, "My sister told me to do this to pay my respects to you. If this is wrong, please don't be mad at me!"

When that was done, I sat quietly next to the Signal Tree and just listened. After a while, I decided to introduce myself and explained why I was there. I stated that I was trying to find out everything I could about the history of the Farnam property and that I was all ears if anyone wanted to tell me something about it. I never got an answer. I wandered out to the woods and did the same thing. By this time, my eyes had adjusted to the darkness, so I scanned the woods for any sign of movement. There was none.

Next, I joined Sam at the carriage house, but not before I had checked to make sure my camera batteries were fully charged. I even brought along some extra batteries just in case. Every picture I took inside the carriage house came out fine, and the batteries remained charged. At one point, Sam and I separated and sat at opposite ends of the carriage house. We took turns talking to any spirits who might have been with us. I even went so far as to tell the spirits that if they didn't like me, they were more than welcome to go hang out with Sam for a while. After a while, we returned back to the house.

As the vigil began to wind down, I decided to walk around the manor and pick a random area to sit for a while. I ended up in the back bedroom on the second floor. Wendy was also in there, and we took turns looking out into the hallway to see if we could see the freakishly tall shadow figure. Then we sat around talking. Wendy and I weren't necessarily talking about anything ghost-related at that point, just chatting away quietly. All of a sudden, I got what I could only describe as a mouthful of perfume—cheap women's perfume—as if I had breathed it in through my nose and it immediately slid down into my mouth. It almost made me gag, it was so pronounced. In fact, if you listen closely to the audio we recorded that night, you can hear me let out a little cough. Almost as soon as I smelled it, it was gone.

I didn't say anything about it, though, because I initially thought that it was Wendy's perfume or deodorant and I didn't want to offend her. If it had been Wendy, you would have thought I'd have smelled it earlier. But I'm a guy, and one of the things I've learned the hard way is that when you're in the presence of a woman and you smell something odd, it's best not to say, "I smell something. Is that you?"

Thankfully, Wendy spoke up. "Do you smell perfume?" she asked. "I did," I said. "I smelled it a couple of seconds ago. It's gone." Wendy looked at me and asked, "Why didn't you say anything?" to which I replied, "I thought I was smelling you." And there it was: mere seconds after feeling like I had sidestepped an awkward moment by not accusing my ghost-hunting friend of wearing cheap perfume, I went and jammed my foot in my mouth anyway.

"You thought that was me?" Wendy blurted. After an awkward pause, we both began laughing hysterically, forgetting for the moment that we had both just smelled something strange. After wiping the tears from my cheeks, Wendy and I began walking around the bedroom, sniffing to see if we could locate the source of the smell. We never smelled it again during the rest of the vigil. The others in the group took turns sniffing around the room, too, all to no avail.

Several hours later, we ended the vigil, packed up, and hung our party hats back up on the wall. It had been a truly memorable night.

FINAL THOUGHTS

Even though I hadn't experienced much in the way of ghost activity during my stay at Farnam Manor, the building stayed with me long after I had left. I was fascinated with the way Kathy and Tim had chosen not only to embrace the spirits of the Manor, but also to invite them to join in celebrations with them. Over the years, I've seen people use everything from Ouija boards and trigger objects to writing implements and even crystal balls to invite spirits to come closer. And of course, there's the most common means—simply asking the ghosts to make their presence known. But Kathy and Tim's way of going about things—put on a fancy hat and enjoy yourself—was a new one for me.

I was also intrigued by the way Kathy and Tim ended up purchasing Farnam Manor. They weren't looking to buy the house. In fact, they weren't interested in it at all, and yet something drew them across the street. It was as if the spirits of the manor house needed someone to help them keep their memory alive and Kathy and Tim were the ones for the job. At least, that's what I'd like to think.

But even if that's not true, Farnam Manor still holds a special place in my ghostly heart. Let's face it: there aren't many places in Ohio where I can say I have an open invitation to come out and party with a ghost or two!

Farnam Manor
4223 Brecksville Road
Richfield, Ohio 44286
www.farnammanorinn.com

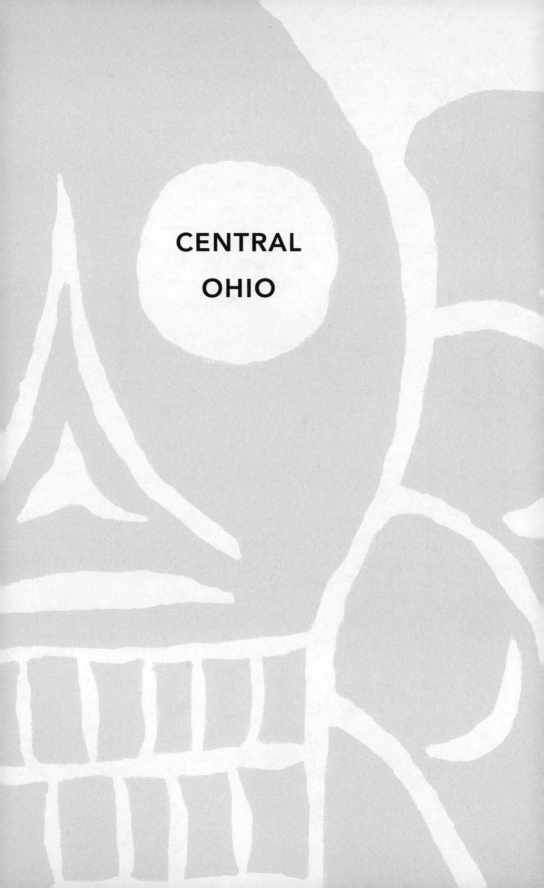

CENTRAL
OHIO

OHIO STATE REFORMATORY

It doesn't matter how much you've read about the building or how many times you've watched *The Shawshank Redemption*. Nothing can prepare you for the first time you crest the hill on Olivesburg Road and get a glimpse of the Ohio State Reformatory. Simply put, it is awe-inspiring and frightening all at once. The massive stone structure somehow seems to beckon you to come closer, to roam its hallways and venture into its deep recesses. Still, there's a little voice inside your head that keeps repeating, "Don't do it. Don't do it." And you know exactly why that voice is telling you to steer clear: if ever a building were haunted, it would be the Ohio State Reformatory. And these would not be your run-of-the-mill motherly ghosts who stop by to tell you they love you and where they buried the family fortune. No, the ghosts here are said to be the worst of the worst: men who cheated, robbed, murdered. They are the type of ghosts you should give a wide berth to.

And yet, even as you're listening to that voice in your head, you suddenly find that you are driving up to the front gate, unable to stay away.

THE HISTORY

The year is 1861 and war has broken out across the United States. Often referred to as the War Between the States, the battle lines of the American Civil War literally divided the United States, often pitting neighbor against neighbor. Several months after the war began, training facilities for Union soldiers began popping up across the Northern states, including several in Ohio. One of these was Camp Mordecai Bartley, situated in close proximity to where the Ohio State Reformatory would come to stand. Named after the eighteenth governor of Ohio, Camp Bartley, as it was often called, would serve as the training grounds for an estimated four thousand young recruits between the time it opened in 1861 and the end of the Civil War four years later. During that time, even though the camp was fed by an underground natural spring, getting clean drinking water was often a problem. In fact, the living conditions at the camp were sometimes less than ideal, which led to the spread of diseases like malaria, typhoid, and chicken pox. Deaths at the camp were not uncommon, leading some to believe that the hauntings at the Ohio State Reformatory all began with Camp Bartley.

When the Civil War ended, Camp Bartley continued to operate for a bit longer before being shut down and dismantled, leaving Mansfield with a huge piece of property and nothing to do with it. Then in the 1860s, the city of Mansfield heard that the state of Ohio was looking for a location on which to build a new prison. This was to be no ordinary prison, though. Rather, this would be a facility for reforming prisoners, turning them into law-abiding citizens who could then be introduced back into society.

Although the theory behind creating "reformatories" was new to the United States, it had been around for many years. At the time, Ohio had two types of penal facilities: juvenile facilities and state penitentiaries, all of which were operating at maximum capacity. An "intermittent" facility for low-risk and first-time criminals would ease the burden of the current facilities with the added benefit of possibly reforming some of the criminals so they did not become repeat offenders.

In 1884, legislation calling for the construction of the Intermittent Penitentiary was officially passed. Mansfield, along with several other Ohio cities, immediately announced that it wished to be considered for the new home for the penitentiary. After two years, Mansfield was finally chosen for the Intermittent Penitentiary, which would be built on a plot of land that included part of where Camp Bartley once stood.

When it came to choosing the designer of the Intermittent Penitentiary, the decision was easy: Levi T. Scofield. A Cleveland native, Scofield had spent the last twenty years making quite the name for himself as an architect. He was known for designing large, industrial-sized buildings that were not only functional, but beautiful to look at. Scofield also designed institutions such as the North Carolina Penitentiary in Raleigh and, closer to home, the Athens Lunatic Asylum.

Part of what adds to the immense size of the Ohio State Reformatory is the fact that the building included multistoried wings to house the warden's family and administration offices.

When tasked with designing the Intermittent Penitentiary, Scofield took the notion of reform to heart and began looking at historic buildings that he felt possessed "spiritual and uplifting architecture." He found what he was looking for in the ancient castles of Germany, although rather than settling on one specific style, Scofield instead chose to incorporate several distinctly different ones into the penitentiary's design: Queen Anne, Richardsonian, Romanesque, and Victorian Gothic.

For the cells themselves, Scofield designed the penitentiary to house close to a thousand prisoners, who would be spread out between two multitiered cell blocks, the East and the West. In breaking with traditional prison design, Scofield's plans called for the cells to be constructed back-to-back, as opposed to facing each other. This way, every prisoner's cell would have a direct view of the windows at either the front or rear of the Reformatory. Between the two cell blocks would be a central guard room, where officers could keep an eye on things.

As the penitentiary was to be self-sufficient, Scofield's plans called for the building to contain not only such essentials as showers, a kitchen, and a dining area, but also a library, a hospital, and even a barber shop. And since the penitentiary's warden would live at the prison as well as work there, there would be a large, three-story building at the front of the cell blocks for administration and living quarters for the warden and his family. All in all, the main building of the Intermittent Penitentiary, including the warden's wing and the administration section, would comprise nearly 250,000 square feet.

The contract for the actual construction of the penitentiary was awarded to a local company, the Mansfield construction firm Hancock and Dow. The initial cost to build the penitentiary was about $1.3 million.

November 4, 1886, was declared a public holiday in Mansfield, Ohio, culminating in a groundbreaking ceremony on the penitentiary grounds. Local masons officially laid the building's cornerstone, and shortly afterward, work began on the penitentiary, continuing almost nonstop for the next decade. It's interesting to note that in 1890, while work was still continuing, Ohio officials began rethinking the idea that this should be a prison. Some began to think that perhaps the building was better suited to be a mental health facility—an "insane asylum," to be precise. Those plans were soon nixed, though, and the following year, 1891, the name of the building was officially changed from Intermittent Penitentiary to the Ohio State Reformatory.

While construction continued on the Reformatory, people, even entire families, stood on the prison grounds, watching the construction. On weekends, people often spread out on the Reformatory's front lawn, enjoying a picnic lunch. Seems strange, but back then, that's the kind of thing people did. The park-like Reformatory grounds and the proximity of the public railroads meant that families could hop off the train, enjoy a nice lunch on the grounds or in front of the Reformatory pond, then jump back on the train and head home. What a nice, relaxing afternoon!

The Ohio State Reformatory officially opened for business on September 17, 1896. The first prisoners to call the Reformatory home were 150 men from the Ohio Penitentiary in Columbus who were either first-time offenders, had been convicted of lesser charges, or low-risk prisoners. Accounts say that the mood in the Reformatory was one of excitement, like a giant celebration. One report states that the incoming prisoners were treated like celebrities and were even handed cigars as they entered the Reformatory.

It's interesting to note that while the Reformatory was officially open and accepting prisoners, the building itself was far from finished. In fact, when it came to the two cell blocks, only the five-tiered West Cell Block was complete. So once the incoming prisoners were checked in, they were often expected to help finish the construction. Ironically, one part of the prison that the inmates worked on was the outside wall—the wall that was supposed to keep all of them securely inside the prison. It seems odd to have prisoners working on such a thing, but since this was considered a low-risk facility, the chance of escape attempts was thought to be slim.

Construction on the rest of the Reformatory would continue for almost fifteen years, when it was finally completed in 1910. The most impressive aspect of the Reformatory was the East Cell Block—six tiers of double-sided cells, for a grand total of six hundred cells, officially making it the world's tallest freestanding cell block.

Since all Ohio prison facilities were overflowing with inmates, as soon at the Ohio State Reformatory opened, the other prisons began considering which prisoners could be transferred to OSR, thereby reducing their prison population. Soon OSR was taking in prisoners from all over the state. It wouldn't be long until it was at capacity.

While OSR had originally been designed to house only low-risk, non-violent, and/or first-time offenders, every once in a while, some borderline inmates ended up at the Reformatory. Combine that with increased overcrowding at the Reformatory, and it wasn't long before tempers flared and violent outbreaks began.

It is also interesting to note that when some of the prisoners at OSR were released after serving their sentences, they thought the fact that it was a low-risk facility might make it easy to help their former cellmates escape. Such was the case of Philip Orleck. In November 1926, after Orleck was released from OSR, he returned to the facility to help his former cellmate escape. Incredibly, Orleck was convinced that he would be able to walk in, find his friend, and walk right back out with him without being questioned. Oddly enough, Orleck almost pulled it off. He had made it through the gates inside the main building and was heading for the cell blocks when he was recognized by an officer, Urban Wilford. When Wilford tried to intervene, Orleck pulled out a pistol and shot the officer dead, making Wilford the first police officer killed in the line of duty at the Ohio State Reformatory. As for Orleck, he found out the hard way that it was a lot harder to escape from OSR than it looked. After shooting Wilford, he attempted to flee but never made it to the front gate. He was arrested and sent to the Ohio Penitentiary in Columbus, where, after being convicted of the cold-blooded murder of Urban Wilford, he was executed in the electric chair on July 18, 1927.

By 1930, even though it could accommodate a thousand prisoners, the Ohio State Reformatory was already operating well above normal capacity. In fact, some of the two-person cells were now being shared by three or even four prisoners. The level of violence continued to escalate while the living conditions continued to deteriorate. On the evening of October 2, 1932, OSR guard Frank Hangar was making his rounds when he stumbled across a small group of prisoners who were trying to escape. Upon seeing Hangar, two of the prisoners, Merrill Chandler and Chester Probaski, jumped the guard and began beating him while the other inmates fled.

After beating Hangar unconscious, Chandler and Probaski headed for the wall surrounding OSR, trying to make good on their escape plan. They never made it and were apprehended without ever stepping off Reformatory property. Frank Hangar, unfortunately, succumbed to his injuries. Merrill Chandler and Chester Probaski were both convicted of the murder and were sent to the electric chair on the same day, November 24, 1933.

Two other OSR inmates, Robert Daniels and John West, apparently had some sort of beef with OSR farm superintendent John Neibel, so much so that even when Daniels and West were both released from OSR, they wanted revenge. On July 21, 1948, both men returned to the Reformatory and headed to the small farmhouse where Neibel lived.

Armed with guns, Daniels and West broke into the house, overpowering Neibel, his wife, and their daughter. The pair then led the Neibels out to a field beside the house and shot them to death in cold blood. Shortly thereafter, Daniels and West fled the scene.

Once the bodies of the Neibel family were discovered, authorities launched a massive statewide manhunt for Robert Daniels and John West. Less than a week later, police managed to track them down, but they were not about to go quietly. Instead, they both drew their weapons on the approaching officers and a shootout ensued. When it was all over, John West was dead and Robert Daniels was in police custody. Sentenced to death for the murders of the Neibel family, Robert Daniels was not returned to the Ohio State Reformatory. Instead, he spent his last days

This photograph, taken from the cell door, shows the size of a typical prisoner's cell at the Ohio State Reformatory. This cell was designed to hold a maximum of two prisoners (note the bunk beds).

behind bars at the Ohio Penitentiary in Columbus until his date with the electric chair in January 1949.

On Sunday morning, November 5, 1950, OSR Superintendent Arthur L. Glattke and his family were getting ready for church. He had lived at OSR since first becoming superintendent in 1935, so Glattke was fairly comfortable with living at the prison. Nevertheless, he kept loaded guns around, just in case.

As Arthur's wife, Helen, prepared for the church service, she went to retrieve something from the bedroom closet. While reaching up to a high closet shelf, Helen accidentally brushed against a shoebox, inside which Superintendent Glattke had been storing a loaded handgun. The gun fell from the shelf and dislodged. Helen Glattke was struck by the bullet and collapsed on the floor. She was rushed to the hospital, where doctors were able to remove the bullet. Unfortunately, Helen Glattke passed away two days later from complications.

In 1957, there was a huge riot at the Reformatory. It is estimated that close to two hundred prisoners took part in destroying property, fighting with each other, and even setting their mattresses on fire. Incredibly, while the Reformatory staff were initially outnumbered, they eventually restored order without anyone being seriously injured. Several prisoners tried to escape during the riot, but none made it to the outside wall. When it was all over, the warden came down hard on the inmates who were suspected of either participating in or otherwise encouraging the riot. Over one hundred prisoners, more than half of those accused of participating in the riot, were sentenced to thirty days in solitary confinement: the Hole. Prison officials ordered all prisoners to serve their sentences immediately, even though the Reformatory's solitary confinement area could accommodate only a quarter of those men.

When news of the riot made the local papers, people began to question whether or not the Reformatory was built for this sort of stress. It was originally designed to hold low-risk offenders, not seasoned, violent criminals—and certainly not so many of them. The state of Ohio began to take a closer look at OSR, and in the 1970s, it officially declared that the Reformatory's conditions were not up to code and that the building did not meet the standards for correctional facilities. The building was in desperate need of repairs, the facilities were outdated, and, of course, there was that little thing known as asbestos. Following the findings, OSR was allowed to continue operating as it had before, but it was becoming increasingly obvious that the facility's days were numbered.

By the dawn of the 1980s, OSR was still overcrowded and parts of the building were nearly a hundred years old. When officials compared the costs to renovate OSR and bring it up to code with simply building a new, more modern facility, the numbers weren't even close. So the decision was made to close the Ohio State Reformatory and build a new facility nearby, so as the new facility expanded, it could take over the land where the Reformatory currently stood . . . after it was demolished, of course.

The last prisoners to call the Reformatory home were relocated in 1990. Some of them didn't have far to move to their new home, though, as the Mansfield Correctional Institution opened the same year, right behind the Reformatory. Once the last inmate had been moved, the gates to the Reformatory were locked up tight one last time and the entire building was left to the elements, silently waiting for its day with the wrecking ball.

In early 1993, as the still-abandoned OSR sat waiting for its inevitable demise, Hollywood producers came to Mansfield, scouting potential locations for a new movie, which was tentatively entitled *Rita Hayworth and Shawshank Redemption*. Since a good portion of the movie was to take place inside a prison, the producers wanted to take a peek inside OSR. Initially, they were shocked at the condition of the prison, but when they heard they could do whatever they wanted inside the building, they chose to film at OSR. In the end, most of the movie would be filmed inside OSR, including portions of the former administration building, which was remodeled and made to look like a halfway house.

Released the following year as simply *The Shawshank Redemption*, the movie, starring Tim Robbins and Morgan Freeman, was only a modest hit, even though it was nominated for Best Picture at the 1995 Academy Awards (it lost to *Forrest Gump*). However, over the years, it grew tremendously popular and came to be considered one of the best movies of all time. As a result, the Ohio State Reformatory—what many people felt was a major star of the film—was put back on the map.

Unfortunately, that resurgence in interest came too late to save some of the Reformatory's brick outbuildings, which had all been demolished. The rest of OSR was still there, though, although apparently the Mansfield Correctional Institution kept eyeballing that prime real estate for potential expansion. But the renewed interest in OSR led a group of locals to realize that the building not only had historical value but could be a prime tourist attraction. So in 1995, the Mansfield Reformatory Preservation Society was formed to restore and preserve the facility.

Today, the Mansfield Reformatory Preservation Society offers a wide selection of historical tours of OSR. They also hold overnight ghost hunts in the building and even turn the prison into a haunted house attraction every October. Between all of that, you could say that OSR offers a little something for everyone!

THE EXPERIENCES

Over the years, OSR's long and violent history has fostered a large number of ghost stories about the building . . . and more than a couple of out-and-out lies. Writing this book gave me the opportunity to get to the bottom of all these stories by interviewing those who had spent the most time inside it: the OSR volunteers.

The first stories I wanted to sort out were related to the tragic event of November 5, 1950, when Helen Glattke suffered a gunshot wound. There are numerous ghost stories circulating on the Internet that center on a vicious lie claiming Superintendent Glattke had in fact planted the gun there, essentially murdering his wife. What's more, these stories claim that Helen's vengeful ghost had returned to the Reformatory, stalking her guilty husband until she was able to exact her revenge by causing him to have a fatal heart attack shortly after her death.

Any ghost stories with a murder-vengeful ghost angle need to be dismissed immediately. There is absolutely no evidence to support that what happened to Helen was anything other than an unfortunate accident. What's more, while Arthur Glattke did indeed suffer a fatal heart attack while working in his office inside the Reformatory, it would happen on February 10, 1959—over eight years after Helen passed away.

But just because there was no foul play involved in the deaths of Helen and Arthur Glattke doesn't mean that their ghosts don't still linger at the Ohio State Reformatory.

Cheryl Kneram has been volunteering at the Ohio State Reformatory for over fifteen years. She has become such a fixture at the building that the other volunteers affectionately refer to her as "Mom." When I asked her about some people claiming to smell perfume over in the warden's quarters of the Reformatory and that the perfume means Helen

Glatkke's spirit is present, Cheryl confirmed she herself had indeed smelled something up there. Even more intriguing, Cheryl told me the smell has changed over the years.

"When I first started here, I used to smell what could have been like lavender or lilac," Cheryl began. "But over the years, that smell sort of went away. Then I would say like my third year, I was in one of the bedrooms that's attached to the pink restroom area on the second floor of the warden's quarters. And I was thinking about the warden's wife, Helen, and the smell of roses came into the room and filled the room. I think that was the first time we ever smelled roses here," Cheryl said.

Cheryl continued: "The smell stayed right there in the room with me for about thirty minutes. It was so strong that people coming into the room could smell it right away. The weird thing was that if people came toward me, the smell would dissipate. But once they left the room, the smell would come back. Then it just left, and I didn't smell it anymore."

At least for now.

Cheryl said that over the years, people have continued to smell roses in that general area. Not rose perfume, though. Actual roses. "At one time, there were old pieces of wallpaper up there that had roses on it. We had to tell people to stop peeling the wallpaper off because they would smell the roses, and I guess they thought somehow it was the wallpaper."

Scott Sukel, who has been involved with ghost hunts at the Reformatory for many years, was present when Cheryl got her first whiff of roses and had something interesting to add: "I was sitting in the corner of the room with another volunteer when Cheryl was smelling the roses. All of a sudden, I started to smell tobacco. It wasn't outside. It was in the room with us. I don't know if that was Superintendent Glattke's ghost or what, but it was strange.

"In fact," Scott added, "we're not even sure if the flower smell is the warden's wife. Sure, it's a female ghost up on the second floor. But is it the warden's wife? Don't know because from 1896 until 1959, there were women and girls and staff who lived here. So who knows if it's Helen? Could be any of the other women," he concluded.

The warden's quarters is also where Cheryl has seen what she refers to as the Shadow Man. In fact, she's seen two of these mysterious creatures.

"The first time I saw the Shadow Man, I was up on the third floor of the warden's quarters with another volunteer and a group of ghost hunters. I was sitting up on the stage, and the volunteer went to go look in a closet near there. So I'm watching her [the volunteer], and all of a sudden, I see this rather large man—I'm talking like six two or six three—standing behind her. I couldn't make him out; it was just a dark figure. He was there, and then he was gone. The volunteer looked at me and said, 'Did you just see that man?' so she saw it, too. We ran around looking for him, but we never did find him," Cheryl concluded.

The next time Cheryl encountered what she thought was the Shadow Man, she was back in the same area of the warden's quarters, only this time, the figure was smaller and less defined than before. "It was after a tour," Cheryl said. "An elderly couple wanted to know if I would take them to the third floor. I did, and as I was walking back, my flashlight beam sort of went across the stage and there was a small shadow figure standing on the stage. It was a dark figure, like the first one I saw, but this one was smaller and was almost oblong-shaped. But like the first one, it just vanished."

The more OSR volunteers you talk to, the more you start to realize that when it comes to shadow figures, Ohio State Reformatory has more than its fair share of them. Brian Wilson Sr. and Matt Buckingham are two OSR volunteers who have the unique distinction of having seen the same shadow figure at the same time. "We were sitting on the stage up on the third floor in West Administration," Brian explained.

"We were just sitting there on the right side of the stage, next to the doorway to another room, and then we saw a shadow person. It would appear in the hallways and in the stairwell. It would just sort of peek around the corner and then go back."

"It was really tall, too," Matt Buckingham added. "When it leaned out into the hallway, it was still over six foot tall."

Incredibly, Brian and Matt continued to watch this shadowy figure for the next forty to forty-five minutes. "That shadow was very busy," Brian said. "But if one of the other volunteers walked by, you wouldn't see the shadow anymore. Once they were gone, you'd see it poke its head out again."

As the pair continued to watch the shadow dart back and forth in the hallway, Brian told me he caught something out of the corner of his eye: a small flicker of light coming from the room to his immediate left. "I turned my head, and there's a full person standing there, looking back at me. He was maybe three feet from me, and I could see every detail. He had on a blue denim shirt, long-sleeved, black belt, and blue denim pants, and he had blond hair. He looked straight at me for a few seconds, and then he was gone."

I asked Brian about what the ghost was wearing, and he told me it looked like a prison uniform. "I know we weren't in an area where prisoners would have normally been, but when the warden lived here, they had prisoners who worked for the warden—cleaned the place or whatever, so maybe it was an inmate that I saw."

On another occasion, Brian was walking through the West Cell Block with two other OSR volunteers, Monique Orbond and Todd Ginther, during an evening ghost hunt. To add to the spookiness, there was a lightning storm going on. "We were on the third tier, going down the right-hand side," Brian explained. "When we got to the corner, there was a bright flash of lightning and we saw it: an inmate, standing there on the rail, just leaning over. Then he just turned around and went back into the cell. It was too dark, though, so we couldn't tell which cell," Brian continued. "We've seen him a number of times after that, and he always does the same thing: comes out of a cell, leans over the rail, and then goes back in his cell. Can't ever tell what cell, though, but it's always in the same general area."

Amy Fortney is another OSR volunteer who has had an encounter with a shadow person. "My first time seeing a shadow person was back in 2008," Amy began. "I was volunteering at a public ghost hunt during the summer. I was all alone up in the chapel, standing on the stage. And then I saw it. It was hard to describe. I would say he was maybe pushing seven foot tall; he was really big. But all I could see was from the shoulders up. I couldn't see any features, but for some reason I could tell he was looking at me. As I'm standing there trying to process all this, it turned and ran out toward the cell block really fast."

Justin Buckingham is yet another OSR volunteer who has seen a shadowy figure inside the building. Unlike the ones the other volunteers have seen, though, the one Justin encountered got a little too close for comfort. In fact, it seems to have a thing against Justin.

"I never really experienced anything here before that night," Justin began. "So that would have been my first real paranormal experience. I'll never forget it."

Justin said he was ghost hunting with several other OSR volunteers, including his father, Matt Buckingham. "We were over near the stairs to the sub-basement, and we were using the Frank's Box. The other volunteers thought they heard something like 'We need help' coming through the Frank's Box, so me and my dad decided to go down into the sub-basement to investigate."

Once in the sub-basement, Justin and his dad decided to split up. "We were both just walking around down there and then I decided to just go back and stand near the entrance. A couple of minutes later, my dad comes back and says, 'There's a shadow right behind you,' and I go, 'Really?' you know, not really expecting to see anything. But I turn around and there's this big, black mass behind me. I left right then because I was kind of surprised and didn't really know what to think of it," Justin told me, his voice cracking.

Justin's father, Matt, picks up the story: "I was heading back to the stairs and I'm looking at Justin standing there and I see this shadow person start to form. It was almost like an elongated oval when it first appeared and then it expanded to a full shadow person. It was less than a foot away from Justin's back and maybe three feet away from me. When Justin got scared and left, I watched that shadow person, and it sort of went back down under the stairs and just disappeared."

Still not sure of what to think about his encounter, Justin went home that night. But whatever it was down in the sub-basement, it wasn't done with Justin yet.

"A few weekends after that, I went back down into the sub-basement again. I guess I just wanted to see if there was anything still down there," Justin admitted to me. "I didn't see anything the whole time I was down there, but at one point, I got pushed—it felt like I was being pushed by something. I kind of resisted but then I lost my balance and fell into the wall. I can't explain it," he said.

Even after all that, Justin still wanted to go into the sub-basement. "I don't know why," Justin admitted. "Maybe I was trying to face my fears or something. But the last time I went down there, I was standing near the wall and all of a sudden, it felt like somebody was rubbing my back. Then I started getting sick. That was probably the worst of it."

Strangely enough, Justin's encounters in the sub-basement stopped almost as quickly as they had begun. When I asked the other OSR volunteers about the incidents, they all agreed that whatever it was, it definitely was focused on Justin. Justin himself can't really explain what happened to him, but recounts a rather strange EVP he captured in the sub-basement during one of his encounters. "It was a woman's voice," Justin stated, "and she's saying, 'You guys really shouldn't be down here.'"

"The interesting thing about the sub-basement," Scott Sukel explained, "is that we've learned it would have actually been the bottom level of solitary confinement. Originally there were three levels of solitary confinement; they were stacked three tall. So what we now have as the lowest level of solitary is actually the second level. The sub-basement would have been the bottom level. There are cells down there. A lot of them are bricked up, though. But from what I heard, a lot of nasty stuff went on down there."

When I asked a group of volunteers if they thought there was something bad at OSR, they all replied "no." But to a member, they all confessed to believing that there was something that wasn't friendly at the Reformatory and it liked to roam around.

"To be honest," Cheryl Knerman told me, "I don't know of a single place in this building where something ghostly hasn't been reported. It's like none of them are tied to a specific spot for long. I do believe there's something not nice here, but it doesn't stay in one place. Areas will feel just fine for the longest time and then, one day, you go in there and things don't feel right," she explained. "For a long time, I would not go to the third floor of this building or the third floor of the administration building by myself. Then one night, things changed and it felt totally fine in that area."

Cheryl continued: "I will walk through most of this place without a flashlight because I'm used to it. But then there's times when I walk into an area, and I'm like, 'Oh, hell, no,' and I'm out of there. No way I'm going through there, even with a flashlight."

Scott Sukel knows exactly how Cheryl feels. "You'll walk into an area and everything's fine and then you leave and come back and it's like, 'Oh man.' It just feels completely different."

"That's happened to me, too," Amy Fortney chimed in. "It only happened once, but it overcame me so fast. I didn't see anything or hear anything. Nothing happened, but it was just this feeling of instant dread."

Brian Wilson has experienced it, too, although he was in the administration area, heading toward the chapel. "I'm walking through that area, and there's nobody around me. I just got this weird feeling, and it was like my body was telling me, 'Don't stop. Get going. You've got to move.' So I went through the chapel, and by the time I got into the East Cell Block, the feelings were gone. But when I was in that area, it was like something was telling me, 'You best leave. You better not be in here by yourself.'"

Solitary confinement is another area of the Reformatory where you might encounter a ghost. Just make sure you "stay in line" or else you might feel the ghost's wrath.

Amy Fortney explains: "I guess it would have been around 2008. I was walking down in solitary with two other volunteers—one in front of me and one behind me. We went down one side and then started coming back the other side—the dark side [side with no lights]. After we got like two or three cells down, I felt something hit me in the side. I turned around and turned my light on and said, 'Did you just poke me?' but I realized they were too far behind me to reach me. Right then, I got shoved from behind and I turned back around, but the person back there was too far away to touch me.

"Later on, at the end of the night—maybe 4:00 or 4:30 in the morning, I was talking to Cheryl [Kneram] and I said, 'I got poked over in solitary,' and she said, 'So did I.' Turns out she got poked within twenty minutes of when I did."

Cheryl picks up the story: "I had been in the back of solitary, where it's dark, and something jabbed me in the stomach so hard that I gasped for air. It felt just like somebody had jabbed me with a nightstick."

"When she told me that, it hit me that was exactly what it felt like to me: a nightstick," Amy stated.

"Since 2004 or 2005, we've had a lot of reports of people experiencing what they thought was a guard down in solitary," Scott Sukel declared. "Most of the time, it's nothing more than footsteps or what sounds like keys jingling. Other times, they see what looks like a guard walking through solitary."

So who might this ghostly guard be? Scott's not sure. "We do know that Frank Hangar was a guard here and he was beaten to death in solitary in 1932 during an escape attempt," Scott offered. "I think his ghost might have been the one who was poking Amy and poking Cheryl. Based on his demeanor and the stuff I've learned about him, it sort of fits."

At the Ohio State Reformatory, the end of the night doesn't mean the ghosts get to go home. After all, the Reformatory *is* their home. Since the Reformatory's ghost hunts often go on until the wee hours of the night (or morning, depending on how you look at it), some volunteers decide to catch a few predawn hours of sleep inside the Reformatory. Those who do often report hearing people moving around, long after the visitors have all gone home. Scott Sukel told me that the first few times he slept in the Reformatory, he heard noises that were so loud, he was convinced there were people still in the building with him.

"The first couple of times I slept here, I slept in the Safe Room because there's no windows in there and it's dark. I would be laying there in bed and I'd hear people talking and walking around and I would think, 'Oh no, what did I do? Lock people in?' But when I'd go out and look, there was never anyone there."

"There were other times I would wake up and think people had showed up early for one of our day tours," Scott continued. "The tours start right outside where I'd be sleeping, so I would get up to go and greet the people, but there's no tour; nobody's out there."

Brian Wilson has also chosen to sleep in the Reformatory. Like Scott, Brian has also heard what he assumed were real people. "I've heard voices here in the morning, when everybody's gone and I'm trying to sleep," he said. Brian was so intrigued with the idea that the ghosts were roaming around after everyone had left that he decided to try to catch them on video. "We had a cleanup weekend, and I just set my camera up in the west administration, right in the hallway, and let it run. I got three hours of what sounds like mop buckets moving around. You can hear a guard talking, people coming out of their offices, and what sounds like tapping, like they are signaling. You can even hear what sounds like an inmate drop his mop—you can hear the handle hit the floor and someone say, 'Oh, s**t.' And this went on for like three hours until I ran out of tape."

I have been coming to the Ohio State Reformatory with my organization, The Ghosts of Ohio, for many years. Every time I've been there, Scott Sukel has spent the night with us. So I decided to give Scott the last word concerning personal experiences at the Reformatory. I asked him point-blank, "Of all the things you've experienced here, what's the one that sticks in your mind the most?" He thought for a moment before he began:

"Over the years, I've experienced so much stuff here. The one that probably made the biggest impact on me was my first year volunteering here." Scott explained that it was early one morning and that other than a woman, he was the only one in the Reformatory. "We had the front doors open because at that time, we had trustees from the prison [Mansfield Correctional Institution] out back who would come out and help us work on the building."

Scott said he was working inside the front entrance when something caught his eye. "I see what looked like one of the trustees walk from the back hall, around the stairs, and into a back room where we had furniture. Maybe fifteen or thirty seconds later, he walks from the back room and out the way he had come in. I know what I saw, but something about the guy didn't seem right," Scott said. So he got on the walkie-talkie and asked the woman in charge, "Do we have trustees here today?"

"She radioed me back and said, 'No, why?' and I said, 'Because I just saw one.'"

"That was a big one for me," Scott explained. "You'll see and hear little things here, and you can try to explain it away. But seeing a guy? You can't explain that away."

THE VIGIL

Over the years, I have spent many a night locked inside the Ohio State Reformatory, usually with massive amounts of equipment. Case in point, the very first time The Ghosts of Ohio spent the night inside OSR, we brought along two generators to power all our equipment. Two of them! Setting up so much equipment inside a building the size of OSR takes time—three hours and twenty-three minutes, to be exact. And while I have experienced more than a handful of weird things at OSR, despite all the high-tech stuff I've lugged through that building, I have yet to capture any of it on video or, for the most part, audio. To be honest, OSR was the building that led me to start an odd ritual that I do after every ghost hunt and vigil. As I'm driving away from the building where I was looking for ghosts, the last thing I do is turn around and look up at the windows of the building. That's because I'm convinced that when I do that, that's when I'll finally see a ghost . . . and the ghost will be flipping me off, saying something like "Thought you were going to find me, huh? Hit the road, ghost boy!"

You see, OSR is the kind of place where weird things happen, almost always off-camera. It's like the ghosts are doing it on purpose, as if they know that without solid evidence, no one will believe you just saw a ghost. So for that reason, I decided that for the vigil for this book, I would go alone with just a couple of hand-helds. I wasn't going to devote hours to setting up the equipment. Rather, I would go into each of the "haunted" areas and sit and wait.

The night of my vigil, I asked Scott Sukel which area of the prison appeared to be the most active recently. Here's some free advice for all you ghost hunters out there who are planning on a ghost hunt at OSR: talk to Scott Sukel when you get there. Scott has been running the ghost hunts at OSR for years, so when people report that they've seen something in the building, the person they're telling is usually Scott. My number one rule for ghost hunting is: hunt where the ghosts are. And if you want to know where the ghosts are at OSR, Scott's the one who can tell you.

That night, Scott said that solitary confinement, the West Cell Block, and the sub-basement had been the places where people were reporting the most activity on recent hunts. With that in mind, I headed to the sub-basement first. Having just purchased a new photography vest, I was able to jam a lot of hand-helds into my pockets, including:

· three digital voice recorders
· one EMF
· one ELF
· one tri-field meter
· one ghost meter/cell sensor
· one K-II meter
· one digital camera
· one non-contact IR thermometer

As soon as I first stepped inside the sub-basement, I immediately felt something was not right down there. I couldn't explain it or even put my finger on it. It just felt weird down there—almost like I wasn't alone, even though, as far as I could tell, I was.

I figured the best way to go about things would be to sit at the bottom of the stairs for a while and get a feel for the sub-basement. I put the devices that lit up—the ELF meter, the K-II, and the ghost meter—on the floor in front of me, sat back, and waited. The longer I sat there, the more the initial creepy feeling I had when I first entered the sub-basement went away. After about twenty minutes, I put my digital voice recorder on the steps, turned on a second one, and decided to walk around the sub-base-ment. If I wanted to see the dark figure who menaced Justin Buckingham down here, perhaps I needed to walk around a bit and then come back to the stairs, which is what Justin's father did right before he saw the dark shape.

I spent about thirty minutes wandering in the sub-basement. It's a weird little place—one that would be really easy to freak yourself out in, espe-cially down here in the dark. You can stand up and walk upright in the sub-basement, but it has a very old "root cellar" feel to it. The floor above you occasionally creaks, too, creating weird sounds that could certainly be mistaken for a ghost scurrying about in the darkness. But I never saw any shadows while I was down there, not even non-ghostly ones that could be a rational explanation for what Justin and his father encountered. If any-thing, my time down in the sub-basement seemed to confirm that the two men had, in fact, seen something ghostly. The sub-basement was almost pitch-black with almost no means for ambient light to trickle in.

Deciding that the dark shape wasn't going to show itself to me this night, I went over to solitary confinement.

There are two sides to solitary and two floors, too. Basically, you walk up one side of the cells in solitary, turn around, and come back down the other side. Since only one side has electric lights, OSR volunteers refer to one side as the "dark side" and the other as the "light side." Of course—wouldn't you know it?—the ghosts tend to like hanging around the dark side.

I started my vigil on the dark side, since that was where some of the OSR volunteers were struck in the chest by what felt like a police baton. I walked up and down the dark side in total darkness (a lot easier said than done) without feeling anything out of the ordinary. So I picked a random cell about halfway down and sat on the floor. After about fifteen uneventful minutes, I began calling out to any ghosts who could hear me to come and tell me their story. I even asked if Frank Hangar, the guard who was beaten to death at OSR in 1932, was nearby. With my recorder running, I told Frank that I had been doing research on him and felt bad that he had to die the way he did, but that I'm sure his fam-ily was proud of him since he died doing his job and protecting others.

As I was saying all this, I heard what sounded like someone walk-ing out in the hallway: six distinct sounds of what sounded like heeled

Hallway in West Diagonal's solitary confinement. Cells can be seen on the left.

shoes on concrete. Since there were other people in the building with me, I immediately thought someone had just come into solitary and didn't know I was there. "Hello?" I said to no one in particular. No one answered. "Is there anybody out there?" I called out. Again, no answer.

It was then I remembered a recent ghost hunt I had done at OSR with The Ghosts of Ohio. Several team members had told me that they had felt "something" like a field of energy move past them while they were in solitary. They thought that was weird, even more so when it happened several times, like a prison guard making his rounds. In an attempt to document the incident, the group had placed a tri-field in the area and adjusted the squelch so that if any type of energy moved past the device, it would give off an audible alarm. It worked: the device seemed to pick up some sort of energy moving through the area.

With that in mind, I took the tri-field and placed it on the floor in the middle of the hallway in front of the cell I was in. Then I went back inside the cell and sat there, alone in the dark. After about ten minutes of nothing happening, I once again called out to Frank Hangar, asking him to come down to my cell so I could talk with him. After a ten-minute conversation (apparently with myself) with no activity, I then asked if maybe I was talking to someone other than Frank Hangar. If so, could they tell me their name? Again, nothing. After another fifteen minutes, I picked up the tri-field and moved over to the light side of solitary, once again leaving the tri-field on and in the hallway. I never heard those footsteps—if indeed they were footsteps—again the rest of the night.

My final scheduled stop for the evening was the West Cell Block. There had been recent reports of people hearing someone walking around outside the cells, and one person said they saw what looked like a guard standing at the far end of the block, up on the forth tier.

Whenever I take a group of people with me to spend the night at OSR, they ask me what they should bring. The first thing I always suggest is comfortable shoes. That's because unless you have been inside the building, you can't begin to appreciate how big it is. Take, for example, the West Cell Block: it's roughly 315 feet long, meaning that if you're planning on walking up one row of cells and down the other, you'll be walking 630 feet. No biggie, right? Except that's only one tier. The West Cell Block is five tiers tall, so if you want to walk the whole thing, that's 3,150 feet, not including the steps between tiers.

I'd been to OSR several times, so I had my comfortable shoes and knew what I was in for. For me, the problem with looking for ghosts in the West Cell Block (or the East Cell Block, for that matter) is that it's almost impossible to cover the whole cell block, even with a group of people. With approximately 360 cells in the West Cell Block, the best you can do is to walk along the tiers and see if you see anything or if a vibe from one of the cells causes you to stop and hang out in that cell for a bit. Well, I walked the entire cell block with nary an odd feeling or a peep out of any of my hand-helds. After reaching the top of the block, I started back down, stopping on the third tier for a little side trip to the OSR chapel and TB ward. No ghosts were hiding up there either, so I made my way back down to the bottom of the West Cell Block.

Having completed my tour of the hot spots of OSR, I spent the next three hours wandering around, inviting any of the ghosts to come out and say "Hi" to me. No luck. Just as the sun was coming up, I packed up my hand-helds and went over to the west administration area just to see if I could stop and smell the roses, so to speak, before I went home. Getting nothing, I headed out to Ol' Blue, my 1997 Honda Accord, and drove toward OSR's front gate and began the long ride home to my warm bed. Of course, I did turn around and take one last look up at the windows of OSR to see if there was a ghostly prisoner up there, flipping me off. There wasn't.

FINAL THOUGHTS

Haunted or not, I dare anyone to spend some time inside the walls of the Ohio State Reformatory and then tell me the place didn't change you in some way. You can't. Simply put, there is so much dark history inside OSR that there's no way you can walk the halls and not be affected by it. Granted, it's not the sort of history we learn about in school or even talk about openly, but it is history just the same.

Maybe that's why the ghosts of OSR are so active—they're forced to go above and beyond in order to get people to stop and listen to them.

Ohio State Reformatory
100 Reformatory Road
Mansfield, Ohio 44905
www.mrps.org

BISSMAN BUILDING

If you ever find yourself driving down North Main Street in Mansfield, take a look to your right as you near the corner of West 5th Street. There, staring down at you, will be the Bissman Building, an imposing Gothic structure that looks like it should be teeming with ghosts. And if the stories are true, perhaps it is. Either way, the building's over a hundred years old, so it's full of history. Want the inside scoop on the Bissman Building? Then look no further than the current owner. He is, after all, a fifth-generation Bissman, so he knows all about the building's history. And its ghosts, too.

THE HISTORY

When it comes to the history of the Bissman Building, you can get it straight from Bissman family spokesman, Ben Bissman IV, who not only represents the fifth generation of the Bissmans to own the building, but who has also been spending his days working (and playing) inside it for over fifty years. "This is just a sweet building because I'm so close to it," Ben confided to me. "My dad and every dad before that were in here."

The Bissman Building, and indeed the entire Bissman empire, began with Peter Bissman. On August 15, 1844, Peter was born to Michael and Louisa in Hesse, Germany. At the tender age of nine, Peter and his family came to America, a journey that would last almost two months. Once in America, the Bissman family settled just outside of Mansfield, in the town of Mifflin.

Peter's first job was working for the Tracy & Avery Company, a wholesale grocer in downtown Mansfield (near where the Mansfield

The Bissman Building stares menacingly down on Mansfield's North Main Street.

Carousel stands today). He enjoyed his work and began dreaming of one day owning his own grocery business.

By the early 1880s, Peter was already well on his way to realizing his dream. All that was missing was a building—a massive building in which to run his business and store all his merchandise, too. With that in mind, he began planning construction of what today is known as the Bissman Building.

With plans well underway for the construction of the Ohio State Reformatory nearby, Bissman hit on a brilliant idea: share the resources with the Reformatory to save on expenses. And that's exactly what he did. Bissman utilized the same materials and even the same workers as the Reformatory. He even used the architectural firm of Hancock and Dow, which was involved in the design of the Reformatory.

Bissman also erected kilns on his property so that he could create bricks on-site. Lumberyard-type facilities were also installed to finish the wood that would be unloaded from the nearby railroad tracks. When it was noted how easily workers were able to unload the materials off the train since the lumberyard was next to the tracks, the decision was made to build the Bissman Building as close to the tracks as possible. That way, the trains delivering the produce and supplies could pull up to the building, thereby simplifying loading and unloading.

When completed in 1886, the Bissman Building, or Bissman Block as it was originally called, was a massive five-story (four up and one basement) Gothic structure of nearly fifty thousand square feet. The top of the building was adorned with a gorgeous clock tower, which some said could be seen across Mansfield. There was even a balcony running across the entire front of the building, which, although ornamental, added a certain look of mystique.

Inside the building, one of the crown jewels, which is still visible today, is a gorgeous hand-painted walk-in safe that Peter Bissman had installed in his office. Emblazoned with the year 1886, the safe was placed within five layers of solid rock, making it impossible to break into. Despite all that, Ben Bissman said that to his knowledge, most of the money was never stored in the safe itself. Instead, it was hidden in a hole in the wall, behind a set of false books.

While originally the building was set up exclusively as a wholesale distributor for food, beer, and wine, Peter Bissman quickly realized that he could increase his profit margins by serving the retail markets as well. Bissman reorganized the internal structure of the building and set it up in such a way they could now cater directly to retail customers, who walked in off the street. They even created several of their own brand of canned goods, labeling the cans right in the building. The most well-known of these brands was Red Band.

Around the 1930s, the Bissmans began roasting their own coffee beans and peanuts on the fourth floor. They had it down to a science, too: coffee beans and peanuts were roasted on the fourth floor, sorted and bagged on the third, then stocked or made ready for shipping on the second floor. They roasted their coffee beans every morning and then switched over to peanuts in the afternoon. What the Bissmans hadn't planned on, but soon discovered, was that the aromas, which wafted up the giant smokestacks that used to be on both the north and south sides of the building and out across Mansfield, helped boost sales of both coffee and roasted peanuts. The smells were essentially free advertising!

In the 1950s, business was going so well that the Bissmans decided to expand the building. In 1956, an additional ten-thousand-square-foot warehouse was added. But just a few years later, beginning in the 1960s, a trend developed that would take its toll on the Bissman family business: consolidation. Gone were the days of a wholesale grocer in every town. The age of giant grocery stores and mega-markets had begun. Little by little, the Bissman business began to suffer. Finally, in 1976, the decision was made to sell off the grocery portion of the business. They held onto the beverage distribution for as long as they could, but eventually sold that as well about a decade ago.

Today, the Bissman family business is commercial real estate, which Ben Bissman believes is still pretty true to his family's first intentions. "You know," Ben points out, "the first thing my family did when they came over here was build a big building for all their people. So that's what we do now: buy big commercial buildings, renovate them, and fill them with people."

In 1993, producers for the movie *The Shawshank Redemption,* which was filming at the Ohio State Reformatory nearby, let it be known that they were looking for a company to produce vintage-looking billboards for the movie. Since Ben Bissman owned a billboard company, he jumped at the chance and created several Schlitz Beer billboards for the movie. When the producers were meeting with Ben, they came out to the Bissman Building and promptly fell in love with it. So although the billboards ended up not making it into *The Shawshank Redemption,* the Bissman Building did.

The exterior of the Bissman doubled as the Brewer Hotel, the halfway house Brooks Hatlen and Red Redding spent time in. Peter Bissman's former office was also transformed into the *Portland Daily Bugle* office for a key scene in the movie. Subsequent movies filmed inside the Bissman include the horror movies *The Rage* and *The Dead Matter.*

In recent years, ghost stories relating to the Bissman have begun to make their way onto the Internet, resulting in the building being featured on such ghost reality television shows as *Ghost Hunters* and *My Ghost Story.* The Bissman now also offers public ghost hunts.

Ben admitted to me that he reluctantly got into the ghost business and worried how it would impact his family's legacy. "Initially, we didn't want anything to do with ghosts. There's still even a lot of stories that I won't share because it's family history. But the fact is that things got out and we kind of planted a little seed and a beanstalk grew. It wasn't an intention, but it just happened," he said.

Still, Ben believes that if there are ghosts in the Bissman, they are comfortable with people coming in trying to find them. In fact, Ben gets the feeling that the ghosts want to be found: "It seems like whatever's here is coming forward and trying to make itself known. It's just like there's somebody in here that wants to get through to some people," Ben pondered.

"So I guess I'm OK with people coming up here looking for ghosts, just as long as they are respectful. We're talking about my family here, so it's an integrity thing. I don't want this to become a Barnum-and-Bailey-type thing," Ben said matter-of-factly.

THE EXPERIENCES

Ben Bissman told me he couldn't remember the first time someone told him that there might be ghosts in the Bissman Building, only that he'd been hearing about them for a long time. "I grew up in this building," Ben said. "And I grew up hearing ghost stories about it, too."

When I asked Ben when his first paranormal experience in the building was, he thought for a minute and then said, "I guess it would have been when I was around eight years old. We used to take wooden pallets apart upstairs and build forts and climb around in the old boxes. I can remember being up there with my friends, and we'd keep asking each other, 'What was that? Did you hear that?' You'd hear things and just get the feeling that we weren't alone up there," Ben said.

"When I was around ten years old," Ben remembered, "my grandfather used to tell me stories about the building. He'd also warn me to stay away from the elevators, and then he'd tell me the story about FW Simon."

According to the story Ben's grandfather told him, FW Simon worked at the Bissman from the day it opened until 1911, when he retired. On his last day of work, Simon allegedly went up to the fourth floor and wrote his name on one of the ceiling beams. His name is still visible there today.

After that, Simon is said to have climbed onto the freight elevator and ridden it down to the third floor, apparently to say good-bye to his now-former coworkers. What exactly happened next is unclear, but it resulted in Simon getting decapitated by the elevator. The most popular version of the tale says that as Simon was standing on the third floor, waiting for the freight elevator to come down, the elevator got stuck on the fourth floor. Not thinking, Simon allegedly stuck his head out into the open elevator shaft, at which point the elevator broke free and crashed down on his head. Another version has Simon standing in the elevator on the third floor and foolishly sticking his head out as it was dropping toward the ground floor. Still another darker version has Simon being pushed out of the elevator by an unknown assailant.

However it managed to knock poor old FW Simon's noggin off (if indeed the event ever took place), his ghost is said to haunt the Bissman, although no one has ever gotten a clear view to be sure it's him. Most of the time, the ghostly activities attributed to Simon are the sort of standard ghostly doings: disembodied footsteps, sounds of objects moving, strange tapping and knocking, and the occasional sighting of a dark human-like shape moving about in the shadows, usually on the third and fourth floors. Is it FW Simon? Hard to say with any degree of certainty, although it should be noted that, as of this writing, all the ghosts and shadow figures reportedly seen at the Bissman have heads attached. So if one of them is Simon, it's nice to know that despite the way he left this world, his head was waiting there for him in the next life.

Even after all the stories he had been told and the odd feelings he has had in the building, Ben told me he still wasn't ready to believe in ghosts. That is, until several years ago, when Ben and his wife, Amber, experienced something that, when they talk about it today, they both describe as "life-changing."

Ben had recently made the decision to allow a ghost-hunting group into the Bissman one hot August night. Curious as to what they were doing, Ben and Amber went up to the third floor, where they found the small group sitting on the floor, talking aloud to no one, with a whole array of gadgets in front of them. Not having had any interest in ghosts, neither Ben nor Amber was sure what was going on, but when the group asked them to sit down, they both agreed.

"We were all up on the third floor," Ben began. "At that point, I was kind of new to all this, so I got kind of embarrassed when they started talking to my ancestors and wanting me to talk to them, too. They were saying things like, 'Talk to your grandfather' and things like that. I found it kind of hokey.

"So they keep saying things like, 'Give us a sign,' 'We're not here to hurt you,' that kind of stuff. Still seemed goofy to me. All of a sudden, like a lug nut or a five-sided bolt came rolling across the floor at us. I didn't think much of it, but the people in the group got all excited," Ben related.

Believing that a ghost had rolled the lug nut at them, the group continued to ask questions and encouraged Ben to speak to his departed relatives. The group was almost giddy with excitement. Ben wasn't impressed, though. He was hot and just wanted to go home at that point.

"It was August and it was 103 degrees up there," Ben said, shaking his head. "It was horrible, and I just wanted to get the heck out of there. But they were all excited, so I said 'Hey, Grandpa, it's Buck [the nickname Ben's grandfather had given him]. We just want to know if you're here. Just give us a sign.' All of a sudden this thing rolls across the floor above us [the fourth floor]. That's when I started freaking out a little," Ben admitted.

"But the group told me to keep talking, so I said, 'I'm your grandson. You just gave us a sign. Can you give us another sign?' And right then, I got hit in the side of the neck with a ball of ice-cold air. And it hit my neck and rolled like a ball around my neck, hit my shoulder, and went off and hit Amber."

"It did," Amber admitted, excitedly. "It hit my neck, went down my arm, and right down the elevator shaft."

"I almost passed out," Ben continued. "I was literally overcome. Whatever it was, it was a feeling like I've never felt.

"That was then I started believing in ghosts. Up until then, I'd have groups in, but it was like, 'Go ahead and see what you can find.' But I never really got an answer. That day, though, Amber and I both got floored.

"There's just no way in hell that could have happened. No reason in the world that building should have gotten that cold," he said.

In 1993, when the crew for *The Shawshank Redemption* descended on the Bissman in order to transform part of the building into the offices of the *Portland Daily Bugle,* Ben said it appeared as though the ghosts came out to see what all the ruckus was about. "When they were in here filming for *Shawshank,* there was a ton of [ghost] activity going on. There were a lot of people in here, running around, doing things. And most of them would come up to me and say, 'There's something in this building and it's like it's trying to get our attention.' People were reporting something following them up the stairs and touching them while they were on the stairs.

"I kind of believe those stories," Ben admitted, "because back then, we didn't say anything to anybody about ghosts here. It was the same thing when they filmed *The Dead Matter* here. We never said anything about ghosts, and yet their crew still said they were hearing and seeing weird things."

When it comes to *The Dead Matter,* Ellis Byrd and Nicole Wallace, who organized the first public ghost hunts at the Bissman Building, both claim to have spoken to crew members who had spooky encounters during filming.

Ellis recalled that when the crew was shooting scenes in the basement, some of them started feeling like they were being watched. "They would turn around and see someone standing way back down on the other side of the basement, watching them," Ellis said. "The first time, they went down to see who it was, but there wasn't anyone there. After that, they just stayed down on this end."

"Up on the third floor, they built like a small apartment up there for the movie," Nicole added. "I know that the lady who was working alone up there, setting up some of the scenes, said there was a lot of weird things going on up there. She said she saw a shadow figure up there." Nicole knows exactly what the woman claimed to see, as Nicole has seen the same thing up on the third floor: "I've seen what looks like the shadow of a man standing up against the wall. Sometimes, almost like when he thinks you're not looking, he'll peek out, like he's trying to see what you're doing. But then he'll step back and even disappear into the wall. I've seen him more than once."

Nicole believes this was the same shadow person that she saw when she had her first paranormal experience in the building, although she was on the second floor at the time. "I was over near the freight elevator," she explained. "It's wide open, so you can kind of look up to the next floor. Well, I happened to look up to the third floor, and I saw a figure standing there—it kind of walked by the opening for the elevator. At the same time, I heard what sounded like someone walking around up there and boxes shuffling, like someone working."

As for Nicole's ghost-hunt partner, Ellis Byrd, while he has had numerous encounters in the building, nothing comes close to the night in 2008, when Ellis believes he was physically attacked by something not of this world.

"I was up on the third floor and, I admit it, I was provoking. I was telling the ghosts to come get me. All of a sudden, I felt something pushing on the right side of my body. It pushed so hard, it pushed up inside my body. It came up to my throat and it literally started to strangle me from the inside. It was weird."

Ellis continued: "I started to swell up, and I couldn't breathe. I tried to call out, but I couldn't. I think that must have been when I passed out and hit my head on the floor."

Nicole was right there when the incident took place: "Ellis was yelling [at the ghosts] and next thing I know, he's down on the floor. I thought he had had a heart attack. It looked like he was dying. Couple of seconds later, he takes a deep breath and sits up. When he did that, I felt something sort of blow past me, didn't see anything, though. It was all over in a couple of minutes, but it was scary."

Part of the first floor of the Bissman Building is home to a local print shop, Pirate Printing and Embroidery. On more than one occasion, people working in the print shop have seen a woman wearing what they describe as "Victorian clothing" standing near the entrance. "They always say the woman has a big dress on," explained Nicole. "They also say that she acts like she wants the guys to follow her. But when they do, she just sort of disappears behind the door."

"Occasionally, you will hear what sounds like rustling of the bottom of a dress coming from that area," Ellis added. "One time, we set up a video camera over there and caught a white mist moving from the print shop over to the door."

Ellis and Nicole said they had no idea who the female ghost was. But then their audio recorders started picking up what sounded like a woman whispering the name "Annabella." One time, they even recorded the woman whispering the name in the old secretary's office, which is very close to the entrance to Pirate Printing. "We can't be sure, but maybe the woman the print shop guys are seeing is Annabella," Nicole concluded.

Even though it has seventy years less of history than the rest of the building, the 1956 addition to the Bissman isn't without its ghost stories. Now functioning as a garage for Ben Bissman's extensive personal collection of automobiles, the building is said to be home to shadowy figures that move about the corners of the building. "We caught two photographs of a pitch-black outline of a person standing near one of the vehicles," Ellis explained. "And both photographs were taken with flashes."

"You'll also hear what sounds like tools dropping out here," Nicole said. "Other times, it's like things are rolling around, but it comes and goes. Sometimes you come out here and it's so quiet, you can hear a pin drop. Other times, it's so loud with things moving all over the place."

But of all the ghosts said to be here, if the Bissman Building were to have an unofficial ghost ambassador, that title would go to the ghost of a little girl whom they call Ruthie.

One of the first ghosts to be reported at the Bissman with any regularity was that of a little girl. Most of the time, she could be seen standing on or near the second floor landing of the main staircase. Sometimes she would even appear to recognize that people were looking at her and she would wave at them before vanishing. Other times, while the girl would not be seen, she would be heard laughing, giggling, and even saying "hello" to people when they first came in the building. Nicole Wallace even mentioned that one of the first times she thought she actually heard a ghost's voice was at the Bissman: "I was on the main floor, and I heard what I thought was a little girl up near the top of the stairs. It was almost like a little giggle and then a 'hello.' I heard it live, too. It wasn't something that I didn't hear until I went back and listened to it on a recorder."

Ruthie got her name from a mysterious photo that appeared out of the blue. "It just showed up one day on my welding table," Ben said. "Nobody would admit to putting it there, so I don't know where it came from."

The faded, sepia-toned photograph shows a woman sitting in a chair with a young girl in a white dress standing to the woman's right and a young boy, also in white, on the woman's left. On the back of the photo is written "Aunt Gladys Bissman, Ruthie and Billy Jr." Noting how the Ruthie in the picture seemed to match the general age of the ghostly girl roaming around the Bissman Building, people decided to take a closer look at who this girl was. Then, when it was mentioned that Ruthie Bissman was not buried in the Bissman family plot with the rest of her family, all hell broke loose.

The story of Ruthie not being buried with her relatives made it onto the Internet, where it rapidly morphed into a bizarre (and completely unsubstantiated) tale about Ruthie Bissman having been murdered when she was eight years old and then buried in the basement of the Bissman Building in order to conceal the crime. Some even claimed that the other resident ghost, FW Simon, was somehow involved in Ruthie's murder. Don't you just love the Internet?

Before you knew it, YouTube exploded with video clips of ghost groups having heart-to-heart talks with Ruthie in the corner of the Bissman basement where her body was allegedly buried. "Psychics" showed up at the Bissman, giving blow-by-blow descriptions of how Ruthie Bissman was murdered . . . and in one case, who actually committed the crime.

When I first heard the story about Ruthie Bissman's murder, I was disturbed by it. Murder is upsetting no matter how you look at it, but when it involves a child, it goes to a whole new level of gut-wrenching. On top of that, I was dreading having to ask the question I knew people would want answered: "So, Ben Bissman, how does it feel knowing that one of your relatives might have been murdered and buried in your basement?" Thankfully, I didn't have to ask that question. That's because Ruthie Bissman was not murdered and she most certainly is not buried in the basement of the Bissman Building.

Through research, I found that the Ruthie in the mysterious picture is Ruth P. Bissman, daughter of Gladys and William H. Bissman Sr.— Gladys is the woman in the picture. The boy is Ruth's brother, William "Billy" Jr. Ruth was born in 1901 and died in May 1972 at the age of seventy. She is not buried with the rest of the Ohio Bissmans because some time after marrying and changing her last name to Weamer, she moved west with her husband and family. Her death certificate lists both her place of death and burial as Los Angeles, California.

Case closed, right? Well, not so fast. While we can most certainly throw out all the claims of people who said that they talked to the ghost of a murdered Ruthie Bissman, we have to keep in mind that all those stories came *after* the initial sightings of the little girl ghost. Just because the stories about Ruthie Bissman aren't true doesn't mean there isn't the ghost of a little girl haunting the Bissman. Put another way, take away all the "murdered girl" stories and sightings and you still have the stories of a little girl giggling at the top of the stairs on the second floor. Oh yeah, and just where did that picture come from anyway?

For now, the search for the identity of this mysterious ghost girl continues, although they still refer to her as Ruthie since they don't have any other name to give her. One of the places in the building where ghost hunters try to make contact with the ghost girl is on the second floor. Near the stairs where she's often seen standing at the top of, visiting ghost hunters have created a makeshift play area for Ruthie. Piled on the floor and on a nearby shelf is a makeshift shrine—a collection of games, toys, candy, crayons, and even fake flowers, all brought there (and then left behind) in an attempt to get Ruthie's ghost to come out and play. "Ghost hunters will come up here and read to Ruthie," Ellis explained. "Others will sit and color or play with the toys and ask Ruthie to come play, too."

THE VIGIL

Prior to the vigil, I had been interviewing Ben Bissman in Peter Bissman's former office. Several other people, including Ellis and Nicole, were also present. We were all sitting around a large table. At one point, I felt what I thought was a draft run across my legs. A few seconds later, I felt it again, although this time, it was moving in the opposite direction. I thought that was odd, although I do remember glancing around to see if there were vents in the walls—the breeze was too low to the ground to have been caused by something like an open window. There were no vents, so I just brushed it off and continued with the interviews without even mentioning it.

Later in the evening, after my group showed up with the equipment, Nicole was telling everyone about Peter Bissman's office when Ellis interrupted: "James doesn't know this, but we had an experience earlier when he was doing the interviews. We all felt a cold wisp run across the back of our legs. It went across and it came back. It went up and then it went across our shoulders."

I asked Ellis if they had ever felt that before in this particular room or what he thought it meant. "Never felt that in here," Ellis stated. "But who knows? Peter Bissman might be wandering about."

For the vigil itself, I decided to try something different. I had recently been mulling over the idea that perhaps ghost hunters get so caught up in monitoring their equipment that they fail to see the ghost standing right next to them. So for this vigil, I wanted to see if the results would be any different if I brought in a group of less-seasoned investigators and set up all the equipment myself, allowing it to run unmonitored the entire evening. So there were no members of The Ghosts of Ohio on this vigil (other than me, of course). Instead, I brought along friends and acquaintances, including my close friend, Dan Stout, and fellow ghost hunter, Troy Ball, whom I brought along as a reward for my "forcing" him to climb into the drainage tunnel at Bobby Mackey's Music World (but that's another story for another day).

Since this was the first time inside the Bissman for everyone in my group, I asked if we could have a guided tour. We started on the main floor and then moved down to the basement. If you've never been to the basement, once you come down the stairs, you walk all the way down one side of it until you reach the front of the building, then you make a U-turn and walk back down the other side of the building.

Our group had already walked down to the front of the building and was making its way back down the other side. Since I am constantly taking pictures, I inevitably end up at the back end of the group, which was the case at the Bissman. So as I was approaching the front of the building, I could look across and see the rest of the group heading back toward the steps.

As I continued to make my way toward the windows at the front of the basement, I suddenly became aware of music playing. I didn't recognize the song, but it definitely sounded like music; it was melodious and had a distinct rhythm to it. But the music sounded like something from a different time period—like something you would hear playing at a circus or an old-time county fair.

Since the music sounded like it was coming from the front of the building, my initial thought was that it was coming from a car sitting outside, even though this did not sound like music anyone would choose to blast in their car. The windows in the basement were close to ground level outside and gave a clear view of the front of the building, so I peeked out. There was nothing there—no cars, no people, nothing that could make that kind of noise. Not even an organ grinder with a little monkey. Yet the music continued. Plus, as I was looking out the window, it felt as if I were looking past the music—as if it were coming from the wall itself.

After about ten seconds, the music abruptly stopped. Whenever I go on these initial walkthroughs, I also have my personal digital voice recorder running, mainly to keep an audio record of events in case I need to refer back to things. On the recording from that night, while there are other people talking (including me, telling people to stop talking), you can clearly hear the music playing in the background. When I play it for people and ask them what it sounds like, the most common response I get is "old-time carnival music." I have no explanation for the sound. Whatever it was, it did not sound like it was from this time period.

The rest of the tour was without incident. When it was finished, I allowed everyone in my group to explore the Bissman while I began the daunting (and slightly foolish) task of setting up all the equipment myself. Two hours later, here's what I had:

Basement
- two DVR night-vision cameras, one on either side of the basement, both facing the front of the building

Staircase (First Floor)
- one infrared DVR camera, pointing up the staircase toward where Ruthie is often seen standing
- one Superlux condenser microphone at the bottom of the staircase, pointing upward

Garage
- two infrared video cameras, one facing north-south and the other facing east-west
- two Superlux condenser microphones, one at the entrance to the garage, facing the center of the garage, and one in the center of the garage, facing the rear wall

Second Floor
- one infrared video camera, pointing toward Ruthie's "shrine"
- one Superlux condenser microphone at the top of the stairwell, pointing toward Ruthie's "shrine"

Third Floor
- · one infrared video camera, pointing toward the freight elevator

Fourth Floor
- · one infrared video camera, pointing toward the beam with "FW Simon" written on it

I decided to begin my part of the vigil out in the garage. I sat out there alone, just listening for anything that might have sounded like tools dropping or rolling around. But everything was quiet. I decided to walk around to see if I could pick up any vibes or sense that someone was in there with me. As I toured the garage, I was struck by the massive collection of automobiles that Ben Bissman had amassed. Many of the cars were clearly classics, while others would fall into the "antique" category. With so much history attached to these cars, I couldn't help but wonder if perhaps the ghosts reported out in the garage had nothing to do with the Bissman Building and were instead attached to the cars themselves. You hear stories all the time of people buying antiques and then claiming there were ghosts attached to them. Knowing how much people have been known to love their cars, who is to say that their love didn't continue from beyond the grave?

After I left the garage, I met up with the others in my group. One by one, I asked them if they had experienced anything and if they thought there were any ghosts here. Surprisingly, none of them had encountered anything they would term "paranormal." None of them felt there were ghosts with us that night. At that point, Troy Ball came the closest to saying there might be ghosts in the Bissman, but then he just shook his head and said, "I really want there to be ghosts here, but I don't think there are." At that point in the evening, I would have had to say I agreed with Troy's assessment. Several hours later, though, that would all change.

We were now in the wee hours of the morning. Most of the group had gone home for the evening, so there were only a few of us left in the building. I was standing in front of the freight elevator on the third floor when all of a sudden, it felt like someone had just dropped cold air over me—it enveloped me in a matter of seconds and made me shiver.

I knew as soon as I felt it that this was no ordinary breeze, but I needed the others to confirm it. So I called them to come over and feel the coldness, too. As the group hurried over, I did what I always do whenever I feel the temperature around me is changing: I struck my Gingerbread Man pose—I widen my stance and stick my arms out at my sides, like a big, portly gingerbread man. The others could feel the cold air around me, but not around them.After about fifteen seconds, it felt as though someone lifted the cold air over my head and took it away. It didn't feel like I was warming up, just that the cold had been taken away. We weren't able to locate the source of the cold air.

Listening to the audio from that particular point in the vigil elicited more than a few giggles from those who listened to it. Since I was with a group of people, including Dan Stout, you can hear me talking to them, saying things like "Dan, take my temperature" and "Lick your hand and put it in the shaft." Seriously, if you didn't know the context, it would be really easy for you to misinterpret what I was asking for (for the record, I wanted Dan to lick his hand and put it in the elevator shaft to see if he could detect a breeze that way).

Oh yeah, and there was something else on those recordings—something that sounds like a little girl talking. Here's the really weird bit: her voice appears twice on the recording, in segments roughly eight minutes apart. It was the first time in all my years of ghost investigation when I appear to have captured the same voice more than once.

When you run it through analyzing software, the two sounds both fall within the range of a human voice. When you line up the two sounds side by side, it's clear that if it is a voice, it's the same voice. The patterns are almost identical, and they don't match the voice patterns of anyone else who was in the building that night.

So if it is a voice, what is it saying? Good question. When it comes to EVPs (electronic voice phenomena), I believe that if you can hear it clearly, you shouldn't start messing too much with the file. I can't tell you how many audio clips I have heard that people have de-hissed, stretched, smashed, and just generally butchered to the point where you could hear just about anything. So I tend to do nothing more than amplify anything odd I record and leave it at that.

I only mention that because I'm not sure what was being said in the first clip. It's very loud and appears close to the microphone, but I can't really make it out. I've played it for lots of people, and they hear all sorts of different things. Most, however, make out only a portion of it, which they think sounds like "I'm not . . ."

The freight elevator on the third floor of the Bissman Building. I was standing in this area, roughly three feet away from the elevator, when I felt the cold spots. The recordings of what sound like a little girl speaking were also recorded in this area.

The second clip is a bit easier to make out. Again, it's very loud and close to the mic, but this time, without prompting, people clearly hear "I said 'no'" when I play it for them.

What does it all mean? Again, not sure. I believe that EVPs are residual. In other words, we are somehow picking up fragments of conversation that somehow managed to get left behind. Sounds trippy, I know. But it's a lot easier for me to accept that as opposed to believing that ghosts have voice boxes and are sitting there, waiting for us to have an intelligent conversation with them. Put another way, while I'm fairly convinced that it is a little girl speaking on those recordings, I don't think there's any context to what she's saying. They are just residual fragments.

No one heard anything like a girl's voice at the time we made the recording. No one is speaking at the time the girl is heard, so as the voice is loud, someone in the group would have commented on it had he or she heard it live. Also, the girl's voice was picked up on another recorder, too. It's not as close to that recorder's mic, but the voice sounds exactly the same, so the recorder didn't misinterpret what it picked up.

Days after the vigil, I reviewed all the audio, video, and photos from that night. Other than the aforementioned old-time music and what sounded like a little girl's voice, there was only one other oddity in all the materials from the vigil.

At approximately 2:18 A.M., there is a loud banging noise in the garage, which was empty at the time. And I do mean loud. It's so loud that it echoes throughout the garage. The noise sounds like something wooden being slammed against the concrete floor. As there were multiple audio and video recorders running in the garage at the time (and they all picked up the sound), I was able to triangulate the sound and determine that it most likely came from somewhere near the center of the garage.

None of the video cameras running in the garage at the time picked up any sort of movement. On top of that, there are no sounds that might indicate something (or someone) was moving in the garage for a good twenty-five minutes before the noise was heard. To my knowledge, the only door that had been left unlocked for us so we could get in and out of the garage was a sliding metal door I referred to as the *Texas Chainsaw Massacre* door. For those of you who haven't seen that movie (shame on you!), there is an infamous scene in which a loud metal door is slid shut. In other words, if someone had tried to open that garage door to enter the garage, the sound of the door being opened would have been picked up on the recorders. They would have gotten only three feet inside the garage before the video cameras would have picked them up, too. So I have no idea what caused that sound. Paranormal? Hard to say, but it is a little odd to hear such a loud noise without seeing any movement in the entire garage.

FINAL THOUGHTS

The Bissman Building, possibly more than any other structure featured in this book, helps illustrate my point that ghost stories and actual history often intertwine. Here you have the history of the Bissman family— several generations of the same family working under the same roof for over a hundred years. Then you have the arrival of a ghostly girl, who not only appears to people, but seems to want to make contact. Who is this girl? No one knows. But in our rush to find all the answers, some people erroneously identified the ghost as Ruthie and invented an imaginary backstory about her. This is where I think we went awry.

I openly admit that ghosts don't make sense to me. Everything about them is an enigma to me: why they're here, why they are doing the things they're doing, why my dead distant relatives don't come tell me where they buried the Willis family fortune. Heck, include the fact that I don't even know what a ghost is in the mix and you get the general idea. It's one of the reasons I don't get invited to speak at many ghost conventions. Why? It's because by and large, the ghost-hunting community wants answers. They need everything to make sense and be totally explainable. But ghosts don't work that way. And some people, in their rush to have everything make sense, subconsciously (or sadly, sometimes consciously) create nonexistent connections and backstories. I think that's what happened in the case of Ruthie Bissman.

Of course, just when I was ready to dismiss the ghosts of the Bissman, I end up having an experience I can't explain, complete with what appear to be disembodied voices—the voice of a child, no less. Looking back, I'm convinced that history was trying to reach out to us at the Bissman Building. Unfortunately, we stopped listening before we had all the answers. But perhaps it's not too late to go back, open our eyes and ears, and see if history is still willing to teach us a thing or two.

Bissman Building
193 N. Main Street
Mansfield, Ohio 44902
www.hauntedbissmanbuilding.com

DELAWARE ARTS CASTLE

Funny story about how I was introduced to the ghost stories of the Delaware Arts Castle. Several years ago, I was asked to give a presentation at the Delaware Ghost Walk. For this particular walk, they had asked for several members of The Ghosts of Ohio organization to accompany the groups on their tours, so I gave a presentation that focused on the different ways The Ghosts of Ohio goes about looking for ghosts. I finished the presentation by playing some audio and video clips of odd things I'd recorded while on investigations, none of which was in Delaware, Ohio. At that time, we had not conducted many investigations in Delaware.

As I was leaving the stage, one of the audience members asked me if I knew of any haunted places in Delaware. After telling them the legends of Blue Limestone Park, I told the woman, "I'm sure the Delaware Arts Castle is haunted." When the woman asked "Why?" I replied, "Because it's a castle. All castles have to have at least three ghosts or at least one headless specter. It's a requirement," I said, with a wink. It was then I heard a soft voice behind me say, "Actually, they do have a ghost; they just don't like to talk about it."

Needless to say, I was hooked.

THE HISTORY

The man responsible for the creation of what would one day be known as the Delaware Arts Castle was William Little. He, along with his business partner, George W. Campbell, owned and operated the Blue Limestone Quarry, the remains of which are visible today inside Blue Limestone Park in Delaware.

Once a wedding gift from William Little to his daughter, Elizabeth, and his business partner, this mighty structure would be reborn as a community arts center for Delaware.

By all accounts, the two businessmen were very close and spent a great deal of time together, even outside of work. So it came as no surprise to those who knew the two men when George Campbell announced his engagement to William Little's daughter, Elizabeth. Little not only approved of the union, but when they married on August 27, 1846, he presented the new couple with a truly unique wedding present: their own castle.

Designed in the Anglo-Norman style, the castle at the top of the hill on West Williams Street featured arched doorways and windows, ornate woodwork throughout, and a stunning turret-like tower. Of course, Little made sure to incorporate some of the blue limestone cut from his own quarry into the house.

George and Elizabeth fell in love with the castle and spent many happy years within its walls, raising several children there. Aside from being a successful businessman, George Campbell was a rather accomplished horticulturist. He was known to sometimes bring back exotic plants and trees from his travels and plant them on his property. One such souvenir was the Chinese ginkgo tree, which still blooms in the castle's front yard. Campbell also built a vineyard next to the castle, where he developed and improved upon a variety of fruits, including grapes. Campbell worked on improving one particular species of grape for so long that even though it was believed to have first been discovered in New Jersey, it is known today as the Delaware grape.

By the 1890s, both George and Elizabeth were getting on in age and were finding that the castle was a bit too much for them to care for. So the home was sold to Rev. Aaron J. Lyons and Mrs. Abbie Parish, who in turn donated the building to Ohio Wesleyan University, a Methodist-based institution of higher learning whose campus was right across the street.

At the time the castle was donated, Ohio Wesleyan University was looking for a home for its art department, which had blossomed since the university had expanded to include a School of Fine Arts in 1877. The castle was a natural fit and was incorporated into the university and renamed Lyons Hall. It would remain part of Ohio Wesleyan until 1966, when the decision was made to return the art department to the main campus. Once the university had vacated the building, it was once again deemed a private residence and put up for sale.

Beginning in the 1970s, the castle passed through several different owners, including an architect and a lawyer. Some made changes to the interior of the home, but by and large, it remained pretty much the same as it had all those years ago.

In the late 1980s, a new nonprofit organization, the Delaware County Cultural Arts Center (DCCAC), was formed. Members of the Board of Trustees were looking for space in downtown Delaware where they could open up an arts center. They actually had their hearts set on one building in particular when one of the board members happened to see the "For Sale" sign in the front yard of the castle. When she showed it to the other members, the feeling was unanimous: this was the building they were looking for. So the DCCAC held a fund-raiser and raised enough money to purchase the building. Once it was theirs, the name of the building was officially changed to the Delaware Arts Castle.

Using mostly volunteer labor, the DCCAC transformed the castle into a community arts center, complete with art studios, kilns, and administrative offices. They even created a small gift shop. The Delaware Arts Castle officially opened in 1988 and has been offering art classes and hosting exhibits and special events for Delaware residents ever since.

THE EXPERIENCES

Joy Kaser has been involved with the Arts Castle since 1986, when she helped start the community arts center inside the building. Even though she was familiar with the building before the committee took it over, she does not remember ever hearing stories of it being haunted. To her, it was just a really cool, unique building. That's what made the events of one particular evening even more head-scratching.

"This would have been earlier on, before we even opened," Joy explained. "We didn't even have lights upstairs yet." Still, that didn't stop Joy and several other members of the committee from having a meeting down on the main floor. At the end of the meeting, one of the members wanted to go look at something upstairs. Taking up flashlights, Joy and the others accompanied the member to the second floor.

"We had just come out of the master bedroom—it's the painting and drawing area now—and were out in the hallway when we all felt a really cold breeze go by us. I remember that there were no windows open. But that cold breeze seemed like it just went past us and toward the staircase," Joy said.

Over the years, items have been known to disappear from the Arts Castle, often showing up out of the blue later on. One of the more popular items to pull a disappearing act at the castle is earrings, leading some to suggest that the ghost here is female . . . or a male with pierced ears!

"A few years ago," Joy Kaser remembers, "I was helping clean up after one of our Castle Arts affairs where we sell some of the artists' works. Whatever we don't sell, we have to give back to the artists. There was one earring that was left, but we couldn't find its mate. It was frustrating because I couldn't find the mate for that one earring. Another woman even helped me and we must have looked for half an hour, but we couldn't find it." That is, until Joy heard a noise "and the earring just fell and landed right between us," she said, incredulously. "I don't know where that earring came from because we'd looked everywhere for it."

Joy took the mysterious disappearance and sudden reappearance of the earring to mean that someone in the castle had taken a liking to the stylish accessory. So what did she do next? "I picked them up and bought them," Joy says, with a smile.

And it's not only earrings that have a habit of disappearing and then reappearing out of thin air at the Arts Castle. One time, Joy needed some scissors, only to have a pair drop down right at her feet.

"I was putting names up on the mailboxes back in the mail area, and I remember thinking I needed something sharp to trim down some of the names since they were too long for the mailboxes," Joy told me. "And no sooner had I thought that when I heard something fall near me: they were a pair of old sewing scissors in the shape of a crane. But they had fallen right under the mailboxes in front of me, which doesn't make sense. I don't know where they could have fallen from."

Joy herself admits to believing there was a ghostly woman here— namely, Elizabeth Campbell, whom the castle was built for. In fact, Joy told me that she would sometimes even talk to Elizabeth's ghost. "It wasn't any big deal," Joy said. "I used to close the building back when I was by myself. And I used to talk to Elizabeth, you know, talk out loud to her like, 'OK, Elizabeth, we're going to go this way now.'" An incident one night at the castle, though, would force Joy to rethink her belief that Elizabeth Campbell haunted the castle. Or if she did, she wasn't the only ghost present.

Joy was getting ready to close up the castle for the night with her husband, Steve. They were up on the second floor in the ballroom when they both heard what sounded like music. "It was pretty loud. It sounded like there was a party going on downstairs," Joy said.

"I think I heard it first," Steve chimed in. "We were in the ballroom, and I heard the music and the talking. So I walked out of the ballroom to the head of the stairs and I said, 'Did you leave a radio on downstairs? Come listen to this.'"

The couple stood together at the top of the stairs, trying to make sense of what they were hearing. "I thought it was coming from outside, but Steve said, 'No, there's nothing out there, and everything's closed for the evening.' It was a lot of chattering, like people were happy and having a party. I couldn't place the music, but it didn't sound modern."

"I kept hearing music and people talking. I couldn't hear much of what they were saying, but I specifically heard a woman's voice," Steve added.

The couple then decided to walk downstairs to see if they could determine where the noises were coming from. "But when we got to the foot of the stairs and turned, the sounds just sort of faded away," Steve explained. "But here's the weird thing: we heard the sounds again. It was hard to pinpoint where it was coming from. But if I had to say, I would say it was coming from the back of the house. It felt like it was on that floor with us—like at the end of that hallway."

Joy agreed: "It was like it was coming from someplace else, but on the same floor with us."

"As soon as we got closer to where we thought the sound was coming from, it just sort of faded away. And at no point was the sound ever loud, no matter where we were. You heard vague talking and other voices with music in the background. We both heard it, too," Steve said.

It was his experience that night that made Steve consider that if Elizabeth Campbell is indeed here, she has company. "People say that Elizabeth is the ghost that's here," Steve told me. "And she might be. But that night, I know I definitely heard more than one person. It sounded like there was a party going on."

When Pat Getha started as a program director for the Arts Castle, she would often work late into the night in the building. For company, Pat would sometimes bring along her dog, Isabella. Most of the time,

Isabella would sleep quietly at Pat's feet while she worked. One night, though, Isabella appeared to have chased something through the castle.

"I was working in my office one night," Pat began. "Isabella was lying down near me. All of a sudden, her ears went straight up and she went tearing from the office and went running upstairs. And I could hear her running from room to room, looking for somebody upstairs. And I said 'Isabella, what are you doing?' and she comes trotting back downstairs and lies back down. For the rest of the night, she stayed with me, but every once in a while, her head would pop up and her ears would go up."

Diane Hodges is the current executive director at the Arts Castle. She hasn't seen any ghosts in the castle (yet), but she does believe that they're here. Diane also thinks they like to play with the door to her office as well as the other offices. "We have to keep checking the doors," she told me. "Doors here seem to lock by themselves. One summer, it got to be a bit of a joke since we'd keep checking the doors."

When I asked Diane who she thought was haunting the castle, without hesitation, she said "Elizabeth Campbell. I just really feel like she is a part of this place."

THE VIGIL

For this vigil, Kathy Boiarski, Darrin Boop, Samantha Nicholson, Sean Seckman, and Adam and Sheri Harrington accompanied me. In order to help raise awareness of the Delaware Arts Castle, The Ghosts of Ohio had recently taken part in a fund-raiser with the winners having the chance to spend the night inside the Arts Castle, investigating with us. Jules Lapp and Rick Gardner were the lucky winners and accompanied us on this vigil.

The minute I first walked into the Arts Castle, I was struck with the energy level that seemed to emanate from every corner of the building. This didn't feel paranormal or ghostly, though. No, this felt different. It felt warm, inviting, and there was an air of excitement to it. I think it had something to do with all the artwork hanging on the walls and on display throughout the castle. It was as if all the creativity and excitement that went into creating these works of art had left their imprint. Whatever it was, it was strong and had me thinking to myself, "If I were a ghost, I would totally hang out here."

Prior to setting up the equipment, I had a briefing session with Jules and Rick. Whenever I have guests with me on a vigil, especially those who haven't ever been on a ghost hunt, I like to let them know what they are in for. Due to the plethora of ghost reality shows currently on air, there are a lot of misconceptions as to what exactly goes into a ghost hunt. There was a time, right around when these shows first became popular, when all of our guests thought they would be participating in the equivalent of a Halloween haunted house attraction with ghosts jumping out at them, scratching them, etc. Obviously, most of those people walked away from a Ghosts of Ohio ghost hunt disappointed. But by and large, once I explained things to them, people began to understand that there's a difference between reality TV and reality. Jules and Rick were no exception, and they were very excited to be taking part in what I later discovered was the first official "ghost hunt" of the Arts Castle.

Here's where we started setting up the equipment:

Back Hallway
- one infrared video camera near the mail area, pointing toward the back door (office doors in view)
- one Superlux condenser microphone near the mail area, pointing toward the back door

Hallway Outside Gift Shop (Beside Main Staircase)
- one infrared video camera beside the main staircase, pointing toward the mail area
- one Superlux condenser microphone beside the main staircase, pointing toward the mail area

Main Staircase
- one DVR night-vision camera at the bottom of the stairs, pointing up the staircase
- one DVR night-vision camera at the top of the stairs, pointing down the staircase
- one Superlux condenser microphone at the top of the stairs, pointing down the staircase
- Vernier LabPro with temperature, EMF, and static electricity sensors running up and down the staircase

Ballroom/Dance Academy
- one DVR night-vision camera in the corner of the room, pointing across the room

- one Superlux condenser microphone in the corner of the room, pointing across the room

Painting and Drawing Room

- one infrared video camera, aimed across the fireplace and focused on the front door
- one Superlux condenser microphone, aimed across the fireplace and focused on the front door

Hallway Outside the Painting and Drawing Room

- one infrared DVR camera, pointing down the hallway toward the front of the castle

After everything had been set up, and after arming Jules and Rick with a full set of hand-helds, we divided up into groups and fanned out across the Arts Castle. I decided to head to the Painting and Drawing Room first as it had at one time been the master bedroom. There was also the added bonus that the cold breeze that Joy Kaser had experienced took place in the hallway right outside the Painting and Drawing Room door. I purposely put Jules and Rick in my group, partly because I'm the "fearless leader," but also because I'm always interested in seeing how "newbies" ghost hunt. I often find myself getting into ruts and just doing the same thing over and over. Since I've yet to find that piece of evidence that proves without a doubt that ghosts exist, I'm clearly not doing something right. So I'm constantly looking for new ways to conduct ghost hunts or how to look for ghosts in general. Jules and Rick didn't bring years of ghost-hunting baggage with them, so I was interested in seeing how they would approach the vigil.

They were both very timid at first and had to be coaxed to conduct an EVP session. But then again, it took me years to get used to sitting in a room, talking aloud to no one. But they eventually overcame their hesitation and jumped in. Despite our invitation to come and talk with us, no ghost took us up on the offer. It was very hard to sit in that room, among all the paints and assorted art supplies, and feel anything other than that creative warmth that continued to permeate the building. During this part of the session, occasionally I looked out in the hallway to see if I could detect a cold breeze or any sort of temperature change. I never was able to.

When each group had finished in a specific area of the castle, we all headed back downstairs to the main room. There, we would talk about anything odd we had experienced in order to give a heads-up to the next group headed to that area. On this particular evening, it appeared to be exceptionally quiet, paranormally speaking. No one reported anything out of the ordinary—no ghost sightings, strange noises, or weird feelings. It was as if the ghosts of the Arts Castle were away on holiday this night.

As the evening wore on and we still weren't getting any results, I started playing with the idea that the ghosts might have gone into hiding. Some say that I've watched too many reality ghost shows, but I've always wondered what it must feel like to ghosts when people come storming into their homes, demanding that they do something to make their presence known. If I were the ghost, I think I would either head for higher ground or else look for the nearest heavy object to throw at these rude people who have invaded my home. Think about it: maybe all these "demonic" spirits that ghost hunters claim to encounter are just the ghosts of former homeowners, angry that they're being treated like a sideshow attraction.

Regardless, for the last part of the vigil, I decided to focus on areas of the castle where I might try to hide if I were a ghost looking for a little peace and quiet: the basement and the tower.

The basement did have a different feel than the rest of the castle— not a bad feeling, just different. Unlike most basements, this one was divided off, with some large rooms and some small. I sat in each room, apologizing for intruding, but stating that I was only trying to interview everyone who was associated with the Arts Castle. In one of the larger rooms, I sat quietly with a K-II, a ghost meter, and an ELF meter around me. I asked that if there was anyone else in the room with me, would he or she do me a favor and simply move closer to me? My hope was that something would move close enough to trigger the hand-helds around me. Didn't work.

In a last-ditch effort to make contact, Darrin Boop and I climbed up the tower and spent some time there, trying to start a conversation with Elizabeth or anyone else who was interested in talking. Apparently, no one had anything to say as we never heard a response and nothing showed up on the audio after the fact. At least not on the recorder I had with me at the time.

Something did show up on the audio from one of the video cameras, though. Reviewing all the materials from the vigil, I found two instances where the video camera positioned in the back hallway—the one pointing toward the offices and back door—picked up a strange noise. Two strange noises, actually, for while the two noises are similar, they do not appear to be coming from the same source. Running the noises through audio-analyzing software shows that while they seem to be coming from the same general area (the hallway in front of the camera), they are not from the same source.

Both noises sound . . . weird. People who have heard them describe the sound as "a talking baby doll" or "bird-like." Although very high-pitched and staccato, they do sound like a voice, especially the first one. I'm not convinced what the first "voice" is saying, but people think it sounds like "look up" or "mama." As for the second "voice," no one's really sure what that one's saying.

But here's the point where these two "voices" get really interesting to me. As I mentioned, they were both picked up by the internal microphone on the video camera in the back hallway. That night, there happened to be a studio microphone, one that was hardwired to the mixing board, sitting right next to the video camera and pointing in the same direction. That microphone did not pick up those odd sounds. In fact, when we went back to the time codes and synched up the video camera with what the microphone recorded, the microphone did not pick up anything at the exact moment the video camera was recording those odd noises. In other words, an internal microphone on a video camera was able to pick up something a studio microphone couldn't hear.

Now, even though the two noises do not sound like the standard types of interference we sometimes record (in fact, I've never heard these noises before or since), we can't rule that out as a possibility. That's because, while we use Sony digital video recorders, we don't use them to record, per se. Instead, we use external burners to burn what we record directly onto DVDs. So there is a possibility that there was an issue with the camera itself and/or the cables connecting it to the burner and somehow the noises got sucked out of the air and onto the DVDs. Otherwise, if we're going to say it was a ghost, we have to entertain the idea that somehow ghosts are able to target specific recording devices since both the video camera and microphone record in the same range. And that just boggles my mind. So for now, the noises remain unexplained.

FINAL THOUGHTS

Any time you combine the words "castle" and "ghost" in a single sentence, it immediately conjures up all sorts of images of spooky, derelict buildings straight out of an old Universal Studios black-and-white monster movie. Nothing breaks that stereotype more than the Delaware Arts Castle. When you stand outside and look up at the building, there's no feeling of impending dread. Rather, it's a warm, comfortable feeling. And that feeling doesn't dissipate when you walk in the door. I'll admit I did hear a scream during one of my visits, but it came from a six-year-old boy, who was apparently quite pleased with his latest art creation.

But there are supposed to be ghosts here, right? How can there be ghosts in the building if it's not spooky? Once again, the Delaware Arts Castle takes that old stereotype and turns it on its head. If there are ghosts here, they're not here to rattle chains and frighten people. If anything, I suspect that they're hanging around here simply because the Arts Castle is a really cool building! There's so much excitement and positive energy going on in the building—who wouldn't want to be around that?

Of course, we need to remember that this building was once a former residence, so perhaps the ghosts of past residents are here. I can't say that's true with any certainty. One thing is for sure, though. If their ghosts are here, they most certainly approve of what's been done with the place.

Delaware Arts Castle
190 West Winter Street
Delaware, Ohio 43015
www.artscastle.org

SOUTHWEST
OHIO

LOVELAND CASTLE

Somewhere in all of our family trees there's at least one do-it-yourselfer. You know, the person who can fix darn near anything and owns a killer set of tools. They probably built a shed or two, put in a new pool, re-shingled the roof. Heck, they may have even designed and built their own house. In short, there's probably nothing they can't fix or build. But you know what? They ain't got nothing on Harry Andrews of Loveland, Ohio. Harry took that age-old saying that every man's home is his castle to a whole new level by building his own castle . . . by hand. That's right, by hand. Using nothing more than rocks he yanked out of the Little Miami River and his own muscle and brain power, Harry built himself a castle.

Harry liked to see things through to the end. So when he said it would take him maybe twenty years to finish the castle and he hit year twenty-one, he kept going. In fact, he worked on his castle for nearly fifty years before he passed away, leaving it unfinished. Or did he? Because there are those who believe that ol' Harry's ghost is still hanging around the castle, waiting for it to be completed.

THE HISTORY

It didn't take Harry Andrews's parents long to realize that their son was different. Born on April 7, 1890, in New York City, it was obvious that from an early age Harry was incredibly intelligent (some believe he had an IQ of 189 and possessed a photographic memory). But more than that, Harry had a unique way of looking at things, and he wasn't content to simply sit by and let things happen. Quite the contrary: if someone told Harry he shouldn't do something, that was all the more reason for him to want to do it.

That isn't to say Harry Andrews was rebellious. Far from it. In fact, he was raised to respect his fellow man and to uphold the basic principles put forth in the Ten Commandments from the Bible. He also developed a deep love for his country, although in his teen years, he became interested in medieval Europe and ancient architecture. So deep was his interest that Harry decided to attend Colgate University, where he could study Greek and Roman architecture.

When he graduated from Colgate in 1916, Harry was unclear as to what he wanted to do with his life. He still felt he had a duty to his country, though, so the following year, when the United States officially entered World War I, Harry enlisted as a medic in the United States Army and was sent overseas to Europe. He ended up being stationed in the city of Toulouse in southwestern France. During his time there, Harry fell in love with the city and especially liked visiting the many castles throughout the region. In fact, Harry would travel all across France if there was a castle for him to see! One in particular that Harry enjoyed spending time at was the Château de la Roche Courbon, which had been built around 1475. Harry was struck with not only its grandeur, but with the sturdiness of its construction, which enabled it to stand the test of time. All in all, Harry was so taken by the entire region that after the war ended, he decided to stay a while longer and study abroad. During this time, Harry began telling people he was working on "becoming somewhat of an expert in medieval architecture."

Upon returning to the United States, Harry relocated to southern Ohio, just outside Cincinnati, and began working for the Standard Publishing Company in Mt. Healthy, Ohio, holding positions as diverse as typesetter and reporter. He also began teaching Sunday school classes. But the more he looked around him, the more disillusioned Harry became with what was going on in America. He began to feel that the country was losing its way, especially when it came to upholding Christian virtues and leading a good, clean life. He began to long for the days of chivalry and medieval knights, which he had learned so much about while overseas.

One of the things Harry enjoyed doing was teaching Sunday school. Often he would take his all-boy class on weekend field trips to camp and fish along the Little Miami River. While the days were filled with parables and stories from the Bible, at night, around the campfire, the stories would inevitably turn to knights and tale of chivalry. One weekend in 1927, it hit Harry: Why not combine the two and create a new organization, a group of "knights" who would honor the Ten Commandments and work to restore noble virtues to society? Harry presented his idea to his small group of Sunday school boys. They loved it, and the Knights of the Golden Trail (KOGT) was formed.

It was further decided that any male over the age of eighteen could become a Knight of the Golden Trail (sorry, no girls allowed). Potential knights would have to officially apply and have their application voted on by the other Knights, of course. But if you were accepted, all you needed to do was to take a solemn vow to live the rest of your life according to the Ten Commandments. From that point on, you were officially a Knight of the Golden Trail and would be addressed as "Sir" whenever engaged in KOGT duties. This explains why, in interviews, Harry always referred to himself as Sir Harry.

If you were under the age of eighteen, you were allowed to join as a Squire or a Page. Only after your eighteenth birthday could you be officially known as a Knight of the Golden Trail . . . or be called "Sir."

Now that they had their name and their rules and regulations in place, they were good to go, right? Well, not really. For as Harry's Sunday school students quickly pointed out to him, you can't be a real knight unless you have a castle to defend. So one weekend, while Harry and the boys were up at their usual campsite along the Little Miami, he took some of the sandstone rocks from the river and created what he termed a "rock tent." That lasted for a while before it fell over. They tried rebuilding it, but eventually it fell apart. Simply put, it just wasn't strong enough to stand up against the elements. If the Knights of the Golden Trail were to have a proper castle, it would have to be a lot stronger. Plus, they had already started taking on new members, so they would need something big. Once he realized all this, it's hard to imagine Harry without a big grin on his face. After all, he had long entertained the idea of building his own castle, so what better excuse did he need?

On the afternoon of June 5, 1929, Sir Harry and his Knights of the Golden Trail gathered on a piece of land that Harry had just purchased: the same location where they had been spending their weekends camping.

They had a small ceremony and officially laid the cornerstone for their new home: Château Laroche—French for "rock castle."

Even though the castle was to become Harry's primary residence in later life, it did not start out that way. In fact, Harry's initial plan for the castle was to use it as a meeting place for the Knights and perhaps for weekend camping trips, so he thought of it more like a retreat house

Harry Andrews's Château Laroche: "Rock Castle."

than a primary residence. In fact, Harry initially worked on the castle's construction only on the weekends as he still had a full-time job. In 1955, though, after he retired from the Standard Publishing Company, Harry decided to move into the castle so that he could work on it full-time.

When people starting stopping by to see Harry's handiwork, one of the first questions they had (after asking Harry what possessed him to build a castle, of course) was what the castle was designed to look like. Truth be told, at one point Harry did have something that vaguely resembled plans for the castle. But by and large, most of the design came from his own ideas and the memories of the European castles he had frequented during World War I. Harry has been quoted as saying that his original intent was to build a full-scale replica of a medieval Normanesque castle, but that he ended up building rooms and additions based solely on what he thought a castle should have. So while there were essential rooms like bedrooms and a kitchen, Harry also set his heart on building an armory, a ballroom, a great hall—and, of course, what castle would be complete without a dungeon?

For the exterior walls of the castle, Harry once again relied on his memory of medieval European castles—in particular, ones built for defensive purposes. Following those models, Harry made plans to install watchtowers and circular holes along the roof line, positioned strategically above the castle's front door—all the better for pouring scalding water and molten lead down upon the heads of unwanted guests! And while women were not permitted to be knights, Harry showed that he still had a soft spot by erecting a special tower just for them . . . or at least one of them. The castle's highest tower would come to be known as the Princess Tower because it housed a tiny room for a woman where she could be made to feel like Rapunzel.

As time went by, more and more people continued to stop by to see Harry and his castle. Those who saw Château Laroche without catching a glimpse of Harry actually working on it missed out on the most amazing and mind-boggling aspect of the castle. This enormous, multi-storied, (mostly) full-scale replica of a castle was built almost entirely by one man using rocks he collected himself from the Little Miami River.

That's right. Every morning, Harry Andrews would wake up, grab two empty five-gallon pails, and head across the property to the Little Miami. Once there, he plunged his hands into the water, grabbed as

Incredibly, Loveland Castle was the work of one man, Harry Andrews, who wanted nothing more than to own his own castle.

many sandstone rocks as his two pails could hold, and then walked back up the hill. Harry kept detailed records of everything he did at the castle and by his count, he had dragged over 56,000 buckets of rocks up that hill to be used for the construction. One would have thought he would have run out of rocks eventually, but the Little Miami also proved to be the perfect "quarry" for Harry because no matter how many stones he took out of the water, every year, the river carried even more downstream, depositing them almost right on Harry's doorstep.

In addition to rocks, Harry also used bricks to build his castle. He even developed an ingenious way to make his own bricks. He would take old cardboard milk containers, cut off their tops, and then fill them with concrete. Once they were filled, Harry would surround the cartons with wooden planks so that they wouldn't bulge while the concrete was hardening. Several days later, Harry would cut away the cardboard and voilà, he had himself some bricks!

It has been estimated that Harry made and used over 44,000 of these bricks. What's more, most of them had some sort of surprise hidden inside. With no public trash pickup at the castle, mainly because there was no road until Harry decided to build one, he needed to come up with alternative means to dispose of his refuse. Harry would burn most of his trash, but what to do with those items that couldn't be burned, such as cans or old lightbulbs? Harry's solution? Put them inside his homemade bricks. This way, he was not only getting rid of his garbage, but helping to strengthen his bricks in the process. Some of the Knights today refer to this as Harry's way of "recycling."

Since Harry needed to cut up the cardboard milk containers, he couldn't reuse them, so those cartons became almost like gold to Harry. Indeed, he often treated them like currency. Since Harry was a notary, people in the area would sometimes show up at the castle to have things notarized. Harry's going rate back then was 25 cents per document. But if you brought Harry a milk carton, he waived his fee and would notarize it for free. Likewise, if you showed up with a milk carton, Harry would give you a free peek inside his castle.

Some of Harry Andrews's homemade bricks, which he made using old cardboard milk containers. Note Harry's unique technique of using garbage to further insulate the bricks.

If you didn't happen to have any empty milk containers handy, there was something else you could bring Harry for his castle: rocks. Unlike the ones he pulled from the river, though, Harry wasn't looking to use the rocks to build his castle. Rather, he wanted them as decoration, so people would bring Harry rocks that they claimed were from faraway places and Harry would proudly display them at the castle. Sometimes he would even mount them directly on the walls with concrete and then carve the date and where the rock was found into the wall. When visitors stopped by, Harry would show them his prized rock collection. Some of the pieces in his collection were alleged pieces of the Berlin Wall and even a hunk of what Harry claimed was a meteor.

But not everything in the castle could be built from stone or brick. Case in point: the front door to the castle. As this was the main entrance to the castle, Harry wanted something unique. But since this was a castle, the door also needed to act as a line of defense and be able to withstand an assault from any knight or, as Harry once put it, "The drunks and punks that come down here at night."

So he pieced together the door, assembling 238 pieces of wood in a crisscross pattern so it would be able to withstand blows from axes. Harry also used 2,530 nails on the door, some of which were designed to dull or break the blade of whatever might be used to bash against the door. Finally, Harry installed what he called a stoop door—a small door within the larger front door.

When the main door was locked at night, people who wanted to come in through the front door would be forced to stoop over to come through the smaller door. Harry used to joke (as least people thought he was joking) that inside the castle, just on the other side of the door, would be a knight holding a sword. Since the first thing coming through the stoop door would be a person's head and neck, the knight, if he didn't recognize or like who was coming through, was in the perfect position to separate the visitor's head from his shoulders.

Harry wasn't content just to build a castle, though. Incredibly, he also landscaped all around the castle. It sat near the top of a naturally sloping hill, but Harry dug up most of the hill on both sides of the castle, creating massive, multitiered formal gardens, including one that was thirty-five feet wide and nearly a hundred feet long.

Harry also set aside a large piece of land for a vegetable garden, which also housed twenty-two hot beds. It is said that people would row up the

Little Miami just to buy some of Harry's tomatoes and his other vegetables. Harry raised crops year-round with the help of a large greenhouse he built behind the castle. When he was digging up the landscape, Harry also built what he referred to as his "dry moat." He never completed the moat, and it never fully encircled the castle either, so whether or not he ever intended to fill the moat with water remains a mystery.

It had long been said that if you wanted Harry Andrews to do something, just tell him it couldn't be done. And once Harry threw himself into a project, he was going to see it through to the end. Case in point: Château Laroche. When he first announced his intention to build the castle, he thought it would take about twenty years to complete it. Over fifty years later, Harry was still working on his castle, even though he was in his nineties. Incredibly, even at that age, by Harry's estimation, he had constructed 95 percent of the castle himself. When asked what his secret was for doing such physical labor at his age, Harry attributed it all to the fact that he never smoked, never drank, . . . and never got married.

One April afternoon in 1981, Harry decided it was time to dispose of the trash. He dragged all the trash outside to the courtyard and set

A view of Loveland Castle in all its glory.

Not content with simply a castle, Andrews also constructed multi-terraced for-mal gardens on the castle grounds.

it on fire. Harry always took great care to make sure the fire never got out of control and would often stand next to the flames with a shovel or rake to keep the fire in its place. On this particular afternoon, there were some strong winds whipping and one gust hit the fire with such force that it caused the flames to shift. It is unclear whether Harry was standing too close to the fire or if he kicked at the flames in order to get them back under control. Either way, Harry was wearing polyester pants at the time and the flames quickly ignited the fabric. Thankfully, there was a woman visiting the castle at the time who was able to come to Harry's aid and help put the fire out, but not before Harry had suf-fered severe burns to his leg. One look at it was all it took for people to see that Harry needed to get to the hospital, and fast. But Harry refused medical attention, saying that he was fine and that he needed to get back to work on the castle.

Stubborn as he was, when Harry was finally persuaded to go to the hospital, doctors told him his leg had been so severely burned that it needed to be amputated immediately lest infection spread through his body. Harry refused to allow the doctors to take his leg, telling them, "You can't build a castle with only one leg." Still, doctors managed to persuade Harry to be admitted to the hospital, hoping that he would come to his senses and allow them to amputate. Harry never gave in, though, and several weeks later, he passed away at the age of ninety-one as a result of an infection in his leg, which spread throughout his body.

At the time of his death, Harry Andrews had spent over fifty years building his castle, only to fall short of completing it. Thankfully, there were those among us who refused to let Harry's dream die. You could say that Harry had taught them well because the men who took up the task of completing Château Laroche were none other than his own Knights of the Golden Trail.

An example of Harry Andrews's ingenuity and creativity: stone archways created from rocks he pulled from the Little Miami River himself.

Today, the Knights not only oversee the construction and restoration of the castle, but they have also opened it up for tours, allowing countless visitors a peek inside the mind of a man driven to complete his dream home, only to die before seeing it finished.

THE EXPERIENCES

Interestingly enough, the first ghost sighting at Loveland Castle might have been by Harry Andrews himself. When interviewed for a segment on the television show *Real People,* Harry told reporter Sarah Purcell that a ghost had been visiting the castle for "nearly twenty years." Harry wasn't sure who the ghost was, especially since it rarely showed itself to him and seemed content to just annoy Harry by knocking on the castle door and ringing the doorbell at all hours of the day and night. Still, Harry felt as though the ghost needed a name, so he settled on Casper Poltergeist.

To date, there is only one known instance where Harry actually claimed to have seen a ghost at the castle, although whether it was Casper Poltergeist or not is still open for debate. Regardless, Harry said that one night, he was sitting downstairs in a rocking chair when he heard a rather odd noise coming from near the fireplace. Turning his head, Harry claimed to have locked eyes with a shadowy figure, standing just beside the fireplace hearth. Harry sat there, transfixed, for several seconds before the ghost yelled out "Harry!" and disappeared.

Sir Fred has been associated with the castle for many years and has even achieved the rank of Noble within the Knights of the Golden Trail. He admits that even before he came to the castle, he had heard stories about it being haunted. "I don't remember specifically what I had been told because it was so long ago," Sir Fred confessed. "You just sort of hear things about the place. I remember hearing them before I came here, but I never gave the stories much thought."

Once Sir Fred started working at the castle, it didn't take long for him to feel as though the stories about ghosts here might indeed be true.

"One time, one of the Knights asked if I would spend the night at the castle all alone, just to keep an eye on the place," Sir Fred began. "We were getting a lot of requests from ghost groups to come here, so we thought I'd spend the night alone and see what happened."

Just before dusk, Sir Fred arrived at Château Laroche. Since he is a professional dog trainer, he thought he'd bring along two of his dogs to see if they could pick up on anything. Settling in for the night, Sir Fred told me that everything seemed normal. As the weather was cold, he decided to build a fire in the fireplace. When it was burning brightly, he settled in a chair nearby and started reading, his two dogs curled up beside him on the floor.

Sir Fred told me that as the night wore on, he started noticing what felt like a cold draft that kept coming down the stairs near him. He didn't think anything of it until one of his dogs, a female German shepherd, suddenly jumped up, stared at the front door for a moment, and then bolted upstairs.

"That dog was a rescue," Sir Fred explained, "and she wouldn't let anyone else touch her. She barely left my side, so I thought it was odd that she just ran off like that." Stranger still, Sir Fred started hearing what sounded like the dog upstairs, playing with someone or something. "You could hear her up there, playing and running around the table. And here's the really weird thing: you could hear feet behind her. It was like someone was walking around behind her. This dog wouldn't go near anybody, and yet she was upstairs running around and playing with someone. She must have stayed up there for about an hour," Sir Fred concluded.

When she was done, Sir Fred's dog quietly came back downstairs, lay down on the floor in front of the fireplace, and went to sleep. "But about an hour later," Sir Fred said, "she jumped up, looked at the front door, and ran up the stairs again. She bounced around upstairs again for about an hour and then came back down and went to sleep."

That was Sir Fred's big experience here at Château Laroche. He's had others, though, but he says he's not ready to say they are the work of ghosts. "Lights turn on and off by themselves here," he explained. "Or you will put all the puzzles near the fireplace together and then, when you come in the next morning, they are all messed up. But does that mean a ghost did that? I don't know. It's weird, though," Sir Fred confessed.

Sir Fred is still waiting to see a ghost at Château Laroche. There have been times, though, where he's felt something strange in the castle. "It's hard to explain, but there have been times when things just don't feel right here. You can feel it. There's something going on—it suddenly feels like somebody's here with you. You can't explain it, but you just know. So my first reaction is that somebody alive is around here. Like they snuck in here. It's like I knew that somebody snuck in here. But when I go to look, there's never anybody here with me," Sir Fred commented.

"Personally," Sir Fred continued, "I've never felt uncomfortable here. I don't think there's anything bad here. But I've had people who won't go into certain places. Usually, it's the chapel or the dungeon. I've also had people come out of the dry moat and say they couldn't even go near it. Those people told me they could feel things or something and that they just couldn't go in the dry moat."

Sir Mike has been involved with Château Laroche for close to a decade. Like Sir Fred, he heard the ghost stories about the castle long before he started working here. He's even sat in with some of the local ghost groups who have come out to the castle. Nothing he's seen, though, has convinced him there are ghosts here:

"Well, I don't really believe. I've been on a couple of the ghost tours, and it just seems like something gets in their head and just starts rolling and they hear and see things," Mike concluded.

Of course, that's not to say that Mike hasn't experienced anything odd at the Loveland Castle. "There was this one night when I was down on the first floor, and I heard something running around upstairs. So I said, 'Did anyone else hear that?' and one of the other Knights said, 'I heard it, too.' I'm not sure if it was a raccoon or something, but we definitely heard something. It sounded like three kids up there, running around in the ballroom and having fun," Sir Mike said.

"That was the same place my dog went to that one night," Sir Fred chimed in.

"So I don't know what that could have been," Sir Mike continued. "Was it a ghost? Who can say? It's like when someone plays you a recording they got here at three in the morning and it sounds like a hammer hitting a rock. Like someone working on the castle. Is that a ghost? Don't know. Only thing you can say is that it wasn't one of us," Sir Mike said.

As the interviews were finishing up, Sir Fred was able to provide some insight into the story behind the Woman in White, a ghostly figure who allegedly can be seen floating above the Little Miami River, right in front of Château Laroche. That's right, floating above the water.

"From what I understand," Sir Fred explained, "the woman lived just up the river with her husband, who was a moonshiner." Apparently, while the husband had a partner who helped with the illegal still, his wife was often called in to assist. "One day," Sir Fred continued, "there was an explosion at the still and Harry went down there to help them. They found the partner dead, but they couldn't find the wife. She was found days later, under a piece of copper tubing."

When I asked Sir Fred why the woman's ghost was always seen out on the water in front of the castle, he surmised, "Maybe it's because she used to come to the castle. I had heard that she would come down here and get vegetables from Harry. She liked his vegetables."

THE VIGIL

Despite the fact that we were dealing with a castle, the way Harry Andrews laid out Château Laroche made it rather easy for just a few people, with equipment, of course, to cover the entire building. In fact, any more than that and you would be falling over each other. On top of that, the acoustics in the castle are such that more than a few people inside at one time might contaminate any potential audio or video evidence. So for this particular vigil, it would just be me and one other member of The Ghosts of Ohio, Jeff Craig.

This was not the first time at Château Laroche for either Jeff or me. The Ghosts of Ohio conducted an overnight investigation here several years ago, during which there was a rather interesting sequence of events that centered on one of our K-II meters, which seemingly took on a life of its own and flashed wildly for over ninety seconds. Initially, those sitting around the K-II when it began flashing thought it was responding to questions that were being asked. Looking back at the video that we recorded during the event, I'm not convinced that was the case. Still, if nothing else, the video does appear to show the K-II reacting to some sort of energy that is really close to the device. What makes this so interesting is that this event took place in a small clearing in front of the castle, down near the Little Miami River, where there's no electricity anywhere nearby. We even tried replicating the flashing by using our cell phones and even walkie-talkies near it. We couldn't get it to work. Afterwards, we learned that the K-II meter had been sitting right next to the same path that Harry Andrews had walked up and down for over fifty years when he was collecting rocks from the Little Miami. Needless to say, for this vigil, I wanted to use some audio and video recorders in the area to see if we could recreate the earlier K-II incident and perhaps capture something new.

Regarding the placement of the rest of the equipment, based on the stories we'd been told, here's where we ended up placing things:

Castle Roof
- two DVR night-vision cameras, one pointing down toward the front door and another equipped with a four-hundred- to five-hundred-foot IR illuminator, pointing down toward the dry moat

Chapel
- one DVR night-vision camera in the doorway, pointing down the hallway
- one Superlux condenser microphone in the doorway, pointing down the hallway

Ballroom
- one DVR night-vision camera in the corner of the room, facing the center of the room
- one Superlux Condenser microphone in the corner of the room, pointing across the room
- Vernier LabPro with temperature, EMF, static electricity, and motion-detection sensors placed around the dining room table

Dungeon
- one infrared video camera at the bottom of the stairs, aimed across the dungeon
- one Superlux condenser microphone at the bottom of the stairs, aimed across the dungeon

Fireplace Room
- one infrared video camera, aimed across the fireplace and focused on the front door
- one Superlux condenser microphone, aimed across the fireplace and focused on the front door

Watchtower
- one infrared video camera equipped with a four-hundred- to five-hundred-foot IR illuminator, pointing down toward the path Harry Andrews took to the Little Miami River

For the first part of the vigil, Jeff and I split up. I wanted to spend some time walking around the castle to see if I could have a few words with Sir Harry. I started up in the chapel, one of the areas Harry was

Harry created these steps, which lead down to the Little Miami River, where he collected rocks for the castle's construction.

said to have been working on when he passed away. I sat there in the dark, introduced myself, and then spoke about how impressed I was with Harry's work. I then asked if he would care to give me some insight into what drove him to build the castle. I asked if he was happy that the Knights of the Golden Trail were keeping his dream alive by continuing to work on the castle. Hearing no response, I moved on.

After I had spent some time alone in every room in the castle, including the rarely opened Princess Tower, I still hadn't seen or felt anything strange. Not even the slightest shiver. So I met up with Jeff, and we headed down toward the river. We sat side by side, a K-II meter between us, asking if Harry could come and sit with us. I brought up the odd series of events that had happened the last time I had visited the castle and asked Harry if he could flash the lights on the K-II meter again. Getting no response, I began to inquire if there was some other ghost here. The Woman in White, perhaps? I asked if she could come forward and tell us a little bit more about herself. Again, no response. When I reviewed the audio I recorded down near the river, other than my voice and Jeff's, there was only the constant croaking of the world's largest bullfrog . . . or perhaps it was the infamous Loveland Frog. Either way, there were no ghostly voices on the recording.

But that's not to say I didn't manage to capture some strange audio during the vigil. Or, to be more specific, during the interview of Sir Fred, which took place several hours prior to the vigil. He and I were seated across one of the game tables in the main room of Château Laroche, to the left of the fireplace and adjacent to the steps leading to the dungeon. There are three audio anomalies that, as of this writing, remain unexplained: two instances of what can best be described as static or interference and one instance of strange knocking noises.

The interview itself lasted fifty-two minutes and fifteen seconds, and the entire time, my digital voice recorder was on the table in front of me, facing Sir Fred. While others entered the room during the course of the interview, there was no one else present when these audio anomalies occurred.

The first instance appears eighteen minutes and forty-two seconds into the interview and sounds like electronic interference or static. It lasts for approximately six seconds and suddenly stops. The noise is loud enough to be heard over Sir Fred's voice, although it is not loud enough to drown out his voice. I do not recall hearing the noise while I was conducting the interview. Coincidentally (or not), at the point when the static occurs, Sir Fred has just begun detailing for me how Sir Harry Andrews died. Specifically, the noise occurs at the point where Sir Fred is saying, "He died in a hospital. I believe it was about sixteen days after the accident."

The same interference-type noise appears again nine seconds later, this time continuing for twenty-five seconds. Again, Sir Fred is talking about how Harry died, how Harry Andrews was burning trash and his pant leg caught fire. The noise occurs while Sir Fred is saying, "He [Harry] was out here and the winds kind of blew the fire out of control. And he was trying to contain the fire and he had polyester pants on and the polyester melted into his legs. They were going to amputate because gangrene had set in, but Harry said no."

The recorder in question was used to record over two hundred hours of interviews for this book. I've never had any problems with it, and this static-type noise has occurred only these two times. I don't have any explanation for it, although I will say that the recorder is freestanding and is not hardwired into any sort of mixer, so it is possible that the recorder somehow managed to pick up some stray signals bouncing around the ozone. There had been a rather severe thunderstorm earlier that afternoon, so that might have contributed to the noise . . . or not.

As for the knocking noise, that's a little harder to explain away. For one, even though the noise is incredibly loud and appears to be happening right up against the microphone, I do not recall hearing it when I was conducting the interview. Oh yeah, and the knocking continues for almost a full three minutes.

I have absolutely no explanation for this bizarre series of knocking noises. I was not making them, and Sir Fred, to my knowledge, wasn't making them either. In fact, I can't explain how I didn't hear something so loud. If I had, I would almost certainly have tried to determine where it was coming from and stopped it. It's so loud that had I heard it during the interview, I would have found it incredibly disruptive. But I never heard it. Sir Fred didn't appear to have heard it either as he just continued talking.

It's hard to describe the noise other than to say it was just loud. It's not rhythmic at all and the tempo of the knocking speeds up and slows down. It's just a series of loud, hard knocks, right up close to the microphone. At one point, there is a rapid series of knocks, followed by a single knock every two to three seconds. In our attempts to explain it, we've explored every possibility, including Morse code (Sir Harry was, after all, in the army), and Ghosts of Ohio member Wendy Cywinski even suggested it might be a deathwatch beetle, which, I'll admit, I'd never heard of before. But after looking it up, I found that while that beetle does make strange knocking noises, it didn't match what I recorded that afternoon, so for now, it remains unexplained.

FINAL THOUGHTS

I have to be honest: I didn't think I was going to find anything ghostly at Loveland Castle, even after we got those weird K-II readings during the earlier overnight investigation. For me, it just seemed like a romanticized story: a man's spirit carrying on his life's work long after he's gone. I've always found the true story of Harry and his castle fascinating enough without the addition of ghosts. But lo and behold, even though I wasn't expecting it, I walked away from Loveland Castle with something I can't explain—namely, that odd knocking noise.

But you know, it's times like these that make me sit back and smile. I spend all my time harping about how ghosts are trying to keep history alive, and here are two examples of just that happening personally to me, in one place, and I'm still trying to downplay it. Guess I just need to keep in mind that Harry Andrews worked on his castle nonstop for over fifty years, so why would he let a little thing like death keep him from finishing it?

Loveland Castle
12025 Shore Road
Loveland, Ohio 45140
www.lovelandcastle.com

WESTWOOD TOWN HALL RECREATION CENTER

Westwood Town Hall is a classic example of a ghostly chicken-or-the-egg story: Which came first to this building, the ghost or the ghost story? If you ask people who either currently live or have lived in the Westwood area, chances are they can tell you all about the ghost said to haunt Westwood Town Hall. They'll probably even be able to tell you the ghost's name. But determining just who this ghost is, why he chooses to haunt Westwood Town Hall, and if he even exists at all proved a lot easier said than done.

THE HISTORY

Ever since it officially became a village in 1868, Westwood, Ohio, had continued to grow and flourish, so much so that less than twenty years later, village officials decided they needed a building to call home—a place not only for village offices but also for a fire department and jail. In December 1884, trustees for the estate of a local family, the Slevins, donated several acres of land along Harrison Pike. Village officials decided it would be the perfect spot on which to build their town hall.

The cornerstone for the Westwood Town Hall was laid on July 28, 1888, with construction beginning shortly afterward. Designed by local architects William Brown and Charles Crapsey, the multistoried building was to include a ground-level jail, complete with several cells, and a fire station. Special archways, still visible on the building today, were designed to allow the horses pulling the fire wagons to go in and out of the building. Upper levels of the town hall were designed to house offices for village officials, including Westwood's mayor, Louis Reemelin. Plans

While the building has undergone several renovations since its construction, much of the Westwood Town Hall Recreation Center looks as it did back in 1888.

even called for the construction of a council hall and a small theater for performances. And, of course, a bell tower was designed to crown the building.

The Town Hall was completed in early 1889 with the official dedication taking place in a public ceremony on Saturday, April 13, 1889. It quickly became a focal point of the village, due largely to the community center aspect of the building and the theatrical performances that took place in it. Five years after it opened, the local YMCA also moved into the building.

Westwood continued to grow, to the point that as the nineteenth century drew to a close, there were rumors that the village might become part of neighboring Cincinnati. Village officials worried that if that were to happen, there would no longer be a use for the Town Hall as the services currently operating out of them, including the fire and police, would then come from Cincinnati. The village officials' fears were realized on January 1, 1898, when Westwood was officially annexed as part of the city of Cincinnati. As a result, there was no longer a need for any of the public offices inside Westwood Town Hall. Initial plans were said to have called for the demolition of the Town Hall, but eventually it was decided to use the building for community programs.

Today, the Cincinnati Recreation Commission owns and maintains Westwood Town Hall, providing art and music classes here as well as after-school programs and even stage performances. It has been renovated extensively over the years, so while the outside looks much the same way as it did when the building was first constructed in 1888, inside it has changed considerably. Of course if the legends are true, one of the ghosts here has been hanging around for over a hundred years.

THE EXPERIENCES

While there are several ghosts said to enjoy hanging out inside Westwood Town Hall, the building's number-one specter is Wesley. According to legend, Wesley was the original caretaker of the Town Hall. One of the perks of Wesley's job was a small apartment in the basement.

Wesley is said to have loved his job, almost as much as he loved the Town Hall. When Wesley heard Westwood would be annexed to Cincinnati, he knew that meant he would be out of a job. Filled with sadness, Wesley is said to have committed suicide by hanging himself inside the Town Hall rather than leave the building. For this reason, Wesley's ghost is said to still linger inside the Westwood Town Hall, keeping a watch over both the building and the people who work here.

Tammi Nuber knew about Wesley for decades, even before she came to work at the Town Hall. "Wesley and the Town Hall go hand in hand. I grew up in the neighborhood and used to come to art classes here when I was little. So the building's always been known as being haunted," she said. But it was when Tammi started working at and spending time inside the building that she really got to know Wesley.

"You never feel like you're alone in this building," Tammi admits. She told me that even when she was working alone in the building late at night, she would feel like there was someone there with her. It wasn't a bad or creepy feeling. It was comforting, like someone watching out for her, making sure everything was OK.

Dina Hanks, who first came to Westwood Town Hall in 1990 as part of the summer theater program, also knew about the legend of Wesley, even though she hadn't met him yet. "I'd heard all the stories about Wesley," Dina told me, "but it wasn't until I'd be working here late at night in the theater that I experienced anything that you could say was his ghost."

Dina told me that when she was alone in the building, working on the stage sets, strange things would happen. "Sometimes the lights would flash on and off. Other times, you would hear doors opening and closing. And sometimes, you would be on the stage and you would look up and it would look like there was someone up inside the sound booth, even though you knew it was empty."

Marlene Trapp has been at the Westwood Town Hall for many years. She likes to think that Wesley is standing guard over the building. As evidence, she points to the fact that not a single serious injury has happened on site for as long as she can remember. "In the beginning, our playground wasn't fenced in," Marlene points out. "And we're on a busy road. So while I hate to think of it, there were plenty of opportunities for children to run out there after balls. But no one ever got hurt. No one."

Dina Hanks said she knows for a fact that Wesley is keeping an eye on things and making sure everyone stays safe. She knows because she believes he came and helped her out of a bad situation.

"We were getting ready to take the kids on a camping trip," Dina began. "I ran back in to use the bathroom and just to make sure everything was closed up." While she was in the restroom, she noticed that the window was still open. "The window was propped open with a roll of toilet paper and since we were leaving, I decided to close the window, but when I pulled the roll of toilet paper out, the window slammed down on four of my fingers."

In excruciating pain, Dina said she tried to pull her fingers free from the window, but she couldn't. "I started pulling on the window with my free hand, but I couldn't get the window to go up." As she continued to struggle, Dina said it just hit her: ask Wesley for help. "So I just said, 'Come on, Wesley, you can help me out of this one!' and all of a sudden, I was able to pull the window up." Stranger still, Dina said that somehow, her fingers weren't seriously injured. "I just went home, put some ice on them, and they were fine."

Tammi Nuber also related a tale to me about how she believes Wesley's ghost stepped in to help a young boy retrieve a toy.

Tammi was down in the Ocean Room with several children, who were all playing. One of the boys was playing with cars on the floor when one of them rolled underneath a locked door in the corner of the room. "It was a door that led to a back hallway, so we always kept it locked," Tammi explained.

The boy was upset over the loss of his car, so Tammi tried to unlock the door in order to retrieve the toy. But she couldn't get the door open, even though she had the key. "The door wouldn't budge. So finally I just said, 'Wesley, can you open the door, please?' and the door popped open."

You'd think that would be the happy ending to the story, but it wasn't. That's because even though Tammi and the boy looked all over the room, they couldn't find the car. Finally, Tammi had to break it to the boy that the car was gone and that he'd have to just play with another one. As Tammi closed and relocked the door and started to walk away, the missing car suddenly rolled out from underneath the door.

"We had looked all over for that car," Tammi said. "I have no idea where it was or how it rolled back under the door. It had to be Wesley."

On the ground floor of the Town Hall is an area that has been transformed into a ceramics room, complete with several kilns. Sometimes, the bottles of ceramic paint and stain have been known to fly off shelves or else rattle and move around. Several people have also reported feeling uneasy in the room, especially when getting close to the kilns themselves.

"From time to time, it would feel like there was something in the room with me," Dina Hanks said. "And there were times when I would be bending over, putting something in the kiln, it felt like someone was going to push you in. I wasn't the only one to experience that either."

If you're thinking this doesn't sound like the protective behavior of a ghost like Wesley, you'd be right. That's because, if a local psychic is correct, Wesley isn't the only ghost here.

"A psychic came in here and said the area around the kiln was an actual spirit portal, where spirits who weren't actual residents could come in and out of," Tammi Nuber explained.

In the back corner of the basement is something like a maintenance room, which also houses some of the electrical panels and the furnace. "It's creepy back there—a really creepy feeling," Dina Hanks told me. Part of the reason for the creepy feeling is that the area was said to be where the original cells were when part of the Town Hall functioned as a jail.

The short hallway leading to the maintenance room has been known to cause feelings of unease when people pass through. Some say it's because the bathrooms off this hallway used to house cells, too. For a period of time, there appeared to be some sort of spirit lingering in one of the restrooms.

"One time," Dina Hanks recalled, "one of the boys went to go use the bathroom in that hallway. He came running back out, screaming to me and Tammi that he couldn't turn the water off. We didn't know what he was talking about, so the two of us went into the bathroom together."

When Dina and Tammi entered the bathroom, they were struck by something odd. The cold water faucet was turned on, full blast. But that wasn't the odd thing: it was the fact that the room itself was hot. "It was like a sauna in there," Dina said.

"The mirrors and window were all steamed up, too," Tami added. "It made no sense, though, because the water coming out was ice-cold."

"There was always something weird about that bathroom," Marlene Trapp told me. "One time I got a call from our maintenance man at 6:00 in the morning. He told me he got so scared he had locked his keys inside the building." According to Marlene, the maintenance man said he walked into the boys' bathroom in the basement and found the water in the sink was turned on. He turned it all the way off and went about his business. Later that morning, he was passing through the area when he heard an odd noise coming from the boys' bathroom. Going back inside, he found that the water in the sink was on once again, going full blast. "He told me he got so scared, he ran out and left his keys in there, so he locked himself out," Marlene relayed.

So who was Wesley? That's the million-dollar question. Tom Fox has spent countless hours digging through old newspapers and historical records and has yet to come up with anything to substantiate that Wesley the caretaker ever existed. "There's no Wesley, no Westley, or even a passing reference to a caretaker committing suicide or dying at the Westwood Town Hall," Tom told me.

"Tom searched from the late 1800s until the city taking over the building. He couldn't find anything that even remotely matched up," Marlene Trapp added.

However, if there had indeed been a caretaker at Westwood Town Hall, it would appear that his apartment would have been down in the basement near what is currently known as the Ocean Room. In that area is what could have been a small bedroom and a bathroom. As for how Wesley's apartment shifted from the basement up to the attic, it appears as though the World Wide Web might be partially responsible for that. Years ago, when the Westwood Town Hall Web site was undergoing changes, a small portion of the site was dedicated to the legend of Wesley. Accompanying the story was a small photo depicting a ghost walking around in a tower. It would appear that even though there was no intended connection between the photo and the story of Wesley, people started making one. Before long, people were talking about Wesley haunting his attic apartment "in the tower."

Diane Hanks remembers that at one point, the Town Hall even got into the act. "In October, we used to take the kids up to the attic for Halloween and tell them the story of Wesley. I think at one point, someone even put a little bed up there, like it was Wesley's room." It appears that right around this time, people walking by Westwood Town Hall at night would claim they could see Wesley's ghost, looking down at them from an attic window.

A final twist in the story of Wesley came in 1997, when a local psychic came for a visit with a local TV crew. While he was there, he claimed that he could sense Wesley's spirit. What's more, the psychic said that Wesley hanged himself in the attic after watching the woman that he loved walk away.

Whether or not the ghost said to haunt Westwood Town Hall is really named Wesley doesn't matter to those who have worked here. They say it doesn't even matter if you believe there's a ghost here at all. Still, it doesn't hurt to stay on Wesley's good side, just in case. "If you were the first one in the building, you would say, 'Hi, good morning, Wesley,'" Dina Hanks said. "And if you were the last one out at night, you'd say, 'Good night, Wesley,'" Tammi Nuber added.

THE VIGIL

The Westwood Town Hall vigil was going to be truly unique. Not only would I be flying solo on this one, but due to Town Hall rules and guidelines, no one was permitted in the building after it closed for the evening. So while I was free to roam the building until approximately 11:00 P.M., I would have to vacate at that time. But that led me to an interesting solution: I would simply set up the equipment and let it run all night. I could then come by first thing the following morning and pick up everything when they opened up for business. My in-laws, Steve and Carol Flee, live in the area, so I arranged to stay with them. Thankfully, I have understanding in-laws who don't think it strange when I call them and ask, "Hey, can I come sleep at your house from, say, 2:00 A.M. until 5:00 A.M.?"

Once my overnight sleeping arrangements were in place, I set about deciding where to place the equipment for the vigil. Keeping in mind that the Town Hall was currently holding classes, I needed equipment to be unobtrusive. Plus, it needed to be in places where I'd be able to leave it all night. Here's where I ended up putting the equipment:

Attic
- one infrared video camera inside the attic door, pointing toward the middle of the attic
- one infrared video camera in the middle of the attic, pointing toward the back of the attic

Theater/Gym
- one infrared DVR camera, stage left, pointing toward the seats at the rear of the theater/gym
- one infrared DVR camera, stage right, pointing toward the seats at the rear of the theater/gym
- one infrared DVR camera, left side of rear seating, pointing toward the stage
- one infrared DVR camera, right side of rear seating, pointing toward the stage
- one Superlux condenser microphone, center stage, pointing toward the seats at the rear of the theater/gym
- one Superlux condenser microphone in the aisle of the seats at the rear of the theater/gym, pointing toward the stage

Cell Room
- one infrared video camera in the corner of the room, pointing toward the back of the room

Kiln Room
- one infrared video camera, aimed across the room and focused on the kiln

- one tri-field meter on top of the kiln
- Vernier LabPro with temperature, EMF, static electricity, and motion-detection sensors placed around the kiln

After setting everything up, the first place I wanted to spend some time in was the kiln room. As the psychic had said there was a portal in that room, I wanted to see how the room felt and if that feeling lasted the whole night or if the atmosphere in the room changed during the course of the evening. While I was setting up the equipment in the kiln room, I didn't feel anything out of the ordinary. Of course, I'm usually so focused on the equipment at that point that if Casper himself showed up, with Beetlejuice in tow, I still wouldn't notice anything. So now that the setup was out of the way, I just wanted to sit quietly in the room and see if I could connect with anything.

When I first got to the kiln room, it felt pretty normal. I had purposely put a tri-field meter on top of the kiln because it is incredibly sensitive when it comes to detecting EMF changes and even has an audible alarm. I turned it off while I was in the room, though, as I often tend to set off the alarm inadvertently.

After I sat in the room for about thirty minutes and felt nothing, I decided to pretend I was putting something in the kiln to see if I'd feel what felt like someone trying to push me into the kiln—what people had reported. I've never put anything into a kiln before, so I just randomly picked up a ceramic piece from a nearby shelf and then said out loud "OK, I'm just going to put this in the kiln here." I didn't feel anything push me, but I'm not sure if that was because there wasn't a ghost present or because he or she saw through my clever ruse.

Then I went to check out the theater/gym. Around the time I got there, it was dusk and the setting sun was starting to cast odd shadows across the floor. To get the best view of the room, I chose a spot in the middle of the seats at the back of the room, about halfway up. While I was sitting there, I began to hear a tapping sound. It sounded as though something was tapping on the windows that ran the length of the theater, on my right. The first time I heard it, it lasted for about ten full seconds and seemed to come from the window on the far right, closest to me as I was facing the windows. After approximately nine minutes of silence, I heard the noise again, only this time, the sound lasted only about four seconds

Kilns in the basement of the Rec Center. A local psychic believes these kilns mark the location of a portal, through which spirits could pass back and forth.

and sounded like something was tapping on the windows farther away from me, still on my right, but more toward the back of the theater.

From where I was sitting, I couldn't see anything moving. In fact, a portion of the windows was obscured: the bleachers had been pushed together up against the windows, partially obscuring the bottom of the windows and the windowsill. So I stood up and walked over to the bottom of the bleachers. As I was standing there, facing the windows, I heard the odd noise again. This time, it went on for a full twenty seconds and seemed as though something was moving up and down outside the windows, tapping them all as it went.

At this point, I ran over to the video camera closest to me, pulled it off its tripod, and began climbing up the bleachers to videotape whatever was making the noise. Thankfully, I had the video camera pointing in front of me, because let me tell you, the vision of me pulling my portly self up those bleachers is not a pretty sight. To be honest, I distinctly remember thinking how embarrassing it would be if I fell off the bleachers and broke some part of my body, especially since I was trying to climb with only one hand while attempting to hold the camera steady with the other. But then I realized that once I became known as the guy who cowrote *Weird Ohio*, my fans wouldn't bat an eye if I ended up in a cast after falling off some bleachers while chasing a ghost.

Regardless, I finally made it to the top of the bleachers and had a full view of both the windows and the windowsills. I didn't notice anything out of the ordinary at first, so I just balanced myself on the top of the bleachers and waited. After about fifteen minutes, I heard the noise again at the far end of the windows, but it was coming toward me. I could also barely make out a small gray shape moving. I kept my eye on the shape while trying to swing the video camera around, all the while balancing myself on the bleachers. It was hard, but I did it: the object was clearly visible in the camera and as it got closer, it started to come into view. It was a pigeon.

Yup, that's right. Yours truly, the mighty ghost hunter, was hot on the trail of a non-ghostly pigeon that had somehow managed to find its way into the theater and was now struggling to get back out. The odd sounds I had heard were the pigeon's wings beating on the windows.

Here's where things get really weird, and in a very non-ghostly way. You see, my wife, Stephanie, not only supports all my ghostly adventures, but she's also a huge animal lover. And I knew that the second I mentioned that I saw a pigeon trapped inside the theater, Steph would want to know what happened to it. And if I couldn't answer with "I helped it get back outside," I'd probably be looking at months, if not years, in the doghouse.

So while trying to decide if I was Dastardly or Muttley (don't worry if you don't get the reference—it just means you're not old like me), I somehow managed to corner and capture the pigeon—with my bare hands, no less—and then release it back outside. Oddly enough, most of it was captured on video as all of the cameras in the theater, including the one I had held while climbing to the top of the bleachers, were running at the time. If you ask nicely, I might let you view some of the footage . . . for a price.

Once I climbed back down from the bleachers and remounted the video camera to the tripod, I sat up on the stage for a while. I called out to Wesley and asked if he had just seen my act of animal-catching prowess. I then changed subjects and asked if he was actually named Wesley.

It was quiet in the theater. Very quiet. Not sensing that there was anything there with me, I decided to move up to the attic for a while.

Knowing that the attic was where a man was said to have committed suicide, I wanted to be incredibly respectful. I always find this type of vigil to be the hardest to conduct. Whenever I attempt to communicate with ghosts, I always speak to them as if they were in the room with me. I ask them their names, how old they are, what they like to do for fun. Basically, I ask questions that, if answered, will help me figure out who this ghost is or was.

But when it comes to ghosts of people who committed suicide, I always feel awkward. I mean, how do you tactfully bring up the fact that they killed themselves? So in this case, I defaulted to my standard "I am writing a book and want to get the facts straight" approach. I asked if the ghost's name was Wesley and if he had worked here as a caretaker. I then brought up the fact that, according to legend, he had passed away up here in the attic. I admitted, out loud, that I was struggling whether or not to put that bit of information in the book since I had no historical documentation to back that up. So I asked the ghost if he could help provide some clarity for me. I waited and I waited, but never received an answer.

I then spent some time down in the area said to have been used to house prisoners. I asked if there was someone here who had been killed in the building after being wrongly accused of committing a crime (another unsubstantiated story that has been making the rounds on the Internet). "If you're here," I said, "this is your chance to clear your name, once and for all." I told the ghost that he or she could take time to respond as I would be staying for a while.

Right around 11:00 P.M., I made one last check of all the audio and video devices, reset the Vernier LabPro sensors, and then let them lock up the building for the night. When I returned the next morning, I packed up the equipment and headed home. When I reviewed the materials, especially those that had been recorded during the overnight hours when no one was in the building, there was nothing out of the ordinary recorded, not even down in the kiln area where the portal is said to be. The battery on the tri-field meter on top of the kiln appeared to have died sometime around 6:15 A.M., but that was because it was left on overnight, not because of anything paranormal. Prior to the point when the batteries died, the meter never made a sound and the levels never deviated at all.

FINAL THOUGHTS

So does the ghost of Wesley really haunt Westwood Town Hall? Better yet, does Wesley even exist at all? While I can't say for certain if there's a ghost in the Town Hall, I can say for certain that Wesley does indeed exist. He may exist only in the hearts and minds of the employees of Westwood Town Hall, but he does exist.

I interviewed numerous people who either worked or volunteered at Westwood Town Hall, and all of them believed in Wesley. When I pressed them for more information, it became clear to me that what they believed in was the *essence* of Wesley and what that represented—a loving, caring fatherly figure who watched over them and the building—as opposed to a ghost. I think that's why, to the people of Westwood Town Hall, the specifics of who Wesley was pale in comparison to what he means to them: he is the building's past who watches over its future.

Westwood Town Hall Recreation Center
3017 Harrison Avenue
Cincinnati, Ohio 45211
www.cincyrec.org/search/facility.aspx?id=40

INN AT VERSAILLES

Even since the movie *1408* came out in 2007, many of my fans, friends, and even family members have been comparing me to the movie's main character, Mike Enslin. Aside from the fact that Mike is one of my least favorite names, I have to admit that there are more than a few similarities between Mr. Enslin and myself. If you haven't seen the movie, it is about a writer who travels around, looking for haunted places to write about in his books. Of course, most of the movie is about what happens when the main character spends the night inside a haunted hotel room.

So when the opportunity arrived for me to spend the night locked inside a haunted hotel room right here in Ohio, I jumped at the chance.

THE HISTORY

The village of Versailles went through several name changes in its history. It was originally platted in August 1819 as Jacksonville, named for a man who had made a name for himself as a military leader in the War of 1812: future president of the United States, Andrew Jackson.

The village of Jacksonville continued to grow and prosper over the years. However, in 1837, residents of Jacksonville were looking for a name change. In December 1837, they filed a petition to officially change the village name to Versailles.

Old habits die hard, though, and five years later, when it came time to name a new section of land that had been platted outside of Versailles village limits, the name North Jacksonville was chosen. In 1855, however, North Jacksonville was officially incorporated into the village of Versailles, where it remains today.

July 6, 1901, stands as the darkest day in the history of the village of Versailles. The Fourth of July fell on a Thursday that year, so villagers celebrated the holiday on Saturday, two days later. While the morning air was filled with sounds of people laughing and celebrating, early that afternoon, smoke began to fill the skies over Versailles and cries of "Fire!" were heard. On the west side of the village, near the railroad tracks, Sheffel Mill, a three-story building that had been abandoned for some time, was ablaze.

Residents ran toward the mill and attempted to put out the fire, but it was too late. In no time at all, the building was fully engulfed in flames and the fire began to spread. Despite attempts to contain the fire, it quickly moved eastward from the mill toward Main Street, no doubt aided by the 30 miles-per-hour winds that were whipping through the village.

Once the fire reached Main Street, it engulfed everything in its path. Entire buildings all along the north side of Main Street were swallowed up by the fire, sending burning debris into the sky, where the winds carried it across the street, igniting several buildings on the south side of Main Street, too.

While the call went out for help, the nearest fire department—in Greenville—was over twenty miles away. So while they waited, residents did whatever they could to stop the flames that were making their way across the village. People threw buckets of water and even slapped at the flames with blankets and stamped them with their feet while citizens dragged what personal belongings they could from the burning buildings. Perhaps one of the strangest scenes that day was a group of men who, after realizing they would be unable to stop the fire from destroying a tavern, rushed into the building to retrieve a keg of beer. They broke open the keg in the middle of the street, poured the beer into their hats, took a drink, and then returned to fight the fire.

The fire managed to burn for almost four full hours before it was finally brought under control. When all was said and done, the fire had managed to destroy six full blocks, including the Snyder Hotel, in the center of the village. Close to forty residences were also lost in the fire. Altogether, the loss was estimated, in 1901 dollars, at $350,000. Miraculously, no one died that day. In fact, there wasn't even a single severe injury reported.

The building on the corner of Main Street in Versailles actually comprises two establishments. Michael Anthony's At the Inn occupies most of the main floor, while the Inn at Versailles is on the upper floor.

The exact cause of the fire was never established, although it is believed that sparks from a passing train may have ignited the abandoned mill. However, given that this was the Fourth of July weekend, the theory that some leftover fireworks might have been to blame can't be discounted. Either way, the village of Versailles was quick to rebound, and only a year later, Main Street was almost entirely rebuilt.

By 1904, the Snyder Hotel had reopened for business at its former location at the corner of Main and Center streets. As it had been before the fire, most of the hotel was on the second floor of the building while the first floor was occupied by various stores and businesses. That's how it would remain for almost a hundred years, when the entire building was sold. The new owners turned both floors of the building into

L'Hôtel de Versailles, with the guest rooms on the second floor and a new hotel restaurant on the first floor, complete with a kitchen and a full-service bar. In January 2004, the building once again underwent renovations and a name change. Now it was the Inn at Versailles. The restaurant was also given a new name: Michael Anthony's at the Inn.

Today, both the Inn at Versailles and Michael Anthony's at the Inn welcome weary travelers and hungry guests from all over the world to come in and relax. As far as they're concerned, it doesn't matter who you are; all are welcome—even if you're a ghost.

THE EXPERIENCES

Telisa Delligatta has been the dining room manager for the Inn at Versailles' restaurant since 2004, when she and her husband, who is executive chef, took over the restaurant. She said that when she first came to the restaurant, she had no idea that it was supposed to be haunted. "But it only took a while for people to say to me, 'Well, you know this place is haunted, right?' Servers and everybody would tell me that. When I asked them who haunts this building, they would all say, 'We call him Fred.'"

Once she started asking around, Telisa soon discovered that while no one was really sure who this ghost known as Fred was, or his real name for that matter, on rare occasions when he was spotted, he always wore what was described as a plain shirt and looked like "a handyman." He also apparently liked to hang out in the basement of the building. And even if you couldn't see Fred, you'd know he was around if you smelled men's cologne or cigar smoke.

Sure enough, before too long, Telisa would occasionally catch a whiff of cigar smoke in the basement. "One of the first things I did when we got here was to start building up our wine inventory. You know, cellaring it in the basement, so I was down there a lot. And since I deal with wine so much, I have a very, very sensitive palate. But there would be times when I'd be down in that basement and I would start smelling cigar smoke."

Fred apparently didn't let the Inn's no-smoking policy prevent him from lighting up in the guest rooms either. "There's been times when I'm upstairs and smelled cigar smoke coming from one of the rooms. So I have to go knock on the door and tell them, 'You can't do that. This is a non-smoking hotel.' But then you find out nobody's smoking

The Inn at Versailles as it sits on the corner of Main and Center streets.

in that room or, better yet, there's no one staying in that room," Telisa explained.

The kitchen of Michael Anthony's at the Inn, known for creating a wide assortment of culinary delights, also appears to attract the attention of the Inn's ghosts. "There's a lot of weird activity in the kitchen," Telisa said, "but it sort of comes and goes in clusters. Sometimes there won't be anything weird for months and then stuff just starts happening almost every night."

Some of the reported activity includes silverware moving on its own, glassware falling and breaking with no one around it, and even a coffee grinder that likes to turn itself on and off. "There have been times when we're just standing in the kitchen and things just fall off the shelves and there's no reason for it," Telisa told me.

Employees working in the kitchen long after the restaurant has closed for the night will sometimes see what they take to be people walk through the kitchen and out into the dining room. But when they go to look, there's no one there.

Telisa has never seen any ghosts walk through the building, but she still doesn't like to be the last one to leave at night, so if she's going to leave late, other employees will often sit and wait for her. Good thing, too, because one night, something happened in the kitchen that made Telisa glad someone else was there to witness it.

The restaurant had been closed for some time, and all the employees had left for the night, except a female staff member who was waiting in the darkened bar for Telisa to finish her final walk-through for the evening. "I was just finishing up and walking through the building, making sure everything was turned off," Telisa explained. "When I got to the bar, almost as soon as I sat down, I heard 'crash, bang, boom' from the kitchen."

The two women stared at each other, each too frightened to go see what the noise was but also not wanting to stay in the darkened bar alone. In the end, they decided they would go together to investigate the kitchen.

As soon as the pair entered the kitchen, Telisa saw what had caused the noise: there was a large breadboard propped up against the wall. But she couldn't figure out, though, how that breadboard got there.

At Michael Anthony's at the Inn, the breadboards are specially designed to fit snugly into place on top of the bread maker so that employees won't cut directly on the stainless steel. They fit so snugly that at the end of the night, employees have to use a spatula to pry them out in order to run them through the dishwasher before returning them to their designated place on top of the bread maker.

"When I came through the kitchen the first time, I swear the board was on top of the bread machine. That's the routine—that's where it goes. There was no breadboard propped up against that wall. There's no shelves there anyway—it's just a wall—so there's no way it could have just fallen," Telisa said.

"There was no place for that bread board to have come from. I know what I saw, I know what I heard, and I know what I saw when I came back into the kitchen. In my opinion, there's not many logical explanations," Telisa concluded.

The ghosts believed to haunt the Inn at Versailles aren't limited to just roaming around the restaurant. They have been known to head upstairs and hang out in the guest rooms. Telisa even let me in on a secret: they say that the ghosts like to call down to the front desk at night. "Sometimes, down at the front desk, the phone will ring and the calls are coming from rooms that we don't have guests in," Telisa admitted.

"What's really weird is that sometimes the calls come from room numbers that don't exist. We get calls from room 100, but we don't have a room 100 at the Inn. And when we pick up the phone, there's no one on the other end. No dial tone either. Just silence and then a click."

Telisa also related a tale involving an extended-stay customer who, while he didn't know it at the time, was sharing the Inn with a ghost.

"This gentleman had been staying with us for a few weeks and he was in room 112," Telisa explained. "One Saturday night, it turned out that he was going to be our only guest, so I told him we would put breakfast out for him, but since he'd be the only guest, if he needed anything, to call me on my cell phone.

"Monday morning," Telisa continued, "the gentleman comes downstairs and says, 'Did you have someone end up booking a room after you talked to me on Saturday?' When I told him, 'No, you were here all by yourself,' he looked at me and said, 'Actually, I wasn't.'"

The man went on to explain that over the weekend, he decided to head down to the local sports bar for an early dinner. He was locking the door to his room when he saw another man walking down the hallway toward him. Surprised to see another customer at the Inn, the man watched as the mysterious figure turned and went into one of the rooms at the end of the hallway. Only the man didn't bother to open the door to the room. Rather, he simply appeared to walk through the closed door. The room number? 108.

Telisa said that there had been reports of ghosts inside room 108 at the Inn long before she came to the building. "Probably the first story I heard was that one night, a Marine who had been staying in room 108 came down to the front desk in the middle of the night and said he couldn't stay in the room anymore." Telisa said the Marine had been sound asleep in room 108 when he was woken up by someone shaking the bed. Opening his eyes, he found that he was no longer alone in the room; there was a shadowy figure of a man standing beside the bed. Without saying a word, the figure turned and headed toward the door to the room. But just as he reached the door, the figure turned to his left and promptly walked through the wall. "They told me the Marine was so shaken up, he didn't even want to stay in the Inn anymore," Telisa said.

Telisa told me that the first time she heard the story about the Marine in room 108, she wrote it off as nothing more than an exaggerated ghost story. But then guests began telling her there was something going on inside that room. "I kept getting reports of people in room 108 being woken up in the middle of the night by something shaking their bed or shaking them—something physically shaking them and waking them up." Sometimes, guests would wake up to an odd smell in the room with them. "Most people described the smell as being like a heavy menthol smell—like menthol or eucalyptus," Telisa explained.

Telisa went on to tell me that sometimes people get so frightened that they can't even stay the rest of the night at the Inn. "I've had people in room 108 get so frightened by what's happening in the room that they go out and sleep in the Breakfast Room because they don't want to stay in the room. And I've had people leave and go stay at other hotels. I literally had people leave in the middle of the night and go get rooms in Greenville [about twenty minutes away]. That's happened twice, that I can recall," Telisa said.

The longer Telisa was at the Inn, the more reports about room 108 kept coming in. And with each new report, Telisa found it harder and harder to dismiss the notion that there were ghosts in that room. "What I find hard to explain," Telisa admitted, "is that none of the people experiencing things in 108 know each other. These people come from all over the country and work for all different companies, so it's not like they could have told each other, 'This is what happened when I was there.' And yet, they all tell the same story."

Before long, word started spreading around Versailles that the Inn had its very own haunted room, attracting the attention of ghost hunters and curiosity-seekers. It even piqued the interest of Marie,* a local businesswoman, who decided one night to see what lurked behind the door of room 108. It would be a night she would not soon forget.

Marie clearly was uncomfortable telling me her story. After a while, she finally took a deep breath and then began: "We had three girls within our department that were getting married. So one Friday night, our department all came uptown—kind of like for a bachelorette party for these girls. So we were just out, you know, doing a little barhopping. And one of the girls said, 'Let's go up to the Inn and get that haunted room. That will be fun. Let's get room 108.'

"So we rented the room, and a few of us went up there. There was a couple of us in the beginning. And we were just sitting around, making

*Fictitious name; she asked that her real name not be given.

jokes, and saying things like, 'Come on, Fred' and 'We want to see you, Fred.' You know, it was like a big joke," Marie said, nervously. As the night wore on, some of the women decided to leave. In the end, Marie and Cathy* were the only two left. "At that point, it was so late that we both just decided to go to sleep," Marie said.

"The next morning, we both woke up early. It was still dark out," Marie said. "Cathy was in the bathroom, so I was just kind of lying in bed. It was pitch dark, but when I looked over at the wall next to the door, I saw these—this is going to sound crazy—but I saw these balls of light, moving in and out of the wall. They were different colors, too— blue, green, and a lot that were red."

Marie paused here for a moment before continuing. It was clear to me that even though this had happened years ago, the memory of it still affected her. Then she continued: "The more I stared at them, it was like each one had a face—just a face. And the faces looked—none of them looked happy—they looked angry or sad. I can't even explain how bad they looked. The most terrible looks I've ever seen on these faces. One of them would go through the wall and then another one would appear. It was eerie and it was almost like they were looking at me. So I kept watching it for a little while, and finally I just turned the light on."

Up until this point, while Marie was telling me this story, she hadn't been looking directly at me. Instead, she was looking over my shoulder, almost as if it made her uncomfortable to look me in the eye while she was relating what happened to her. But then she turned her gaze toward me, and we made eye contact. I could tell from the look in her eyes that Marie was trying to determine whether or not I believed what she was telling me. Apparently satisfied with what she saw, Marie resumed telling the story.

"When Cathy came out of the bathroom, I didn't say anything to her because I thought she was going to think I was nuts. So we left, and when I got home, I told my husband, but he was like, 'What are you talking about?' I've tried researching it and looking things up online to try and explain what it was I saw, but I still have no clue."

Telisa picked the story up at this point: "At first, I didn't know any of that had happened. But after lunch one day, Marie told me about it and

*Fictitious name; she asked that her real name not be given.

The interior of room 108 at the Inn at Versailles. The alleged portal is located directly behind me.

she had tears in her eyes when she was telling me. When she was done, I was like, 'Oh my god, Marie, why didn't you tell me?' She said, 'I just thought that everyone would think I was crazy.'"

Almost as soon at Telisa took over the restaurant, renovations began on most of the guest rooms at the Inn. A year later, two of Telisa's friends, Joerdie Fisher and Susan Fantz, came to the Inn for dinner. Knowing that Joerdie was supposed to have some psychic abilities, Telisa decided to take the two women upstairs to show them the remodeling . . . and to let them take a peek inside room 108. "But I deliberately did not tell Joerdie anything about room 108 before I took her up there," Telisa points out. "I wanted to see if she would pick up on anything."

"We'd never been in the building before that night," Susan Fantz explained. "Joerdie and I knew Telisa from her other restaurant, so we thought we would come out here and support her."

Joerdie Fisher told me that she wasn't picking up on anything prior to entering room 108. But once inside, that all changed. Here is what Joerdie told me she experienced in room 108:

I first felt something as soon as I walked in the door. I walked in the door, and where the bed is, I saw a desk and there was a man in a uniform that looked like he was some sort of official. And he had a huge sword. As he's sitting there, his sword is touching the ground, but it was standing straight up. The room was set up like an office, and where the chest of drawers is [currently positioned in the room], I saw a door. And a younger man dressed in a simple military uniform, walking back and forth, bringing papers to this commander. And he was signing them and saying things to him, and this young man would go back.

At one point, Susan and Telisa were standing where this [ghost] door was, and he [young ghost] just stopped and put his arm around them. Then the whole thing just faded.

When I asked Joerdie for more details about what she saw in room 108, she added, "It was very detailed, but it was transparent. Sometimes when I see them, they are dense—you can't see through them. I don't know what the difference means." She also allowed me to sketch out where things in her vision were in relation to the real items in the room. She placed the desk in the center of the wall where the headboard to the bed currently is. As for the door the young ghost kept walking in and out of, she put that directly opposite the wall where the headboard was, along the same wall Marie had seen the ghost faces moving in and out of.

Neither Telisa nor Susan reported seeing anything out of the ordinary while they were standing in room 108 with Joerdie. Hearing that the young ghost allegedly put his arms around Telisa and Susan, I asked the two women if they had felt anything touch them while they were in the room. They both said "No" with Susan adding, "The room felt weird, but I didn't feel like a touch or anything."

THE VIGIL

While I had previously investigated the Inn at Versailles with The Ghosts of Ohio, this was going to be a truly unique vigil for me because not only was I flying solo on this one, but I was also planning on spending the night—alone—inside room 108.

When I first arrived at the Inn, I immediately unloaded Ol' Blue, my 1997 Honda Accord, and brought all the equipment up to room 108. If you ever decide to rent room 108, the first time you open the door and walk in, you'll probably be disappointed, not because it's not a nice room. Quite the contrary. It's just that after hearing all the spooky stories about this room, you'd be forgiven if you were expecting to walk into something straight out of Stephen King's *The Shining*. But it's just a small, cozy little room. As I was setting up the equipment in the room, I didn't feel the least bit creeped out. I was actually quite excited.

You see, room 108 at the Inn at Versailles holds a special place in my ghostly heart due to a strange thing that happened during my previous investigation with The Ghosts of Ohio. Having heard the stories about a "portal" in the room where ghostly soldiers and glowing faces come and go, we decided to hang all the remote sensors from the Vernier Lab-Pro on that wall, including a static electricity sensor. I use a static electricity sensor because I believe that ghosts, if nothing more, are a form of energy. And since static electricity is, at its very essence, an imbalance of electric charges that can have an impact on humans (mild shocks, hair standing up), then perhaps "ghost energy" can have an impact on static electricity—in theory, at least.

On every single investigation and vigil where we have used the static electricity sensor, it has recorded the same exact thing: a steady buildup over time of the level of static electricity. It happens like that everywhere, not just in places that are supposed to be haunted. Static electricity naturally builds up over time. Not a lot, but it does build up. However, on ghost vigils, we set our sensors in such a way that we are continually re-setting the static electricity sensor because it increases over the course of an evening. But like I said, that's normal and the static electricity almost always elevates over time. The one exception was inside room 108.

During the vigil with The Ghosts of Ohio, the static electricity sensor recorded a drop in static electricity in room 108, which doesn't make sense. The levels should have gone up, especially since we kept adding people into the room. Stranger still, the levels weren't gradually dropping. They would drop only when there were women in the room. During the course of the evening, we tried an impromptu experiment where we kept changing the assortment of people in room 108, resetting the static electricity sensor each time. One time, it was all women, then all men, then a mix of men and women. Finally, all women again. Oddly enough, the levels dropped only when there were only women in the room. If there were all men or a mixture of men and women in the room, the levels either remained steady or else steadily climbed, which is normal. Needless to say, I was eager to see what would happen to the static electricity levels when I was in that room all alone.

Here was the equipment I set up inside room 108:

- three infrared video cameras, one on either side of the bed, each pointing toward the wall near the door (where the Vernier LabPro sensors were hanging)
- one Superlux condenser microphone in the far corner of the room, aimed across the bed and toward the door
- one tri-field meter on top of the dresser, facing the bed
- Vernier LabPro with temperature, EMF, static electricity, and motion-detection sensors hanging on and around the section of wall believed to be a "portal"

After all the equipment was set up, I headed downstairs and did a walk-through of the entire Inn, as well as Michael Anthony's. As the restaurant was open for business, I spent most of my time down in the basement, sniffing around to see if I could detect some of the smoke from Fred's cigar. I also sat in the wine cellar, asking Fred for an interview. He wasn't talking this night, so I headed back upstairs.

Prior to the vigil, I asked Joerdie Fisher, Susan Fantz, and Telisa Delligatta to accompany me to room 108. I wanted to see if any of the women, especially Joerdie, felt anything out of the ordinary. I should probably state here that when it comes to psychics, I have developed something of a love-hate relationship with them. I firmly believe that there are certain people who are more in tune with the surrounding environment and are able to pick up on things most people can't. In fact, I believe that we are all "psychic" to a certain extent. Put it this way: we've all walked into a party and immediately determined that we don't like a certain stranger based solely on the vibe he or she is giving off. I believe that's what psychics do, only on a much grander scale. What I struggle with is that many psychics tend to make generic, blanket statements that can never be independently confirmed or else are so vague that individuals can attribute all sorts of different meanings to what is being said. Put another way, when it comes to psychics—and I have used them on investigations over the years—I need to have my equipment react to something at the same time that the psychic is sensing things in order for me to consider an event as possibly supernatural.

Almost as soon as we walked through the door of room 108, Joerdie turned to me and said, "My ears are popping." When I asked her

LabPro sensors arranged along the wall said to contain the portal in the Inn at Versailles's room 108.

what that meant, she replied, "That there is all kinds of energy swirling around here—a lot of concentrated energy. It's like I'm on an elevator that keeps going up and down."

When I played back the audio from this point in the evening, as Joerdie is describing the energy she is feeling, I found that I had managed to record what sounds like a woman saying "stop" over and over, a grand total of three times. Examining the "voice" with audio-analyzing software shows that it does not match the voice imprint of any of the people who were in the room at the time. Regardless, I don't recognize the voice, nor do I remember any of the others in the room commenting on hearing the "voice" at the time.

Joerdie began walking around the room and commented that as long as she was moving, the feeling in her ears would stop. But if she came to a stop near the wall directly opposite the bed, she said her ears would pop and it felt like she had water in her ears. "Something's going to happen," she told me. "I just don't know what it will be."

When I asked Joerdie if she could tell if there was someone else in the room with us, she told me, "No, I just feel energy. It just feels like a collection of energy." At this point, I noticed from the Vernier Lab-Pro ambient temperature devices that the temperature along the wall was dropping. In fact, it dropped roughly five degrees in thirty seconds, which doesn't sound like a lot, but it is. Until this point, the temperature had been a steady sixty-nine degrees for roughly the past four hours. Now that there were additional people in the room, the temperature had dropped to sixty-four degrees, even though you'd think the addition of people to the room would cause the temperature to rise, not fall, so it was a little odd. This was the only strange temperature variance to be recorded the entire evening.

After a while, the ladies left me for the evening, but not before Joerdie told me, "It just feels really heavy in here. I think you're going to experience something tonight."

Once they were gone, I checked all the equipment to ensure it was still running correctly. Then I changed and got ready for bed. Now, I'm sure the idea of sleeping in a haunted hotel room sounds really exciting and spooky. Exciting? Yes. But spooky? Not this night. I had a 5:30 A.M. wake-up call waiting for me, so when I finally turned off the lights and lay there, prepared to wait all night for the ghosts to appear, I was out cold in less than fifteen minutes. Good thing I had set all the equipment to run all night.

Days later, when I sat down and went through everything I'd recorded that night, other than my realizing how heavy my breathing is when I sleep (and that I barely moved at all during the night), there were no anomalies captured on video or audio. As for the static electricity sensor, after steadily climbing for the first two hours after I had reset it, around 2:45 A.M., it suddenly did an about-face and started dropping steadily. It did that for about ninety minutes, at which point the levels started climbing again. No idea what caused that, probably because I was sleeping like a baby at that point.

FINAL THOUGHTS

So what are we to make of the strange occurrences inside room 108? On the one hand, this was one of the few times that I have had a psychic's claims/impressions backed up by variances noted by the equipment, most notably the temperature gauges. And then there's the whole notion of what appears to be a woman's voice on the recorder at almost the same exact time that Joerdie was having her experience. So this could be some rather compelling evidence, if you will. But on the other hand, the temperature change could simply be dismissed as a coincidence. And while the woman's voice is very clear and distinct, we can't simply ignore the fact that everyone who saw a ghost in room 108, including the psychic, stated what they saw was male—the only exception being the "faces" Marie saw coming out of the wall (she was not able to determine the gender of the faces).

When it comes right down to it, room 108 at the Inn at Versailles is one of the most perplexing and fascinating places I've ever had the honor of spending the night in. I have no idea what the spirits of this room or building might be trying to tell me, but then again, the best part of ghost hunting is the thrill of the hunt.

Inn at Versailles
21 W. Main Street
Versailles, Ohio 45380
www.innatversailles.com

MUSEUM AT THE FRIENDS HOME

Waynesville, Ohio, has long been known as one of the favorite haunts for antique seekers. Somewhere along the line, it managed to acquire the moniker, "The most haunted village in Ohio," so naturally, I wanted to find a place in Waynesville for my book. Finding a location that was alleged to be haunted wasn't a problem. In fact, I had many to choose from. But I wasn't just looking for ghosts; I wanted history, too. And what better place to get history than at the local museum? And wouldn't you know it? The museum's supposed to be haunted, too!

THE HISTORY

George Fox, born in England in July 1624 and credited with starting the religious movement known as the Quakers, grew up a very confused man. His family was very religious, as were most of his neighbors and friends. Yet Fox saw something lacking in the Christian-based faith he was brought up in. He was also confused by the fact that he was told God would never speak directly to him. Rather, God would speak to other religious individuals, who would then interpret the message and relay it to Fox via a public sermon. Fox didn't think that people needed a middleman and that God, being God and all, could speak to whomever he wanted. Fox also found the church somewhat hypocritical in that it was teaching followers to live peaceful, simple lives, all the while waging war against other faiths and building huge, ornate churches. Fox decided to start preaching his own ideas about both the Bible and God and was instantly labeled a heretic and a blasphemer.

Around the early 1650s, George Fox had acquired a rather large group of followers who believed in his teachings. Calling themselves the Religious Society of Friends, Fox's followers believed in what they termed the four basic testimonies: Integrity, Simplicity, Equality, and Peace. While everyone today would agree that those are good ideals to live by, in seventeenth-century England, those ideals were very controversial because they were not put forth by the Church of England. Fox and his followers were frequently harassed and, on more than one occasion, arrested.

In 1650, Fox was hauled in before the court on charges of blasphemy. His journal, published in 1694, recounts that as he stood before his accusers, he told one of the justices to "tremble at the word of the Lord." He recounted: "This was Justice [Gervase] Bennet, of Derby, who was the first that called us Quakers." The name stuck. And Fox was found guilty of blasphemy and sentenced to a jail term.

Although Fox continued preaching after his release, it became almost impossible for him to escape constant harassment from local officials. Seeking answers, Fox sat down with a few of his close friends, including real estate entrepreneur (and fellow Quaker) William Penn. It is believed that Penn first suggested to Fox that they should move to America to escape the religious persecution. And that's exactly what they did. Beginning in the 1670s, William Penn brought a large constituent of Quakers to America with him, initially settling in an area now known as the state of New Jersey. They would quickly expand and settle in Philadelphia.

By the 1700s, the Quakers had continued to grow and thrive. In the process, their reach began to expand, too. Eventually they moved out of Philadelphia and down the Appalachian Mountains into Virginia, North Carolina, and South Carolina. Near the end of the eighteenth century, Quakers were the third largest religious group in the entire United States.

In 1797, the town of Waynesville was founded in an area that was still considered part of the Northwest Territory. Several years later, Quaker Abijah O'Neall and several other "Friends" from South Carolina—Quakers don't like titles as they believe everyone is equal, so fellow Quakers are always referred to simply as "Friends"—purchased a piece of land in Waynesville and moved their families, making them the first and only Quakers to settle in the area. In just a few short years, that would all change: on March 1, 1803, Ohio was admitted into the Union as a free state. In South Carolina in the same year, at a historic gathering of Quakers known as the Bush River Meeting, Zachariah Dix stood up and reminded everyone at the meeting that one of the founding Testimonies of the Quaker faith is "Equality"—namely, that all men, women, and children are created equal. Dix argued that Quakers could not claim to be upholding the Equality Testimony as long as they were living in a state that condoned and practiced slavery. Many Quakers agreed, and a mass exodus from Southern slave-holding states began. Many of the Quakers from South and North Carolina chose to relocate to Waynesville, Ohio, causing a population explosion there almost overnight. In fact, so many Quakers relocated to Waynesville that before 1803 ended, they had enough members to set up their very own local meeting (the "meeting" is the Quaker equivalent of a church service).

The first Quaker meeting was held in Waynesville in October 1803. Shortly thereafter, Waynesville sent representatives to the Indiana Yearly Meeting, the annual gathering where Quakers from Indiana, Ohio, and Illinois would gather to discuss business, including proposals for new construction.

The Quaker community at Waynesville continued to thrive and expand over the years. As they approached the settlement's one-hundredth anniversary, discussions had begun to take place as to how to best care for some of the elderly original settlers of the area. One idea was establishing a Friends Boarding Home, where people, including the elderly, could rent rooms, making the building a combined boardinghouse and retirement home. As many Quaker communities centered around agriculture and farming, often when a husband passed away, the wife would be unable to care for the farm on her own. A review of the Indiana Yearly Meeting Minutes shows that the idea of creating a Friends Boarding Home in Waynesville was brought up for discussion as early as 1900.

Regardless, construction was put on hold until the required monies could be raised: $15,000. It took several years and several donors to gather the funds, but in May 1904, a local newspaper, the *Miami Gazette,* announced that construction of the Friends Boarding Home was to begin "soon." An October issue of the same newspaper even ran the "official plans" for the Home, which included, in part, that:

The building is to be 58 feet front by 50 feet deep, two story with basement below and unfinished attic above. The foundation and all walls are made of concrete, outside walls to be veneered with dressed brick, roof to be tile, supported by an iron post above the square.

The contract includes complete installation of both city and rain water, the latter hot and cold in bathrooms, closets, wash stands and laundry.

The original design called for most of the rooms to be single-occupancy, with a few suites that could accommodate two people, such as a husband and wife or, as was more likely the case, a patient and a nurse. The building was also equipped with common areas such as living rooms and even a dining room with seating for forty people.

The Fox Brothers, a contracting firm in Cincinnati, was originally hired to construct the Boarding Home, but they soon had a falling-out and the final construction was overseen by Aaron B. Chandler, who would be named superintendent of the building upon its completion.

In September 1905, Lydia Conard began her duties as the matron of the Friends Boarding Home. The following month, the building officially opened for business and accepted its first boarder, Mrs. Mary Terrell of New Vienna, Ohio. The following year, all the rooms at the Friends Boarding Home were filled and they had to turn people away. In the early days of the Boarding Home, $3.50 a week got you room, board, and your laundry done. You could even invite a friend for Sunday dinner, but that would cost you an extra 25 cents. And while most of the rooms were occupied by seniors and widows, that didn't mean there wasn't opportunity for love to bloom. Case in point is what could be termed a "workplace romance." Home matron Lydia Conard married the home's superintendent, Aaron Chandler, on October 27, 1908. They lived together at the Boarding Home until 1910, when they purchased their own home.

In the ensuing decades, the Friends Boarding Home continued to accept new boarders, especially those in the later years of their life. The Home was often filled to capacity, so much so that before long, there was a need for a larger facility. In the late 1960s, pastureland behind the Boarding Home was donated and set aside for the construction of a larger, more modern assisted-living facility. In 1972, the Quaker Heights

View of the Museum at the Friends Home from Fourth Street.

Nursing Home opened for business and some of the Boarding Home residents were relocated there. Since it opened, the nursing home continued to expand. Today, the facility is known at the Quaker Heights Care Community and can accommodate almost 160 residents.

But the expansion of the modern facility literally in its backyard meant that there was not much need for the older Boarding Home. In 2000, the Friends Boarding Home was leased to the Waynesville Area Cultural Center, which turned the building into the Museum at the Friends Home. Today, the museum contains over twenty rooms, each filled with historic artifacts and exhibits focusing not only on aspects of Quaker life and the history of Waynesville, but also on memories of local communities and schoolhouses. One of the most intriguing items the museum currently houses is a detailed record book with the names of everyone who ever stayed at the Boarding Home. Of course, that runs a close second to the old cot from the Phillips Hotel that Abraham

Lincoln is said to have taken a nap on during a stopover on his way to Washington.

THE EXPERIENCES

Linda Morgan was here when the Waynesville Area Cultural Center first took over the building in 2000. She doesn't recall ever hearing stories of it being haunted. "There was a gentleman in town who would sometimes tell ghost stories about places in Waynesville," Linda explained, "but nothing about the boardinghouse." So the first time people told Linda they saw a ghost in the boardinghouse, she was skeptical, to say the least. "It was shortly after we moved in here," Linda recalled. "Two women were here for the art show, and they said a lady came down one of the main staircases, looked at them [the women], and then went back up. It was the first time anyone said they saw a ghost here, so to be honest, none of us really took it seriously."

The following December, Linda was inside the museum, working at their Christmas Open House, when a middle-aged woman came in. "She asked me if a little girl ever lived in the boardinghouse," Linda recalled. She told the woman that it was not common for children to live in the boardinghouse as it was designed as accommodation for seniors or single people. In fact, Linda could recall only one instance of a child living here—a young girl named Ruthie, who lived at the boardinghouse briefly with her mother before they moved on. Intrigued by the question, Linda asked the woman why she wanted to know if children ever lived in the boardinghouse.

"The woman told me her daughter was afraid to walk past the building because of what she saw here," Linda confessed. The woman told Linda that her daughter and a friend were walking home from a local football game one night. As they were passing the Friends Boarding Home, the daughter looked up and saw a young girl in a white dress standing on the porch. While she could clearly see the girl, right down to the bow in her hair, the daughter told her mother that she just felt there was something not right about the girl. For one thing, she was wearing a dress that looked to be from a different time period. "So the daughter turned to her friend and said, 'Why is that girl standing up there on the porch, dressed like that?'" Linda relayed. When the daughter and her friend turned back to look at the girl, they found the porch empty. The little girl had simply vanished in a matter of seconds.

"The other thing that started happening around that time," Linda continued, "was that we all started smelling pipe tobacco in the building, especially in the dining room. And nobody smokes in here. You would just be sitting in there and you would smell the tobacco. And then it would just disappear." Linda even remembers a time when a group of people gathered in the kitchen and they all smelled the pipe smoke. "We were having our book club meeting," Linda said. "Somebody said, 'Who's smoking?' and then we all smelled it. Went through the whole building but never found where the smoke was coming from. It was there one minute and then it just disappeared."

Mary Bunker has been the curator at the museum since 2002. Like Linda Morgan, Mary hadn't heard any stories about the building being haunted prior to starting work there. Mary was also quick to point out that she's not really sure if she even believes in ghosts. However, her relationship with a former museum docent, Carol,* has made Mary consider reevaluating her stance on the afterlife. Mary explains: "Carol had a lot of health problems and was even on oxygen. But she loved working here, even though it meant she had to tote her oxygen tank down here with her."

Mary continued: "So Carol and I became friends. Around 2002 or 2003, I noticed her health was starting to deteriorate. One day, she told me, 'I know I'm not going to live a lot longer. But when I pass away, I'm going to come back and let you know that I'm OK.' We had several conversations like that," Mary told me.

Sadly, Carol did pass away a short time later. Then one afternoon, after the museum had closed for the day, Mary was working in her office in the basement when she heard the doorbell ring. "So I went upstairs, thinking someone wanted to come in and see the museum," she said. Only when she got upstairs, there was no one there. "So I went back downstairs and maybe ten or fifteen minutes later, the doorbell rings again. And like last time, when I got up there, nobody was there." A bit annoyed this time, Mary once again went back downstairs to her office and started working again. Before long, the doorbell went off again. "This happened like eight

*This is a pseudonym.

times," Mary said, sounding exhausted just telling me about it. "Finally, I just said out loud, 'OK, Carol, I got it!' And you know something? That doorbell didn't ring again that afternoon, and it hasn't happened since," Mary concluded.

Linda Morgan has also had the museum's doorbell act strangely in her presence, even apparently alerting her to an unlocked door. "I was here one day by myself, doing the Saturday tour," Linda told me. "At the end of the day, I turned off all the lights and went out to my car." But as Linda got ready to drive away from the museum, a thought crossed her mind: Did she lock the front door?

Returning to the museum, Linda found that she had indeed locked the front door. But fearing that shaking the door to test the lock would set off the museum's burglar alarm, she unlocked the door and went inside, turning off the alarm with the intention of resetting it and leaving as soon as the alarm was ready. "Just as I turned the alarm off," Linda explained, "the doorbell in back of me rang. So I went over and discovered that the other door to the house wasn't locked. I locked it and I don't know why, but I said, 'Thank you, Carol.' I just felt the alarm was her doing."

Bill Stubbs has spent a lot of time helping out at the museum. He thinks that Carol's ghost might indeed be responsible for ringing the doorbell. "We've kidded each other about the doorbell ringing," Bill stated, "but it seems like something Carol would do. She had serious breathing problems, so she couldn't do much physically. But ringing a doorbell she could do. And she would tell us that when she died, she would come back and let us know. So who knows?"

One local historical figure who may not have even stepped inside the Boarding Home, at least not while he was alive, is Capt. William Rion Hoel. Born in Cincinnati, Captain Hoel would eventually relocate to Wayne Township, barely a mile away from Waynesville. By the time he moved to the area, he had already established himself as a talented and respected Ohio River captain as well as a Civil War hero. He was also quite the character, and his life was filled with colorful stories and interesting anecdotes. He was just the kind of man Linda Morgan found interesting, especially since the museum has several of his personal belongings on display, including a plaque dedicated to him.

"One night," Linda remembered, "we were having a public ghost hunt at the museum and there were a bunch of people just sitting around downstairs." As several guests were disappointed that there didn't appear to be much ghostly activity taking place, Linda decided to entertain the guests with stories about Captain Hoel.

"I just think the captain is an interesting character, so I just started telling the guests about him," Linda said. "All of a sudden, the K-II meter on the table where everyone was sitting starts blinking. And every time I mentioned a fact about Captain Hoel that you could verify—a historical fact—it would light up. It was really bizarre and really fantastic," Linda admitted.

On the second floor of the museum is the Children's Room, so named because it is decorated with toys and other items a child would have used. But according to the Boarding Home records, no child ever lived in this room. Regardless, it is said that the ghost of a little girl named Ruthie haunts this room, although who Ruthie is remains a mystery. Some say she is the mysterious little girl who was seen standing on the front porch while others say she drifted over from the Charity Lynch House across the street, which has often been referred to as the most haunted house in Waynesville. As for the name Ruthie, there seems to be some confusion as to where it originated, and it is attributed alternately to something psychics picked up on to a name local ghost hunters identified during an EVP session or when their K-II meter flashed in response to questions. It can't also be dismissed that perhaps after discovering a child named Ruthie did very briefly live in the house, the name just began to be associated with the ghost. Of course, that hasn't stopped people on public ghost hunts from coming into the room, placing a K-II meter on the floor, and trying to communicate with her.

Chuck Feicht has been a part of the museum for some time now. During that time, he's noticed something interesting about the Children's Room. "People say the Children's Room is haunted because of a 'feeling.' No one ever says they see anything."

Chuck has some interesting insights into the feelings certain rooms in the museum have. That's because every year, he rents out the entire museum for his family's Christmas Eve dinner, after which he lets everyone roam the building.

"The last couple of years," Chuck explained, "I've been telling my family, 'Go into all the rooms, look at the exhibits, then come back and tell me which rooms you think are the most haunted.' I do that with my ghost tours when we come up here, too. And until recently, it was always the Children's Room. But," Chuck added, "in the last few years, it's been the Boarder's Room."

"That's the room people usually feel uncomfortable in," Linda Morgan added. "She's right," Mary Bunker concurred. "People say that the Boarder's Room creeps them out. I don't know what it is, but there is something about the Boarder's Room that is cold and uninviting to a lot of people."

Just like the Children's Room, there has not been a single sighting of a ghost in the Boarder's Room. Psychics, however, claim to have made contact with a "grumpy man" in the Boarder's Room and in the hallway right outside the room. One psychic went so far as to state that the ghost belonged to a man who might have taken his own life inside the building. "If that's true, and his ghost is still here, I feel sorry for him," Linda said.

Linda also doesn't believe that if there are ghosts here, they are unhappy. "It's a friendly thing that's going on here," she told me. "If there are ghosts here, I really think they just want to share that they're here.

"I think they just don't want to be forgotten," Linda said.

THE VIGIL

I arrived at the museum around 1:00 P.M. As this was a smaller building, I had brought along only one member of The Ghosts of Ohio to help out with the vigil: Julie Black. In the parking lot, we met Chuck Feicht, who brought me inside while Julie decided to grab a quick smoke.

Once inside the museum, Chuck introduced me to Linda Morgan and the rest of the group, and we started the interviews. It was then that I heard the faint rattling of a doorknob, a clear indication that Julie was trying to get in. Sure enough, the rattling was soon followed by a light knock on the door. Linda remarked, "Is the door locked?" and got up to look.

We all waited for the door to open, but it didn't. In fact, a minute or so later, Linda called out "Chuck, did you lock this door?" Bill Stubbs immediately got up and went to the door. I then heard the knob turn, apparently without hesitation. As Julie walked into the museum, I heard her say to Linda and Bill, "I could turn the knob, but the door wouldn't open."

I really didn't think anything of this incident until later on, when I asked the group about who they thought might be haunting the museum and the name Carol, the former docent, came up. As the group talked about how much Carol had loved the museum, they brought up an interesting fact: Carol had been a smoker, but that didn't stop her from getting annoyed if other people were smoking in the building.

Once I heard that, I immediately recalled Julie not being able to get inside the museum . . . right after she had been smoking. So I asked the group, "Does anybody here smoke?" Only Julie raised her hand.

This raises an interesting question: Was Carol's ghost trying to keep Julie out of the museum because Julie had been smoking? That's hard to say with any certainty. Is does seem a bit, odd, though, that the only time the door refused to open that day was the first time a stranger, who just happened to be smoking at the time, tried to gain access to the museum.

I asked Julie to describe what happened when she tried to enter the museum. "I turned the doorknob and there was no give at all," she said. "There was no play in the door, and it wouldn't budge. I was even pushing on it. Then I got to thinking maybe there was a dead bolt in the inside and maybe you guys accidentally locked it or something, so I knocked."

"When I came up to the door, the knob on my side wouldn't turn at all. It was like it was glued," Linda Morgan said. "But then when Bill came up, he just turned the knob and it opened right up. I use that door a lot," she added, "and it's never been like that. It wouldn't budge."

During the rest of the afternoon, we watched several visitors and staff members come in and out of that door with no problems. We even ran several tests on both the door and the doorknob but were unable to recreate what had happened to Julie. The door moved smoothly in and out of the frame without sticking, and there was a lot of play in the doorknob. It's also interesting to note that while Julie said she was able to turn the doorknob on her side of the door, Linda said the knob on her side, inside the museum, refused to turn. Examining the door, we found that the two doorknobs were actually connected to each other. So if one side turned, the other side did, too. We were left scratching our heads over why Julie couldn't get into the museum.

After running the tests on the door, we set up the equipment. For this particular vigil, we decided to incorporate trigger objects. As mentioned in an earlier chapter, trigger objects can be anything that a ghost might want to touch or play with—for example, using a doll to attract a child ghost or reading aloud from a book to raise the curiosity of a librarian ghost. Ghosts may be more inclined to interact with us if we're doing something that's of interest to them. Of course, it's always helpful if your trigger objects are light and easy to move, so you can tell if someone or something is moving them.

For the vigil at the Museum at the Friends Home, here's where Julie and I placed the equipment, based on where we'd been told paranormal activity had taken place:

Children's Room
- two DVR night-vision cameras, one inside the room, pointing down at the two trigger objects and one outside the room, pointing into the room
- one Superlux condenser microphone in the center of the room
- two motion detectors, one at chest height and one on the floor
- two trigger objects: a set of keys and a stuffed animal, placed on the floor in the center of the room

Boarder's Room
- two DVR night-vision cameras, one inside the room pointing across the room and the other outside the room, looking into the room
- one Superlux condenser microphone in the center of the room

Second Floor Sitting Area
- one Superlux condenser microphone, positioned in the far corner to pick up any noise coming from the entire sitting area and/or the front rooms

Front Staircase
- Vernier LabPro sensors, including two ambient temperature devices, one electromagnetic sensor, and one static charge sensor, running up the center of the whole staircase
- 30 milliwatts laser grid at the bottom of the staircase, pointing upward toward the landing

Ground Floor
- one infrared video camera, with 100-watt IR extender aimed across the entire lobby area

Basement
- one infrared video camera in the small hallway between the rooms
- one infrared video camera in the "canning kitchen"

While we were setting up, Linda Morgan mentioned that she would need to step away for a while to help out on one of the Ghostly History Walking Tours. Not wanting to pass up an opportunity to get some additional local ghostly history, as well as the chance to set up an experiment, I decided that once we had set up all the equipment for the vigil, we would turn everything on and then leave to go on the walking tour, allowing the equipment to run unmanned. That way, we would have a "control" with the building completely empty, which we could compare against later in the evening, when we were in the museum conducting the vigil. Plus, as I've always said, I'm convinced that ghosts go into hiding whenever I show up, so this was a chance to see if maybe the ghosts come out to play only when I'm not around!

So after getting everything up and running, Linda locked the museum up tight, and Julie and I joined her for dinner and a ghost walk. Approximately two hours later, we returned to the museum, made note of the time we returned, swapped out some DVDs, and got ready for the vigil. When we went back and looked at the materials that were recorded while we were away, there was nothing out of the ordinary.

During my interview with Linda, I was intrigued with her account of how the K-II meter had reacted when she was telling people the story of Captain Hoel. If indeed Captain Hoel's ghost had come forward because Linda was talking about him, perhaps we could recreate that and get the same results. So when we returned to the museum, with Linda's permission, I had her sit at a table in the middle of the main floor and placed a K-II meter in front of her. I then placed an additional K-II, an EMF, an ELF, and a natural tri-field meter around her on the table. When those were in place, I had Julie and Chuck Feicht join Linda at the table. After getting a baseline reading off the hand-helds, I backed away from the table, turned off the lights, and told Linda to tell Julie and Chuck the story of Captain Hoel.

While Linda was talking about Captain Hoel, I positioned myself at the desk in the corner of the main floor, where I had placed the monitor for the DVR cameras, the sound mixer, and the laptop that I use to monitor the readings from the Vernier LabPro sensors. I also had an unobstructed view of Linda as well as the laser grid on the front staircase.

After approximately twenty minutes of no activity, including nothing from the hand-helds sitting on the table in front of Linda, Julie, and

Chuck, I decided to see if perhaps the ghosts were frightened off and lurking either on the second floor or in the basement. So while Linda continued her story of Captain Hoel, I went up to the second floor.

The first thing I did was use my hand-helds on both the front and rear landings and around the tops of the staircases. My thought was maybe Captain Hoel's ghost was uncomfortable being around all the equipment, but that he still wanted to hear people talking about him. So what would be better than to hang out near the landing, where he'd be out of the way, but still able to hear Linda sharing stories about him? Sounds good in theory, but the reality is that on this particular evening, the equipment did not detect any form of energy on the landings or anywhere near the staircases or in the rooms on the entire second floor. If there was a ghost in the building while Linda was telling her story, it wasn't on the first or second floor. In a last-ditch effort, I headed down to the basement, stopping briefly on the main floor to ask Linda if she could keep talking for a few more minutes.

In the basement, I could still hear Linda's voice, although it was a bit muffled, so I began taking readings in the areas of the basement where I could make out her voice, again using the theory that there might be a ghost down there with me, eavesdropping. There didn't appear to be as I was unable to detect any anomalous readings. In fact, the entire basement, with the exception of an area near a rather large grouping of electrical wires, had very low EMF readings.

When I returned back upstairs, Julie, Chuck, and Linda told me that none of the meters, including Linda's personal K-II meter, had reacted at any point during this particular part of the vigil—not so much as a single light flicker.

For the last part of the vigil, which actually lasted several hours, I spent time inside each of the rooms on the second floor. For most of them, I simply sat quietly or else conducted an EVP (electronic voice phenomena) session, asking if there were any ghosts present and, if so, if they could make themselves known to me. I asked for names, ages, even what their connection to the museum was. I called out to the people whose ghosts were thought to haunt the building: Captain Hoel, Carol, Ruthie. No one answered.

Since there had been specific ghost activity reported in the Boarder's Room and the Children's Room, I wanted to spend a significant amount of time there. I began in the Children's Room doing what came naturally: playing, or at least pretending to play as many of the items in the room could be classified as antiques. I lay down on the floor and asked Ruthie if she wanted to come play with me. I tried to make a connection with Ruthie by telling her that I had a daughter of my own. I even asked for advice from Ruthie regarding what would be the best toys for me to get my daughter, Courtney. Not getting any responses, I tried a different approach and asked if there was a ghost here who was *not* named Ruthie. If there was, I said I wanted to make sure I got the story straight for my book, so could they please tell me their real name. Once again, I didn't hear, see, or feel anything out of the ordinary. The equipment didn't pick up anything either.

Finally, I spent some time in the Boarder's Room. People have reported odd feelings in this room, but while I was there, it felt just like any other room. I was at a bit of a loss in this room because it wasn't associated with a particular ghost. In fact, while it was made up to look like a boarder's room, the fact was that *all* the rooms on the second floor of the museum were boarder's rooms. This particular room was simply recreated to resemble what a traditional boarder's room would have

The Boarder's Room—an example of what a typical boarder's room might have looked like at the Friends Home.

looked like. So while the ghost here might have indeed been a boarder in this room, it could have been brought in with one of the many items used to decorate the room.

That being the case, I once again called out to the ghosts of the building whose names I knew. Getting no response, I decided to sit quietly and see if I would experience the odd feeling that others had reported here. After about twenty minutes in the darkness, I decided it was time to move on to another room. Eventually, Julie and I decided that there didn't appear to be any ghosts with us and packed up the equipment and headed home . . . although before we left, I made Julie go back outside for one last cigarette and then see if she could get back inside the museum. She did, but the door opened easily. "I told Carol I'd quit smoking and she let me in," Julie told me with a smile.

FINAL THOUGHTS

The whole incident with Julie not being able to get in the door has me scratching my head. On the one hand, it seems like too much of a coincidence that Julie, the only smoker in the group, couldn't get in the building and one of the reported ghosts was supposed to have been antismoking. On top of that, I personally fiddled with that door for a good twenty minutes, trying—unsuccessfully—to get it to stick or otherwise jam. But let's face it: it's mind-boggling if a ghost could somehow have managed to bar a door in such a way that two people couldn't get it to open. Still, I have no explanation for how that happened. What I can tell you is that I showed up for that vigil not knowing a single thing about Carol. When the night was over, I knew plenty about her, including the fact that she didn't like smokers and may or may not have locked my friend, Julie, out of the museum.

If nothing else, my visit to Museum at the Friends Home is the only vigil or investigation I can ever remember when I repeatedly encouraged a team member to keep taking smoke breaks.

Museum at the Friends Home
115 S. 4th Street
Waynesville, Ohio 45068
www.friendshomemuseum.org

SOUTHEAST
OHIO

ZANESVILLE COMMUNITY THEATRE

I'm always skeptical when I hear about a theater that's supposed to be haunted. If anything, I'm more intrigued when I hear about a theater that's *not* haunted. I'm not sure why, but it seems like almost every single theater—not just in Ohio—has a ghost story or two (or three) associated with it. Still, when I heard about the ghosts of the Zanesville Community Theatre, I was excited. Here was a theater operating in a building that wasn't always a theater. On top of that, it was an old building with a rich history. Now that's the kind of theater I like!

HISTORY

From the outside, the Zanesville Community Theatre does not look like the typical place to catch a play or performance. That's because when it was originally constructed in 1910, it was designed to be a synagogue. In fact, in order to accommodate the large Jewish population in the area, it was one of two synagogues constructed at the time, with the other on 7th Street in downtown Zanesville.

Over the years, the local Jewish community continued to grow, so much so that in 1925, the synagogue at 940 Findley Avenue built an addition, but it wasn't enough, and by the 1950s, both of Zanesville's synagogues were operating beyond capacity. So construction began on a new, larger synagogue, capable of accommodating members from both of the current synagogues. In 1958, the Beth Abraham Synagogue opened on Blue Avenue in Zanesville. Shortly thereafter, both of the older synagogues went put up for sale.

The front of the Zanesville Community Theatre still shows signs, such as the closed-up arched window, from the days when it functioned as a church.

A Baptist congregation would be the first group to move into the former synagogue on Findley Avenue. They held services in the building for several years before selling it to another religious organization, the Mormons. Like the Baptists before them, the Mormons held services in the building for several years. In the early 1980s, after their larger church was completed nearby, the Mormons moved their congregation to the new building and put 940 Findley Avenue up for sale. Fortunately for the Mormons, it didn't sell right away. Shortly after their new church was opened, it was struck by lightning, so they moved their services back to Findley Avenue for a short period while the lightning damage was repaired.

When the Findley Avenue building was put up for sale, one of the Mormon board members suddenly thought of a group that it would be perfect for. You see, the board member was also on the board of the Zanesville Community Theatre, and they just happened to be looking for a new location to call home.

Founded in 1963, the Zanesville Community Theatre was (and still is) the oldest continuously operating theater company in the area. Having previously operated out of the Zanesville campus of Ohio University and another theater in downtown Zanesville, the Zanesville Community Theatre wanted a new place that they could call their own. While the former synagogue would need a lot of work to be turned into a theater, everyone who saw it fell in love with it. So in 1985, the new address for the Zanesville Community Theatre officially became 940 Findley Avenue.

Almost as soon as the theater company moved in, renovations and remodeling began. In the beginning, the stage was elevated and all the seats for the audience were flat on the ground. After a major overhaul, the stage was lowered and the seats were all elevated, which is how the current theater is arranged. A portion of the wall behind the stage was cut out and removed in order to increase the depth of the stage by five feet, which doesn't sound very deep, but the Zanesville Community Theatre has been able to do some amazing productions in that small area over the years, including *Sweeney Todd* and *M*A*S*H*.

Other parts of the building were also transformed over the years. Former kitchens became makeup areas and Green Rooms. Dressing rooms were added behind the stage. And of course, no theater would be complete without lighting and sound. Those were all added to the balcony area behind the seats at the back of the theater.

Today, six to eight theatrical pieces are produced annually by the Zanesville Community Theatre. Tickets are available online and at the theater box office. Group discounts are also available. Get your tickets early as the shows have been known to sell out. Keep that in mind should you choose to attend a performance and remind yourself that just because the seat next to you is empty, that doesn't necessarily mean it's unoccupied. You just might not be able to see who's sitting there!

THE EXPERIENCES

Carl Underwood, Zanesville Community Theatre's treasurer and lighting guru, first arrived at the theater in 1985. He told me that he didn't know much about the building when he first got here, least of all that it might be haunted.

"I remember that I was doing a Google search online and came across people saying you could hear music playing backstage," Carl recalled. "It's funny, but in all the years I've been here, I've never heard ghostly music from backstage." In fact, Carl told me that he had been at the theater for almost twenty years before he had his first paranormal experience.

"It was back in 2003," Carl remembered. "We were doing *The Diary of Anne Frank* and everyone had decided to go outside because they were going to shoot some video so people would have something to watch while we changed scenes during the show." Since he was now alone in the theater, Carl took the opportunity to think about how he would light the show. At the time, the only thing on the stage was a round table with a vase of flowers on it. "All of the flowers were nice and neat," Carl said.

As Carl worked, he had his head down, but he would occasionally look up at the stage as he tried to work out the lighting in his head. At one point, Carl looked at the vase on the table and noticed something different: the flowers had all moved. "It looked like somebody had taken their finger and twirled it from the inside so the flowers were all spread out," Carl explained.

Carl told me his first thought was that since the windows were open, a breeze might have done it. But as he rose and walked to the windows, he realized there was no breeze, so he headed toward the door, thinking one of the actors had come in and moved the flowers while he was focused on his lighting. Opening the door, Carl found that there was no one near the theater; they had all moved down the street to film there. At that point, Carl said he was willing to brush off the whole thing— that is, until he went back inside and found that this time, the entire vase had moved. "The whole vase was tipped up. And it was tipped upstage, against the slope of the stage. That didn't make sense to me," Carl admitted. He also admitted that at the time, he found the whole thing a bit unnerving. "After I saw the vase tipped up, I decided to go outside and wait for everyone to come back."

Carl was quick to point out to me that the vase incident didn't really scare him—it was just something odd. Of course, he did admit to being scared in the theater. But let's be honest, who wouldn't be a little freaked out hearing a disembodied voice telling you to get out? No wonder the incident still sticks with Carl, right down to the day it happened and even the play he was working on.

"The only time I've ever experienced anything malicious or threatening act was on March 12, 2003, when we were rehearsing *Taming of the Shrew*." Carl recalled that rehearsal was over, but that he still had some work to do up in the balcony. So as the last person was leaving the theater, Carl asked him or her to lock him in so he could work in peace.

No sooner had Carl gotten back up in the balcony and started working when he heard a voice in his head, ordering him to "get out." Carl told me "It was all I could do to pick up my stuff and get out, shutting off the lights as I went."

When I asked Carl to describe the voice, he told me he heard the voice in his head as opposed to something out loud. "It was something I felt. It was not an 'out loud' voice. But it was a male voice that was dark and rough and very distinct."

As to why Carl took off after hearing the voice, he explained, "My sister told me, if you hear something like that, you just go. You don't ask questions."

Confused as to why the voice wanted Carl to leave the theater, he began thinking of possible explanations. One possibility was maybe the voice was just letting Carl know it was time to go. So Carl started paying attention to the time whenever he was in the theater, even going so far as to publicly announce how long he planned to stay each time he arrived.

"Generally, if I'm the first person here, as soon as I walk in the door, I'll say out loud what my agenda for the day is," Carl told me. "I'll even say what my stopping point is, although that [is] usually in terms of work I have to complete as opposed to a time." That tends to quiet things down at the theater, to a point.

"Sometimes," Carl explained, "I'll be working in the balcony and I will hear this noise—it's a crunching noise, like the sound of a plastic bag being squashed." Oddly enough, Carl tells me that he usually hears the noise thirty minutes before he's planning on leaving, almost as if the ghosts of the theater were telling him it was time to wrap things up. "That noise tells me it's time to finish up," Carl said.

When he hears that noise, Carl says he can't ever tell where it's coming from and he never sees anything. Still, he takes the hint: "When I hear that noise, I say out loud, 'I only have this much more to do. Give me thirty more minutes.' And they do because the noise will stop. So I'll finish, pack up, and go."

It's not just odd noises either. Carl recalls another instance when it seemed as though the spirits of the theater had to remind him it was time to leave. "It was after a performance and everyone was out of the theater except for myself and the producer," Carl said. "The lights were still on, but everything had been broken down. There were just some chairs up on the stage." Carl was in the back of the theater, talking to the producer, the only other person in the building at the time. As they were talking, they both heard a loud noise coming from the stage. Carl said that as he and the producer headed toward the stage to investigate the sound, he wondered aloud if the noise was their cue to leave the theater.

As Carl and the producer reached the stage, they noticed that two of the chairs that had been on the stage were now lying upside down. "I looked at the chairs and said, 'That's our cue,' and we left," Carl said.

But Carl's not the only one the ghosts get impatient with when people appear to outstay their welcome. One night, a woman was alone in the building, painting some set pieces. She was working near the theater's ghost light—an electric light often left on in an unoccupied theater so the building isn't entirely dark and people coming in can navigate their way through it—when the light suddenly flashed on and off, startling the woman. But what really creeped her out was when she realized the light managed to turn on even though it wasn't plugged in. Around the same time, she started hearing weird noises coming from the basement. "So she said out loud, 'I need thirty more minutes,' and the noises stopped," Carl said.

In all the years that Carl has been at the Zanesville Community Theatre, he's never actually seen a ghost. He has heard stories from people who claim to have caught a glimpse of a specter, though. Oddly enough, people who saw one particular ghost up in the balcony at first thought they were looking at Carl's daughter, Cary, who is very much alive.

"One weekend, a group of people were in the theater, rehearsing," Carl recalled. "I wasn't there, but the following week, people kept coming up to me and asking if I had come in to the theater on Sunday afternoon with Cary." Intrigued since neither he nor Cary had been at the theater at all that weekend, Carl asked why people were curious as to his whereabouts on Sunday. They each told Carl that while they were all on the stage Sunday, they noticed a young girl standing up in the balcony area, where Carl's lighting controls are. The girl stood there watching them, so the group just assumed that Carl had come in to do some work and brought his daughter, Cary, with him. They didn't think anything of it and just went about their business and ignored the girl. No one was really sure where she went. They just looked up at some point and noticed that she was gone.

Even though Michelle Duke had been investigating haunted places for a very long time, she admits that prior to 2009, she knew very little about the alleged ghosts at the Zanesville Community Theatre: "I had heard a couple of the ghost stories, like the music playing and the little girl, but it was just stuff from the Internet."

In 2009, Michelle was given permission to investigate the theater with her group. It was a night she would never forget. "For me, truly, this theater is one of the most haunted places I've ever investigated," Michelle said.

She told me that the unexplainable activity started even before her group began investigating. In fact, they had been at the theater for only a short time and were getting their initial tour of the building when things started to get a little strange. "We were all downstairs, near the Green Room, when we all heard three distinct knocks on the outside door," Michelle recalled. Thinking someone was outside and wanted to come in, the woman giving the tour excused herself to answer the door. A few moments later, the woman returned to Michelle's group. "She told us she opened the door, but there was no one there. But we all heard it; it was three distinct knocks," Michelle said.

Since there had been very little ghost activity reported at the time, I was curious as to how Michelle's group set about picking places to put their recording equipment for the investigation. "One of the areas we picked was around the dressing room," she told me. "We just thought it would be an active area since back when it was a theater, there was probably a lot of hustle and bustle going on back there." This move would soon prove to be a good call.

At one point during the investigation, Michelle and Carl Underwood were sitting at the monitors, watching two male investigators checking out the dressing room area behind the stage. For a while, nothing happened. But then Michelle and Carl saw something totally bizarre on the monitor. "There is a set of cupboards back there," Michelle told me "and right near them, Carl and I both saw what appeared to be someone peek out and then peek back in, then actually stick their head and shoulder out and then go back in—almost like they were coming out of the wall."

Michelle immediately radioed to the investigators in the dressing room area and asked them to look for anything strange near the cupboards or at least something that could explain what she and Carl saw. They looked, but they couldn't find anything out of the ordinary or a logical explanation for the odd images Carl and Michelle had just witnessed. Stranger still was what Michelle discovered when she reviewed the video from that night. "What we didn't see at the time," she said, "maybe because of the excitement, is that a full-body apparition walks in front of the camera, maybe seven seconds after we saw that thing pop out near the cupboards. You clearly see it walk by."

And that wasn't all Michelle's group caught that night. At some point during the evening, a game of ghostly cards must have taken place on the stage. That's because Michelle recorded what sounds like someone shuffling a deck of cards, followed by a disembodied voice saying, "my turn."

On a return visit to the theater for another investigation, Michelle was sitting in the first dressing room with Cary Underwood and another female investigator. Michelle explained: "We were talking and asking if there was anything there that wanted to communicate with us." Suddenly, all three women saw a series of bright flashes of light, moving down the hallway past the dressing room they were sitting in.

"It was the brightest, whitest light that I have ever seen in my life," Michelle said. "It went from one end of the hallway toward the other, and then nothing. We looked down the hallway, but there was nothing there. But we all saw the light through the dressing room curtains."

There was a video camera running in the hallway at the time, complete with an infrared extender. But when they reviewed what the camera had recorded that night, there was not a single flash of light to be seen.

Later in the evening, Cary Underwood was sitting in the darkened back hallway with Michelle Duke when she felt someone or something touch her. "Something touched me on the foot. And I was wearing flip-flops, so I started freaking out," Cary admitted. She immediately told Michelle that something touched her foot. Michelle had a video camera with her at the time, so she panned the camera down toward Cary's feet. There was nothing there. "Whatever it was," Cary told me, "it was so cold, it gave me chills."

Around 1:30 in the morning, as the group was getting ready to leave for the night, something in the theater apparently wanted to say goodbye to Cary in its own special way. "We were going to leave and someone said, 'Give us a hug.' And all of a sudden, I felt that same feeling—almost like a chill—around my arms. It gave me goose bumps, and it was like eighty degrees outside."

"It was like whatever it was, it responded to what we were saying," Michelle added. "That, to me, proves [that] whatever's here is intelligent. It's listening to you."

One final note: should you ever decide to take in a show at Zanesville Community Theatre and want the chance to sit next to a ghost, your best bet would be to sit in row H—specifically the seats that are stage right (audience's left): H106, 107, and 108. These are the seats in which people have sat and suddenly felt like they were being touched by unseen hands. "And during the show, too," Carl added. "That's what is interesting to me: people are not up there to investigate ghosts. But things still occur in those seats."

THE VIGIL

As soon as Ghosts of Ohio member Julie Black and I pulled up in front of Zanesville Community Theatre, I knew we were in for a unique vigil. Even from the outside, the building just looks and feels . . . different. It's hard to explain, but the stately brick building certainly doesn't look like there would be a theater, let alone ghosts, lurking inside it. It does, by its very appearance, imply that it is still a place of worship, so knowing there was something different waiting for us once we walked through those doors—namely, a stage and theater seats—immediately gave the building an air of mystery.

After meeting fellow Ghosts of Ohio member Amy Kaltenbach outside the theater, we went inside and were greeted by Carl Underwood, who had set up some interviews for us. I'm not sure if Carl was being theatrical or whether it was just a coincidence, but he had the interviewees sitting in the theater seats while I was up on the stage. It was a wee bit intimidating, but totally cool at the same time.

While I was conducting the interviews, I noticed out of the corner of my eye that both Amy and Julie kept glancing over to stage left, near the lobby. I can remember thinking that maybe someone had walked in and was waiting for me to stop talking so he or she could make an entrance. But when I looked over in the direction they were looking, there was no one there, so I just kept talking. About five minutes after that, Julie

View of Zanesville Community Theatre, taken from the audience seating area, near the three seats of the "haunted row," row H.

interrupted me and said to Carl and the group, "I'm sorry, but do you guys have a cat?" Carl said, "No," while the rest of the group shook their heads, agreeing with Carl.

I glanced over at Julie with a "What was that all about?" look on my face, but she just smiled. After the interviews, I asked her why she asked if they had a cat. "When you were talking, I saw a dark shadow dart across the floor in the lobby. It was small. The only thing I could think of was that it was a cat," she said.

Amy chimed in and said that she saw the dark shadow, too. Neither one of them could make out what it was; it was just a small, dark mass that was close to the floor and moving very fast. It was broad daylight, so it didn't seem possible for the shadow to have been caused by any sort of external light source such as car headlights, a reflection off a streetlight, or someone outside the building with a flashlight. Of course, we couldn't rule out the possibility of it being caused by a shadow coming through from outside. We tried to recreate what Julie and Amy had seen, but we were unable to. Amy and Julie didn't report seeing the dark mass again the rest of the time we were at the theater.

After the interviews were finished, Carl took Amy, Julie, Michelle Duke, and me on a tour of the building, pointing out the places where paranormal activity had been reported. As always, I had my digital voice recorder running, although I usually run it during the tours just to record information about the building and the reported activity than to capture ghost voices via EVP.

Carl had just finished showing us the dressing rooms behind the stage, and we were starting down the back stairway toward the Green Room. As we were going down the stairs, Carl can be heard on the recording, mentioning that there is a hallway near the Green Room where people "feel weird." Michelle Duke can also be heard talking about how her group had recorded EVPs while in the Green Room. At a point in the recording when no one is talking, a sound can be heard that sounds like a woman saying "Hey!" The sound is very loud and appears to be very close to my recorder, which was clamped to the clipboard that I always hold in front of me when I'm walking. When I went back and examined the "voice" with audio-analyzing software, it falls in the range of a human voice. It also does not match the voice pattern of anyone else who was in the area at the time it was recorded, and it didn't occur again the rest of the night.

After the tour, Julie, Amy, and I looked at the interview notes I had compiled, and we had a brief discussion about where we should set up the equipment for the vigil. Here's what we decided:

Stage
- one infrared video camera with 100-watt IR extender, stage right (rear) and aimed across the entire stage
- one studio microphone, center stage, facing the audience

Seating Area
- one DVR night-vision camera in the aisle on the main floor, facing the stage
- one Superlux condenser microphone in the aisle on the main floor, facing the stage

Backstage
- two DVR night-vision cameras, both in the backstage hallway—one at the far end of the hallway and the other halfway down the hallway
- one DVR night-vision camera, pointing down the stairs toward the Green Room

- one Superlux condenser microphone at the end of the backstage hallway, pointing down the hall
- Vernier LabPro sensors, including two ambient temperature devices, one electromagnetic sensor, and one static charge sensor, running the entire length of the backstage hallway

Green Room

- one infrared video camera in the corner of the room, facing the staircase to the backstage area
- one Superlux condenser microphone positioned in the far corner, facing the center of the room

Balcony

- one infrared video camera at the top of the stairs, facing the lighting desk
- one Superlux condenser microphone in the far corner, facing the lighting desk

Row H

- one infrared video camera in row H, facing across the aisle

After everything was set up, Julie, Amy, and I talked about where in the theater we each wanted to go first. I chose the stage area because I wanted to perform a special experiment. I wanted to see if I could get a ghost to play cards with me.

The idea had occurred to me when I was interviewing Michelle Duke and she mentioned how her group had captured what sounded like the sound of cards being shuffled up on the stage. She even played the recording for me, and it did indeed sound like cards being shuffled. So I thought that if I sat up on the stage and played cards, perhaps I could get a ghost to come play with me, maybe even move some of the cards or do something else that I could capture on video. There was only one small problem: I'm horrible at cards. I can play poker against myself and still find a way to lose. And forget about solitaire. So I opted for a good old-fashioned game of blackjack. I figured that if I were the dealer, it would open up more opportunities for the ghosts to interact with me as they would need to let me know if they wanted to "hit" or "stand."

So with all the audio and video running, we turned off the lights in the theater and I took a seat up on the stage at a small table, where we also added a second chair, directly facing me. I also put an EMF detector and an ambient temperature sensor on the table, near the empty chair. I started by shuffling the deck and introducing myself, saying I would be their dealer for the night. After shuffling, I put the deck in front of the presumably empty chair across from me and asked if they wanted to cut the deck. Then I sat and waited. And waited. Finally, I took back the uncut deck, shuffled some more, and dealt out two hands of blackjack, one for me and one for the empty chair.

"Hit or stand?" I asked the empty chair, with my hand poised on top of the deck of cards, ready to slap down another card. Getting no response, I said, "You need to let me know if you want another card. Give me a sign, please." After waiting several minutes and not hearing or seeing anything, I said, "OK, you hold," and gave myself another card. Believe it or not, I actually won that hand.

I dealt several more hands, each time asking if the empty chair wanted another card or not. After a while, I decided to see if I could get a response by continuing to "hit" the empty chair until it eventually went bust. I thought maybe my incompetence would annoy the ghost to the point where he or she would give me a sign to let me know, "Enough, already! Quit giving me cards!"

When that didn't work, I decided to take it up another notch by openly cheating. I would deal out a hand and then say out loud, "Soooooo, should I hit or stick? Well, lemme see. What have you got?" and then I would peek at the empty chair's cards before I decided to hit or stick. That didn't work either, and when I went back after the vigil and reviewed the audio and video, the only thing I managed to record was confirmation that I'm really bad at cards, even when I'm cheating.

For the next part of the vigil, I wanted to spend some time up in the theater seats, specifically row H. Since there were three seats in the "haunted row," I took an extra ELF and a K-II meter with me. I chose these devices because they light up, so I'd be able to see them better in the dark. I put the ELF on the floor in front of seat H106 and the K-II meter on the floor of seat H108. I sat between the two devices in seat H107.

Before I sat down, I looked directly at H107 and asked aloud, "Pardon me, is this seat taken?" I took the nonresponse as a "no" and sat down, introducing myself to seat H106 and H108 as I did. Settling into my seat, I attempted to strike up conversation with my invisible seatmates. I asked if this was their first time at the theater or if they had been coming here for a while. I inquired as to what their favorite play was and even how they managed to score such great seats. Regardless of what I asked, I never got any response. The hand-held on the floor in front of me never blinked once.

I then decided to spend some time down in the Green Room with Amy. Of all the places I went to during the Zanesville Community Theatre vigil, the Green Room was the one area that felt a little off. At first, sitting on the couch in the darkness with Amy, I thought there might be someone else in the room with us. But as I became more accustomed to my surroundings, it was clear that the feelings I had were more than likely the result of the way the room was set up. The couch is against an exterior wall, with a staircase to the immediate left. It creates this weird feeling that at any moment, someone could come down the stairs, but it's not a ghostly kind of feeling. It's more like you don't feel you have enough personal space around you. Once you get up from the couch and go to the middle of the room, that feeling quickly dissipates.

Still, I wanted to see if there was anything ghostly to the feelings I had while I was sitting on the couch. The hand-helds weren't picking up anything, so I started taking pictures of the room. Then, considering the fact that I might be dealing with ghostly actors and actresses, I said aloud that I had thoroughly enjoyed the performance and asked if I could please take a picture of the cast. I took a few random pictures of the room before realizing that even if there were ghosts in the room, I didn't know where they were. So I asked if the cast would be so kind as to sit on the couch with Amy. I then asked everyone to say "cheese" and took several pictures. In all the pictures, Amy is the only one sitting on the couch.

After returning to the main floor and checking all the equipment, I then headed with Julie backstage to the dressing rooms. I wanted to sit first in the dressing room where Michelle had been sitting with the other investigators when they witnessed the bright flashes of light.

Once inside the dressing room, I positioned myself so that I could see out into the hallway. These dressing rooms have curtains over the doorways, so I pulled them back just enough that I could peek out into the hallway, replicating what Michelle said she had done the night she saw the flashes of light.

While I had been very vocal at all of the other places I had been during the vigil, I decided that I wanted to remain quiet while I was backstage. Recalling Michelle Duke's comment about how the backstage area had been a place of much activity with all the actors and actresses running around back in the day, I thought that if any of that energy was still lingering, if I were quiet enough, I might be able to hear some of it.

On most vigils, when I decide to sit quietly, it takes a good fifteen or twenty minutes for me to settle in and get used to all the normal noises a building makes. Not at the Zanesville Community Theatre, though. It was perfectly quiet, at least in the dressing room area, from the moment Julie and I sat down.

After about forty-five minutes in the first dressing room when absolutely nothing happened, I began to wonder if perhaps I was in the wrong room, so I moved down the hall to another area. Still nothing. Slowly but surely, I continued down the hallway until I was at the far end, right above the steps down to the Green Room. This location gave me a good view of the entire hallway, so there would be no way I could miss any flashing lights that might appear. So I hung out in this area for another forty-five minutes or so, but never saw anything out of the ordinary.

For the final part of the vigil, I wanted to see if I could catch a glimpse of the girl up in the balcony, so I told everyone in the group where I was going and that I would be ready to wrap things up within an hour. Unbeknownst to the group, I had no intention of leaving in an hour. In fact, I was planning on staying in the theater for several more hours. So why did I lie to them? It was part of another experiment I had decided to try. Carl Underwood had said that sometimes he would hear a weird crunching noise up in the balcony when it was about thirty minutes before his announced time of departure from the theater. So my plan was to announce when I planned to leave and then stay a lot longer to see if I could hear that crunching noise in the balcony.

The balcony has a great view of the entire theater, so when I first got up there, as soon as my eyes readjusted to the dark, I spent some time just sitting, watching to see if any card-playing ghosts appeared on the stage. When they didn't, I went over to the other side of the balcony and leaned over the railing to keep an eye on row H. When it was about thirty-five minutes before my announced time of departure, I went over to the desk where Carl Underwood works his lighting magic, sat down, and pretended to work on something.

I stayed like that for the next forty-five minutes. Occasionally, I would raise my head and pretend that I was looking for something—I was really peeking to see if there were any ghosts standing in the corner, impatiently tapping their foot and looking at their spectral watches. I never saw or heard anything. After I was officially forty-five minutes past my announced departure time, I called it a night and we started packing up the gear. We ended up leaving two hours later than we had originally intended, partly because of my little experiment and also because we had problems breaking down the equipment. Through it all, the ghosts of the Zanesville Community Theatre sat and quietly bit their tongues.

FINAL THOUGHTS

While I was reviewing the materials from the Zanesville Community Theatre, I was reminded of the movie *Beetlejuice*—in particular, how the main characters had died, but because they hadn't read their *Handbook for the Recently Deceased* yet, they were having trouble communicating. Yes, I know both the movie and that book are works of fiction, but I've always wondered if some of the ghost activity (things moving, weird EVPs) is the result of a ghost not yet knowing how to communicate properly. Let's face it, if I were to die tomorrow, I'm not sure I would know how to make contact with the living. Hopefully, there's a handbook.

But back to my point. None of the activity at the Zanesville Community Theatre, even that which was reported by others, made sense. It all seemed so random: moving flowers, shuffling cards, a ghostly girl in the balcony. Maybe it all seems random simply because the ghosts haven't learned to communicate properly yet. Hey, it's just a theory.

But just because they haven't figured out how to communicate doesn't mean we should stop listening. I think perhaps Michelle Duke summed it up best when she told me, "It's like the ghosts here are listening. They're probably listening to you right now, trying to figure out how to tell their story."

Zanesville Community Theatre
940 Findley Avenue
Zanesville, Ohio 43701
www.zct.org

CLAY HAUS

I was born and raised in a little town in upstate New York. When I was growing up, my parents always insisted that no matter where our family vacation destination was, we would drive instead of fly. So that meant that we'd be driving down two-lane roads through a whole lot of nothing until we reached what my dad called "civilization."

One of the staples on those journeys was a stop at the Red Apple Rest, a cafeteria-style restaurant near Tuxedo, New York. No matter where we were headed, we always stopped at the Red Apple Rest, both coming and going. Sometimes it was for a meal, other times it was just for my dad to get his cup of coffee, but we always stopped. It was as if the Red Apple Rest became something of our own personal oasis, signaling either the start or end of our vacation (depending on which way we were headed). Either way, every time I walked into the Red Apple Rest, you could feel the buzz from all the travelers, excited to be embarking on a new adventure or basking in the weary contentment of having survived another family vacation. It was a feeling like no other.

So when the Clay Haus popped up on my list of potential locations to cover for my book, I knew right away that I wanted to pursue it. Much like the Red Apple Rest, Clay Haus was designed as a place for weary travelers to stop, relax, and reflect upon their journey. I'd always felt that sort of environment was what drew people in, making them want to stop and stay a while. I was intrigued with the notion that perhaps that same environment would draw ghosts in, too.

THE HISTORY

The original deed to the property where Clay Haus currently stands dates back to 1812 and shows a transfer from Jacob Miller to Phillip Grelle. There is a structure—believed to have been made of logs—listed on the deed, but it no longer exists as part of the current building. As for the current building, while the exact date of its construction is unknown, most agree that it was built sometime in the 1820s. After Phillip Grelle, the next two owners were Frederich Mains, a tinsmith, and Jesse Morris, a doctor. Over a hundred years later, when the Clay Haus basement was excavated to remodel part of the building, remnants from each of these previous owners were uncovered. Mains apparently operated his business out of the basement, as it was found to be filled with ash and the wooden walls were charred. As for the good doctor, Morris left behind lots of glass medicine bottles.

After Morris, the property was then sold to George Jackson, one of the builders of the Somerset Courthouse, still located just a few blocks away from Clay Haus. It would remain in the Jackson family for several generations. The building would then pass through several other families before being rezoned and turned into a commercial building. The last people to use the building as their primary private residence were Bert and Gertie May.

In the late 1970s, local businessman Carl Snider was enjoying a successful career in construction. He had also started making plans for his retirement: Carl would purchase rundown buildings, renovate them, and then rent them out, essentially earning his retirement fund from the rent he collected from tenants.

When Carl first laid eyes on the building that would become Clay Haus, it had been abandoned for several years. There was no running water, and the electrical system was far from being up to code. In fact, since the building hadn't been a private residence for many years, the only working bathroom and kitchen were in the basement. In short, the building was a mess, which is why everyone was shocked when Carl's wife, Betty, announced that she wanted to turn the building into a restaurant. What's more, Betty wanted to run the restaurant herself, despite a complete lack of experience.

The West Main Street entrance to Clay Haus in Somerset.

Both Betty and Carl had always enjoyed traveling cross-country, stopping at quaint little inns along the way. They especially loved the Pennsylvania Dutch heritage that was so prevalent in Somerset. Betty explained to Carl that since Somerset was along the Zane Trace Highway (Route 22), the main route between Zanesville and Lancaster, the restaurant would get a lot of business from weary travelers who needed a place to stop for a while and enjoy a good meal before hitting the road again. When Carl heard that, he purchased the building for Betty, and its transformation into a restaurant began.

Obviously, when turning what used to be a private residence into a restaurant, one of the first things that needs to be addressed is the kitchen. While there had been a kitchen added to the back of the main floor of this building in later years, the original kitchen was in the basement, so that meant not just relocating the kitchen, but remodeling as well.

But that wasn't the only work that needed to be done with the basement. When the Sniders took over the building, the only working bathroom was in the basement. The electrical system originated from the basement, too, with the upper floors sometimes being fed by nothing more than extension cords. And in order to get the basement up to code, the Sniders needed to dig down, dropping the original floor almost a full foot.

As for the top floor, while it consisted of a master bedroom and two smaller bedrooms, the Sniders took down the partitions between the rooms, creating one large dining room. In recent years, the Sniders purchased the building next door and punched through the wall, creating a separate dining room for Clay Haus. Nicknamed Helen's Room, after the last woman who owned the building, the part of the building that now houses the dining area used to be a gift shop. Helen's bedroom was upstairs while her kitchen and bathroom were in the basement.

From the very beginning, Betty Snider wanted the restaurant to be a family affair, right down to the name: Clay Haus. Part of the restaurant's name comes from Betty's father, Irwin Clay Priest. Then, looking to her husband's Pennsylvania Dutch heritage, Betty took the word *Haus,* Pennsylvania Dutch for "house."

THE EXPERIENCES

Around the same time Carl and Betty were purchasing their soon-to-be-restaurant, their son, Scott Snider, was graduating from college. He returned home to Somerset to help his parents with the renovations and never left. "Their project became my project . . . and my curse," he joked.

Having spent over thirty years inside Clay Haus, almost from the very beginning, Scott, who is currently the restaurant's manager, is the perfect person to ask about the origins of the building's ghost stories. Interestingly enough, while he is a lifelong resident of Somerset, Scott doesn't remember hearing any ghost stories about the building before his parents bought it. "I know the building looked kind of spooky because it was abandoned, but as far as ghost stories, I don't think my family was aware of any until we came here." He thought for a moment before adding, "I guess you could say the ghost stories started with my family because we started talking about things that were happening to us inside the building."

When it comes to ghosts, one of the first things Scott remembers is that he didn't like being in the restaurant alone after dark. "When I was younger, I never tried to be here much later than closing because I would get scared. I would hear noises, and the hair on the back of my neck would stand up," Scott admitted.

Once in a while, that feeling would be accompanied by what sounded like someone wanting to come into the restaurant. "Sometimes you would hear what sounded like someone knocking on our kitchen door out back. And you'd go to the door, and there would be nobody there," Scott said. "Back then, the other manager, Rosemary, would tell me she heard the knocking, too."

Today, well over thirty years later, Scott still hears that same knocking, although he admits it's not as often as in the past. When I asked Scott why he thought that was, he thought for a moment and then said, "I don't know. Maybe it's because I'm immune to them and I'm not as afraid as I once was."

That's not to say Scott doesn't occasionally feel like he needs to leave the building—fast. "Once in a while, I'll get a weird feeling, like somebody's coming up the stairs. Whenever I feel that, I'll get my stuff done as fast as I can and get out."

One of the earliest ghost experiences at Clay Haus that Scott can recall involves his younger brother, Brett. Scott explains: "Back when Brett was in high school, he would come out with his friends and girl-friends and they would hang out here at night. He swore that they'd sit downstairs and hear chairs moving around upstairs [on the main floor]. So that became the thing to do: come sit in the basement and see if you could hear anything."

One night, Scott said Brett and his friends were down in the basement of Clay Haus when they heard noises, which they thought were coming from the main floor. But when they went upstairs, they could still hear the noise. This time, it sounded like it was coming from the third floor.

Going up to the third floor, Brett and his friends went into the Blue Room dining area and found that the sound was coming from near the furnace, which was behind one of the original plank doors the Sniders had saved during the renovation.

"Brett said it sounded like the floor was vibrating behind the door, even though the furnace wasn't on," Scott said. "One of the girls start-ing pointing at the furnace room door and saying, 'There's something in there!'"

Scott said that at this point, his brother decided to put his friends' minds at ease. "My brother's a big football-type guy and he's like, 'Oh, let me show you, there's nothing there.'" Except that on that night, it appeared as if there was indeed something there because just as Brett reached for the handle, the door started violently shaking and banging. At that point, Brett decided he'd had enough. "He told me he was out of there so fast, he almost knocked the girls down trying to get out of that room," Scott said.

"My mom always had the idea of the Clay Haus being an inn. So in the middle of the winter, if we had a blizzard, she would make me stay open in case some weary travelers were stuck out on the road and needed some place warm to stop and get something to eat."

Scott said that during one bad snowstorm, he walked down to the Clay Haus and made sure it was open, even though the sidewalks and streets were all snowed in. "There was something like a twenty-below chill factor that night, but I made sure we were open," Scott chuckled.

There were a few guests that night—some locals who had decided to trudge down to the restaurant in the snow. But by and large, the restaurant was deserted. So Scott had come out of the kitchen and was just sitting in the dining room, chatting. "All of a sudden, there's a really big crash upstairs. Just a crash and a thud and I thought, 'Oh my gosh, the way that the wind's blowing, the window's blown in.'"

Going upstairs, Scott found all the windows secure and nothing out of place—that is until he came to the Blue Room dining area, where he found a large ceramic bed warmer lying in the middle of the floor.

"That bed warmer usually sat on one of the wood shelves on the wall. How it got on the floor I don't know because this house is brick—it doesn't vibrate," Scott explained. Scott also noted that while there were several other items on the shelf, including some glass items, the bed warmer was the only thing that fell. Nothing else on that shelf appeared to have even been moved in the slightest.

Scott has an interesting theory about what happened that night. Prior to the Sniders' renovation, the area known as the Blue Room had actually been several small bedrooms—the Sniders just removed the walls and opened it up into one big room.

"So these were bedrooms up here," Scott explained. "Maybe on what was one of the coldest nights of the year, something needed a bed warmer to take the chill off," he said, with a smile.

Chris Riffle was only seven years old when his grandparents bought the building. But by the age of thirteen, he was already bussing tables, so he knows all about Clay Haus and its ghosts.

"When I was younger, I remember hearing my grandma talking about the ghosts. I'd hear employees telling stories about ghosts, too," he told me. As for his first paranormal experience at Clay Haus, though, Chris said that happened around 1988 during the Christmas holidays.

"I was up near the top floor, sweeping the steps," Chris remembered. "There was no one else in the building. "I heard a lady say 'Hello,' and I thought it was a customer, so I said 'Hello' back. But there was no one else in the building with me."

I asked Chris if he could tell where the voice came from, and he said he couldn't. "I couldn't even tell what floor it was coming from. But it wasn't a familiar voice."

Another family member who has spent most of her adult life inside Clay Haus is Carla Liss, Carl and Betty Snider's daughter. Like most of the Snider family, Carla has had a paranormal encounter at the restaurant.

"I guess it was around Halloween 1991 or '92," Carla began. "A friend of mine from Columbus had heard stories about ghosts at the Clay Haus, and she wanted to come down and spend the night. I told her, 'Sure, come down. We can sleep downstairs at the restaurant and see if we see any ghosts.'" A short time later, when Carla's friend got to the restaurant, she came prepared: she brought along her sleeping bag and even a Ouija board. "We were planning on just hanging out downstairs, kicking back, and relaxing," Carla joked. Unfortunately, the friend chose a night that happened to be one of the busiest nights of the week at the restaurant, so Carla wasn't able to get off work until close to midnight. "At that point, I was exhausted, so I was like, 'Let's just go downstairs, unroll our sleeping bags in front of the fire, and go to sleep,'" Carla explained. "Didn't even get the Ouija board out. Just got cleaned up and got ready for bed."

After going downstairs, the women stoked the fire a bit, then pushed all the tables to the other side of the room and unrolled their sleeping bars near the hearth. Settling in, Carla said she had shut her eyes and was just about to drift off to sleep when she heard what sounded like a slap, followed by her friend yelling out, "Why did you do that? Why did you throw the Ouija board at me?"

Carla explained: "We had left the Ouija board on the table on the other side of the room. And it was still in the box. So something lifted the whole thing off the table and hit my friend in the head with it. We were the only two people in the room, and we were still in our sleeping bags."

Carla still shakes her head when she remembers that night. "I don't know how it happened. Maybe the ghosts were upset that we had brought a Ouija board in. Either that or they wanted us to get up and use it. But something definitely moved that board off the table."

The place where this incident took place—the dining room off the tavern area downstairs—was also the site of perhaps the most memorable ghost sighting in the history of Clay Haus. It involved Betty Snider and her friend, Rosemary. Over the years, Betty has told the story so many times that all her family know most of the story by heart.

"It was at the end of a long night," Carla told me, "and my mom was downstairs with Rosemary, sitting near the fire, just relaxing and enjoying each other's company." Both women were sitting at a table with their backs to the fireplace, looking out toward the tavern. At almost the same exact moment, Betty and Rosemary saw something moving on the stairs. Rosemary would tell people she saw only a blur, but Betty described something more. "My mom said she saw three people—two men and a woman—coming down the stairs," Scott said.

"Mom said they were wearing dark, old-fashioned clothing," Carla remarked. "She said she and Rosemary looked at each other like 'Are you seeing this?' She said when she looked back at the spirits, they gave her a look like 'I think she sees us' and then 'poof,' they were gone."

"The interesting thing about those stairs," Scott points out, "is that they are not original to the house. We had to add those on later."

"Yeah, I've always thought it was strange that those aren't the original stairs," Carla added.

Scott told me that while there have not been any additional sightings downstairs, there are still odd things happening down there. "Camera batteries tend to just die in that area," he said. "There was a camera crew here one time, filming me for a local news show, and the video camera just stopped working. Another time, I was being interviewed over by the fireplace and the same thing happened: the video camera just quit working. The guy said, 'I can't figure out what's wrong. The battery was fully charged.'"

While there is no concrete evidence regarding who the ghosts are that are said to be haunting Clay Haus, there is a name associated with at least one of them: Mariah. According to Scott, that name originated from relatives of former owners of the building. "They were relatives of George Jackson, the man who lived in this house back in the early days. Some people believe George even built this house," Scott explained.

According to the way Scott remembers it, members of the Jackson family stopped by the restaurant after it had been operating for only a few years—back in the early 1980s. "They were talking to my parents about the house, and I guess somebody mentioned something about if there were any ghosts in the building. And the Jacksons said, 'Well, if you're having things getting thrown around and broken, it's probably the ghost of Mariah Jackson.'"

The Jackson family members went on to explain that Mariah Jackson had a bit of a temper and was prone to throwing tantrums . . . and china. Scott went on to tell me that when they were digging out the ground floor of the building during renovations, they came across an enormous amount of smashed china—buckets of it, in fact. "After that, my mom starting telling people about Mariah, and the name sort of stuck. Now if anything falls or breaks here, or even if you jostle something, we say 'Mariah must have done it,'" Scott admitted. "But to my knowledge, no one's ever seen Mariah's ghost here. I certainly haven't." Scott waited a moment and then added, "Well, I did see what I think was a ghost of a woman, but I don't know who she was."

Scott's ghost encounter came at the end of a busy Saturday night. He was in the kitchen, rushing back and forth between the grill area and the dishwasher when something caught his eye. He looked up at the window in the kitchen door and saw a woman standing on the other side, smiling and waving at Scott.

"She was smiling at me and just waving to beat the band," Scott recalled. "She just looked so happy to see me." There was just one problem: Scott didn't recognize the woman at all. Scott told me that there was a bit of glare on the glass, so he squinted a little to see if he could get a better look at the woman. And that's when she simply disappeared. "That's when I thought to myself, 'I think I just saw a ghost.'"

I asked Scott to describe the woman to me. "She was short and dressed funky. I would say it was like chiffon—kind of period—clothes and a big hat. A bigger hat with some sort of brim. I'm pretty sure she had long, gray hair. She looked real. At first I thought she was a real person. She wanted me to see her and looked really happy when we made eye contact."

To this day, Scott still doesn't know who the mysterious woman was. "I don't know if she was someone from this house or someone from my life, but I did not recognize this person."

Since that encounter, Scott told me that from time to time, he will still feel as though someone is watching him when he's back in the kitchen. But each time he looks up at the window in the kitchen door, there's no one looking back at him . . . so far.

Betty Snider was a fixture at Clay Haus and truly seemed to enjoy each and every moment she worked at the restaurant. There were many who believed that Betty would always be a part of Clay Haus, which is why, when she passed away unexpectedly, it came as a shock to her family and friends. Out of respect, Clay Haus closed for a few days. On the evening they were scheduled to reopen for dinner, Chris Riffle had gone in a few hours earlier to get things ready. "I had been there a while, just working. Around 3:00, I heard the front door open," Chris recalled.

Thinking it was a customer who didn't realize the restaurant wasn't open yet, Chris went to the front door, only to find no one there. The front door was still locked from the inside. When Scott Snider arrived for work a short time later, Chris told him what had happened. "Scott said it was probably just the wind," Chris relayed. "But there was no wind that day and the door was still locked."

It wouldn't take long for Scott to have his own encounter with the front door seemingly opening on its own. "The very next day," Chris began, "Scott was sitting in the salad bar area and right around 3:00, he said he heard what sounded like someone trying to get in the front door." Going to the front door, Scott found it still locked, with no one standing outside either, and that's when it hit him. "Scott said my grandmother [Betty Snider] would always come in around 3:00, hang around for a while, and then leave."

"It still happens today," Chris said when I brought up the noises at the front door. "Usually in September, right around the time she [Betty Snider] died. It doesn't seem tied to 3:00 anymore, though."

THE VIGIL

For this vigil, I was accompanied by two members of The Ghosts of Ohio, Mark DeLong and Julie Black. We also had a special guest for the evening: Beth Santore, who, aside from running the amazing and informative Web site, Grave Addiction (www.graveaddiction.com), was also instrumental in my getting permission to investigate Clay Haus.

After conducting several interviews and visiting the infamous Bloody Horseshoe Grave in nearby Somerset, we headed back to Clay Haus for a quick dinner before setting up the equipment. As I was sitting there, enjoying my meal, I was struck by the overwhelming feeling of warmth that seems to come from literally every corner of Clay Haus. Betty Snider's idea that Clay Haus should function as a haven for weary travelers was evident everywhere you looked, from the warm, inviting fireplace to the assorted family photos on the walls, mixed among the antiques and assorted bric-a-brac. It was obvious that Clay Haus truly was a family affair, right down to Betty's son, Scott, cooking our dinners and her grandson, Chris, serving it to us.

When we had stuffed ourselves, we brought in all the equipment. As

Clay Haus is a functioning restaurant, we were not able to put most of the equipment in place until after the building had closed down for the night and everyone had gone home.

Given that on this particular evening, the downstairs tavern room and dining area were not being used, we decided to use it as our staging area. That way, we could get all the video cameras on tripods and the microphones attached to their shock mounts and mic stands and then just move them all into place once the building was locked up for the night. Knowing that, with the exception of the Ouija board incident, there had been little in the way of ghost activity in the downstairs dining area, we decided to keep all our monitors in that room, which would also allow us to have a full view of the staircase, where people had reported seeing ghosts walking.

Once we had everything staged in the downstairs dining room, we waited for the "all clear" signal and started moving everything into place. Here's where all the equipment ended up:

Entryway
- one infrared video camera, pointing toward the front door
- one infrared DVR night-vision camera, pointing into the dining room
- one Superlux condenser microphone next to the cash register, pointing toward the front of the building

Main Dining Room
- one DVR night-vision camera, pointing across the dining room toward the front door

Salad Bar Area
- one DVR night-vision camera, pointing toward the kitchen door

Kitchen
- one DVR night-vision camera, pointing toward the kitchen door
- one Superlux condenser microphone in the far corner, facing the center of the room

Main Staircase
- two infrared video cameras, one at the top of the stairs, pointing down toward the landing and the other at the bottom of the stairs, pointing up at the landing
- one Superlux condenser microphone at the center of the landing

The basement dining area of Clay Haus. People sitting at the rectangular table in front of the fire, with their backs to the fireplace, have reported seeing ghosts walking down the staircase in front of them.

- Vernier LabPro sensors, including two ambient temperature devices, one electromagnetic sensor, and one static charge sensor running the length of the bottom portion of the staircase and the landing
- laser grid, pointing up from the bottom of the stairwell toward the landing

Blue Room Dining Area (Third Floor)
- one infrared video camera in the doorway, pointing across the room toward the shelf with the ceramic bed warmer on it
- one Superlux condenser microphone in the doorway, pointing into the room

For the first part of the vigil, Julie and Beth were going to sit in the main dining room and I was going to spend some time alone on the third floor. Mark would stay in the basement and monitor things. When we all headed off to our designated locations, I suddenly realized

I had forgotten to change the batteries in the hand-helds I always carry with me, so while the others got into position, I stayed in the basement with Mark and replaced the batteries. I was still doing that when Mark called me over to the monitors, stating that the Vernier LabPro sensors were acting "strange."

Before we go any further, perhaps I should give a bit of background on the Vernier LabPro sensors. By and large, most of the sensors are ambient, meaning they take readings from a general area—roughly up to a few feet away from the sensor/probe—as opposed to a specific location. We set up the sensors so that they take a reading every half second, so two readings every second. I realized a long time ago that despite what some people will tell you, there is no reading or number that means there's a ghost nearby. Believe me, I wish there were. But basically, we are looking for readings that are strange, like changes in temperature when there's no breeze present or the sudden detection of EMF when there haven't been any readings for most of the night—that sort of thing. We will even go so far as to put ambient temperature sensors at opposite ends of the area we're monitoring (e.g., a hallway) in an effort to determine which way the temperature variance is moving. So, for example, if there is a drop in temperature recorded by the sensor at the left end of a hallway, followed by a drop at the right end, we can infer that whatever that cold spot represents, it was moving from left to right. That's the sort of thing that helps us find out where drafts (and sometimes ghosts) in a building originated from.

The other thing to note about the Vernier LabPro is that the sensors are incredibly sensitive. Even someone walking within six feet or so of the sensors will probably affect the readings, so you have to spend some time staring at the monitor in order to see what patterns are "normal" and which ones are not.

So when Mark called me over to the monitor and pointed at the real-time graph that was being plotted by the sensors, I first thought I was looking at the telltale signs of Beth and Julie walking up the stairs on their way to the main dining area: one temperature sensor at the end of the stairs registering a temporary increase in temperature, followed by the EMF sensor in the middle of the stairs reacting, and finally, the temperature sensor at the other end of the stairs registering a temperature increase.

"That's Beth and Julie," I said, somewhat annoyed.

"Well, that could be," Mark commented, "except for one small problem. Beth and Julie went *up* the stairs. This," he said, pointing to the graph the sensors were plotting, "indicates that something came *down* the stairs."

Sure enough, when I took a closer look, that's exactly what the chart was showing: something coming down the stairs. The order in which the sensors reacted was as follows: temperature sensor near the landing, EMF sensor in the middle of the bottom portion of stairs, and finally, temperature sensor near the bottom of the stairs. Looking at it all together, it appeared as though something came down the first set of stairs (from the main dining area), went across the landing, and then down a portion of the lower set of stairs. And then—get this—turned around and went back up the stairs!

The Vernier LabPro system we use hardly ever records anything out of the ordinary for us. Make no mistake—it works and works well. But if you were to look at how many times we set up the system and it recorded something we couldn't explain, you could probably count all those instances on one hand. Again, the system works. One reason the Vernier LabPro system may rarely record inexplicable events is because what we think of as ghosts may not be as prevalent as some would have us believe. This is why I was so intrigued by what I was looking at in the Clay Haus basement. It was also why I immediately began to suspect that perhaps the system was malfunctioning.

So Mark and I spent some time resetting the sensors and even repositioning them on the stairs. For a while, they would perform as expected. But every so often, they would appear to detect the same sort of movement: something coming down the stairs, across the landing, and down the first few steps toward the basement before reversing and heading back up and disappearing.

We even conducted experiments with each of us taking turns walking up and down the stairs to see if the sensors were somehow picking up our residual energy. While the sensors would certainly react to us when we were in close proximity to them, once we were clear of the stairs and the landing, they would return to normal and start recording essentially steady readings.

During the course of the evening, there were five instances or events when these odd variances occurred. The EMF readings increased from an average of 1.2 milligauss to a 4.9 milligauss during each event. The temperature variance was seven degrees. Oddly enough, despite the age-old claim that it gets cold when ghosts are around (cold breezes, etc.), the temperature rose rather than fell during the events. In essence, both the EMF and temperature readings closely mimicked those that occur when a live person walks by the sensor. Yet at no point during any of the five events did anyone present during the vigil see a person or anything else, for that matter, standing or walking on the steps even though the portion of the stairs where the events were taking place, including the landing, were in full view. Simply put, there is currently no explanation for the activity we witnessed and recorded that night. The Vernier LabPro, including all the sensors, had not behaved like that prior to or following that evening in the Clay Haus, and it is still in use today. I should also note that at no point did anything appear to break or disturb any portion of the laser grid set up on the stairs.

As amazing as that was, the Clay Haus wasn't done sharing its strangeness with us.

Later on in the evening, Julie and I were sitting together in the main dining area. As we sat there in the dark, trying to make contact with the spirits said to roam Clay Haus, Julie mentioned that earlier in the day, when we were getting a tour of the building, she had gotten "a weird feeling" when we first went into the newer dining area, Helen's Room. When I asked her to explain it, Julie said, "I don't know. It was just creepy. It wasn't a good feeling." So, of course, even though there hadn't been any ghost activity reported in Helen's Room, I immediately wanted to check it out.

Once we were in Helen's Room, Julie and I walked around in silence for a few minutes before I asked her if she was still getting the same feeling as she had earlier. "Not really," she responded, "but it still doesn't feel right in here." I was just about to ask her if she could pinpoint where the feeling was coming from when we both heard it—a noise that I can only describe as a scream.

To say that this noise could be heard with the naked ear would be an understatement. It was loud and we both had no problems hearing it in real time. When we heard it, we were both standing almost one third of the way across Helen's Room. We had been walking side by side, I on the left—with the back of the building to my left—and Julie on my right.

Staircase from the main dining room leading down to the basement dining area. This is the staircase on which the ghosts are most often sighted.

As for where the sound emanated from, it appeared to come from the window on the far left (when facing the windows) that looked out at the rear of the building (Julie later confirmed she thought that as well). The odd thing is that when you look out any of those windows at the back of Helen's Room, you're basically looking out at empty space since you're almost two stories off the ground, and yet this screaming noise seemed to be coming from just on the other side of the window.

The noise itself lasted 4.2 seconds and, as I said, when I heard it in real time, my first thought was that it was someone screaming. When I went back and listened to it on my digital voice recorder, the only recording device we had in Helen's Room at the time, while it does still sound scream-like, there are parts of it that sound animal-like. As for what type of animal, I have no idea. I've played it for all sorts of people, including hunters and nature lovers, and have yet to come up with a definitive answer as to what kind of animal could make a noise like that. But theories range from owls and raccoons to squirrels and even domestic cats. I've yet to find anything that sounds like what Julie and I heard and recorded. On top of that, whatever it was sounded like it was literally on the other side of that window. But when I looked, there was nothing there.

Even with two strange incidents in one night, Clay Haus still had one left for me. Toward the end of the night, while we were all downstairs taking a break, I started hearing this weird tapping noise coming through the stereo mixer. The sound was coming from the microphone we had moved into Helen's Room earlier in an attempt to catch the strange scream-like noise Julie and I had heard before. This wasn't a scream, but it was odd and definitely merited a closer look.

As soon as I went into Helen's Room, it was fairly obvious that what I was hearing were raindrops hitting the roof. It had just started to rain, which explains why we hadn't heard the noise before. It was a passing shower, though, and things quickly quieted down again. But while I was in Helen's room, I noticed that the light fixture hanging from the middle of the ceiling was moving. I should probably choose my words wisely here; it wasn't swinging wildly about. It was just slowly moving back and forth, maybe a half-inch in either direction. Knowing that the rest of the group was downstairs, listening through the mixer's headphones, I said out loud, "The ceiling light in here is moving." Immediately after that, I reached up and steadied the light to see if it would start moving again. As I held the light, I noticed that there wasn't much play in it. It felt like it would have taken a lot to get it to move at all. Either way, after I steadied the light and let go, it didn't move again.

Having heard that there was a light moving, Mark DeLong came up and joined me in the room. We played with the light a bit more, trying to get it to move. We even took my notebook and waved it around violently to see if a strong breeze could move it. It couldn't. Then we decided to go up to the floor above to see if there was anything up there that could have caused the light to move.

The floor above Helen's Room is just used for storage. There's only one way to get up there: a separate set of stairs off the main room. When Mark and I went upstairs, we didn't pass anyone or notice anything odd. Once upstairs, other than some boxes and assorted decorations, the room was empty. The ceiling was fairly low, too, so while you could walk upright there, it wasn't easy. Either way, I made my way across the room to

Helen's Room at Clay Haus. The window where a strange "scream" was heard is immediately to the left. The hanging light fixture that seemed to move on its own is visible on the far right.

the part of the floor that was directly above the light fixture in the ceiling of Helen's Room. Once there, I moved around while Mark kept an eye on the light to see if it moved. All my attempts were in vain, though, as I was unable to get the light fixture to budge.

FINAL THOUGHTS

I have absolutely no explanation for what the Vernier LabPro sensors picked up on the staircase that night at Clay Haus. I can't say it was a ghost, simply because I don't know what it was. It was weird, to be sure. The fact that the sensors picked up something coming across the landing and partially down the bottom staircase before reversing and going back up the stairs mirrors what employees claimed to have seen ghosts doing is, well, bizarre. And it is one of the few times, even outside the scope of this book, that the equipment appears to support the emotional claims that people have reported.

But what does it mean? That's hard to say. I wasn't that surprised to find that the staircase was where we appeared to have captured the most activity. If we think in terms of a residual ghost being the result of energy left behind, in what area of a building are people using most of their energy (and get your mind out of the gutter)? Staircases. And in the case of Clay Haus, where there have probably been countless people walking up and down those stairs, the level of residual energy might be incredibly high.

You don't need to be on the staircases of Clay Haus to feel the energy, though. It's all over the building, literally on every floor. In fact, almost every bit of wall space is covered with photos and mementos of days gone by. Those are the real spirits of Clay Haus. And they're waiting to tell you their stories. It's a fact that's best summed up in the oft-quoted words Betty Snider used to describe her pride and joy, Clay Haus: "Take a moment as you sit by our hearth to let your mind wander back to pioneer days. To the days of a little Pennsylvania Dutch village nestled in the wilderness. You may hear it; the past reaching out to the future."

Clay Haus
123 West Main Street
Somerset, Ohio 43783
www.clayhaus.com

TWIN CITY OPERA HOUSE

Several years ago, I received an invitation to speak at the Great Appalachian Spook Show, a paranormal convention that was to be held in McConnelsville, Ohio. Intrigued by the location for the convention, the Twin City Opera House, I readily accepted the invitation.

The night before the convention, my wife, Steph, and I made the trip down to McConnelsville in what was easily the nastiest lightning storm I have ever had the pleasure of being forced to drive in. Never having been to the Opera House before, we decided to go by it that night so that I wouldn't have to try and find it early the following morning, most likely before my caffeine had kicked in.

As we drove through the center of town, we hit a traffic circle. While we whirled around inside it, the sky was suddenly lit up by a huge bolt of lightning that was so bright, it literally made me squint, but not so much that I didn't see the ominous building looming up in front of me: the Twin City Opera House. I must have made an audible gasp because Steph suddenly looked at me and said, "What's wrong?" "Nothing," I said. "That's just a really cool, spooky-looking building. Probably lots of history, too. All it needs is a ghost or two and it's totally going in my book," I told my wife.

The next day, after my presentation, Steph and I were standing outside the Opera House, chatting with one of the organizers, Marty Myers. I told him how much I liked the building and how you could see its rich history everywhere you looked.

"Well, you know this place is supposed to be haunted," Marty said.

"You don't say," I replied, smiling and nodding at Steph.

McConnelsville's Twin City Opera House on the eve of a performance.

THE HISTORY

Beginning in the mid-1800s, Morgan County, Ohio, became quite the happening area, spurred on by the booming coal-mining facilities. The town of McConnelsville was also making a name for itself. Sure, it was known for its cigar-manufacturing plant, but by and large, the coal-mining industry helped build this town, so much so that it became the county seat. Multiple railroad lines crisscrossed the area, too, bringing visitors from all across the state to this thriving town. Even riverboats would make their way up the Muskingum River and moor at the McConnelsville docks while passengers disembarked and spent some time wandering the streets and visiting the various shops and vendors in the town.

To bring more tourists into McConnelsville, hotels began popping up throughout the town. They were successful, but still, the leaders of the town were worried that there was a certain stigma associated with being a coal-mining town. They wanted to present McConnelsville as a distinguished, refined town. It was, after all, the county seat, so after much deliberation, they came up with an idea. What better way to shed the rough-and-tumble image of a coal-mining town than to erect a giant Opera House?

As with all government-related issues, there were disagreements right from the start. For one, government leaders disagreed as to whether or not the building should function solely as an Opera House. Some politicians wanted a new Town Hall instead. In the end, it was decided that the building should function as both an Opera House and a Town Hall.

In 1889, two lots on the northwest side of the town square, an area referred to as the Burned District, were purchased for $4,000. Ground was officially broken in a simple ceremony on October 20, 1889. H. C. Lindsay, a Zanesville architect, was hired to design the building. Lindsay's approved plans called for a three-story building, complete with a clock tower over a hundred feet tall, to be erected at a cost of $16,000.

Construction didn't go according to plan, though. The money dried up and construction costs went way over budget, so much so that the original plans for a clock tower had to be scrapped. Sure, the tower is still there, but the holes that were originally designed to hold multiple clock faces ended up being just windows. Still, construction was completed by the spring of 1892. All in all, the seating capacity of the building was a little over 650, with single-ticket prices costing between 25 and 50 cents.

The grand opening of the Opera House took place on Saturday, May 28, 1892. The first performance was Gilbert and Sullivan's *The Mikado,* which was performed by the Arion Opera Company. Aside from the excitement of opening night, there was also the fact that the Opera House was one of the first buildings in McConnelsville to have electricity. That excitement was short-lived, however, when the main generator broke down even before the curtain went up on Act One. The owners scrambled to fix the generator, which they were finally able to do. Unfortunately, roughly half the audience had already given up and headed home by that time. For that reason, it was not long before the Opera House owners installed gaslights to be used as backup should the electric generator break down again. Some of the original gaslights are still visible inside the Opera House today.

The Opera House continued to stage plays and musical performances and even magic and other variety shows until 1913, when a movie screen was added to run silent films and a projection booth was constructed and added to the rear of the building. In the 1930s, the Opera House upgraded the movie equipment in order to make the jump from silent films to "talkies." In the process, a new projection booth was added. Since then, however, the Twin City Opera House has remained pretty much the same as it was when it first opened over a hundred years ago. So think about that: over a hundred years of history, remaining virtually unchanged, under one roof. Is it any wonder some patrons and employees apparently don't want to leave?

THE EXPERIENCES

While known for many years as a haunted locale, the Twin City Opera House and its ghosts were a bit of an enigma until 2007, when Eric Glosser arrived and began conducting ghost hunts in the building. Impressed with the building and its history, Eric convinced the current owner to open the Opera House for overnight public ghost hunts. And that's when things really started jumping.

In the beginning, Eric and his associate, Marty Myers, were the only ones running the ghost hunts, so at the end of the night, it was up to the two of them to make sure everyone was out of the building before they locked it up.

Eric recalled: "One Saturday night, Marty and I had just finished up with a group. They had all left, and we were in the lobby, getting ready to go. And then we heard someone coming down the stairs from the balcony. I mean, there was no doubt—there were footsteps coming down."

"We thought maybe somebody from the ghost group had come back inside or maybe we'd missed one of them and left them in the building by mistake," Marty added.

Both Eric and Marty went and looked at the stairs that led to the balcony, but there was no one there. In fact, there was no one inside the Opera House except for the two of them.

"Next week, the same thing happened," Eric said. "We'd be ready to leave and we'd hear someone coming down the steps. This happened three weekends in a row."

When Eric and Marty started digging into the history of the building, they found that while there had been whispers about it being haunted for many years, the more detailed accounts could be traced back to one man: Galen Findlay. Findlay owned and operated the building from the early 1960s until the 1990s. He also lived in the building, literally on the stage, for a period of time. Given the amount of time Galen spent inside the Twin City Opera House, it was only a matter of time before the ghosts made their presence known to him.

"Galen might not have been the first person to experience a ghost in the building," Eric confessed, "but so far, we haven't heard stories from anybody from before he took over. When Galen took over, that's when some of the things he had experienced sort of got out and got around."

"Almost all the early stories of hauntings here at the Opera House originated with Galen," Marty confirmed.

Since Galen still lived in the area, Eric and Marty were able to track him down and talk with him about the Opera House and its ghosts. "One of the first things Galen told me," Eric said, "was that the big, heavy curtains on either side of the stage would close on their own. He said they would always stop at the same distance apart—about the distance they would have been when they ran the old silent films here." "The curtains are automated now, but back then, they were manual. You needed two people to move them, they were so heavy. Galen said that when the curtains moved on their own, it was always hard to find someone to help him move them back because everyone was too scared to go back there."

When Galen was running the Opera House, he was also very involved with the church and even ran a youth ministry. One evening in 1963, he had a small group of boys out to the Opera House when they asked Galen if they could go play hide-and-seek in the auditorium. Galen told them "yes," and they quickly bounded off to play. A few minutes later, the boys all came running back, asking Galen who he had hiding out in the auditorium, waiting to scare them. When Galen told them that they were the only ones in the building, the boys began to describe seeing a man dressed in white, standing in one of the aisles. "As they're describing the man they saw," Marty said, "Galen realizes they're talking about Everett Miller, who worked as an usher for almost thirty years. Only problem was that Everett had passed away several years ago."

During the time when Galen was living in the building, they were only showing movies, not doing any stage performances, so Galen was able to block off the area behind the screen and create his own little living space.

"One summer night," Marty began, "Galen and a friend were sitting up on the stage, on a couch in the living room he'd arranged up there." Even though it was late at night, since it was summer, it was very hot inside the building. "But all of a sudden, they start feeling it getting really cold," Marty said.

"Galen said it was so cold, they could see their breath," Eric added.

As the temperature continued to drop, the two men became aware of a strange white mist up on the stage with them. To their horror, the mist began to twist and move, eventually taking on the form of a woman.

"This misty woman starts walking across the stage," Marty explained. "She went from one side of the stage to the other and then up the stairs to the door where one of the dressing rooms used to be. Then she disappeared."

Panicked by what they had just witnessed, Galen and his friend bolted for the back door and ran up the street to Galen's mother's house. "Galen was in his thirties at that point," Eric said, "and here he is, running home to his mother's house. He must have been really scared."

Indeed he was. When Galen recounted the night's events to Marty, he ended the story by saying, "Needless to say, it wasn't too long after that that I was no longer living on the stage."

But before he moved out, the Opera House still had one last scare for Galen.

"Galen was alone in the building and he was down in the orchestra pit, playing the piano," Marty said. "Then he starts hearing someone coming up behind him."

Thinking it was just one of the boys from the youth group sneaking in to scare him, Galen said he decided to keep playing the piano as if he didn't hear the boy. Then, when the boy was right behind him, Galen was going to whip around and give him a good scare.

"So he keeps playing the piano," Marty continued, "and he hears the boy coming closer and closer. The noises get right up on him, and that's when Galen turned around to scare the boy." Only there was no boy standing behind Galen. In fact, there was no one there at all.

"So out the door I went . . . again," Galen told Marty.

Galen Findlay might have left the building, but apparently the ghostly woman still remains. "We've had people tell us they've seen a woman dressed in Victorian clothes up on the stage," Eric said, "but we've never been able to capture her on video. The closest anyone's ever come is a video where the whole stage just slowly illuminates. It's not a bright white—just a glow. And it stays that way, maybe for almost a minute, and it just goes back down. And then there's a little white ball of light that moves out when it's done. It's really weird."

The ghostly woman, whom they've dubbed Victoria, might not be the only ghost haunting the Opera House stage. Some visitors have actually reported seeing a second ghost: a man.

"One night," Marty began, "I was with another investigator, and we were on the main floor, heading toward the steps that lead up to the stage. We were about halfway to the stage when I noticed a guy about twenty feet ahead of us, walking the same way we were—toward the stage. I watched him take about fifteen steps and then walk up the steps to the stage. I could see him perfectly. He was wearing dark clothes and had short hair. He was kind of short, too, like five foot six or so."

Marty told me that the image was so clear he initially thought he was just looking at another investigator, even though he didn't recognize the man. Of course, Marty's opinion changed when he got up on the stage and found that the man he had just seen was nowhere to be found. What's more, the other investigator who had been walking alongside Marty never saw the man.

"I've seen that guy, too," Eric confided. "We were filming in here for a documentary we were doing on the Opera House. Marty was in the basement, and I was on the stage, at the top of the basement steps. I wanted to get some footage of Marty coming up the steps. So I have my video camera and I'm looking down the steps, when all of a sudden, here comes this guy, walking on the stage toward me. Walks right beside me, up by the light panel and out through the curtains. I didn't even think to film it. I just froze."

Eric paused for a moment and then continued: "You know, I think it was the same guy that Marty saw on the stage, except the guy I saw was a little different. The guy I saw was black and shadowy, but it looked like he had a coat and a brim hat on. But he was walking in basically the same place where Marty saw his guy."

If there were an area of the Twin City Opera House that people who are afraid of ghosts would fear to tread, it would be the basement. And apparently, employees have been avoiding it for a long time. At one point, since part of the basement ran beneath the concession stand, the syrup canisters were stored down there—that is, until the delivery-man refused to go down into the basement again. "He told the owners, 'You're gonna have to put those canisters down there yourself because I'm not going down there. There's some weird stuff going on down in that basement,'" Eric Glosser related.

When it became clear that Opera House patrons were starting to leave thirsty because no staff members wanted to go down into the basement either, the decision was made to move the canisters upstairs, where they've remained to this day.

Who or what is lurking in the basement of the Twin City Opera House is currently unknown. What is known is that whatever it is, it's not very friendly.

"We've had dozens of reports of people seeing a black mass or a shadow down in the basement," Eric said. Rather than frighten people away, this creepy visage has instead encouraged a pilgrimage of sorts among ghost hunters, who take to the basement and sit in a circle on folding chairs in an attempt to see the dark shape. Some go away disappointed, though. "Things in the basement aren't very cooperative at all," Marty explained.

"It's hit-and-miss down in the basement," Eric agreed. "But if it's there, you'll feel it. And you can see it, too, even though the basement is pitch-dark. It's because this thing is darker than the dark, if that makes any sense. You can see it moving around."

Apparently, if you want to increase your chances of seeing or inter-acting with something in the basement, you just need to make yourself vulnerable. "It's like if it thinks it can sneak up on you, it's more likely to react," Marty told me. "So I tell people, 'Go make yourself vulner-able; take your chair out of the circle and go sit all by yourself.' I've seen grown men try that, then pick up their chairs from where they were and move them back into the circle!"

If moving out of the circle doesn't work, you could always try being belligerent. Of course, if you do that, I'm of the mind-set that you get what you deserve. "We had a guy down there, provoking, and I see his chair move back six inches, on its own. The guy looked scared to death. It's a dirt floor down there, so you could see how far the chair had moved," Eric said.

Eric and Marty have been able to capture the strange black mass on video. Eric explains how they managed to do that: "We were using a 4-channel DVR system, and we had two of the cameras down in the basement, sort of facing each other. Near the end of the evening, both cameras pick up this black blob forming. Then part of the blob breaks free and covers the lens of one of the cameras—blacks it out. But you can still see it on the other camera. Then it just moves away, and the other camera starts working again."

"During this time, the other two cameras kept working fine, so it wasn't a power fluctuation or anything of that nature," Marty added.

"And there was no one in the building at the time. No one," Eric em-phasized.

In January 2009, Eric and Marty were at the Twin City Opera House, preparing for a very special event: the premiere of the documentary they produced on the Opera House.

They had both arrived early before the Opera House was open, so that they could do a test run of the DVD. Eric and Marty were upstairs in the sound booth and had just put the DVD in and it started play-ing. But since there was no way to communicate with people down in the main seating area to see how the sound levels were, Marty left the sound booth.

"I was walking down one of the balcony aisles," Marty explained. "I was going to lean over the railing and sort of yell down and ask how the sound levels were. I'm coming down the steps, and I see this guy out of my peripheral vision, sitting in one of the seats in the balcony as I pass by. So I turn around right after I pass the guy, and he's not there. So at that point, I'm thinking, 'Well, that was weird.'"

But that wasn't the weirdest part. This was: As Marty was looking at the empty seat where, seconds ago, he had just seen a man sitting, something caught his eye. As his eyes scanned up, across the balcony seats, he saw that same man, now sitting in a different seat, rows away from him.

"He's just sitting there, looking down at the screen on the stage. He was there for maybe two seconds and then he was gone. The seat he had been sitting in was up and it wasn't moving, so I assume it was always up."

When I asked Marty to describe the man, he told me: "He just looked like a normal guy. Nothing unusual about him. He was clean-shaven and had relatively short hair. I didn't notice anything at all about his clothes," Marty said.

But of all the locations inside the Twin City Opera House where paranormal activity is said to occur, the most active location is on the catwalks, high above the stage.

"The first spirit we encountered up on the catwalk was during our first investigation here in 2007," Eric said. "We were up on the catwalk, stage right, and we were asking questions. And we said, 'Tell us your name. We want people to remember you,' and we got an EVP of a young girl saying 'Elizabeth.'"

Since that investigation, the ghost now known as Elizabeth has not only imprinted her voice on numerous EVPs, but she will often cause the lights on K-II meters and ghost meters to flash, often apparently in response to questions. Through this method, ghost hunters claim to have established that Elizabeth is a ten-year-old girl and that she has been haunting the Opera House for a long time. In an effort to make Elizabeth feel more at home, Marty Myers went out and bought her a tea set and a doll to play with, both of which are still visible up on the catwalk, along with other assorted toys that ghost hunters bring and leave behind for her.

But Elizabeth is not alone on the catwalk. Far from it. Another spirit, who first made himself known to Eric and his group in 2008, is Robert Lowry, a former stagehand at the Opera House. Lowry has acquired the moniker "Red Wine Robert" due to an EVP Eric recorded where Lowry's ghost is said to remark, "I've got red wine." Like Elizabeth, Lowry likes to communicate by flashing K-II and ghost meters in response to questions asked of him. And as they do for Elizabeth, ghost hunters bring gifts for Lowry: bottles of red wine and corks from wine bottles. But Lowry doesn't take too kindly to people who touch his stash. "Robert doesn't like it when you touch his bottles," Eric said, "So we tell people to just leave them alone."

Interestingly enough, while both Elizabeth and Red Wine Robert are said to be extremely talkative (through the hand-held devices, that is) and have been known to carry on conversations for upwards of fifteen minutes, it is rare that you can catch them "talking" at the same time. Elizabeth's ghost is said to show up earlier in the evening. When she's done, Robert will show up and take her place.

THE VIGIL

I arrived at the Twin City Opera House with Ghosts of Ohio members Mark DeLong and Sean Seckman. There was a live performance going on at the time, so we had to wait for that to finish before we could start setting up the equipment. Regardless, having heard that public performances tend to stir up the ghosts of the Opera House, I was quite excited to see what, if anything, would happen during this vigil.

After meeting with Eric Glosser, Marty Myers, and Ted Williams, we got a tour of the reported paranormal hot spots, after which we talked about where to place the equipment. When all was said and done, here's what we ended up with:

Stage
- one infrared video camera, stage left and pointing across to stage right
- one infrared video camera, stage right and pointing across to stage left
- one Superlux condenser microphone, center stage toward the back, facing the audience

The catwalk high above the rear of the stage at the Twin City Opera House. This view is leading away from the shrine for Eliza-beth and Red Wine Robert.

· Vernier LabPro sensors, including two ambient temperature de-vices, one electromagnetic sensor, and one static charge sensor, run-ning stage left to stage right

Main Auditorium

· one DVR night-vision camera, pointing toward the stage
· one Superlux condenser microphone, pointing toward the stage

Catwalk (Stage Left)

· one DVR night-vision camera, pointing across the stage toward stage right
· one studio microphone, pointing across the stage toward stage right

Under the Stage

· one DVR night-vision camera on the right side of the room, point-ing to the left

- one Superlux condenser microphone on the right side of the room, pointing to the left

Sub-Basement

- one DVR night-vision camera in the corner of the basement
- one infrared video camera, shooting across the circle of chairs toward the opposite corner of the basement
- one Superlux condenser microphone in the center of the circle of chairs

In addition, we had toyed with the idea of putting some video and audio equipment up on the catwalk on stage right—the area where both Red Wine Robert Lowry and Elizabeth were known to communicate. The problem was that so many people have added to the tea set and doll that Marty Myers had put up there for Elizabeth that the collection had grown into a full-blown shrine. And to be honest, the addition of bottles of red wine and corks for Robert Lowry make this a bizarre display that is a little creepy to look at. Anyway, having such a large display, coupled with the chairs positioned around the area, left little room for equipment. So I made the decision that in lieu of equipment, we would just spend most of our vigil up on the catwalk. When we weren't going to be there, we would leave behind a digital voice recorder and put it right in the middle of the shrine/display.

The first odd incident that occurred during this vigil came during the initial setup of the equipment. I was running cables down into the basement. To reach the basement, there is a small hallway off the room that runs under the stage. At the end of that hallway is a small metal door, a fire door of sorts, that opens up into the dirt-floor basement.

As I'm running the cables, I get to the metal door and pushed on it, but it wouldn't open. In fact, there was no give at all, leading me to believe that it was locked. I looked and felt around for a lock or even a handle or knob, but the door is nothing more than a flat piece of metal. Unable to get the door open, but knowing that both Mark and Sean had been setting up equipment in the basement earlier, the same equipment I was currently trying to run cables to, I walked back out to the stairs leading up to the main stage and called out, "How do you open the door to the basement?" to which Sean yelled back, "Just push on it." A bit perplexed, I walked down to the basement door and pushed on it. Just like before, it wouldn't budge at all. A little cranky now, I walked back out to the stairs and called up to Sean, "I pushed on it, but it's locked." At this point, I heard Sean walking across the stage toward the stairs before he yelled down, "There's no lock on that door. Just push it."

Determined to prove Sean wrong, I marched back down to the door and really threw my shoulder against the offending door, which promptly flew open, nearly causing me to fly headlong into the basement. Unlike the previous two times, I felt absolutely no resistance when I put my shoulder to it. As soon as my shoulder made contact with the door, it popped open. Coincidence? Possibly. But personally, I'd like to think there were ghosts on the other side of that door, holding it closed while they tried to stifle their ghostly giggles. Then when I went to throw my shoulder against the door, they ran (or floated) away to hide, peeking out just long enough to see me come hurtling into the basement like a bad reenactment of a *Three Stooges* episode.

As soon as all the equipment was set up, the first place Mark, Sean, and I wanted to spend some time in was the catwalk. We wanted to see if we could start up a conversation with Elizabeth and/or Red Wine Robert. During the interviews, both Eric and Marty mentioned that the ghosts' favorite way of communicating was through a ghost meter, known to most people as a cell sensor (unless you get the version that has the cool "Ghost Meter" sticker on it). Basically, this meter picks up electromagnetic fields with a special nod to those put out by cell phones and cell towers. The top of the device is made of red plastic with a light inside. The light flashes when it picks up electromagnetic fields, and the device also beeps, both of which are a benefit to ghost hunters who are sitting in the dark. With that in mind, I made sure I had my cell sensor along with the other hand-helds I took up to the catwalk.

Once up in the catwalk, Sean and Mark sat around the "shrine" while I leaned against the back wall. We began by taking turns asking questions, all of which went unanswered. But after about twenty minutes with no results, the cell sensor meter started beeping and blinking, slowly at first, but then it became constant, meaning there was a rather substantial level of EMF around me.

The entire time we were up on the catwalk, the cell sensor I had with me had remained in the same place—in the front right pocket of my vest. It was almost completely covered with only the top portion of the

The shrine for Elizabeth and Red Wine Robert. The wall where we encountered strange EMF readings is directly behind the shrine.

device—the red plastic portion—sticking out. I had been in the same spot since I got up there: leaning with my back against the rear wall of the Opera House.

After beeping wildly for approximately one minute, the cell sensor began to slow down. While this was going on, Mark DeLong stood up and began taking readings around me with an EMF gauge. Mark was able to find an EMF reading of 8.2 milligauss immediately to my right, but it kept moving farther and farther away from me. It was as if whatever was putting off the EMF was moving down the wall, away from me. Shortly after my cell sensor stopped beeping, the EMF level Mark had been tracking disappeared, and the entire length of the wall I was leaning against was now reading a fairly constant 1.2 milligauss.

While Mark and Sean searched for the source of the strange EMF level that appeared to have moved across the wall, I maintained my current spot, waiting and hoping for the cell sensor to start beeping again. After about fifteen minutes of no activity, Mark suddenly announced that he had found the source. Almost dead-center of the rear wall, Mark had found an area about two feet wide and running from the floor to

Using a ghost meter (a.k.a., cell sensor) to track anomalous EMF readings across the rear wall of the Opera House.

as high as he could reach. The EMF meter, when placed flat against the wall, was reading 9.3. If Mark moved the meter two feet to the right or left, the EMF level would suddenly drop to a 1.2. I can't stress enough how this makes absolutely no sense. The reason for this is simple: electricity "bleeds."

Put another way, let's say that a television in the corner of a room is putting out an EMF level of 5.0 milligauss. Well, if you place your EMF meter directly against that TV, you'll get a reading of 5.0. Then as you back away from the TV, the levels will gradually decline as you get farther and farther away. But the levels never just suddenly drop all the way down. Never. Electromagnetic fields don't work that way. It's actually one of the things that helps us determine where any odd levels of EMF are coming from. You just start moving slowly in different directions and watch to see if the levels on the meter go up or down. It's sort of like playing a game of "hot or cold" and trying to find where the EMF is hiding.

So while Mark and Sean marveled at this truly unique event, I was standing still against the wall. All of a sudden, Mark announced, "It's moving." What he meant was that the EMF levels were widening. Initially, the area of wall that had the 9.3 reading was only about two feet wide. It was now three feet wide . . . and growing. And it seemed to be growing in both directions, moving both to the left and the right of where Mark's initial readings had been. It was basically spreading out across the wall—the wall I was leaning against. As Mark continued to track the EMF, he kept moving closer and closer to me. Eventually, the cell sensor in my pocket began beeping, too.

When Mark reached me, he paused for a moment and then, meter still in hand, he skipped over me and continued down the wall. Whatever was causing the EMF levels, my portly body wasn't enough to keep it from spreading. However, once it got to the end of the wall, the levels stopped and remained right there, where the two walls met. As before, there appeared to be a line drawn between the high level of EMF and the low level; no bleeding. Mark kept getting levels upwards of 9.0 milligauss on the one wall, but as soon as he slid it over to the other wall, the levels would immediately and significantly drop down an average of 8.0 milligauss. Again, this is not something, as Mark said, "that happens in nature."

After a few minutes of steady levels, the high EMF reversed its path and started back down the wall from where it came, with Mark and his EMF in tow. As before, it didn't let me get in its way, hopped over me, and made its way back to the center of the wall where Mark had originally found it. As it passed over me, the beeping from my cell sensor slowed and eventually stopped altogether. At no time did I feel or see anything out of the ordinary. So, you know, it's not like I felt a ghost move through me or anything. I was blown away by what I was witnessing, though.

Once it got back to roughly the spot it had been originally, that twofoot-wide area continued to give off a high level of EMF and then, inexplicably, it disappeared. Sean and Mark were unable to locate it. We waited another twenty minutes or so for it to come back, but it didn't. So thinking we might be able to find a rational explanation for it—such as faulty electrical wiring—we decided to go behind the Opera House to see what was on the other side of the brick wall I had been leaning against.

I didn't think we were going to find anything. For one, we were way up high above the stage area and there were no visible wires, outlets, or anything of that nature along that wall. It was also a solid brick wall, which meant it was highly unlikely that there was anything inside the wall that could be causing those strange levels. But most of all, I didn't think we'd find anything because I had no idea what we were looking for. I had never experienced an instance where EMF levels not only seemed to move freely, but, as I mentioned earlier, I've never encountered a field that had such clearly defined lines.

Once the three of us got outside, while we did see a power line attached to one of the exterior walls, it was nowhere near the wall where we'd tracked the high levels. In short, we couldn't find anything to substantiate or explain what we'd just encountered up in the catwalk. Strangely enough, the exterior walls didn't register any EMF levels above a 2.0.

Deciding to try another area to explore, we asked Eric, Marty, and Ted to join us in the basement and show us how ghost hunters have traditionally sat in the circle of chairs to attempt to have an experience with the dark shape that's so often reported in the basement.

The entire group sat in a circle, in the darkness of the basement, for a while. Not getting any results, I decided it was time for me to "make myself vulnerable" and to wander off, alone, to the depths of the basement to see if the shadow would come for me.

I picked a spot far away from the circle of chairs, so far that I could identify where they were only by the faint glow coming off of one of the hand-held video cameras. Incidentally, it was very near where the syrup canisters had originally been stored.

This part of the basement is a little odd. While you can stand up in most of the basement, here you have to stoop a bit, lest you risk smacking your head against an exposed beam. After climbing back as far as I could, I crouched down, turned off my flashlight, and waited patiently for something to come and get me.

Waiting for a ghost to show up is sort of like being a child lying in bed on Christmas Eve. Even though the lights are out and everything is quiet and calm, your heart's pounding and your mind is racing. Everything—and I do mean everything—is amplified. Every small noise becomes a ghostly footstep. Shadows seem to dance across the walls. It takes some practice to ground yourself so that you're not jumping at shadows. So that's what I did: I took a couple of deep, cleansing breaths, tilted my head back, closed my eyes . . . and waited.

Nothing happened. The whole time I was there, alone and vulnerable, I didn't see, hear, or feel anything strange. After a while, I seriously considered provoking—basically yelling at the ghost, calling it names, and daring it to do something—but I've never been able to do that. Ghosts were people once, too, and it just seems rude. So instead, I stayed there, crouched, until my legs and back pretty much let me know it was time to go.

After that, Eric, Marty, and Ted went out to the lobby, leaving Mark, Sean, and me to continue exploring. We decided to split up and spread out across the auditorium to see if we could catch a glimpse of a ghost up on the stage or perhaps the gentlemen who have been seen walking around and even sitting in the seats. I chose to go up to the balcony, where Marty Myers had reported seeing the ghost of a man who jumped from seat to seat.

As soon as I got there, I sat next to the seat where Marty had first seen the ghost. I decided to try an EVP session and asked the ghost what his name was and why he had chosen that seat to sit in. I then remarked that perhaps the view would be better elsewhere and that he should go and check out another seat. My thought was that if I could get the ghost to sit in another seat, I might see the seat move in some way. Sounds good in theory, but in reality, it was a long shot. In fact, it completely backfired on me as none of the seats moved at all.

Next, I moved down a few rows, closer to the front of the balcony. From my seat, I not only had a clear view of the stage, but I could also lean over to take a look at the main auditorium below me. I again tried an EVP session, all the while keeping an eye on the stage. Once again, it was in vain as nothing out of the ordinary took place.

We then decided it was time to go back up to the catwalk to see if we could recreate the strange EMF readings that moved along the wall. I also asked Marty, Eric, and Ted to join us to see if their presence would affect the level of odd activity in any way. Upon reaching the catwalk, I positioned myself where I had been earlier in the night. I made sure the cell sensor was back in my front pocket again, too. Mark took some baseline readings of the wall with his EMF and confirmed that the levels were averaging around 1.3 milligauss.

Since Eric Glosser is supposed to have a special connection to Red Wine Robert, we asked Eric if he would reach out to Robert and see if he would talk with us. As Eric was doing just that, Mark announced that he was getting readings on the back wall again. As we all watched Mark, just as he had done earlier in the evening, he began to track an ever-widening area of EMF across the wall. Once again, as the levels got closer to me, my cell sensor began going off. Almost as if we were reenacting a scene from earlier that evening, the EMF moved down the wall, over me, and to the end of the wall. There, it paused before reversing and moving back down the wall and then disappearing.

We continued to track the EMF's movement for several hours over the course of the evening. There didn't seem to be any sort of pattern related to how often it would happen or even how long each incident would last. But each time the field appeared, it would start at one spot on the back wall, extend the whole length of the wall, and move back down the wall before dissipating. I've never been able to find a rational explanation for what occurred that night.

Days later, while reviewing the materials we had collected during the vigil, we found that there was one more surprise waiting for us. At approximately 3:14 A.M., when Mark and I, the only two people in the Opera House, were up on the catwalk tracking the EMF, the video camera located stage left picked up something truly bizarre: something that sounds like a man singing.

The sound appeared to be coming from the opposite side of the stage— stage right. It is soft, but it is definitely there. It lasts for approximately four seconds, sounds very melodious, and has a distinct rhythm to it; it sounds like a song, although no one who has heard the recording has been able to identify it. Some, however, say it sounds like someone warming up his vocal cords before a performance. Either way, the voice pattern does not match that of anyone who was in the Opera House that night. Stranger still, while there were multiple recording devices in the general area where the video camera that recorded the sound was, including two studio microphones, the singing sound was recorded only by the one video camera.

FINAL THOUGHTS

Of all the possible evidence I recorded for this book, what happened to me up on the Opera House's catwalk was some of the weirdest. In fact, I would argue that it was one of the strangest things I've ever encountered in my almost thirty years of conducting ghost research. There's just no reason for EMF to behave like that.

But is that proof that the Twin City Opera House is haunted? Certainly not. Even if we never find a rational explanation for what happened, until we have concrete proof that a ghost can cause EMF to act like that, we simply cannot call the activity that happened on the catwalk ghost-related.

Still, that's not to say the activity has no effect at all on the Opera House ghosts. Far from it. Eric Glosser and Marty Myers have become obsessed with determining not only who haunted the Twin City Opera House, but why. It's the not knowing that frustrates and motivates them to uncover the building's secrets and assemble a portion of its history that, so far, remains unknown. And that's where the bizarre EMF readings on the catwalk come into play. They are weird, bizarre, unexplained—just the kind of thing that Eric and Marty need to motivate them on their quest to complete the Twin City Opera House's history. That is the best part of it all because, once again, ghosts are trying as hard as they can to keep actual history alive.

Twin City Opera House
15 West Main Street
McConnelsville, Ohio 43756
www.operahouseinc.com

WAREHOUSE STEAK N' STEIN

Back in the canal days of the early nineteenth century, Roscoe Village was quite the happening place. Boats moved up and down the canal system, pausing only long enough to load or unload merchandise and let people disembark to explore Roscoe Village, visiting the stores or perhaps staying overnight in one of the hotels. And at the center of all this hustle and bustle was a warehouse situated a mere stone's throw from the two locks of the village. The building was full of activity, with businessmen, merchants, and warehouse workers scurrying about, stocking shelves, and loading boats.

Much has changed since those days. The canals are all but a memory now. Most of the original shops and businesses in Roscoe Village, while still in operation, have been renovated and renamed. Even the old warehouse, while it still looks the same on the outside, has been transformed into a restaurant on the inside. Out with the old, in with the new. Change, it would seem, really is inevitable. Or is it? Because there are some who believe that late at night, the past awakens inside the old warehouse, time stands still, and the dead walk the hallways.

THE HISTORY

In the early 1800s, merchant James Calder was running the store he owned in Coshocton, Ohio. The only problem was Calder was not much of a businessman and his store went belly up. But what Calder lacked in business smarts he more than made up for in determination, for instead of giving up and picking another line of work, Calder went the other way and decided to go even bigger. Rather than own just a small busi-

A view of Warehouse Steak N' Stein at night. According to legend, even when the restaurant is closed for the evening and all the employees have gone home, there's still activity taking place inside.

ness, he would own a whole town. With that in mind, Calder decided to leave Coshocton and hop across the Muskingum River in 1816, settling on a small plot of land that he proudly named Caldersburg. After building his new home, a log cabin, Calder purchased over sixty adjacent lots and built a log building that functioned as both a tavern and a hotel.

Surprisingly, James Calder's endeavor was a success and Caldersburg began to prosper, becoming something of a small river town. Calder, however, passed away before a major turning point in Caldersburg's history came in 1825: the state of Ohio announced its plans to develop a canal system.

Ohio's plan was to develop a canal system that would run from Cleveland up north through the entire state down to Portsmouth in the south. When it came to the Muskingum River, planners had to decide which side of the river to put the canal on, the Coshocton side or the opposite side of the river, where Caldersburg was currently located. Residents of both towns held their breaths, but when canal workers showed up in the area in the late 1820s, they started digging on the Caldersburg side of the river. A few years later, the first canal boat arrived in Caldersburg in August 1830. And with that, the town really began to thrive and prosper, so much so that it was decided that Caldersburg needed a new name, although how it got it is one of the area's great mysteries.

The man often credited with renaming the town is Noah Haynes Swain, a local judge and politician who, years later, would become the first Republican appointed to the United States Supreme Court. Swain and several other area residents got together and came up with a new name for Caldersburg: Roscoe Village. They chose to name the town after William Roscoe, an English historian and poet, who is probably most remembered for being one of the earliest abolitionists. Why Roscoe? Good question. Not only are there no records to suggest that William Roscoe ever visited the area, but it doesn't appear that he ever set foot in the United States. On top of that, Roscoe died right around the time Caldersburg was renamed, leading many to snicker that Roscoe probably went to his grave without ever knowing a town had been named after him.

The newly named Roscoe Village continued to flourish, aided largely in part by its close proximity to the canal system. However, right around the time that Caldersburg residents were considering the idea of renaming their town, another life-changing event occurred: the arrival of the railroad.

In 1828, the first commercial rail service, the Baltimore and Ohio Railroad, arrived in Ohio. At the time, the canal system was still the preferred method for shipping and transport, but not for long. While the canals could certainly get you from one side of Ohio to the other, they couldn't do it year-round. Once winter came and the canal waters froze, you weren't going anywhere. Not the case with the railroads. With trains, you could go anywhere you wanted to, year-round, as long as there were tracks to roll across. So naturally, when the railroads showed up in the area, trying to decide which side of the Muskingum River to put the tracks on, the residents of Coshocton and Roscoe Village once again held their collective breath. Having lost the canals years earlier, Coshocton ended up winning big this time as the railroad chose to put the tracks on the Coshocton side of the river.

In the 1850s, there was a railroad boom where tracks were being laid everywhere. This was Coshocton's turn to flourish while Roscoe Village had to take a back seat of sorts. They still had the canal system, though, and while the number of shipping and pleasure boats continued to dwindle, Roscoe Village still managed to hang in there, even though it could no longer be said that the village was prospering. Years later, yet another life-changing event took place. In 1913, one of the worst floods in Ohio history swept through the area, carried along in no small part by the canal system.

After the cleanup from the flood, the state of Ohio made it official: they were done with the canals. They considered the canals an antiquated means of transport, and the flood had caused major damage to the canal system. According to the state of Ohio, the cost to repair it was too much, and with that, Roscoe Village began a slow and steady decline.

By the 1960s, Roscoe Village was but a shell of its former self. Almost all the signs of the once-thriving village were gone, leaving nothing more than old—and in some cases abandoned—buildings in their place. As luck would have it, though, a chance drive through the area by a local businessman would revive Roscoe Village.

Successful area businessman Edward Montgomery was enjoying a leisurely drive with his wife, Frances, when they ended up driving through the deserted streets of Roscoe Village. Having grown up in the area, the Montgomerys were quite familiar with how successful Roscoe Village had been back in the day. They were both extremely saddened as to what had happened to the village. They decided that they would fix up the village to return it to its previous glory. They also hit on a unique premise: they would model Roscoe Village after Williamsburg, Virginia, a historic community that is open to the public. And that's exactly what they did.

They began by creating a nonprofit organization whose sole intention was the restoration and preservation of Roscoe Village. Once the organization was in place, they began purchasing and restoring the existing buildings in the village. The first building to be restored was the original Toll House, which was completed in 1968; following that, the old warehouse was transformed into a restaurant.

Some buildings at Roscoe Village were in such decay that they could not be restored. In those cases, the Montgomerys just brought in other buildings. An example of this is the Craftsman's Building, which is not original to Roscoe Village but was relocated to the village as part of the restoration process as it was from the same time period as the heyday of Roscoe Village.

Before Ed and Frances Montgomery passed away, they took steps to ensure their vision for Roscoe Village remained. To that end, the Montgomery Fund still exists and is the operating foundation for Roscoe Village. Today, visitors can literally walk through history by simply wandering up and down the streets of Roscoe Village, taking in the sights and sounds of a canal village brought back to life.

THE EXPERIENCES

The Warehouse Steak N' Stein (or simply, The Warehouse) is a huge, five-story building that sits at the center of Roscoe Village at the oddly named corner of Whitewoman and North Whitewoman streets. The Warehouse is so named because originally that was the building's function in Roscoe Village. The tavern downstairs at The Warehouse is named Lock 27, which got its name from the fact that all the locks in the Ohio and Erie Canal were numbered. Locks 26 and 27 were located in Roscoe Village with lock 27 located right outside the back doors of the Warehouse.

John Larson, current owner of The Warehouse, admits that he takes all the talk about ghosts in the restaurant with a grain of salt and a smile. "We had a psychic come in here one time and tell me that the spirits here are friendly. So I told her, 'Well, they must get into our liquor,'" John said with a grin.

Still, John is quick to point out that some things have happened at the restaurant that defy explanation. "I don't know what it is, but there are a lot of things that happen in this building that are unexplainable. That's how I look at it," he said.

One such incident, which the restaurant owner and patrons still talk about even though it happened years before John Larson took over the building, involved two women who felt like they were chased out of the building. The event took place even before the restaurant underwent its most recent renovations. Back then, there used to be a booth that, oddly enough, was known as Booth 13. Superstitions aside, all the tables and booths in the restaurant are numbered and that booth just happened to be number 13. There was nothing ghostly or unlucky associated with the booth, at least not that anyone could remember. But all that changed the day two women came in for lunch and sat down.

The waitress serving the table had come over, dropped off two glasses of water, and had just started heading back toward the kitchen when she heard a woman scream, accompanied by the sound of shattering glass. Turning around, the waitress saw the two women struggling to get out of the booth as fast as they could. As the pair rushed past the waitress, they hurriedly explained that there was no way they were staying because while they were sitting at the table, the two glasses of water flew off the table and smashed on the floor.

Another famous story involves a male employee, Gene, who was working during Roscoe Village's Canal Days Festival. The employee was heading to The Warehouse's basement storeroom when he remembered that his wife, who also worked at The Warehouse, was on break and was sitting downstairs at the Lock 27 Tavern, eating her lunch, so he decided to swing by the tavern to say "hi."

As he was walking toward his wife at the bar, Gene told me he saw another man walking toward the bar, too. "He had on old clothes, like he was one of the Canal Days vendors in costume or something like that," Gene said. Thinking the man was looking for a table for lunch, Gene said to the approaching man, 'Let me get you a waitress' and turned to find one. But when Gene turned back around, he found the man had simply vanished.

"It looked like a regular man—like I'm looking at you now," Gene said to me. "I looked him straight in the eye."

A few weeks later, people at the restaurant were passing around some pictures of The Warehouse before it had been restored. Included in the stack of pictures were some taken years ago, when the building was a general store. "In one of those old pictures, I see the guy who walked up to me down in the tavern," Gene told me. "Nobody knows who he is, but it's the same guy."

Just because John Larson hasn't been at The Warehouse as long as some of the other employees doesn't mean he hasn't had his share of strange encounters. One week night he was finishing up a few things in the restaurant with Craig, a bartender. "It was ten minutes to eleven. Our kitchen closes at ten during the week, so there was no one back there. Everyone's gone for the night," John said.

John told me that he was walking with Craig toward the kitchen and that as soon as they entered, they heard the printer that prints out orders, printing. "We both just sort of looked at each other and I remember thinking, 'Who would be doing that? Kitchen's closed.'"

John went over to the kitchen printer and saw that four different orders were printing out, including one that appeared to come from John himself. "It was an actual order from me," John exclaimed. "That makes no sense because to place an order, you have to first log onto the computer with your password. Then you put the order in and it prints out in the kitchen. But I'm the only one that knew my password, and I know I didn't send the order."

The order itself was even more bizarre. "The order was for four rare burgers and three loaded baked potatoes. They were different burgers, too: one bacon mushroom Swiss, two cheeseburgers, and one plain burger," John explained.

John told me he found the receipt so strange that, while he threw the other ones away, he kept the one that had his name on it. "I still have

Receipt from Warehouse Steak N' Stein showing the mysterious order that was placed after hours from a locked computer, using owner John Larson's password—all without Larson's knowledge and while he was in the building cleaning up.

it on my bulletin board," he said, "because it sold me a little bit about ghosts being here. I'm not really a believer or a disbeliever, but I know there could be things out there that are hard to explain. And that receipt is extremely hard to explain. I don't know how it happened."

Another time, John was upstairs in his office, doing some paperwork. Once again, it was after hours and The Warehouse was locked up tight. As John was busying himself with paperwork, something on the security system monitor near his desk caught his eye. The monitor was divided up with each section showing a different image, captured live by the various video cameras placed around The Warehouse. All the images appeared normal, except the one near the interior doorway to the Lock 27 Tavern. That's the one that caught John's eye.

As John watched the live feed, the entire doorway to Lock 27 Tavern lit up with a weird, off-white glow. "It was the doorway near the end of the bar," John explained. "All the lights were off, so it wasn't a reflection or anything. It was like there was just a glow—and the whole entrance, the whole door—was just covered by a glow."

The weird glow lasted for approximately ten to fifteen seconds and then quickly faded away. "I have no idea what could have caused that," John told me. "It was kind of nerve-wracking, to tell you the truth, especially being here all by myself."

As someone who has known the building for several decades, all the way back to the early 1970s, when he took art lessons in the building with the local art guild, Ron Cummings now not only works in the restaurant, he has become its unofficial historian. Of course, that means people don't just come to Ron to share stories about the building's history. They want to tell him about the ghosts, too.

"I think the thing that I hear the most is people tell me they feel these phantom pats on their back," Ron explained. "I've had employees and customers tell me they will just be sitting there and it's like someone comes up behind them and pats them on the back." When the people turn around, there's never anyone there. Ron told me that while people are sometimes startled to find they're not alone after just feeling someone touch them, the pats themselves are reassuring and comforting and seem to come at a time when they're upset or sad about something. "It's usually when they are feeling down," Ron said. "That's when people feel it the most. It's like someone's telling them, 'It's going to be all right.'"

Ron's never felt a ghost pat him on the back, but he did have a rather disturbing encounter with something up in the attic in 1993.

"They sent me up there to clean and sweep," Ron explained. "Back then, the attic was set up with like a stage in the center and then it drops off on either side. As I'm sweeping, I heard a real loud whimper. It was like a big dog or something. But I looked around and there wasn't anything there. But I heard it, and it was really loud."

Ron said he thought that maybe he was hearing something coming from the floor below him. So he went downstairs and looked around. Finding nothing, he decided he needed to go back upstairs, finish sweeping as quickly as possible, and get out of there—fast.

"That was the first time I thought there might be ghosts here. I'd heard stories, but that was the first time I heard or saw anything here," Ron confessed.

So where is the most haunted spot at The Warehouse? That award would be the sub-basement. "That's the area that people don't like going to," Ron Cummings told me.

Employees tend to avoid the sub-basement at all costs because of what is said to lurk down there. It doesn't appear to be very friendly, or perhaps it's just misunderstood. Either way, it's been known to push and shove people who go down there.

There is also said to be an overwhelming feeling of fear and dread that overtakes you the further you go into the sub-basement. Employees often report not being able to take more than ten steps into the room before they start to feel uneasy. One woman even reported that it felt like something was trying to smother her.

"One time, a well-known local psychic came in and said she was having conversations with ghosts down in the sub-basement," Ron related. "She said they were nice, though, so I don't know why they would push anybody."

Ask anyone familiar with the ghosts of The Warehouse to name a ghost who haunts the building, and one name will keep coming up: Phoebe. So who is Phoebe and, more importantly, why does she haunt The Warehouse? Those questions proved to be a lot harder to answer than first thought.

"As long as I can remember, there's always been a 'house ghost' here and they kind of think of it as a female," Ron explained. "But as far as I know, no one's ever seen the ghost of a woman here."

That's true. Of all the people I interviewed, none of them reported seeing the ghost of a woman inside or even on the grounds of The Warehouse. In fact, according to the people I interviewed, only one of them claimed to have actually seen a ghost, and that ghost was clearly male. To further cloud the ghostly water, several books and Web sites call the ghost "Matilda" instead of "Phoebe" and claim she haunts the building because she was murdered here. "There was a Matilda, and she was indeed murdered," Chris Hart, Roscoe Village's living historian, told me. "But she wasn't murdered in the building or even on the property where The Warehouse stands today."

OK, so we're back to square one. Where did the name Phoebe come from?

The name comes from Phoebe Medberry, wife of Arnold Medberry. Together, the couple was responsible for erecting several of the original buildings in Roscoe Village, including The Warehouse. To honor her, one of the banquet rooms upstairs was originally named The Phoebe. Some claim that at one point, there was even a sign reading "Phoebe" above the doors to the room (the rooms have all since been renamed). Apparently, with stories of a ghostly woman in the building circulating, someone just took the name Phoebe from the door and assigned it to the ghost, and the name stuck.

As for the story that Phoebe died in the building, that, too, is false. While Phoebe Medberry is indeed buried near Roscoe Village, her body was returned to the area after she passed away in Kansas.

THE VIGIL

Even though Wendy Cywinski and Samantha Nicholson were to accompany me on The Warehouse vigil, I arrived several hours earlier as I needed to interview Ron Cummings. That interview took place at the back of The Warehouse's dining area, which was empty except for the two of us as it was not yet dinnertime.

At one point in the interview, Ron and I were discussing the ghost known as Phoebe and where that name originated. Ron was talking about how it's just a name that has been given to the ghost and that no one is really sure what the ghost's name is. At one point on the recording, there is a very strange noise that occurs immediately after Ron tells me "Around here, it's always 'OK, Phoebe, go ahead and play,' because that's just the name that's associated with her." The noise goes on for approximately three seconds and it sounds like the digital voice recorder is violently bouncing up and down—only the recorder never moved, at least not that I saw. During the entire interview, the recorder remained in the same spot. Whenever I'm conducting interviews, my recorder is usually sitting on an angled, flip-out stand. That's where it was when it picked up the strange sound. It was in the middle of the table, pointing directly toward the people I was interviewing. The recorder ran the entire length of the interviews, roughly one hour and twenty-eight minutes. The noise was heard only once during that entire time. I've not heard this type of sound on this or any other recording device before or since.

Once Wendy and Sam arrived, we tried to figure out a game plan for the night's vigil. The Warehouse posed an interesting problem for us as it is both a restaurant and a tavern. So not only would there be a lot of traffic moving throughout the building, but it would also be open quite late into the evening. Based on that, we decided to use very little of the big audio and video equipment and instead use hand-held devices almost exclusively. As for the bigger equipment, we would keep those mainly down in the sub-basement as that area, for the most part, did not have any foot traffic coming through. Of course, the fact that it was rumored to be one of the most haunted spots in the building helped, too.

So here's where the equipment ended up in the sub-basement for The Warehouse vigil:

- one infrared video camera just inside the first doorway, pointing toward the second doorway
- one infrared video camera just inside the second doorway, pointing across the back room
- one infrared video camera in the far corner of the back room, facing toward the camera in the second doorway
- one Superlux condenser microphone just inside the first doorway, pointing toward the second doorway
- one Superlux condenser microphone in the center of the back room
- Vernier LabPro sensors, including two ambient temperature devices, one electromagnetic sensor, and one static charge sensor in the center of the back room

Prior to setting up the equipment, I wanted to try a little experiment with Sam and Wendy. They had not been involved with any of the interviews, so they knew nothing of the reported ghost activity. Even if they had looked online or read books about The Warehouse ghosts, there was something I learned during the interviews that I had never heard of before—namely, the overwhelming feelings of dread that some people have felt in the sub-basement. So when Wendy and Sam arrived, I wanted to take them on a tour to see if they could pick up any weird feelings in the sub-basement.

Without telling them anything, I asked Wendy and Sam to come on a tour and let me know afterwards where, if anywhere, they felt ghosts might be lurking. We started up in the attic and then went through every single room of The Warehouse, even walking through the dining areas. When the tour was over, I pulled Sam aside first and then Wendy and asked if they felt anything. They both told me that overall the building felt "fine" or "normal," except for one area in particular. Guess which one? Both Wendy and Sam said they felt uncomfortable in the sub-basement. What was even more intriguing to me was the fact that they both picked a specific area in the basement, an area that also happened to be where, according to Ron Cummings, the psychic was standing when she claimed to be talking to ghosts.

Later that evening, when Sam and I were setting up the Vernier LabPro sensors in the basement, I thought it would be interesting to set them up near the spot where the psychic had been standing (and where Sam and Wendy had felt strange). But when we placed some of the EMF sensors on the ground, they started behaving oddly. They were shooting out random pulses where the EMF appeared to jump from 1.1 milligauss up to 6.9 milligauss in two seconds' time. Sam and I actually thought the sensors had malfunctioned until we put an EMF meter directly on the floor and watched the numbers dance around. We put a K-II meter next to the EMF, and the K-II started lighting up like a Christmas tree. As Wendy, Sam, and I stood there, trying to figure out what sort of electrical charge could be coming up through a solid concrete floor, the levels suddenly dropped and returned to a steady 1.4 milligauss. It remained that way for approximately twenty minutes before it jumped up to 14.6 milligauss and remained there for over five minutes.

Knowing that there had to be electrical wires running throughout the basement, especially near the furnace, somewhere in the sub-basement, Wendy, Sam, and I fanned out across the room to see if we could determine

Sub-basement of Warehouse Steak N' Stein. Some people report feeling strange as they make their way down this passageway, and in one instance, a psychic claimed to have had conversations with ghosts here. The area where we picked up the anomalous EMF readings coming from the floor is located just on the other side of the doorway, approximately four feet from the seam on the floor.

where the EMF levels were originating from. Try as we might, we couldn't find it. While crawling on the floor with our EMF meters, it appeared as if the high EMF levels were originating from that spot on the floor.

Throughout the evening, the EMF levels continued to shoot up and suddenly drop back down again, seemingly at random. There was no discernible pattern to it. I timed how long the incidents lasted, and even those varied widely. The events also did not seem to be at all related to when the furnace turned on or off. When I asked John Larson about the strange levels and what, if anything, was under that portion of the floor, he had no answers.

When the restaurant and tavern finally closed down for the evening, Wendy, Sam, and I wandered around a bit in the darkness, spending some time in each of the rooms. When it came to the upstairs banquet rooms, I even sat and asked if Phoebe was in any of the rooms with me. I introduced myself, said I was writing a book about The Warehouse, and wanted to hear her side of the story so that I would get it right in my book. I never heard back.

Rejoining Wendy and Sam, we walked through the main dining area. I did a mini-EVP session at a table in the dining room, the same table where I interviewed Ron Cummings when the recorder picked up a sound as if the recorder were being bounced up and down, even though it hadn't moved. This time, though, nothing odd showed up on the tape. At one point, Wendy swore she saw something small and dark, almost shadow-like, dart across the floor. Of course, as is usually the case when something weird or ghostly makes an appearance, I was looking the other way, so I missed it. The fact that Sam didn't see it either was of little solace.

At the end of the evening, after we had packed up everything and were heading off, I decided that I would alter my usual ritual of taking one last look up at the windows of the building I had just investigated to see if a ghost was looking back at me. This time, I decided I would take some pictures of those windows. That way, if there was a ghost up there, I'd have it documented. Alas, no ghost showed up in those photos.

FINAL THOUGHTS

I'd have to say that if I were a ghost, I'd really like to hang out at Warehouse Steak N' Stein, provided, of course, I was permitted to partake in one of their sensational hamburgers!

All joking aside, The Warehouse does have a certain ghostly aura about it—not in a bad way, mind you. It's just that as you're sitting in the restaurant, or especially in the tavern, you can feel the history around you, right down to the original stone foundation the building was constructed on. Touch those walls and you can almost feel the building's nearly two hundred years of history.

The Warehouse also provides an interesting example of how ghost stories and actual history sometimes become intertwined. Here we have unexplained activity, allegedly being caused by a female ghost. She has apparently been at it for years, but just who she is remains a mystery, mainly because no one has ever really seen her. But over time, the name of a real woman, Phoebe Medberry, a historical figure from Roscoe Village, became associated with the ghost. But is it really Phoebe Medberry's ghost? As of this writing, I can't answer that any more than I can answer what caused the weird EMF levels in the sub-basement or the shaking noises on my digital voice recorder. For now, they are all just random pieces of an unfinished puzzle. Hopefully, one day I'll be able to find all the pieces and fit them together. Until then, I have a pretty good reason to want to return to the Warehouse Steak N' Stein in Roscoe Village: the ghosts there haven't finished telling me their stories yet.

Warehouse Steak N' Stein
600 Whitewoman Street
Coshocton, Ohio 43812
www.warehousesteaknstein.com

CONCLUSIONS

What a long, strange trip it's been!

There is no way I could have prepared myself for what lay ahead when I started this project some three years ago. That's right, what you've just read (unless you cheated and skipped to the back of the book) is the culmination of over three years of active research and investigation. In my mind, the scope of the book was fairly simple: visit some historical locations that were reportedly haunted, interview people who believe they've encountered ghosts there, then spend the night and see if I could have a paranormal experience. Simple, right? In theory, yes, but once I got into it, the project just snowballed. Here are some interesting numbers related to this project:

- 5,048 miles driven in Ol' Blue, my 1997 Honda Accord
- 3,153 digital photographs taken
- 756 hours of video recorded during the vigils
- 639 hours of audio recorded during the vigils
- 211 hours of recorded interviews
- 126 hours of Vernier LabPro data to analyze
- 14 pounds of handwritten notes and photocopies

My initial goal with this project was to show that ghosts, whether or not we have proof of their existence, can work to keep actual history alive, and I think I've proven that within these pages because even if, after reading my story about the Warehouse Steak N' Stein, you walk away refusing to believe that the ghost of Phoebe Medberry haunts the building, well, you now know the name of Phoebe Medberry, a real historical figure.

In the field of paranormal research, we are always trying to look at things differently to get a new perspective. In doing so, we hope to get the answers we've been searching for. In much the same way, I'm hoping that my research and this book get people, if only a few of you, to stop looking at ghosts and ghost stories as things whose sole purpose is to frighten us. Rather, I want people to embrace ghosts and their stories and to see, perhaps for the first time, what the stories are trying to do: teach us all real history. And we don't need proof of ghosts in order to learn history.

And yet, things did happen during my overnight vigils—things that I couldn't explain. Granted, it wasn't the type of activity you see on those ghost reality shows. I wasn't punched, kicked, scratched, or made to write bad checks. I wasn't possessed, and not a single demon tried to follow me home. But let's face it. That's not reality; that's reality TV. And it's the kind of stuff that makes all of us who take paranormal research seriously look foolish. I know for a fact it was one of the reasons why so many of the locations I contacted for possible inclusion in this book said "Thanks, but no thanks."

When I looked at all the unexplained events from my vigils, the most frustrating part was that I had no idea why they happened. Of course, if you take a look at the stories in this book, no one was sure why the reported activities took place in the vast majority of these places either. It was all very confusing to me. At times like this, I always ask myself, "If I were a ghost, what would I do?"

So let's put ourselves in the ghost's shoes for a minute. If you were choosing to haunt a specific location, there would probably be a reason for that, right? Sure, one of the first things we probably would all like to do when we become ghosts is to scare the heck out of anyone who pissed us off when we were alive. But after that, where would you go? More than likely, you would return to the people and places you loved and cared about while you were alive; at least that's what I would do.

Taking that into account, it's not that much of a stretch to say that if ghosts exist, then the ones haunting the locations in this book are somehow connected to those locations: they are part of that building's history. And yet, we don't know who these ghosts are. Therefore, until we know who these ghosts are and why they are choosing to haunt these buildings, we can't claim that we know the entire history of the buildings. The ghosts are the missing chapter, so we need to figure out who they are.

That is easier said than done. Again, let's just step over the gigantic elephant in the room that says ghosts don't exist and assume that they do. Now, take a look at some of the locations in this book—The Warehouse, Westwood Town Hall, and Oliver House, for example—and you'll see that even when names are assigned to the ghosts, more often than not, those names are either just educated guesses or, in some cases, just randomly assigned with no real evidence, so there is clearly more work to be done.

That's where you come in. So go ahead, visit these locations and see for yourself, only don't just go looking for ghosts. If you do, you're likely to be disappointed as ghosts don't perform on command or on cue (oh, how I wish they did).

Rather, go to soak up the history of the location. Experience all the sights, sounds, and smells that it has to offer. Be polite and introduce yourself. You are, after all, guests in the ghosts' home (although you might want to say it quietly if others are around just so people don't give you funny looks). Tell the ghosts that you are a fan of history and that you'd love nothing more than to hear them tell you a little bit about themselves. Then try to find a quiet place where you can sit back, relax, and try to imagine yourself in a different time period—a time before the Internet and the airwaves were full of phony psychics, taunting ghost hunters, and fake demonologists. Just sit quietly and wait.

Only then, and if you're really lucky, the historical ghosts of Ohio just might speak to you.

ACKNOWLEDGMENTS

First and foremost, I want to collectively thank all the owners and managers of the twenty-one locations covered in this book. There is no way this book would have been possible if you hadn't gotten behind this project and given me access to your buildings. Thank you, not only for allowing me into your second homes, but for also understanding this project and realizing that I meant to treat your buildings with the utmost care and respect. Hopefully, I've done my job right and it will help continue to keep the rich history of these locations alive for years to come.

I want to thank each and every one of you who shared your personal stories with me. There are too many names to list here, but suffice it to say that if you are quoted in this book, I thank you from the bottom of my heart. Your stories and personal experiences really brought this book to life.

I am also forever indebted to all the members of The Ghosts of Ohio organization, especially those who participated in the vigils. There is no way that I could have done all the necessary fieldwork, reviewed all the evidence, and then written about it without the support of these individuals: Julie Black, Kathy Boiarski, Darrin Boop, Jeff Craig, Wendy Cywinski, Mark DeLong, Adam Harrington, Sheri Harrington, Amy Kaltenbach, Samantha Nicholson, Sean Seckman, and Ted Seman.

And now, in no particular order, I would also like to thank the following people without whose support this book would not have happened: Mark Moran and Mark Sceurman, thank you for being the first to allow me to explore my "weird" side; Kurri Lewis for letting me "borrow" a couple of extra blank DVDs for the Merry-Go-Round Museum vigil; Telisa Delligatta for offering my wife and me the gorgeous suite for a night, even though it wasn't haunted; Michelle Duke, thank you for all your help with the Zanesville Community Theater vigil, including the use of SOPI's infrared extender; Troy Ball—gone too soon, my friend—feel free to stop by some night to chat about music and to tell me how I'm going about this ghost-hunting stuff all wrong; Beth Santore for the killer guided cemetery tours; Brian Littier, you promised you'd come visit me in the new house, and I'm holding you to that; Courtney Willis for never letting me go talk to the big kids about ghosts before getting a kiss and a hug; Joyce Harrison, thank you for believing in the project right from the start; Rosalie B. Willis, I know you waited as long as you could for me to finally write this book, so here's hoping that you can find a way to see the results; my nephews and nieces—Heather, Jason, Amber, Matthew, Julian, Evan, Michael Jr., Jennifer, and Ryan—for allowing me to frighten them all these years; my sister, donna, for making me the weirdo that I am today; my sister, Patsy, whose big eyes always let me know when I'd told the story correctly; Troy Taylor, My Invisible Friend, thank you for allowing me to stand ghostly guard over the state of Ohio; Stephanie Willis, "These memories lose their meaning when I think of love as something new"; the little girl at the Lancaster Library who made me tear up when you said my books make you happy—I never had the chance to get your name, but your words will continue to touch me for a long, long time; Billy Timmermeyer for helping me sleep at night, safe in the comfort that the next generation of paranormal enthusiasts will do me proud; Aubree Kaye and Cara Stombaugh for all the years of support, even if you still can't get me inside a certain building that shall remain nameless; Kory Young for getting me the hookup with the sound mixer and mics and for helping me rock out with . . . well, you know; Chris Hart of Roscoe Village for going above and beyond and giving me my own personal tour of the Village; Steve and Carol Flee for room and board and for continuing to trust me with your beautiful daughter; Carl Kolchak for showing me the way to get to the bottom of every story; Arthur Willis, I don't think you ever understood, but I hope you're proud of me: "Hey, Dad, what do you think about your son now?"; Barnabas Collins for being just as scary in color as you were in black and white; the entire cast and crew of the Delaware Ghost Walk; Brian Fielder for waiting patiently for the next round of pizza and beer; Tom Fox for his invaluable insight into Wesley and the history of Westwood Town Hall; Milton Cook for the amazing history lesson about the Quakers; Jules Lapp and Rick Gardner for participating in the Delaware Arts Castle overnight. And last, but certainly not least, I want to thank my fans for supporting me all these years, no matter how weird things got. As always, never stop looking for what's not there.

BIBLIOGRAPHY

Armentrout, Mary Ellen. *Carnegie Libraries of Ohio: Our Cultural Heritage.* Mansfield, Ohio: Rainbow Publishing, 2002.

Austin, Joanne, ed. *Weird Encounters: True Tales of Haunted Places.* New York: Sterling Publishing, 2010.

———. *Weird Hauntings: True Tales of Ghostly Places.* New York: Sterling Publishing, 2006.

Baskin, John, and Michael O'Bryant, eds. *Ohio Almanac: An Encyclopedia of Indispensable Information About the Buckeye Universe.* Wilmington, Ohio: Orange Frazer Press, Inc., 2004.

Brake, Sherri. *The Haunted History of the Ohio State Reformatory.* Charleston, S.C.: The History Press, 2010.

Carlson, Bruce. *Ghosts of Ohio's Lincoln Highway.* Wever, Iowa: Quixote Press, 2010.

———. *Ghosts of the Ohio River.* Wever, Iowa: Quixote Press, 2005.

Casper, Teri, and Dan Smith. *Ghosts of Cincinnati: The Dark Side of the Queen City.* Charleston, S.C.: The History Press, 2009.

Cassady Jr., Charles. *Cleveland Ghosts.* Atglen, Pa: Schiffer Publishing, 2008.

Ciochetty, John B. *Ghosts of Historic Delaware, Ohio.* Charleston, S.C.: The History Press, 2010.

Clay Haus Restaurant. http://clayhaus.com/.

Colson, Michelle. *Ghost Hunter's Field Guide to Ohio.* Baltimore, Md.: PublishAmerica, 2007.

Crosier, Andy, and Richard Shane Reinert. *True Ghost Stories from Ohio with Richard Crawford,* vol. 1. DVD. Directed by Andy Crosier and Richard Shane Reinart. Loveland, Ohio: Dark Figure Productions, 2006.

———. *True Ghost Stories from Ohio,* vol. 2. DVD. Directed by Andy Crosier and Richard Shane Reinart. Loveland, Ohio: Dark Figure Productions, 2007.

Dalton, Curt. *How Ohio Helped Invent the World.* Dayton, Ohio: CreateSpace, 2013.

Day, Sandra, and Alan Craig Hall. *Steubenville.* Charleston, S.C.: Arcadia Publishing, 2005.

De Wire, Elinor. *The Lightkeepers' Menagerie: Stories of Animals at Lighthouses.* Sarasota, Fla: Pineapple Press, Inc., 2007.

Ellis, Bill. *Aliens, Cults, and Ghosts: Legends We Live.* Jackson: Univ. Press of Mississippi, 2003.

———. *The Farnams; One of Richfield's Early Settler Families.* Richfield, Ohio: Richfield Historical Society, 1983.

Everett, Lawrence. *Ghosts, Spirits, and Legends of Southeastern Ohio.* Haverford, Pa.: Infinity Publishing, 2002.

Fairport Harbor Bicentennial Committee. *A History of Fairport Harbor, Ohio.* Painesville, Ohio: Lake Photo Engraving, 1990.

Fairport Harbor Historical Society. *Fairport Harbor.* Charleston, S.C.: Arcadia Publishing, 2003.

Finch Studio, ed. *Historical Souvenir of the Fremont Flood: March 25–28, 1913.* Fremont, Ohio: Finch Studio. 1913.

Folzenlogen, Robert. *Hiking Ohio: Scenic Trails of the Buckeye State.* Glendale, Ohio: Willow Press, 1990.

Fort Meigs: History. http://www.fortmeigs.org/history/.

Friends Boarding Home. http://www.friendshomemuseum.org/first_decade.html.

Gnap, Bernie, and Stephen Kelleher. *Construction of O. C. Barber's Anna Dean Farm.* Barberton, Ohio: Press of the Barberton Historical Society, 2009.

Hard-Luck House Stands the Test of Time. http://articles.orlandosentinel.com/2003–10–05/business/0310030068_1_farnam-zaruba-house.

Hauck, Dennis William. *Haunted Places: The National Directory.* New York: Penguin Books, 2002.

Haunted Oliver House. http://www.clipsyndicate.com/video/play/1674378/haunted_oliver_house.

Historic Roscoe Village. http://www.roscoevillage.com/.

Holzer, Hans. *Great American Ghost Stories.* New York: Barnes & Noble Books, 1993.

Infamous Floods. http://www.enquirer.com/flood_of_97/history5.html.

Katz, Michael Jay. *Buckeye Legends: Folktales and Lore from Ohio.* Ann Arbor: Univ. of Michigan Press, 1994.

Kelleher, S. E., and Jessica King. *Ghosts Along the Tuscarawas.* Barberton, Ohio: Press of the Barberton Historical Society, 2009.

Kermeen, Frances. *Ghostly Encounters: True Stories of America's Haunted Inns and Hotels.* New York: Warner Books, 2002.

Kimber, Jo Lela Pope. *Ghostly Tales of Lake Erie.* Wever, Iowa: Quixote Press, 2005.

Lanigan-Schmidt, Therese. *Ghostly Beacons: Haunted Lighthouses of North America.* Atglen, Pa.: Schiffer Publishing, 2000.

Laven, Karen. *Cincinnati Ghosts.* Atglen, Pa.: Schiffer Publishing, 2009.

———. *Dayton Ghosts.* Atglen, Pa.: Schiffer Publishing, 2009.

Martin, Jessie A. *The Beginnings and Tales of the Lake Erie Islands*. Detroit, Mich.: Harlo Press, 1990.

Moor, John, and Larry Smith, eds. *In Buckeye Country: Photos & Essays of Ohio Life*. Huron, Ohio: Bottom Dog Press, 1994.

Moran, Mark, and Mark Sceurman. *Weird US*. New York: Barnes & Noble Publishing, 2004.

———. *Weird US II: The ODDyssey Continues*. New York: Sterling Publishing, 2008.

Morris, Jeff, and Michael Morris. *Cincinnati Haunted Handbook*. Cincinnati, Ohio: Clerisy Press, 2010.

———. *Haunted Cincinnati and Southwest Ohio*. Charleston, S.C.: Arcadia Publishing, 2009.

Myers, Arthur. *Ghostly American Places: A Ghostly Guide to America's Most Fascinating Haunted Landmarks*. Avenel, N.J.: Random House, 1995.

My Ohio: Following the Trail Taken by the Moviemakers Who Filmed "Shawshank Redemption" in Mansfield. http://www.newsnet5.com/news/local-news/my-ohio/my-ohio-following-the-trail-taken-by-the-moviemakers-who-filmed-shawshank-redemption-min-mansfield-ohio.

Norman, Michael, and Beth Scott. *Historic Haunted America*. New York: Tor Doherty Associates, 1995.

Ohio's Scenic Railroads. http://www.touring-ohio.com/day-trips/scenic-railroads.html.

Oscard, Anne. *Tristate Terrors: Famous, Historic Female Ghosts of Ohio, Indiana, and Kentucky*. Dayton, Ohio: Hermit Publications, 1996.

Parsons, Brian D. *Handbook for the Amateur Paranormal Investigator or Ghost Hunter*. Raleigh, N.C.: Lulu Press, 2008.

———. *Handbook for the Amateur Paranormal Investigator, Part II: The Art and Science of Paranormal Investigation*. Raleigh, N.C.: Lulu Press, 2010.

Past May Linger in Richfield Manor. http://www.ohio.com/news/first/past-may-linger-in-richfield-manor-1.188200.

Quakenbush, Jannette, and Patrick Quakenbush. *Haunted Hocking: A Ghost Hunters' Guide to the Hocking Hills and Beyond*. Bloomington, Ind.: Xlibris, 2010.

———. *Haunted Hocking: A Ghost Hunters' Guide to the Hocking Hills and Beyond II*. Bloomington, Ind.: Xlibris, 2011.

———. *Ohio Ghost Hunting Guide: Haunted Hocking III*. North Charleston, S.C.: CreateSpace, 2012.

Richfield Historical Society. http://www.richfieldohiohistoricalsociety.org.

Rule, Leslie. *Ghosts Among Us*. Kansas City, Mo.: Andrews McMeel Publishing, 2004.

Scenic Stops: Sullivan-Johnson House. http://www.youtube.com/watch?v=qC8 5dFlYVj0.

Shriver, Rick C. *Twin City Opera House*. Raleigh, N.C.: Lulu Press, 2007.

Stanfield Jr., Charles A. *Haunted Ohio*. Mechanicburg, Pa.: Stackpole Books, 2008.

Summers, Ken. *Haunted Cuyahoga: Spirits of the Valley*. Raleigh, N.C.: Lulu Press, 2006.

Taylor, Troy. *The Ghost Hunter's Guidebook*. Chicago, Ill.: Whitechapel Press, 2010.

Thay, Edrick. *Ghost Stories of Ohio*. Edmonton, AB: Ghost House Books, 2001.

Willis, James A. *The Big Book of Ohio Ghost Stories*. Mechanicsburg, Pa.: Stackpole Books, 2013.

Willis, James A. et al. *Weird Ohio*. New York: Sterling Publishing, 2005.

Wlodarski, Robert James, and Anne Powell Wlodarski. *Dinner & Spirits: A Guide to America's Most Haunted Restaurants, Taverns, and Inns*. Lincoln, Neb.: iUniverse.com Inc., 2001.

Woodyard, Chris. *Ghost Hunter's Guide to Haunted Ohio*. Beavercreek, Ohio: Kestrel Publications, 2000.

———. *Haunted Ohio*. Beavercreek, Ohio: Kestrel Publications, 1991.

———. *Haunted Ohio II*. Beavercreek, Ohio: Kestrel Publications, 1992.

———. *Haunted Ohio III*. Beavercreek, Ohio: Kestrel Publications, 1994.

———. *Haunted Ohio IV*. Beavercreek, Ohio: Kestrel Publications, 1997.

———. *Haunted Ohio V*. Beavercreek, Ohio: Kestrel Publications, 2003.

———. *Spooky Ohio: 13 Traditional Tales*. Beavercreek, Ohio: Kestrel Publications, 1995.

Zanesville Community Theatre, Inc. http://zct.org/.